STRON　　　　　EATH

THE JAKE SAWYL　　　.IES (BOOK 2)

ANDREW LOWE

GET A FREE JAKE SAWYER NOVELLA

Sign up for the no-spam newsletter and get a FREE copy of the Sawyer prequel novella **THE LONG DARK**.

Check the details at the end of this book.

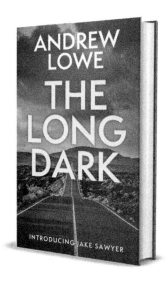

Email: andrew@andrewlowewriter.com
Web: andrewlowewriter.com
Twitter: @andylowe99

First published in 2018 by Redpoint Books
This edition July 2023
Cover photographs © Shutterstock
Cover by Book Cover Shop

ISBN: 978-1-9997290-5-9

For Tom and Josh

To progress again, man must remake himself. And he cannot remake himself without suffering. For he is both the marble and the sculptor.

— ALEXIS CARREL

PROLOGUE

'Adult trauma call!'

The two paramedics hustled the trolley from the back of the ambulance and wheeled it into A&E. Running.

The man at the front glanced back at the unconscious young woman. She had been wedged into a rigid plastic scoop, head squashed between two stabilising blocks.

The waiting obstetric trauma team swarmed around and escorted them along the corridor.

The paramedic at the far end of the trolley addressed the senior A&E doctor. 'Unidentified female, involved in a high-speed road traffic collision where she was the restrained driver of a motor vehicle involved in a head-on collision with an HGV. The airway has been secured with an endotracheal tube. She's not making any respiratory effort, and she's currently being mechanically ventilated. Oxygenating at ninety-nine per cent, with the ventilation. She currently has a blood pressure of seventy over thirty. Heart rate is one hundred and five.'

They crashed through double doors into the ward.

The paramedic took a breath, steadied himself. 'She's cool to the touch and peripherally shut down. Mottled.

1

There are no external signs of significant haemorrhage. BM is six point seven. GCS of three throughout.' He paused again, and the doctor caught his eye. 'She's sustained significant left-sided head trauma and it appears she is at least thirty weeks pregnant. No information on past medical history or allergies. Unable to verify identity. Her passenger was deceased at the scene.'

The obstetrician stepped forward. 'Late stage gravid uterus causing IVC compression.'

The A&E doctor conducted his primary survey: a rapid head-to-toe assessment, looking for evidence of airway compromise. 'We need to maintain cervical spine immobilisation, but I want this woman put into a left lateral position.' The trauma team—three men, two women —eased the woman over onto her right side. 'She has a blown left pupil. I'm concerned there might be raised intracranial pressure. Possible haemorrhage.'

The anaesthetist looked round at his colleagues; the fight was fading from their eyes. 'Still no respiratory effort. I'm using extremely high ventilation pressure.'

The doctor felt around the woman's neck and shook his head. 'No carotid pulse. We've lost cardiac output. Starting CPR.'

The paramedics wheeled the trolley into a bay.

'This woman is continuing to deteriorate,' said the obstetrician. 'We need to perform a perimortem section before we lose the baby, too.'

The A&E doctor screwed his eyes shut and ran through his final checklist. 'No circulation. Major head injury. No respiratory effort.' He opened his eyes. 'Irretrievable.'

The general surgeon and obstetrician gathered their instruments.

The doctor whipped a curtain around the trolley.

PART ONE

A DESIGN FOR LIFE

1

Jake Sawyer jumped down from the grass verge onto the Tarmac path that ran parallel with the Hope Valley railway line. He bowed his head and drove forward. The soles of his running shoes were cushioned, but his steps fell heavy on the solid ground and the impact rippled through his core.

He sucked in the thin morning air, feeding his scorched lungs. The pain was a pleasure; it was one of the few things he trusted as proof of his existence, his aliveness.

A tremor in the track. Sawyer checked his stopwatch. The Sheffield train would be rounding the corner as it crossed the River Noe, levelling for its approach into Edale, three miles down the line.

He slowed, plugged in his earphones and started the music.

He reached around into the pocket of his backpack, and pulled out a chestnut-brown balaclava. He rolled it over his head. The fabric scratched against his shaven scalp and flattened his week-old beard.

He pocketed the watch, took in another gulp of air, and sprang away, easing into a jog.

Sawyer had been planning the move for weeks. Observing. Rehearsing. Mapping it out. Marking down the stats in a notebook: the average speed of the trains, his running times from this end of the path to the level crossing.

There was a chance he had miscalculated.

There was a chance he might die.

But, as ever, the idea was detached, abstract, irrelevant.

There was only the pain. And the howling guitars, the clobbering drums. He had selected 'Faster' by the Manic Street Preachers: a rallying cry for self-empowerment.

He was sprinting now: along the path, in the shadow of the fence that separated the Tarmac from the scrubland at the edge of the railway track. The verge kept him hidden from drivers and walkers over on Edale Road.

Ahead, the level crossing lights flashed to herald the train's approach. He knew that the red-and-white boom barrier would already be down, and it was unlikely there would be a car waiting to cross. Not this early.

Even if there was a car, he might just do it anyway.

Sawyer turned his head, saw the lights of the train sparkling through the mist.

He forged ahead. Maybe it was his time. Maybe this morning, his measurements wouldn't apply. A distracted driver. A fresh security protocol.

If it was his time, he couldn't have picked a more spectacular backdrop for his final view of the world: at the other side of the track, the meadow thinned to an olive green span of eternal moorland, rising to the heather plateau of Kinder Scout: the highest point in Derbyshire. The peak of the Peak District.

He could see the road now, at the level crossing. No cars.

The track popped and creaked. He turned his head again.

The horseshoe of yellow at the front of the driver's carriage. The lights, close enough to dazzle.

Sawyer ran harder. At the crossing, he vaulted a low dividing fence and snaked around the boom barrier. He was exposed to the train driver now and, as he lunged for the rails, the horn sounded: two tones. More greeting than warning, but still piercing through the music.

He was seconds from the track, from the crossing point. The wool had gathered around the balaclava eyeholes, constricting his peripheral vision. He angled his head to the right and saw the driver leaning out of his cab window, arms waving, shouting.

The horn sounded again.

Sawyer faced forward and sprinted for the track.

He knew the risks. If he was lucky, the train would hit him square on, and it would be an instantaneous shutdown. A millisecond flash of impact, and then emptiness.

If he was unlucky, he would survive.

He knew the risks, and yet felt nothing.

No panic for life. No pain of potential loss.

No fear.

His running shoes crunched into the trackside gravel.

The train rattled and roared, somewhere to the right. Impossibly close.

At the nearside rail, he dug in his foot and launched himself over the sleepers, onto the other side.

He scrambled forward, stumbling into the scrub at the edge of the field. Into safety.

Behind, the train clattered past his crossing point.

He crouched, out of sight, in a shallow ditch rendered

boggy by the weekend's first dousing of autumn rain. He pulled off the balaclava and listened to himself, straining for something deeper than the familiar surface prickles of adrenaline.

But still, there was nothing.

2

Sawyer drove over the private driveway bridge and parked his orange-and-black Mini Convertible at the side of the cottage. He killed the engine and sat there, alone with the silence, gazing out at the single track road separated from the cottage by a thin stream of reservoir run-off. He liked to think of the divide as a moat, but it was barely a ditch, and easily jumpable. A few weeks earlier, the light had been dappled by the dense canopy of birches. But now, the trees were shrinking back from the road, shorn and skeletal, revealing a shallow climb of farmland that blended to a tangerine blush of sphagnum moss on the lower slopes of Kinder Scout.

He had taken the cottage on a long-term rental—annual, rolling—from a sheep farmer who seemed keen to hand off the tourist turnover. It was an old outbuilding, barely converted. No hot tub or underfloor heating, but, miraculously for the area, the phone signal and Wi-Fi were tolerable, and Sawyer had worked fast to carve it into his own corner of the world.

Inside, he closed the blind on the sitting-room window and crouched beside the modest TV. He sifted through his stack of old-school DVDs, acquired in an eBay head rush: *Paranormal Activity*, *The Texas Chain Saw Massacre*, *Suspiria*, *Halloween*, *Don't Look Now*, *The Orphanage*, *The Strangers*. The room was low-beamed and L-shaped: long section with the window, sofa and TV, and, round the corner, a galley kitchen and dining table, with bedroom and en suite bathroom at the back of the house. A side door opened onto a scruffy patio with a wooden picnic bench. When he had first moved in, he had used the bench as an outdoor reading retreat. But the air now carried a wintry sting, and he had hibernated to the overheated interior: one man and his horror.

Sawyer's phone blipped with a message alert. He ignored it and switched on the PlayStation, settling too close to the screen, cross-legged. As the Japanese logos announced his favourite retro shooter, *Bullet Symphony*, he saw a flash of the train's yellow front, heard the two-tone horn. If he had died, the coroner would have probably called it accidental: he was in the running zone, didn't hear the train over the music. Death by guitar solo.

It would have been an edgy way to go, affording a noble eulogy from his freshly saved father.

He checked his message. Maggie.

Jake. Talk to me. Remember Wild At Heart? Don't turn away from love? I've found someone who can help. But you need to blink first. x

David Lynch had been their thing at university; Sawyer had been drawn to Maggie as the first woman to show an unironic appreciation of *Eraserhead*. He had wanted more from her, at a time when she wasn't ready to give it. And when she finally got round to him, he had moved on.

He ground through the first few waves of *Bullet*

Symphony: weaving his insectoid spaceship through the pixel-wide gaps in the geometric downpour of pink and blue pellets. To the uninitiated observer, the game was comically hostile, but for Sawyer it was respite: a chance to divert his churning brain to the sole business of smiting his digital enemies.

He paused the action, opened his message app, and navigated to his chat history with Eva Gregory. He scrolled through the string of blue speech bubbles. The messages were all marked as 'Read', but there were no corresponding grey replies. Two signs of madness: talking to yourself, repeating the same thing and expecting different results.

The trimphone ringtone broke through; the screen turned black and switched to a call alert. One-word Caller ID.

Keating.

He could have screened it. He was technically off duty, on holiday.

Sawyer restarted the game and watched, passive, as a phalanx of enemy craft flew in and sprayed a barrage of glowing pellets towards his ship's position. When the missiles were millimetres away from his ship's vulnerable core, he paused it again and tapped the 'Answer' button.

'Sir.'

'It lives!'

'Technically. Social call?'

'Whatever gives you that idea?' Traffic in the background. Birdsong.

'It's Saturday.' Sawyer turned off the PlayStation and took a sip from a glass of tepid Coke, poured yesterday.

'You're due back on Monday. We stopped working five-day weeks back in the eighties, DI Sawyer.' Keating's Welsh twang broke through when he was joshing.

Sawyer gagged at the Coke. 'You've spoken to Maggie.

She's worried about me. She asked you to check I was okay to come back.'

Keating sighed. 'Three out of three.'

'Any movement on Crawley since I've been away?'

'Pre-trial hearings. Psychiatric reports. Insanity plea won't hold. They rarely do. Too much load on the defence.'

'He's nodded for manslaughter?'

'Yes. Diminished. Abnormality of mind.'

'Where is he now?'

A pause from Keating. 'Manchester. Although I still think of it as Strangeways. DI Sawyer. Are we done?'

'With what?'

'The pleasantries. Catch-up.'

Sawyer fell back onto the sofa and rocked forward, reaching for the coffee table. He rummaged in the fruit bowl: Club biscuit wrappers, Haribo, a blackened banana. 'I was going to ask after the wife and kids.'

Keating scoffed. 'You need a mission.'

'Like *Apocalypse Now*? For my sins?'

'Never seen it.'

'It's a bit of a plunge. Maybe start with *Hamburger Hill* and work your way up.'

Keating cleared his throat. 'We have something.'

3

He took the scenic route: through Hayfield and the western moors, weaving along the Snake Road to the alpine lakeland of the Hope Valley. He had thrown on a white T-shirt and black blazer, but hadn't bothered to shave. As he joined the forest road that led to the Fairholmes Visitor Centre, Sawyer calculated the last time he had spoken to another soul, face to face: almost two weeks.

He drove past the roadblock signs and parked in a lay-by near a huddle of FSIs, de-suiting and transferring equipment into a Scientific Services Unit van. A tall, fifty-something woman with a crop of peroxide blonde hair directed the group with short, sharp commands. She was the only one who kept on her Tyvek suit. Turquoise.

Sawyer drew in a slow breath and released it through pinched lips. He got out of the car and approached the cordon manager: a swaggering young officer in a new uniform, probably pressed by his mother. He rummaged for his warrant card.

'He's with me!' The blonde woman strode away from her charges and squinted at Sawyer, looking him up and down.

He nodded at her. 'Sally.'

She waved a hand. 'Excuse me. I'm looking for a man called Jake Sawyer. Good detective. Dresses a bit like you.'

Sally O'Callaghan was posh, strident. She sounded like royalty alongside Sawyer with his languid Northern vowels.

He shook her hand. 'Comedy isn't your thing, Sally.'

She smiled. 'Fuck it. I'll stick to tragedy.'

The cordon manager logged Sawyer's attendance, and Sally angled her head towards the trees. They trudged, in silence, up a slope, into thinning woodland. As they stepped over the inner cordon tape, Sally turned to him. 'Channelling Walter White, Jake?'

'I'm on holiday.'

'Not any more.'

The forensic tent had been erected over a stone wall that marked an underused walking route up to Lockerbrook Farm. The fabric flapped and scraped against an overhanging branch as Sally led Sawyer inside.

DCI Keating stood at the far side with his back to them, finishing a phone call. Sally had left a pair of suited male FSIs to oversee the tent, and one of them—short, with calm, kind eyes peering over the top of a face mask—handed him a pair of latex gloves.

'Scene is fully documented,' said Sally. 'But I'll be taking the bag, obviously.'

Sawyer snapped on the gloves and crouched by the extra-large black leather holdall. He unzipped the main compartment. His green eyes glinted in the Paladin light as they moved over the contents.

Keating loomed behind. 'Nice of you to make an effort, Detective.'

Sawyer didn't look back. 'Sally's done that one, sir.'

The bag contained the naked body of a woman in her early sixties. She was white and pale, with long black hair matted into the grooves of her collarbone. Her arms had been crossed over her chest and she had been tightly rolled into a polythene sheet, sealed by several strips of silvery grey gaffer tape. No blood, no immediate sign of injury. She looked clean, fresh. Like shrink-wrapped meat.

Sawyer pinched at his beard. 'Who found her?'

'Dog walker,' said Keating. 'Fella who works at the Visitor Centre. Early morning. He brings his dog to work some days. He says it ran up here and didn't respond when he called. He came up and found the dog sniffing around the bag.'

'Who is she?'

'No ID,' said Sally. 'Dabs and DNA in the system.'

Sawyer peeled away one of the strips of tape and lifted the polythene from the woman's head and shoulders, as if he wanted to give her a chance to breathe. He lifted her left arm; it was rigid, and, as he tucked the left hand under the right, the movement raised the other arm. He checked over the chest area and rested the arms back in place. He lifted two more tape strips at the body's lower end and slid his hand underneath the woman's ankles, lifting the legs, as if weighing them. 'Nothing else found? No jewellery? Watch?'

'No,' said Sally.

Sawyer replaced the tape strips. He turned and stood upright. Keating and Sally had been joined by a young detective, almost as short as the FSI who had handed him the gloves. His suit was well fitted, but his tie knot was rushed and untidy.

'Good to see you, sir,' said DC Matt Walker.

Sawyer gave him a dimpled smile. 'Dedication, Detective. Not the most life-affirming way to start your weekend.'

Walker shuffled slightly. 'Heard you were coming, sir. Wanted to get in at the beginning.'

Sawyer nodded, glanced at Keating. 'Moran? Myers?'

'Not around. Shepherd's in Liverpool. Family stuff.'

Sawyer nodded. 'I'd say she's been dead for twenty-four to forty-eight hours. Rigor is just leaving her legs.' He looked at Walker. 'It comes in head to toe but leaves toe to head.'

Walker frowned. 'I knew that.' He crouched by the bag, mirroring Sawyer's previous position. 'He bothered to cover her breasts. Wouldn't it have been easier to get her in the bag with her arms by her sides?'

'It would,' said Sawyer. 'So what does that tell you?'

Walker thought for a moment, then turned. 'Could be that he has respect for her. Doesn't want to leave her exposed.'

'In my experience,' said Sally, 'men with genuine respect for women don't kill them.'

Sawyer nodded. 'Maybe he sees those breasts as belonging to him, and he doesn't want anyone else looking. Or he might just be a bit anal. Likes things to be just so. The strips of tape are all pretty much the same size. And he's cut them with scissors rather than tearing them off. How's the rest of the scene, Sally?'

'Clean. Plenty of footprints on both sides of the wall. Lots of footfall round here.'

Walker stood up. 'Trace and eliminate?'

'Yes, please,' said Sawyer. 'Let's look into sexual motive first.'

Keating clicked his tongue. 'Wasn't she a bit old for a predator?'

'Maybe that's his bag,' said Sally.

'Get her to Drummond. We need to know who she is and why someone would want to stab her.'

Sally stepped forward. 'Stab?'

'Single entry wound, just below the left breast. Looks like he's sealed it, too. Cauterised. That might explain why it's all so clean.'

Walker leaned in and studied the body. 'Left breast?'

'Yeah,' said Sawyer. 'Straight through the heart.'

4

The Murder Investigation Team occupied the whole of the first floor at Buxton Police Station. It was supposed to be interim, while the permanent premises were set up in Sheffield. But the positive outcome in the Crawley case had cast the project into bureaucratic limbo, and the unit had gone native.

Keating had parked Sawyer in a large room next to his own, on the back side of the building. They both enjoyed an expansive view of the Tarmac Silverlands football stadium: currently hosting the second half of an afternoon game. The planners had positioned Sawyer's desk facing away from the window, but he had shifted it side-on, so he could keep one eye on the street and the other on approaches from the open-plan office outside.

A shadow filled the frosted glass of his door. Two taps.

Sawyer waited, rolled his eyes. 'Come in.'

DS Ed Shepherd entered and made for the chair in front of Sawyer's desk. He was a big man, and struggled to disguise the waddle in his walk. But he seemed fresh, clear-eyed. He had lost his dated goatee and, by Sawyer's reckoning, at least twenty pounds.

Sawyer sat back in his chair. 'Thought you were up in the homeland?'

'I got Keating's message,' said Shepherd, taking a seat. 'Family wedding. Good excuse. Daggers from the better half, but duty calls.'

'You don't have to wait to be admitted, you know. This isn't the headmaster's office.'

Shepherd shrugged. 'Says Mr Approachable now. Never know when I might catch you on a bad day. Pick up a bollocking.'

'How've you been? Looking good. Although I don't mean that to imply that you didn't look good before.'

Shepherd smiled. 'Thanks. Running, cycling. No booze, no sugar. And not a single carb passes these lips. Don't stress. It gives me a pass to comment on your new look.' Sawyer nodded, waiting. 'Bass player in a nineties rap-metal band. Standing at the back in a press shot, trying to out-cool the singer.'

Sawyer studied him. '"Bass player". That sounds like an insult in itself.'

'If I was trying to insult you, I'd have gone for keyboards.' Shepherd looked around. 'Nice place. Keating keeping you close. As a friend?'

'I assume so. He's finally given me HOLMES access. Are you up to date?'

He nodded. 'Can you cover the first briefing, though? I'll take it from there.' Cheers from the football crowd. Concentrated, but muted. 'Away goal. Sounds like they're getting a spanking. Although you wouldn't know about that, being a glory hunter.'

Sawyer flinched. Either Shepherd's banter was cloying, or Sawyer just hadn't calibrated yet, after his time out of touch. 'I'm a Liverpool fan. I know better than to hang my hopes on silverware.' He opened a drawer. 'Speaking of trophies, I've got something of yours.' He took out a chunky metal tactical pen with a textured grip.

Shepherd shook his head. 'Keep it. I got a new one. Better than that.'

'I'm not going to engage in pen envy. How's the head?'

Shepherd shifted his gaze to the window. 'Better. Exercise is helping. No problems lately.'

'You getting some help?'

Shepherd craned his neck, as if to catch a better view of the football. 'I'm dealing with it.'

———

'At around six-thirty this morning, an employee at the Fairholmes Visitor Centre up in Bamford followed his dog up a walking trail and discovered the body of a sixty-one-year-old woman, Susan Bishop.'

Sawyer took a breath and looked around. The MIT detectives had gathered in their usual cliques, facing the briefing area. Most were perched on desks to get a better view, while DC Walker stood beside Sawyer and DS Shepherd, head raised, surveying the audience.

'DC Walker was FOA,' said Shepherd.

Sawyer glanced at Walker; he was struggling to suppress an odd little smile. Behind Sawyer, the whiteboard carried a large monochrome headshot of Susan Bishop. Posed, side-on, pouting to camera. It was a professional shot, not a selfie. 'Susan's professional name was Suzie Swift. She was an actress and model who did a lot of TV work in the seventies and eighties. Variety shows, a few bit parts.'

Walker stepped forward and checked his notebook. 'She was a regular on something called *The Dicky Emery Show*.'

Titters from a group near the back. Keating emerged from his office and they fell silent.

Myers, a hefty detective with rolled-up sleeves and a tall, shiny quiff, raised a hand and waggled his pen. 'Was she local?'

'Miller's Dale,' said Sawyer. 'Maggie and the FLOs are with the husband. Says he was about to call her in missing when they turned up.'

He turned to the whiteboard. Susan Bishop was still there, smiling at him, suspended in time, brimming with the composure of a natural performer. Gleaming teeth, salon-fresh hair: inky black, crimped at the edges. He saw it plastered into the grooves at her neck. He saw her skin: bloodless, blanched.

He saw Jessica Mary Sawyer, beaming from the garden gate in his wallet Polaroid. Christmas morning, 1987. Black hair, fanned around her neck by the winter wind. Eyes shining with love and pain, freighted with secrets.

'Why?'

His heart lurched. Susan Bishop had been given sixty-one years. His mother only thirty-four.

'DI Sawyer?'

Keating's voice, swimming up from somewhere. He turned back to the group. Side-glances. Shepherd and Walker implored him with raised eyebrows.

'That's... what we need to find out,' said Sawyer.

A silence. Murmurs. Sawyer was struck by a queasy possibility: he had become absent for a few seconds. Drifted off. Answered an imaginary question.

'Find out?' said Keating.

Shepherd moved in front of Sawyer. 'The body is with pathology, but we believe that Susan was stabbed. Once.'

'Once?' A new voice, from a scrawny detective in wire-frame glasses in the group near the back.

'Yes, DC Moran. Once.' Sawyer stepped to the side,

into Shepherd's place, regaining ground. 'Prelim from Drummond shows marks around wrists and ankles.'

'She was cuffed,' said Walker.

A beat. Sawyer continued. 'Wound on forehead from blunt instrument. He knocked her out, restrained her, delivered the stab wound and waited for her to die. Then he wrapped her up, packed her into a vehicle and dumped the body at Fairholmes.'

'He?' said Shepherd.

Sawyer sighed. 'Women don't stab.'

'Apart from Joanna Dennehy.'

'The exception that proves the rule.'

'Passive data? said Moran.

Sawyer shook his head. 'No cameras or ANPR on the Snake Road or the path into the Visitor Centre. Speed camera near the reservoir bridge but I assume he wasn't joyriding. Questions. Where was she killed? Wherever it was, why not leave her there? Myers, find out what you can about the route from the murder scene to Fairholmes. Check phone mast data. And *why* was she killed? Moran, take victimology. Tell me everything about her and find me a good reason. Old showbiz connections, possible grudges. DC Walker, work with Sally on the holdall and plastic sheeting. I want to know where and when the holdall was bought. I'll talk to the husband in the morning. From here in, DS Shepherd is your case manager. I'm SIO. He'll coordinate briefings and keep me up to date. Everything into HOLMES, please. And Stephen? Details out of the press for as long as you can.'

Stephen Bloom, the tall, Nordic-looking media manager stood up to speak. As ever, Bloom's tailoring was more suited to a corporate conference than a provincial police station. He wore a royal blue waistcoat, sky blue shirt, grey tie. 'Fairholmes have already had ITN on the phone, sir.'

'They won't know anything,' said Walker. 'The guy who found the body didn't open the bag. He just called it in as, uh—'

'Suspicious package?' said Moran.

'Keep it dark,' said Sawyer. 'We might get something significant from Drummond's findings. And, technically, we're already questioning a suspect.'

'The husband,' said Walker.

Sawyer nodded and headed back into his office. He was about to close the door behind him when he realised Walker was on his tail. He beckoned him inside.

'Sir. Would it be possible for someone else to look into the holdall? As first officer attending, I'd like to work on victimology if possible.'

Sawyer took a red boiled sweet out of a bowl on his desk. He unwrapped it and squeezed it into his mouth. 'It's possible.' He whipped his jacket around his shoulders and shrugged it on. 'But that's DS Shepherd's call now.'

5

The lift clunked into place on the basement level of Sheffield's Northern General Teaching Hospital. It took a few seconds for the mechanism to oblige, and the doors squealed and parted, as if prised by invisible hands. Sawyer turned side-on and slid out into the corridor before they were fully open.

As usual, the place smelled like an old car park: chalk and cement, a tingle of ammonia. But there was comfort in the lack of front, the disregard for subtlety.

As he turned the corner by chemical storage, he saw a vast figure ducking into the office adjoining the mortuary. Frazer Drummond turned and caught Sawyer's eye as he approached, but then entered the room and closed the door behind him. Sawyer picked up his pace and followed him inside.

'I'm impressed with your new welcoming approach, Frazer. Hearts and minds, eh?'

Drummond dropped into his desk chair and yanked a handful of tissues from a box. He blew his nose. 'I've got a fucking cold coming on, Sawyer. I could have done without a weekend bat signal from Keating. So pardon me for not cupping your balls.'

The voice—sonorous, Glaswegian—rattled the windows of the box-room office. He peered up at Sawyer over the top of his semi-rimless glasses. 'Interesting new look. Going undercover or just breakdown chic?'

Sawyer looked around the room. The walls remained bare, but Drummond had gathered a collage of family photographs on a corkboard by his desk. Signs of life. 'Crawley is in Manchester. Says he's insane.'

Drummond scoffed. 'He's as sane as you and me.' Sawyer caught his eye. 'Well. Me, at least.' A silence lingered. Drummond sat back. 'You're not seriously seeking professional validation from the man whose wife you tried to steal.'

'That's not what happened. And even if it were true, it didn't work, did it? You won. Might be time to move on.'

Drummond sprang to his feet and lifted a folder out of his filing cabinet. He flapped it onto the desk and sat back down. Sawyer ignored it and gazed through the windowed side door into the autopsy room.

'I hear she was an entertainer,' said Drummond. 'Bringing a bit of light into a dark world.'

Sawyer turned and sat on the edge of the desk. Drummond bristled. He only kept one chair in the office, but hated his desk being used as a rest spot. 'TV. Minor roles. Early retirement a few years ago. Husband runs a talent agency.'

Drummond sat back. 'There's no business like it, apparently.' He opened the file. 'Uniform bruising around the lips. He put gaffer tape over her mouth. To keep her quiet.'

'Why take it off?'

Drummond shook his head. 'Something that had done

its job? Something he didn't need to leave behind. He probably forced her to strip at knifepoint, cuffed her...'

'Tell me about the wound.'

Drummond nodded and zoned out a little. 'Closing it up. That's a new one. Looks like he might have used a soldering iron.'

'Cauterised? It looked like a fresh burn.'

'Yep. Old Hippocrates was doing that way back in the fifth century BC. Heats up the tissue and blood, causing it to coagulate.' He fixed Sawyer with a patrician stare. 'Protein denaturation. But you knew that, right?'

'Of course. And no worries about infection from the burns.'

Drummond smiled. 'Very good! Dead people don't suffer from infections, though.'

'Everything intact, internally?'

'Nothing removed, no. Just the stab.'

'Any way to tell the weapon from the wound?'

'It's hard to even tell the depth. And the cauterisation means it's impossible to tell the shape of the blade. So, he knocks her out, positions the knife tip where he wants it.' Drummond held up his left hand, fingers closed. He held his right-hand index finger over the gap between two left-hand fingers. 'He drives the blade in...' Drummond slotted his right-hand finger between the left-hand fingers, then reversed the motion. 'He pulls it straight back out. And his aim was true. She would have been shocked awake by the stab, and then, as her heart wouldn't have been able to pump enough blood to her brain, she would have lost consciousness again within seconds. Brain death in minutes.'

Sawyer hitched off the desk and walked to the windowed door. Gurney: surface recessed, like a shallow bathtub. Body drawers, stacked three high. All-seeing spot lighting. Stainless steel, and not a stain in sight. Not a molecule out of place. 'Anything else?'

Drummond took a pen out of a holder and scribbled something into the file. 'Heavy bleed into the chest cavity. To be expected. Grim Reaper ETA was less than two hours before she was dumped. Do you know what it takes to kill someone like this, Sawyer? Apart from really, really wanting to do it?'

Sawyer turned. 'Precision.'

Drummond jammed the pen back into its holder. 'Precisely. It has something of the abattoir about it, don't you think? Efficient. Cold.'

'But also specific.'

'Well, yes. If you were just out to end someone, there are equally effective methods that aren't quite so—'

'Ritualised?'

Drummond angled his head. 'That's a reach.'

'So why, then? Why do it that way?'

'Out of my jurisdiction, Sawyer. I do the how. The why is your department.'

Sawyer picked up the file. 'Why do I get the feeling you're holding something back?'

Drummond smiled. 'Because I am?'

Sawyer frowned and flicked through the file.

'I'm disappointed you didn't spot the old scar when you looked over the body.'

Sawyer worked through the pages: read, swish; read, swish. 'Cardiomyopathy?'

'Bingo! Our fair Susan had ticker troubles. She had a transplant last year. Looks like the new heart was working well. Until someone stuck a knife through it.'

6

Amy Scott eased her ageing purple Corsa into a rare space a few doors down from her house in Crosspool, a bland suburb of Sheffield. She stepped out of the car and flattened down her nurse's uniform. On the short walk up the steps, she stole a look at the sky. The light was fading earlier in the day now; autumn turning in for the winter slumber.

She let herself in, closed the front door, and called out. 'Myra?'

A young woman—spindly thin with long, parted red hair—stepped out of the sitting room and pulled on a cheap-looking leather jacket. She flicked her hair over the collar and flashed a pained look at Amy.

'I'm so sorry. It's been a crazy day. Emergencies. And—'

'It's okay.' Myra's voice was tiny, constricted. She gathered her things, not bothering to soften her irritation. 'Wish you'd called.'

'I know. There wasn't time.'

Another look. Doubtful. 'Ava has been fine. Gave her tea, read a few stories.'

'She likes Dr Seuss.'

Myra nodded, without smiling. 'I've got to go. I'm

really late.' She pushed past and hurried out of the front door.

'Here. Take something extra.'

Myra paused on the step. Amy turned to the empty hall table. 'Oh! I must have left my bag in the car. Wait here. I'll get you—'

'It's okay.' Myra scurried down the steps and headed off along the narrow street, towards the main road and bus stop.

Amy bounded up the stairs, two at a time. There was still a chance that Ava would be only half asleep and she might get in a few last-minute cuddles before retiring with her lasagne and Netflix.

She eased the bedroom door open a few inches and poked her head into the darkened room. 'Ava? Sweetheart?'

She slipped inside and closed the door.

Her eight-year-old daughter lay on her side, beneath a crumpled fuchsia duvet, using her battered old plush unicorn as a comfort pillow. Amy straightened the bedclothes and stood there for a while, basking in the sound of Ava's slumber: her whispered breaths, regular and clear. She leaned in and pressed a light kiss to her forehead, then tiptoed out to the landing.

Back downstairs, Amy gazed into the wall mirror and saw a weary, winded character in a blue-and-white uniform. She winced at the dark smears beneath her eyes, the limp hair: unstyled and borderline mousey. She was a bright soul: kind, empathic, and, according to her friend Lisa, "a catch". But lately, the job was washing out her colour, leaving her drained and desolate. During a recent video chat with a potential Match date, she had made the mistake of asking the man to guess her age (thirty-four). He had studied her image and announced, with confidence, that she was 'somewhere in the early forties.'

She latched the front door and dashed down the steps to the Corsa.

The handbag sat in full view on the passenger seat. She rolled her eyes and unlocked the driver's door.

As she leaned in to retrieve the bag, something caught her eye. One of the windscreen wipers had been lifted and an item placed underneath. She took the bag, locked the car and moved around to the windscreen.

Pinned beneath the wiper: a single red rose with a small card in a plastic wallet taped to the stem.

Amy lifted away the flower. She stripped off the wallet and took out the card.

On one side, in smudgy lettering, the sender had used an old-school typewriter to mark out a single sentence.

A reminder of our arrangement.

7

Sawyer leaned on the wooden bench and stared out at the sweep of yellowing fields and balding trees. He had dug the Mini into a lay-by off Bradshaw Lane and finished the last ten minutes of the journey on foot. The dusk was settling and the Barrel Inn car park was only half full, but the car's distance gave him a psychological buffer; it allowed him to step out of his detective role and slip into the shoes of Lloyd Robbins, investigative journalist. It was an uneasy masquerade, but necessary. For now. Until all was well.

He squinted and tracked a white van as it slid along a farm track towards Wardlow, his home village, but then turned left, away from his old house and his mother's old school; towards the lane and the end of his old world.

———

Sawyer had over four hundred years on the Barrel Inn, but it caught the top of his head as he ducked inside, scraping the albino patch at the back of his scalp. The place engulfed him like an embrace: oak-beamed bar, nail-studded doors, flagstone floor, a maw of a log fire. Marcus Klein had found a spot in a dark corner, near the entrance to the restaurant. His rectangular glasses were unchanged, but he had taken to wearing a tweed cap over his salt-and-pepper hair, had grown a neat beard, and was leaning so far over the top of his jug of bitter, Sawyer thought he might be asleep.

Sawyer slid into the seat opposite Klein. Just inside the restaurant entrance, a group of three men—chunky farm types—raised a rowdy toast. Two of them were perched on chairs, but the biggest of the three had taken a bench for himself. He downed his drink and sat back, manspreading over the width of the seat. Sawyer caught his eye for an awkward second.

'Mr Robbins.' Klein raised off his chair and held out his hand. Sawyer gripped it. Lean, bony. 'It's a pleasure to see you again. How are you? How is the book?'

Sawyer wriggled out of his jacket and draped it over the chair. 'Fine. I've been busy with research for a few weeks.'

Klein took a sip of beer, wiped the froth from his moustache. 'Do you have an editor? A deadline?' His voice wavered; not far from a whisper.

Sawyer nodded and glanced over at the big man, who was laughing about something with his two colleagues. 'Both. My editor is a big help. The deadline, not so much. I need to deliver it early next year.'

'Who is publishing?'

'Small press based in London. Mostly non-fiction. The case is quite old and my agent didn't have much success with the bigger places. No need, these days, anyway. The story is evergreen and the marketing will be easy. A strong human interest, too. As well as the murder and attempted murder, there's also the injustice suffered by yourself.'

Klein sighed. 'There's one person I doubt you'll get a sale from. Harold Sawyer. He tried to block my release. It was fine in the end, though. I transitioned in a Cat D for a few weeks. I'm living at my brother's place near Castleton now. He's away a lot so it's easy.' He looked wistful for a second, then gathered himself. 'I got a dog.'

In the restaurant area, the big man bellowed at the waitress. 'All on me tab. No danger! You won't get these cheap bastards paying for anything, anyways.' Bristled head poking from a black polo-neck. Flushed. Already half-cut.

'Mr Klein, I just wanted to check that you're up for this? The investigation?'

Klein flinched and the overhead light caught his forehead wrinkles: pronounced, premature. Sawyer had heard that every year in prison puts half a year on you. Klein had only just turned twenty-four when he had been convicted of the murder, thirty years ago. 'I would like to clear my name, yes. I did not kill Jessica Sawyer. As you know.'

'I do. And I'll try my best to keep you on the side lines. But I don't know what I might uncover once we get going. If the real killer is still out there, then there's a chance he might be nervous about you being out.'

'After all this time?'

'He's got away with murder for this long. He'll want to keep it that way.'

Klein took a long drink. 'Christ, I wish you could still smoke in these places.' Sawyer eyed him, waiting for an answer. 'Yes. I'm up for it. No fear. What have you found out?'

Sawyer rose. 'Let me get a drink and I'll fill you in.' As he turned, he had to step around the group of three men as they headed for the bar with their drinks. The big one took a sidestep at the last second and shouldered into Sawyer. Most of his drink sloshed over the rim of his glass and splatted onto the stone floor.

'Fuck's sake, mate!' He stepped towards Sawyer, eyes

bulging. He was close in height but almost twice Sawyer's width.

Sawyer looked down at the puddle of beer and lifted his eyes to meet the big man's. 'Looks like you need another drink.'

The big man's companions exchanged a look.

He moved in closer. Beer breath, unbrushed teeth, stale sweat. A few grains of white powder clung to his flaring nostrils. 'Yeah. Cheers. Pint of Grolsch.'

Sawyer smiled and moved around him. The barman raised his eyebrows. 'Just a lemonade, please.'

The barman eyed the big man. 'Half or pint?'

'Half. No ice, thanks.'

Sawyer turned his back on the group and looked up and around the room as the barman took up a soda gun and aimed it into a glass. 'How old is this place, exactly?'

The barman stole a nervy glance over Sawyer's shoulder. '1597. Highest pub in Derbyshire.'

'Has it changed much?'

The barman placed the full glass on a beermat. 'Used to have a thatched roof, I think. Tiled now. Two-forty, please.'

'Hey!'

Sawyer ignored the shout from behind him, and paid, taking his time. The barman caught his eye and Sawyer offered a slight nod, hoping it conveyed reassurance.

He turned, straight into the big man's leering face. The three had formed a tight cluster, blocking his way back to the table. Sawyer took a sip of his drink. 'Can I get past, please?'

The big man tapped at his earlobe. 'You got a hearing problem, pal?'

Sawyer took a breath and closed his eyes, listening to himself. Still nothing. But he saw it all: the *Jeet Kune Do* solution.

Move first. End it quickly. A swift biu jee *strike to the big man's nose, probably dislodging a clump of unsnorted coke. Drop back, create distance. One of his pals tries a haymaker. Sidestep, gut punch, follow up with an elbow to the back of his neck. Second guy wades in. Drop further back and dodge. Stomp kick to his knee, side on. Break his leg. Longest weapon to nearest target.*

He opened his eyes and leaned to the side, peering around the group. Klein had shifted his chair, watching the show.

Sawyer faced the big man. 'Are we really doing this? The old, "you spilled my pint" routine?'

'What's that?' He nodded at Sawyer's glass. 'Shandy? Tough guy eh?'

Laughter from the other two.

The barman spoke up. 'Shaun. You've been barred once before. Leave it.'

Shaun leaned in closer, forehead to forehead with Sawyer. 'I *said*, a pint of fucking Grolsch.'

Head-butt. Elbow into one of the other two. The third will probably bottle it.

Sawyer flicked his eyes over Shaun's shoulder. Klein was transfixed. 'Okay. My fault.' He held out a hand. 'No trouble. Fresh pint of Grolsch for Shaun. On me.' He pulled out a five-pound note and flicked it onto the bar. 'Stick the change in the tip jar.' Shaun accepted the hand. Sawyer shook and slapped him on the shoulder. 'Have a good night.' He picked up his lemonade and squeezed past, back to Klein. He sat down, with his back to the group, watching Klein's eyes.

Shaun slurred a parting shot. 'Too fucking right! Watch where you're going next time.'

The barman poured Shaun's drink and the group shuffled to a table near the back of the bar.

Klein puffed out a whistle. 'Nicely done, Mr Robbins. You should offer yourself to the UN.'

Sawyer smiled and took a deep drink. 'Arseholes. Forget about them. Let's talk about what matters. Where were we?'

Klein gathered himself. 'You were telling me what you've found out.'

Sawyer glanced over his shoulder. Shaun and his boys were grinning to each other, relaxed, enjoying the victory. 'The last time we spoke, you said you remembered the summer before it happened. It was a hot night and you were restless and couldn't sleep. You heard a noise downstairs. As I said, I think that was someone stealing the hammer that was used to kill Mrs Sawyer. It was either the killer or someone told to steal it by the killer.'

'I used the hammer to fix a number to my door a few weeks before, and then I didn't use it again. I didn't see that it had gone missing.'

'Yes. I think someone saw you do that and used the hammer in the attack, implicating you.'

Klein took off his glasses, revealing ruptured, bloodshot eyes. He pulled out a handkerchief and pinch-cleaned the lenses. 'So how are we going to find out who this might have been? Have you spoken to anyone else involved in the case? Family members? Police?'

'As far as the police are concerned, it's a closed case. We wouldn't get any cooperation because it would be embarrassing if we unearthed anything. Best to keep it freelance.' Sawyer took a slug of his drink. 'I approached the sons. They were both present at the murder, as you know. I did get one of them to speak to me. Michael.'

Klein sat forward. 'Anything?'

'Let me lay it out for you, Mr Klein, as I understand it. Someone sees you with the hammer. They somehow steal it, probably on the night you say you heard the noise. A few weeks later, Jessica and her sons are walking with their dog along the lane near Wardlow. A lane they often use. The killer, wearing a balaclava, ambushes them. He kills the dog, attacks the two boys. Michael is hurt but, as he tells me, he hears Jessica say something to the attacker as he's killing her. The killer is interrupted by another walker and he has to leave. He dumps your hammer and it's found later, convicting you.'

'I like the way you call her "Jessica". Not "Mrs Sawyer".'

Sawyer dropped his gaze. 'Too easy to forget the victims.'

Klein pulled himself closer and replaced his glasses. Fumbling fingers. Unsteady. He smelt of perfumed soap and tobacco. 'So what did Michael hear Jessica say to the killer?'

Sawyer found Klein's eyes. 'He says he heard her say one word: "Why?"'

Klein slumped. 'How does that help?'

'A lot. I think she knew him. Most people would say, "Stop!" or, "Don't!" or, "No!". But "Why?" implies confusion, outrage, maybe disappointment. Some kind of connection.'

'Romantic?'

Sawyer sloshed the remaining lemonade around in his glass. 'When I saw you at the prison a few months ago, you said that Jessica told you she was trying to "change her life". Get out of something difficult. Was your relationship obvious? You were both teachers at the same school. Would other staff have noticed? Might her husband have suspected something? Was it possible she was involved with someone else who worked there?'

Klein took off his cap. The hair on his head was too long. Silvery, waxed and parted. He propped his elbows on the table and massaged his temples. 'We thought we were pretty discreet. But, you know. It's hard to gauge it. You think she knew her killer. Well... She knew *me*. Didn't make much difference in the end, but I suppose I'm lucky that didn't come out in the trial.' He tipped back his glass and drained the drink. 'You still think I'm innocent, Mr Robbins?'

Sawyer blinked. 'Of course.'

'So what's the next step?'

'I have a good police contact who might be able to get me access to the local arrest records from a year or so around the time of Jessica's death. There may be something that sticks out. I think you were burgled, Mr Klein. There may be a burglar who was active at the time who was involved in taking the hammer. Career burglars in the area who might know something.'

Klein shook his head. 'It was a long time ago. It sounds like a long shot.'

'You know how it goes. You miss every shot you don't take.'

'Mr Robbins. A question. What if we do find a link to the person who did it? You say the police won't even be interested in investigating because of the embarrassment.'

Sawyer shrugged. 'Depends what we find. They might have good reason to not want to re-open the investigation. You might get compensation.'

Klein grimaced and dropped his chin to his chest. 'I was a good teacher, Mr Robbins. It was an asset that kept me sane, and alive, inside. I don't want money. I just want a clear name. So I can work again.'

Sawyer sat back. 'We'll get you justice. But we have to keep it low profile.'

———

They talked for another half an hour, mostly around Klein's prison war stories. Sawyer maintained his persona by reworking old case detail into tales from his days as a 'local crime reporter'.

Sawyer turned his head at the sounds of an altercation from Shaun's table. The men were arguing amongst themselves, with Shaun's the loudest voice, sounding a note of protest and apology.

He smiled and stood up, pulled on his jacket. 'I have to go. I'll be in touch if my police friend discovers anything.'

Klein stood, shook Sawyer's hand. 'I'm going to stay and read my book by the fire for a while. I'm learning about online teaching. Something I can do anonymously. Probably best we don't leave together, anyway, eh?'

Sawyer grinned. 'You're getting the hang of it already.' He turned and headed for Shaun's table.

'Guys! I always pay my fucking share!' Shaun was on his feet, pleading with the other two. 'I've never had this before. Honest!'

The two seated men caught Sawyer's approach. Shaun saw their attention shift and pivoted to face him. 'What's the problem?'

'Just hoping I can help,' said Sawyer. 'Sounds like you're having trouble paying.'

Shaun pushed his chair out of the way and took a step towards Sawyer. 'What the fuck has it got to do with you?'

Sawyer slid Shaun's tatty black wallet from his jacket pocket and placed it on the table. 'I think you must have dropped this, tough guy.'

———

Outside, the fields had been smothered by starless night, and an impish wind swooped around the high ground.

Sawyer used the light of his phone to navigate down the lane to the lay-by. He started the Mini and cued up a playlist recently shared by Maggie: The Flaming Lips.

As he crunched onto the A road towards Edale, a burgundy BMW pulled out of the Barrel Inn car park and rumbled its way down the lane, keeping a cautious distance.

8

Ronald Bishop poured himself a whisky and limped over to the sofa. He paused and gazed into the glass. The liquid caught the light from a wall lamp and cast a golden shimmer across his crumpled forehead. Maggie Spark stepped in and guided him down onto the sofa. She took the glass from his trembling hand and transferred it to a side table.

Sawyer sat opposite, beside Shepherd on a second sofa. He had suited up, but Shepherd was dishevelled, in an ill-fitting overcoat with jacket and tie underneath. Ronald hadn't opened his curtains, and the features of the vast, high-ceilinged room were sunken beneath the low wattage gloom. Cloth-covered piano, stone-cut fireplace, black-and-white portrait photos hung in elaborate frames: a young Ronald and Susan with dogs gathered at their feet; Susan in various costumes and guises; Ronald with clients, mostly TV stars of the eighties.

Maggie strode over to the French windows. 'Quite a nice morning out there, Ronald. Remember what we said yesterday? We should let the day in.'

'Just a little.' Ronald knitted his fingers together and

writhed them around, as if washing his hands. He kept his gaze straight ahead, avoiding Shepherd and Sawyer. He was approaching seventy, with a dense mane of oyster-grey hair framing a rugged face set in a permanent squint. His tone was military, dampened by grief. 'Suzie loved Sundays. When we were younger, it was our running day.' His eyes flashed up to Sawyer and Shepherd. 'She had to keep fit, you see. She was forever on diets. Then it became our walking day. That's how it goes. You slow down, scale back. It all catches up with you in the end.' He sighed and reached for the whisky.

Maggie parted the curtains halfway. Watery sunshine seeped in. The front garden was modest: tightly mowed with multicoloured fringes and a low hedge bordering the lane into Miller's Dale village.

'How did you meet Susan, Mr Bishop?' said Shepherd.

He winced. 'Ronald, please.' His gaze drifted. 'Twenty-five years ago. I was looking after her first husband. Magician. It was the end of the working relationship, and they'd ran their course. I later found out he was... *physical* with her. He died many years ago. Cancer, I think.'

Maggie walked over and lowered herself into an armchair. She had grown out her rust-red hair a little since Sawyer had last seen her, and pinned it back into a stubby ponytail. She caught him watching her and narrowed her eyes.

Sawyer sat forward. 'Your agency. Everything amicable there? Any clients or ex-clients who might have issues with you or Susan?'

Ronald shook his head. 'Not that I can think of. Suzie took on more of the admin. I kept up with the "warm" work. Meetings, casting directors, ego massages, what have you. A lot of the younger performers bypass agencies, these

42

days. Bloody technology lets them manage themselves. We mostly have the old hands on our books.'

'Can you take us through your activities yesterday evening?' said Shepherd. Ronald glared at him. 'We need to account for everyone and everything. You understand.'

He took a sip of whisky. 'In the afternoon, I was working in the office. Suzie had been home most of the day. Gardening, reading. She made us an early dinner. Salmon. I left just before seven to drive to a friend's house in Chapel, where we played bridge. I came back around midnight, very tired. Suzie's door was closed and I assumed she'd gone to bed. I went to my room, didn't sleep well. I took her some tea early in the morning and was shocked to see she wasn't there. Her bed hadn't been slept in, and her purse was still in the drawer. As far as I know, she wasn't planning to go out anywhere. Is there evidence? Of intruders?'

Sawyer shook his head. 'Not that we can see. Was your bridge evening a regular event?'

'Yes. Every Saturday.'

Sawyer looked up and ran his eyes around the patterns of the interlocking oak beams. 'Mr Bishop, did you and your wife enjoy a transparent relationship?'

Ronald looked at Maggie, then Shepherd, then back to Sawyer. 'What does that mean?'

Sawyer trained his gaze on Ronald. 'Romantically. Is there a possibility that your wife was seeing someone else?'

'Certainly not. I was devoted to Suzie, and the feeling was mutual.'

Sawyer could feel Maggie's eyes on him. 'I'm not making any moral judgement. I just have to explore every possibility, palatable or not.'

Ronald tilted his head back. 'Consider that possibility fully explored, Detective.'

Shepherd pointed at one of the portrait images of Susan

Bishop. 'Can you tell us what happened with your wife's heart transplant, Ronald?'

'She developed cardiomyopathy after the birth of our daughter. She was in her forties and it was difficult. Unplanned. She managed the condition for a long time, but, as I say, things catch up with you. It became worse last year and the transplant became necessary. She had the operation at Wythenshawe Hospital in Manchester.' Ronald took a drink. He screwed his eyes shut, weathering something. When he opened them again, they were filled with tears. 'Why would someone do this to my Suzie? What... what happened to her?'

Maggie reached forward and squeezed Ronald's hand. 'We're still working that out.'

'She was stabbed.' Sawyer brushed down his orange tie and looked at Maggie.

Ronald gasped and reeled back. '*Stabbed*? Why? Did she suffer?'

Maggie glared at Sawyer. He peeled his eyes away and focused on Ronald. 'I don't believe so. I would tell you if I thought otherwise.'

Ronald rubbed at his eyes with a handkerchief. 'I'm sure you would.'

———

Sawyer strode through the Bishops' back garden, ahead of Shepherd and Maggie. He heard Maggie tell Shepherd to wait by the house for a second.

He stopped and turned, denying her the lecture. 'Get a contact for his bridge buddies. Look into their agency. Cross-ref for anyone with a record or arrests.' He paused. Shepherd took out his notebook. 'Find some detail on the

44

transplant. Is someone unhappy that she got higher up the list? Maybe because of her minor celebrity?'

Shepherd nodded. 'Disgruntled patient. Or patient relative?'

'Or maybe it's symbolic. A jealous lover stabbing her through the heart. Creative. She broke his heart, and so he's doing the same to her. Get a victimology cell on Susan Bishop's showbiz history. Anyone who sticks out. Trace and eliminate. And check out the ex-husband.'

Shepherd looked up. 'He's dead, sir.'

'Do it, anyway. Connections. Grudges.' He glanced at Maggie; she stared him down. 'We need to know more about their relationship. Can you find out more?'

Maggie folded her arms. 'Shall I push him on their sex life? Now you've "softened him up"?'

Sawyer sighed, held her stare. 'Okay. I was a bit heavy-handed. But it's better that he knows now. Then he can start getting used to it. Rather than living in limbo.'

Maggie stepped forward. 'It's *better* that he's given time to absorb the blow of his wife's death before he learns of any—'

'No sign of a break-in. So, Ronald's out playing bridge. Someone calls, probably not too long after he left. Not too late, or she might not answer the door. It fits what I said in the briefing. He knocks her out, cuffs her, delivers the stab wound, waits for her to die. He wraps her up, gets her into a vehicle, and cleans the scene. Sanitises the body, cauterises the wound, dumps her up at Fairholmes.'

Shepherd frowned. 'Why would he risk her husband coming back?'

'Ronald said the bridge night was a weekly event. The killer must have known he'd have time to do his work in the house, then get her out to the car. As you can see, it's pretty private round the back here. This was planned. She was targeted. We need to find out why and we need to find out who's doing the targeting, the stabbing, the sanitising. Because whoever it is, is certainly arrogant enough, fearless enough, to do it again. I want Sally here with a full forensic team as soon as possible.'

'It *could* be random,' said Shepherd. 'And he got lucky she was alone.'

Sawyer shook his head. 'Think about what stands out. The meticulousness. The cauterising. The respect for Susan's body.' He looked up at the handsome, three-storey limestone house and thought of Ronald, rattling around, dragged from cosy, middle-class companionship and dropped into a hollow half-world of regret and sympathy. 'There's no opportunism here. Drummond said it felt impassive, emotionless. Like a dirty job that had to be done. But there's a bigger picture. This is not the work of your standard empty soul getting his kicks from the big three. Domination, manipulation, control. He's not killing because he wants to. He's killing because he needs to.'

9

Sawyer spooned out a clump of raspberry jam and daubed it over his buttered teacake. He had planned to head home and kick back with a binge of J-horror, but Maggie had dragged him to their favoured breakfast spot: the Nut Tree, a comfort café on the edge of The Roaches.

She spread a napkin across her knees and dug in to her avocado and salmon. 'I hear you were a bit wobbly at the briefing.'

He shrugged. 'It was Shepherd's gig. I should have prepared better.'

'You should hand over more. Take some weight off your shoulders.'

Sawyer squashed together both halves of the teacake and took a bite.

Maggie raised an eyebrow. 'Jam sandwich.'

He wrinkled his nose. 'More of a doughnut, I think. And, yes. I'm trying to pull back, train up the support troops. Keating has made me his neighbour at Buxton. I get the feeling he wants me where I can't cause trouble. The very idea.'

Maggie sipped her tea.

Sawyer nodded to the cup. 'Twig and thistle? Wormwood and peat?'

She smiled. 'You're not happy.'

'No?'

'No. You're off balance. Making bad decisions. Your self-awareness isn't quite on the channel.'

A waitress handed Sawyer a mug of milky tea. He tossed in a couple of sugar cubes. 'Mags, I appreciate the concern. But I'm not having a breakdown.'

'You do realise that if you were, you'd be the last to know?'

He slurped his drink, keeping his eyes on her over the rim of the mug. 'I had a tough case. Had to put myself back together.'

'You've isolated yourself.'

'It's self-care.' He shook his head. 'This is how it always goes with you therapists. You mould the evidence towards your theories. You always see the worst in people.'

Maggie laughed. 'I suppose that's because we usually only see people when they're at their worst.'

Sawyer took another bite of his teacake, braced for a bollocking.

'You were harsh with that poor man.'

'Harsh?'

'Insensitive. Mean. You're never mean.'

'He needed to know what happened.'

'Do your job, Jake. Gather the evidence.'

He sighed. 'Leave the emotions at the door?'

'Save them for someone else.'

He held her gaze, pushed out a half-smile.

Maggie stared down into her cup. 'The last time we sat here, you said you felt something you'd never felt before. In the cave with Crawley.'

'I hadn't slept. I was trying to keep a nine-year-old boy

48

safe from a multiple killer. And I was halfway to hell. Underground.' He shrugged. 'Stress.'

'It was something new. Something you've been told is beyond your emotional functioning. And yet there it was. Maybe it was the lack of oxygen in the cave. Maybe it was one of the most stressful situations you've ever experienced. It hardly matters why it happened: now you know it's in there somewhere. You know that you're not completely beyond fear. It must feel like a strange new toy. And I bet you want to bring it out for a second look.' She caught his eye again. This time he flinched, looked away. 'You can't do that yourself, Jake. You need a professional.'

Sawyer stirred his tea. 'We talked about this. Keeping our friendship strictly personal.'

'I told you. I know someone who I think could help you.'

He sighed. 'The flashbacks are getting stronger. And I'm dreaming of the murder. It's feeling more vivid.'

'Are you sleeping?'

'Barely.'

She sat back. 'If I tell you a secret—'

'Will I promise not to tell?'

She nodded.

Sawyer looked up at her. 'Is it that Keating has asked you to keep an eye on me?'

She rolled her eyes. 'Yes.'

'But you don't want him to know that I know.'

'I would rather you sought help for yourself. Not because someone else wants you to. I'm telling you about Keating's concern as a trust thing.'

'And to bank a favour.'

Maggie's shoulders slumped. 'I'm not that cynical. But if that's how we're doing this, then yes. I would like you to return the trust by taking a trial session with a therapist who is excellent at tailoring to individual client needs.'

He took another bite of teacake, chased it with a slurp of tea. 'I'm not doing EMDR.'

'People scoff at that. But it is the kind of therapy that could help you to detach the traumatic memory and give you the freedom to move forward. I'm talking about something else, though. The therapist I'm thinking of is more psychodynamic.' She opened her purse and slid out a card. Creamy background. Sky blue border. Black text.

Sawyer took it and turned it over in his fingers.

ALEX GOLDMAN
Goldman Counselling Centre

'I'll send you the address. It's not far. Tuesday at one?'

He laughed. 'I hope you're getting a commission.'

She lifted her chin in triumph. 'And in the meantime, you can use me as a buffer between yourself and your boss. Just be happy that he wants the best for you.'

'And you're the best?'

'Oh, you don't know how lucky you are. The both of you. Have you finished the book yet? *The Gift Of Fear*?'

'Started it. Lost it in the move. I'll get a new one.' Sawyer's phone buzzed and he took it out. 'It's Shepherd. I have to get back.'

He stood, whipped on his jacket. Maggie reached a hand across the table, but he snatched his away and deflected by fumbling in his pocket.

'Whatever you're going through, Jake, try to be decent to people. You know how it works. True to your own spirit. Don't compare other people's gains to your own loss. Susan Bishop had a good life, but it didn't end well.'

Sawyer leaned down to the table. 'Nobody's does.'

10

Sawyer pushed through the double doors into the MIT unit and propped himself against the wall outside his office. He watched as DC Walker fussed with the whiteboard. Shepherd gathered the team and motioned for Walker to take a seat. He complied, with some reluctance.

Shepherd turned to the room and cleared his throat. 'We've spoken to Susan Bishop's husband, Ronald. Susan's first husband, Peter, died ten years ago. Ronald claimed that there was some domestic abuse, but I can't see any relevance.'

Walker rose in his chair. 'And we see no reason why Ronald himself might be involved.'

'Apart from the fact that he's the husband and the most likely suspect?' DC Moran tilted his head and looked round for support.

'Story holds up.' Sawyer ran a hand over his cropped hair. 'He was crushed.'

'He runs an acting agency,' said DC Myers. 'Might be a decent performer himself.'

Sawyer shook his head. 'Not even close. I bought every word.'

'Or he sold you,' said Moran, not looking at Sawyer.

'They had dinner,' Sawyer continued. 'He went out to play bridge. He came home late and didn't realise she wasn't there. Separate bedrooms. If he's a murderer, Moran, then you're a ballet dancer. There's no evidence he was ever at Fairholmes.'

'There's no evidence that *anyone* was there,' said Sally O'Callaghan, parked on the edge of the desk beside Shepherd. 'Way too many footprints to trace and eliminate, and nothing on the route from the road to the scene. Nothing on the holdall or materials. Cleanest scene I've ever worked on. It's like he's winched the poor woman in place via helicopter.'

'Any more from Drummond?' said Shepherd. 'Sexual assault?'

Sally sighed. 'He says not. Single stab wound. No other violation.'

Sawyer pulled open a bag of Skittles and scattered a few into his palm. He spoke without looking up; his position in the room forced the others to turn slightly. 'And the Bishop house?'

Sally eased herself up off the desk. 'My team are wrapping up now. There's no evidence of intruders. Nothing in Susan's bedroom, or the garden. She must have gone outside of her own—'

'So we're looking for a ghost?' Sawyer tossed the Skittles into his mouth. 'Is that your professional opinion, Sally?'

She angled her head. 'It's not an opinion, DI Sawyer. I'm just laying out the forensic findings to date.'

'You missed something.'

Chairs scraped as the others turned to Sawyer, away from Shepherd and Walker and their whiteboard.

Sally took a breath, trying to reclaim the moment. 'My team do not "miss" things.'

Sawyer stared at the floor, chewing. 'Are your team human beings, Sally?'

'Yes, they are.' She looked away for a second, then counterattacked, bright and sarcastic. 'Wait a second. That would mean that they might make *mistakes*, right?'

Sawyer smiled and raised his eyes to her. 'She was targeted. It was close to dusk. She didn't go for a stroll and get jumped. Wherever he killed her, he wanted it to be private, efficient. No mess. No fuss.'

'Sterile?' said Sally.

'Yes. No contamination, either physical, or potential compromise from the public. He did it there and then. Either inside the house or somewhere private close by.'

'Vehicle?' said Shepherd.

'A mobile murder lab,' said Walker. 'Fits his psychology. It's like he wants complete control over every single detail.'

Sawyer nodded. 'Including what he leaves behind. Killing inside a vehicle gives him that privacy. He can take his time. No danger of getting caught in the act.'

And then, there he was, in the lane. Crawling. Clenching at the soil.

Henry, his dog. Twitching. Trembling. Was he cold? He wanted to cover him.

Michael, his big brother. In a heap, near to their mother.

At once, Sawyer was in two separate places: his physical form in the MIT room, but his perception had shifted in space and time.

He could hear his mother's cries. Her sorrow and agony. Her submission.

Sawyer looked up at Sally. Her mouth was moving but he could only hear the ambience from that day, like an aural imprint on his six-year-old eardrums: birdsong, a distant car engine, leaves rustling in the breeze.

The impotence. The screams, dwindling to sobs, braced for each hammer blow.

Metal on bone.

'DI Sawyer?

A rumble of nausea.

He swallowed the half-chewed sugary mush and screwed his eyes closed, grinding his teeth together. He pinched at the flesh around his thigh muscle, focusing on the physical sensation.

'DI Sawyer, are you with us?'

He was. The nausea faded. He retuned back into the room. 'Yeah. Sorry. Bit of heartburn.'

Sally squinted at him, nodding. 'I said, do you want me to tell my team to take another sweep?'

'Yes, please.'

'And if there's still nothing?'

Sawyer blinked the moisture from his eyes. 'DS Shepherd?'

He was ready. 'Myers. Get time of death from Drummond, as close as you can. Work with Rhodes on CCTV and ANPR, two hours either side. Larger vehicles: vans, people carriers.'

'What about victimology?' said Sawyer. 'What's he got against Susan Bishop?'

'Not a lot coming up,' said Moran. 'Focused mostly on her TV past. She was easy on the eye in her younger days. Lot of casting couches around back then. We're talking to a couple of her old directors later. Maybe there's still a beef or two over spurned advances. They're knocking on a bit now, though.'

'This is a younger man,' said Walker.

Moran scoffed. 'Good job we've got Poirot on our side.'

Walker ignored him. 'Even if he did murder Susan in

her own home, he still had to carry the body to a vehicle, and then from Fairholmes to the deposition.'

Moran widened his eyes. 'Deposition? Haven't heard that one since training college.'

'What about Susan herself?'

'Pretty boring,' said Myers. 'One daughter, Charlotte, now nineteen. Studies in America. Flying back later today. Susan was part of a local book club. Romance. Kept an allotment near Chelmorton. Lots of walking. Weekly group hikes. The group leader said she used to go every week but she hadn't seen her much since the heart op.'

'Tell me about that,' said Sawyer.

Myers shrugged. 'Husband's story checks out. Transplant last year at Wythenshawe. Records are confidential, but Ronald showed me the paperwork, photos.' He checked his notes and struggled with the pronunciation. 'Cardio... my... o... pathy.' He looked up, satisfied. 'Heart struggles to get blood around the body.'

Moran turned back to face Shepherd and muttered into his desk. 'It's certainly doing that now.' A couple of titters from his colleagues.

'DC Moran.' Sawyer took a step towards him and pivoted his chair around. He leaned in, close to Moran's shoulder. 'Can I ask you a question?'

Moran squeezed out a weak smile. 'You're the boss.'

Sawyer leaned back, stood upright over Moran. 'Have you ever lost someone?'

Moran shrugged. 'My cat died when I was twelve.'

Sawyer smiled. 'You say you went to training college. But I'm not sure your victim awareness skills are up to speed. When we're done with this case, let's get you on one of the new support courses. There's a really good six-weeker. You can do it weekdays, before or after work.'

Moran smiled. 'I'm sure I'll learn a lot. *Sir*.'

Sawyer turned away. He caught the eye of Stephen Bloom, seated in the corner. Bloom flinched and averted his eyes. 'DS Shepherd.'

'Sir?'

Sawyer kept his gaze trained on Bloom. 'Are you ready yet?'

Shepherd frowned. 'Ready?'

'To tell me. I'd say it's something media-related. You were probably waiting to tell me privately after this. Let's get it all out in the open, though. We're all friends here.' He smiled at Moran, who responded with an even bigger grin.

Shepherd slumped. 'Local press are running something tomorrow. Exclusive. *Death Of A TV Star*-type thing. Dean Logan.'

The temperature dropped. Sawyer let the information settle. Dean Logan was a *Derbyshire Times* hack who delighted in stirring up petty crusades against the police. He was a Wapping reject with a nostalgia for pre-Leveson tabloid culture. 'DC Walker. Special mission for you. I want to know more about Susan's heart transplant. Did she milk her celebrity and jump the queue? If so, is there anyone who got bumped down the list or maybe even died? Any unhappy relatives who might have a problem with Susan? Look into connections with the surgeon, the hospital. The stab in the heart might be a coincidence but I want to be sure.

'And, Stephen?' Bloom rose to his feet. 'Get Logan under control. If ITN spoke to Fairholmes, I imagine they summoned him as their local bin-dipper and he's shafted them for the exclusivity.' Bloom nodded, nervous. 'Either that, or someone in this room wasn't listening when I said I didn't want the press involved.'

11

Back at the cottage, Sawyer abandoned *Audition* for *The Texas Chain Saw Massacre*, a film the back cover review quote insisted 'should come with a free change of underwear'. He'd seen it before, as a student, and had found himself more interested in the reactions of his flatmates than the content of the film. This time, it felt slow and pointless, with too much screaming.

He stripped to boxer shorts and headed into the bedroom, where he'd laid out a rubber training mat, a barbell and bench. In the corner, he had jammed a full-size Wing Chun training dummy, with protruding wooden poles to simulate an opponent's arms and legs. He used Wing Chun techniques for meditation, and as a base discipline for his beloved Jeet Kune Do. The 'wooden man' was a powerful tool for honing technique, combination blocks and strikes, and to improve sharpness.

His back muscles cracked and pulsed as he worked, distorting the Greek tattoo across his back: *Κατά τον δαίμονα εαυτού* ('True to his own spirit'). He had lost some weight since the Crawley case, but his hand speed was exceptional, and he revelled in the pain as he worked his core and upper body, driving his wrists and forearms into the dense wood.

He completed a flurry of movements. As he rested, he tuned in to a soft, intermittent drilling sound from the sitting room.

Sawyer took a hand towel and swiped at his forehead and neck, then hurried next door and snatched up his vibrating phone.

He checked the Caller ID and took the call. 'Eva. I've told you. You have got to stop pestering me like this.'

She laughed: soft and sweet, with a hint of indulgence. 'How are you? You sound out of breath.'

'Working out. If you want to find out how I am, you could just read through the string of messages I've been sending.'

'You mean the stalking?'

He took a slug from a bottle of water. 'Semantics. Honestly, these days you can't relentlessly pursue a woman without being accused of harassment.'

Eva sighed, but didn't laugh this time. 'We have to be quick.'

'How's Luka?'

She took a deep breath. 'Difficult. Playing up at school. He's having some counselling but he doesn't want anyone to know. Especially his mates.'

'No ill effects from the car accident?'

'He's had check-ups. He's fine. They think he might have ADHD.'

'I could talk to him.'

Eva jumped in. 'We're separating. Me and Dale.'

Sawyer switched the phone to speaker and set it down on the coffee table. 'Is he moving out?' He opened his wallet and shuffled through the contents: coffee shop loyalty schemes, bank cards, expired V&A Museum membership. He dug into the inner pocket and took out the tatty polaroid of his mother, standing at the gate on Christmas morning, 1987: awkward smile; orange bathrobe; coal-black hair bundled into the hood of the robe, with a few strands spilling over her shoulders.

'He wants to live closer to Manchester. Still keen to see Luka. I told him not to tell Luka yet. But he did, anyway.'

Sawyer pulled out a European Health Insurance card. 'Gives him the moral high ground. Makes it look like his decision, like you're too difficult to live with. If you'd spoken to Luka together, it would have seemed too mutual and made him look weak.' He studied the front of the card.

Name: BROOKS
Given names: SHAUN CHRISTOPHER

Eva sighed. 'I don't care about any of that.'

'You just want him out. You think he'll be a better influence on Luka with occasional access. Summer trip to the Heights of Abraham.' She didn't answer. He heard the clink of a Zippo lighter. 'You're smoking?'

'Yes. That's still legal, right?'

'Depends where you are. I can talk to Luka, you know. He might listen to the guy who rescued him from an underground cave network.'

She puffed out smoke. 'I don't want to put him in that awkward place. Between you and his dad.'

'Is that how you see Dale? There's your father, and there's your dad? One is biology. The other is a *relationship*. Sometimes they go together. Not in this case.'

'Is this an audition for stepfather?'

He laughed. 'Does Dale know someone called Shaun Brooks?'

'Haven't heard the name, no.'

59

He replaced the cards and photo and closed the wallet. 'Come and see me.' The crackle of burning tobacco, another puff of smoke. 'You know you want to.'

'It was a mistake. You know it can't be repeated. For everyone's sake.'

'Including mine?'

'Especially yours.'

Sawyer pulled on a T-shirt. 'You can't just plot your life from moment to moment. Neat little segues from one phase to the next. It's messier than that.'

'No, but I want the separation to be smooth. Dale knows it's over, but he also knows about you. He's wary.'

'I'm a big boy. Dale likes to intimidate people. It's his currency. Bullies need victims, though, Eva. He doesn't scare me.'

She barked out a laugh. Contemptuous, exasperated. 'Always the same with men. It all comes down to a pissing competition in the end. I work for an accountant, remember? Not everything is zero sum.'

'You don't make a "smooth" separation from people like Dale. I did a bit of checking. Jason Haig. The driver of the car that hit Luka. *Accidentally*, remember? It was Luka's fault?'

'Jake...'

'Haig was badly beaten in his own house a couple of weeks ago. In front of his wife and son.' Sawyer picked up Shepherd's tactical pen from a pot on the table and doodled on a stack of Post-it notes. 'The lad was ten years old. They threatened to hurt the bloke's wife unless he joined in with the beating.'

'Please.'

'They made a ten-year-old boy punch his own dad in the face. That's not a robbery with violence. That's calculated humiliation.'

'You don't know that Dale had anything to do with that.'

'Yes, I do. And so do you.' Silence at Eva's end. 'Come and see me.'

He checked the phone. She had hung up.

12

'Is it in?' Keating tapped something into his corner computer with a flourish. He pivoted his chair to face Sawyer and Shepherd.

Sawyer glanced at Shepherd. 'You haven't seen it online?'

Keating waved a hand. 'I don't look at anything online. There's just too fucking much of it.'

Sawyer smirked. 'Of what?'

'Of...' He sighed. '*People*. And their opinions. What does it say?'

On cue, Stephen Bloom entered, trailed by DC Walker. By his standards, Bloom was dressed down: dark blazer, white shirt, no tie. Walker was Monday-morning fresh, and Sawyer wrinkled his nose at his excessive cologne.

Bloom laid the morning edition of the *Derbyshire Times* on Keating's desk. The front page showed a large archive shot of Susan Bishop as Suzie Swift, clearly taken sometime during her TV heyday: beaming in period dress, huddled in for a promo shot with TV variety star, Ronnie Barker.

The headline was a screamer. A Logan classic.

Keating scanned the story. 'How does he know she was stabbed?'

'We saw the husband yesterday, sir,' said Shepherd. Keating raised his eyes to Sawyer, then across to Shepherd. 'We gave him the details. '

Sawyer shook his head. 'Logan must have doorstepped him.'

Keating sat back. 'Evidently. When you say "we" gave him—'

'I told him,' said Sawyer.

'And you didn't think it might be worth keeping that private? Cards close to chest? At least until Drummond has finished his work.'

'He's her husband. He has a right to know.'

'Yes. But he also has a right to expect us to catch the bastard who killed his wife. And that's a fuck of a lot easier if the killer doesn't know what we know.'

Walker stepped forward. 'Shall I arrange some support for the FLOs at the Bishop house, sir? There's bound to be more press interest now.'

Keating smiled. 'That's up to your case manager, son.' He flashed a glare at Shepherd. 'Let's stay ahead of the story from now on. I'd rather the public got their details from us, not from serpents like Logan. Any hard news?'

'Just spoke to Sally,' said Shepherd. 'Her team have completed two sweeps of the Bishop house and surroundings. Nothing.'

Sawyer turned to him. 'Don't you find that a bit strange?'

'He might have forced her outside,' said Walker. 'Weapon threat.'

Shepherd nodded. 'Or he's just meticulous. It's

happened before. Killers who do their homework. They know what we look for. One guy in Baltimore used a black light torch to make sure he'd caught all of the fluids.'

'I agree with Walker,' said Sawyer. 'He surprised her. Forced her out to a vehicle. Subdued her.'

'Find me the vehicle,' said Keating. 'This could be pretty straightforward if he's stupid enough to be driving something we can link to him directly.'

'Myers is on it, sir,' said Shepherd.

Walker cleared his throat. 'I spoke to the husband about Susan's heart transplant. He said there was no hint of any resentment, no accusations of queue jumping. They were asked if they wanted details on the donor, but declined. The operation was textbook, apparently. He said her condition went from life-threatening to being as manageable as something like asthma.'

Sawyer sat down, leaving himself and Keating as the only ones not standing. 'And nobody in her life was opposed to organ donation on religious grounds or whatever?'

All eyes were on Walker. 'I didn't pursue that angle. I'll look into it.'

'I don't think any religions are opposed to organ donation,' said Shepherd, 'apart from Christian Scientists. They let their kids die rather than submit to medical care.'

Bloom spoke up. 'They wouldn't see it that way. They would see their child as being chosen by the Lord.'

Sawyer nodded. 'And *He* has that "mysterious ways" disclaimer. Handy. Although, of course, there's also that inconvenient commandment about not killing. Which is what the parents are doing to their kids by refusing the medical help.' His phone buzzed. He stood up and spoke to Shepherd. 'I have to take this. Brief the team and call an update for 3pm.'

He strode into his office and closed the door. The low autumn sun flared through the half-closed window blind, mottling the room in solid strips of shadow.

He sank into his chair and connected the call. 'Max.'

'Jake. Good to hear you.' Male voice. Middle-aged. London, close to cockney. 'How are things up North? Grim?'

'Green. Just about.'

'Winding down for the winter?'

Sawyer rummaged through a drawer. 'Hardly. Plenty of excitement up here lately.'

'Bloodshed at the Nell Gwynn Tearooms?'

Sawyer laughed. '*Fawlty Towers*.'

DI Max Reeves tutted down the phone line. 'Still can't get much past you. I've been busy. Got your message. Not like you to come running. You must have got the internet up there, by now?'

'I'm calling in the favour.'

Reeves went quiet for a second. 'I've got the files for your mum's case, from general registry. They were outsourced to the Met about fifteen years ago. Also dug out the Buxton station records for a year either side, as you said. And I've sniffed out a few repeat burglars from that time. And when I say "that time", Sawyer, we're basically talking fucking Jurassic era on the police admin clock.'

Sawyer pulled out a notepad and pen. 'I get that it wasn't easy, Max. You can lose the crown of thorns.'

Reeves laughed: too loud and long. 'This is a lot more than calling in a fucking favour. I don't see why you couldn't do this yourself. Bit of research not beyond a man of your talents? Or do I not want to know?'

Sawyer squinted through the blinds. 'It's personal. I don't want anyone knowing that I'm looking into it.'

Reeves sighed. 'Like I say, a few names pop up. If you

could tell me a bit more about what you're looking for, I could narrow it down.'

Sawyer scratched out a doodle in the corner of a clean page. 'I'll cover that.'

'Top of the table of repeat appearances is one Owen Casey. No fixed abode. Notes say he was part of a community of Irish travellers that settled around Uttoxeter in the seventies and eighties. He was nineteen at the time of his last arrest. June 1988. A few weeks before...' He trailed off. 'Now. Apart from being so prolific, here's the thing that makes Casey stick out. I think he was used as an informant, around this time. June.'

'Unusual for travellers.'

'Yeah. I thought that. Not usually a rich seam of snitches. But this last offence was pretty nasty. Aggravated. And yet he was released without charge. Homeowner chased and caught him. Given his history, it's unthinkable that he would have just walked.'

Sawyer wrote the name Owen Casey on the top page of the pad. 'Any paperwork? Anything formal? Any record of a specific enquiry he might have helped with?'

'Not a scrap. Source handling was different then. You know that. These days, it's regulated up the arse by RIPA. Back then, it was all informal. Snouts down the pub.'

Sawyer sat back. 'I didn't realise you were that old, Max.'

Reeves snorted. 'Comedian. Are you not getting this, Jake? I'm catching the bad smell from here.'

'Who nicked him?'

Reeves slurped at a drink. He was building to something. 'Ready for the fun bit? The arrest record. I went through hundreds from that period. With respect to your humble beginnings, Jake, this is Buxton, Derbyshire. It's not Bogota, Colombia. Out of all the records outsourced to the Met from that station at that time, including the murders, this is the only arrest record with *no paperwork*. I only know Casey was nicked because he's mentioned in the victim statement. Someone didn't want his arrest to go on record—'

'But they forgot to bury the victim statement.'

'Yeah. The victim clearly knew Casey, because he mentions him by name. Must have done him over before.'

'Is he still around?'

'Kenneth Townsend. Died about ten years ago.'

Sawyer sketched jagged lines around the O of Owen. 'So where is Casey now?'

Reeves laughed. 'We are *so* square now, Sawyer. In fact, I think it's you that owes me a favour.'

13

Amy Scott slotted her phone into the dashboard cradle and pulled out of the hospital car park. It had been a busy shift: an endless staff meeting on new NICE guidelines, training up an assistant nurse, fighting a few minor admin fires, and a depressing end-of-life care meeting with the parents of a twenty-nine-year-old who would not be seeing thirty. Her friend Lisa worked in oncology, and although Amy's work never directly involved breaking bad news, their roles often overlapped.

For lunch, she had inhaled a bowl of greenery from the hospital M&S, and she was craving a hit of carbs. Ideally, with a glass of something red and barely affordable, in the company of someone with half a brain.

Amy glanced out at the ugly modern church on the corner of Barnsley Road. A sign advertised the latest Alpha Course: Bear Grylls on some mountainside, staring off into the distance, surrounded by think bubbles ('Is there more to life than this?', 'Does God exist?', 'What happens next?').

She unlocked her phone screen. 'Hey, Siri. Call Lisa.'

The phone's virtual assistant confirmed her request and connected the call.

'Hey, babe.'

Lisa was loud and lively, and Amy squeezed the volume decrease button a couple of times. 'You still in?'

'Tell me about it. I feel like I've only just got here! Won't be out until at least seven, at this rate. We'll have to do another night. Sorry, darling. No hot dates on call?'

'Oh, I'm fighting them off. Got to have a break sometime, though.'

Lisa laughed. 'Seriously. Anyone on the scene?'

'Had two good ones recently. The first seemed okay in messages, but then we did a live chat and he was pretty dull. Didn't directly respond to what I was saying. Just seemed to use my messages as a sort of bridge to get to what he wanted to say next.'

Lisa made a buzzing sound; shorthand for 'rejected'. 'What about the other one?'

'He was really nice.'

'And?'

'I mentioned Ava.'

Lisa sighed down the phone. 'Schoolgirl error. They're men. They're looking for sex. Don't make them think of bedtime stories.'

'I want more than just—'

'The more than just sex stuff comes after the sex, not before. Look. You wanna get off Match. Soulmates is loads better for your type.'

Amy laughed. 'Easy for you to say, with the steady consultant boyfriend.'

Lisa coughed. 'It's an open relationship.'

'Does he know that?'

'He seems okay with it when it comes to his wife.'

Amy's phone screen showed an incoming call waiting, from 'Broomfield'.

'Oh. It's Ava's school. I'll have to take it. Call you later.'

Amy tapped the End & Accept icon. 'Hello?'

'Ms Scott? It's Rose from the school office. Are you able to collect Ava today?'

Amy recognised the voice. Chatter in the background. 'Of course. I'm on my way. Is there a problem?' She checked the time: 3:06. The drive was barely ten minutes. Pick-up at 3:20.

'No. Everything is fine. But Ava's uncle called. He left a message.'

'Uncle?'

'Yes. He seemed to think he was picking up Ava today?'

Amy's mind spun through the options. 'I don't have any brothers. Are you sure you've got the right Ava?'

A pause. Muffled conversation. 'Yes. Ava Scott. We don't actually have any other children called Ava.'

Amy squeezed the accelerator. She bullied her way around a queue of turning cars and crossed over the Neepsend canal bridge. 'What was the message?'

More muffled conversation. 'The caller asked if we could write it down and pass it on to you. He said, "I can't take Ava today. But I can do it any other time."'

14

Keating took a chair at the side of the MIT whiteboard and shifted it side-on, to give him both a presiding position and a full view of the room. Sawyer sat at the desk outside his office, behind the perched Sally O'Callaghan and just out of Keating's eyeline. Sally didn't turn to acknowledge him; surely she wasn't still sulking after their exchange yesterday?

'We've completed two full sweeps of the scene at Fairholmes and the Bishop house. Susan's killer has barely left a blade of grass out of place.'

'I've never known a scene like it,' said Sally. 'No blood, no DNA. No fibres. No prints. Patent, latent or impressed. Susan was naked, so we couldn't use any soil samples from footwear. K9s found a few spliff butts at the Derwent site, nothing else.'

'Did you use different personnel for each sweep?' said Sawyer, behind her.

Sally didn't turn. She tilted her head and addressed her response to Shepherd. 'I didn't, actually. They're professionals, and if there was anything to find then they would have found it. We completed several searches. Linear, grid, quadrant, spiral. We're testing the soil samples under her fingertips but I'm guessing it'll be from her allotment. If the killer has left any trace, then Almighty fucking God himself would have trouble finding it.'

'Tyre tracks?' said Keating.

'Plenty. But both the road outside the Bishop home and the Derwent scene were wet. Even if we could separate them, the results would be too distorted to be meaningful.'

A brief, despairing silence. Myers raised his hand. 'Rhodes has been busy on passive data that fits time of death. No ANPR near either scenes. Couple of larger cars caught on shop CCTV in the village, but no plates in view.'

Shepherd sighed. 'Moran? Victimology?'

'I spoke to Ronald Bishop's bridge buddies. Everything tallies. They were a bit touchy about the questions over Ronald's relationship with Susan, but they're adamant that there was nothing going on. Solid as a rock. I also looked into their talent agency. He still does it all by paper. Not too many clients south of sixty. Hardly A-listers. A couple of tax avoidance cases, all wrapped up now. Nothing to suggest any problem with Susan or Ronald. And not a whiff of Yewtree. Surprising, given the demographic.'

'Local press are all over it,' said Keating. 'Stephen is managing the nationals. Let's keep focused and dead-bat any badgering. Usual reasons. We don't want the murderer to know what we know.'

'Hardly worth knowing at the moment, anyway,' said Moran.

Keating glared at him. 'I trust that Logan has got his information from the husband and he isn't enjoying any insider access? Until we decide to actively involve the press, I want all information confidential, on HOLMES, and I do not want to find out that somebody in this room is leaky.'

Walker stood up, taking an attention-drawing trick

from Bloom's book. 'I'm looking into the heart transplant. Meeting a consultant at the Wythenshawe heart unit later.'

'Find out what you can about the donor,' said Sawyer. Keating leaned forward, craning his neck to see where Sawyer was sitting. 'I'm not seeing much relevance, but it'd be good to get the full picture.'

'I also called Ronald Bishop.' Walker awkwardly switched his gaze between Shepherd, Sawyer and Keating. 'We talked about the organ register and I said I was on it, and that I was in favour of the opt-out system. Seemed to strike a chord. He's willing to talk to me later.'

Sawyer's phone buzzed once in his pocket. 'Nice. You warmed him up. Go easy.'

He looked at the screen. Voicemail.

Sawyer listened to the message as Shepherd wound up the briefing.

'Detective Sawyer. My name is Dean Logan. I'm the crime correspondent on the Derbyshire Times. I wonder if you could spare me a few minutes to talk? I understand you're currently in a meeting, but I'm downstairs at the police station. Happy to wait for five minutes. I think you'll be very interested in what I've got to say, but I would prefer to keep it private.'

———

Sawyer met Logan in reception and led him into one of the ground floor interview rooms. He was a vast, ogreish man in his late fifties, shovelled into an unflattering grey suit, unimproved by a lopsided statement tie. The handshake, as expected, was damp and flabby, and Sawyer made a mental note to head for the bathroom hand sanitiser once they were done.

Logan sat at the table in the centre of the room and

tilted his chin up, fixing the standing Sawyer with a constipated perma-squint. He smiled, for effect.

'Let's start with my private number,' said Sawyer. 'How did you get it?'

Logan's eyes found the table top. He shrugged, and held his shoulders high for a few seconds before letting them slump. 'You know better than that, DI Sawyer. I'm a journalist. I don't reveal my sources.'

Sawyer sat down. '"Journalist" is a lofty term for what you are.'

Logan sighed. 'And what term would you use?'

'You're a hack. You know it, too. Which makes you a pretentious hack.'

'Now you're getting high minded. I use journalistic skills to unearth stories that are in the public interest. Just because something is popular, that doesn't mean it has no worth.'

Sawyer sat back, warming to the debate. 'I'd say that journalism is a noble calling. Getting to the truth. Sniffing out the bad guys. Exposing them. For the greater good.'

Logan slid a notepad and pen from his inside pocket. 'For someone who's spent so much time in the big city, you don't half sound naive.'

Sawyer smiled. Logan was getting defensive, maybe winding up for a low blow. 'Do you seriously think you're reporting the "news"? You're a muck-spreader. It's why you fit in so well round here.'

Logan opened his pad. 'One of my old editors said that "news" is what someone, somewhere doesn't want you to print. And the rest is just PR. Puff pieces.' He clicked his pen. 'I'm a bit more base than that. My philosophy is simple. If it bleeds, it leads.'

'Or the more literary version. "Happiness writes white."'

'Eh?'

'French writer. De Montherlant. You'd like him. Went blind and shot himself.' Logan tapped his pen against the table and stared. 'Why are you here? And it's not an existential question.'

'I've got a proposal for you.'

Sawyer leaned forward, ready to raise himself off his chair and show Logan out. 'Talk to Bloom. You won't get much. He's already been chewed out for this morning's front page.'

Logan laughed. 'You boys really do live in the seventies, don't you? You probably think *Life On Mars* was a reality show.' He shook his head. '"Media relations". An analogue job in a digital age. You still think you can "manage" information? You're like those fuckers in the dome at the end of *The Crystal Maze*.'

Sawyer stood up. 'Do what you need to do. But you won't get an inside track from me. Now, Mr Logan. I'm busy, trying to deny you another lead.'

Logan looked down at his notepad. 'It's not about the Bishop case. Boring. Probably turn out to be a jealous younger lover. She looks like a cougar type to me.'

'You should retrain. Come and work for us. We could use that kind of insight.'

'It's about you.'

Sawyer sat down again. 'Me?'

Logan nodded, kept his eyes on the pad. 'I want to do something on you. The Crawley case is a good hook. Tragic past of hero cop. And it's got a great backstory.'

'Backstory?'

Logan looked up. 'Yes. The public loves a bit of the old triumph over adversity. Young boy sees his mother horribly murdered right in front of him. Barely survives the attack himself. His brother suffers a breakdown. But he rises up, becomes a bigshot policeman. Now fights the kind of monsters who robbed him of his mother.'

Sawyer raised his eyebrows, nodded. 'Plenty of blood, too. An ocean of claret. It would definitely make the front page.'

'I expect so.'

'Warm blood. Not the type that runs through your veins.'

Logan sat back in his chair. 'I would have thought that *ad hominem* attacks were beneath a man of your reputation.'

'Why would I even consider this?'

'*Interest*. The public's. But mainly mine. See, I'm wondering why you've come back to your old stomping ground around the time of the release of the man convicted for your mother's death.'

'Long time ago. Justice has been done.'

Logan studied him. Sawyer's eyes sparkled, unwavering. 'He who fights monsters, Detective. I'm sure you know your Nietzsche.'

Sawyer stayed silent, waiting for more.

Logan wrote a number onto the pad. 'Your father tried to block Marcus Klein's release. But you didn't.' He tore off the paper. 'You've got to admit, that is kind of interesting.'

Sawyer took a deep breath. 'Like I said, I'm busy and I'm afraid I will have to respectfully decline your request for an interview. Now, unless you have any other information relating to the current case...'

Logan stood up. He pushed the strip of paper with the number across the table towards Sawyer, and tucked his pad and pen back into his pocket. 'Don't get me wrong. I'm not making judgements. You've given me plenty to write about. The local body count has certainly spiked since you've been back.'

Sawyer stood, opened the door.

Logan walked towards it and paused in the frame. He turned to Sawyer and took a step forward. 'Hacks. Journalists. Whatever you want to call us. We follow our instinct. And my instinct is screaming at me to leave you well alone, DI Sawyer. But I'm the stubborn type. I like trouble. And trouble certainly seems to follow you around.'

15

Sam Palmer bundled his kitbag into the boot and looked back at the floodlit training ground. The Astro pitch was pea-green and shimmering under a fine spray of evening rain. A few of the Chesterfield first team had stuck around to work on set pieces, and their coltish shouts filtered through the tall wire fencing.

It had been a good session. The players were sharp and hungry for his insight. His assistant had carried the team through pre-season and managed the first few match days. But he'd struggled (two losses and a draw), and Sam was keen to re-impose his defensive philosophy: sit back, steal the ball in midfield, use width to counter-attack.

Sam drove out of Hasland and aimed for Bamford. His stomach flipped at the thought of the midweek game: his first in charge since his recovery. The team were ready, but was he? Had he come back too quickly? Probably. But it would soon turn around: the football and his health. He was an optimist, and as he told the players, he believed that 'mistakes are the building blocks of learning'.

He stopped at a temporary light on the Baslow Road. The rain scattered across the windscreen: light but relentless. He set the wipers to a two-second delay and cued up a Roxy Music album. He would call in at the Angler's Rest for a meal and then head home. He was meant to avoid pubs, or any situation that lent itself to alcohol. But he had a stubborn streak, and felt that if he could cope in trickier settings, then it would make everyday life less of a trial.

The light changed, and he moved off, turning onto a single-lane track at Eastmoor, slotting in between the low stone walls. He entered the National Park to the incongruous strut of 'Love Is The Drug'.

At the Angler's Rest, the dining area was busy and noisy, and the waitress seated him at a lousy table on the edge of a central lane of staff, scurrying between the kitchen and bar. But he was hungry and there seemed to be few other options. He took a steadying breath in through his nose and slipped on his glasses to study the menu. It was a challenge. It would all be a challenge from here.

He ordered the beef wellington and called Judy. As he waited for the call to connect, he felt a hand on his shoulder and looked up to see a red-faced man in a blue-and-white Chesterfield FC polo shirt.

The man grinned. 'The *real* Big Sam!' He was happy drunk. He leaned down and Sam caught his alcohol breath: sweet and heartbreaking, like an ex's perfume. 'Be good to get you back in that dugout. First win of the season on Wednesday, eh?'

Sam smiled. 'That's what we're working for.'

The man backed away, offering an exaggerated palms-up gesture of deferral. 'Ah. Course you are. It's a tough job. Up the Spireites! Can I get you a drink?' He winced. 'Soft drink, of course.'

'No, thank you.'

'Ah. No problem. I'll leave you in peace, mate.' He

bowed his head, too close to Sam's ear, and patted him on the back. 'Take care of yourself.'

Sam nodded. 'I will. Thank you very much. Hope we can give you a reason to celebrate on Wednesday.' He turned his back slightly. The man hovered.

'Hello?' Judy answered. 'It's noisy. Where are you?'

Sam pointed at the phone and smiled. The man gave him a clumsy thumbs-up and staggered away. 'Angler's Rest.'

Judy sighed.

'It's okay. I'm not daft. Getting something to eat.'

'Glass of Coke, right?'

'Not even that. Water.'

'How was training?'

He sipped his drink. 'Better than I thought it would be. It'll take time.'

'*You* need more time. It's only football. And don't give me the Shankly crap. It's not more important than life and death.'

'I agree.'

'You didn't used to!'

'Looking forward to seeing you tomorrow. I'm feeling good.'

She paused. 'Really?'

'Yeah. Really. Let's go out.'

'Fischer's?'

He laughed. 'I'll save that for the proposal.' She scoffed. 'Look. This is why I'm calling from here. It's the new, transparent me. It helps with the recovery. To be more accountable.'

'You could get a proper sponsor, Sam.'

'I'm not doing that. I can fix this myself.'

'Nobody is giving out medals for martyrdom. This is in your blood. You need *help*.'

'Honestly, love, I'm good. I really do feel like I've been through the worst. I'm looking forward to things. Football. *Us*.'

She sniffed, warming to him. 'In that order?'

'Jude. I've been given a second chance, I know that. I'm not going to screw it up.'

———

Sam passed through the rural suburbs of Bamford and turned into the twisty lane that led to his single-storey semi. The path tapered into a cul de sac as it reached the house, set deep at the back of a neat front garden, behind high hedges, almost fully moulted for the chill to come. He had been born here, forty-one years earlier, and his parents had handed it down when they'd moved to a less isolated place near Onecote. It was perfect for Sam and his dog, Buddy: a small but tenacious Staffordshire Bull Terrier.

He parked at the end of the drive and killed the engine.

Barking.

It was Buddy, inside the house. A local vet friend called in to feed the dog on training and match days, but he would have left a couple of hours ago.

Sam frowned. Buddy wasn't a noisy dog; he only barked when there was something to bark about. And this was persistent. Full volume. Ripping and roaring. Barely pausing for breath.

He opened the door and walked round to the boot to retrieve his kitbag. The rain had stopped, but a damp mist hung in the air.

A movement down the lane made him turn his head. A small van, dark purple, had parked up on the scrap of pavement. The back doors were ajar, and someone was sitting by one of the back wheels, head in hands.

Sam squinted through the darkness. The figure was short and slight. A child?

He closed the boot. 'You okay there?'

He moved towards the van.

The figure looked up and rose to its feet. A man. Chunky black hiking jacket. Dark-striped beanie. No more than five-three. Sam had at least forty pounds on him, and he barely reached up to his shoulders.

The man smiled. Worried but friendly eyes. He gestured towards the van. 'Oh, hi. Are you local? I've come up from Nottingham. I'm trying to find a friend's house but my phone's just died. Used all the charge on Google Maps.' He leaned to the side, looking round to Sam's parked car.

Barking.

'What's your phone?' said Sam.

'Galaxy. Can't believe I've been so stupid.'

'I've got an iPhone. I don't think the charger—'

The man stepped towards Sam. 'Can I just use your phone to have a quick look where I am? Ten seconds and I'm gone. Just need to get my bearings. I've got his postcode.' He fumbled in his pocket. 'Happy to throw you a few quid. I'm desperate, mate.'

Sam shook his head. 'No. Don't worry. No problem at all.' He dug out his phone. 'Just tell me the postcode. Where does your mate—'

In the time it took for Sam to glance at his phone screen and find the Google Maps app, the man dashed forward from the van, and stopped within touching distance. The smile had gone. The long, broad blade of a kitchen knife extended beyond his hand by at least an inch at the hilt.

'I'm sorry, Sam. But I need you to put these on.' He withdrew the knife to his hip and held out a pair of sturdy handcuffs.

Sam stared at the cuffs, frozen. 'And why would I do that?'

'Because if you don't, within ten seconds, then I'll stab you with this. And then I'll drag your body around that wall and you'll die, Sam.'

The man was still and steady. Waiting. Almost polite. It all felt like some woozy hallucination.

Barking.

'What happens when I put the handcuffs on?'

The smile again. 'That's a surprise. But there's your choice. Certain death or possible survival.'

Sam felt a little bloated from the food, but he could take this guy. He had the size advantage; the man had the knife. He looked skinny, though, underneath the jacket. Barely strong enough to lift the knife, let alone do any damage. But the man's attention was focused. If Sam complied now, he could disarm him later, when he was distracted.

Sam took the cuffs and examined them. 'I'm not putting on handcuffs and getting into a van with a stranger.'

The man nodded. 'Ten... nine...'

'Look. Where are we even going? What do you want?'

'Eight... seven...'

Barking.

Was he an ex-player with a grudge? Someone who hadn't made the grade?

'Six... five...'

There was no menace in the tone of the man's countdown. He seemed more irritated by the delay.

'Okay!' Sam put on the cuffs but kept the strands unfastened.

The man paused. 'Through the ratchets.'

Sam bluffed it. 'I've put them on, okay? Now what?'

The man regarded him. 'Four... three...'

Sam carefully clicked the strand through the end ratchet, leaving the cuffs locked but with maybe enough room for manoeuvre.

The man was on him in a flurry. He felt something flat clunk against his forehead. Had he been punched?

His fingertips touched the ground: stony, wet. Then his cheek.

Then.

Barking.

Black.

―――――

Sam awoke with a ferocious headache, and opened his eyes, into stinging white light.

He was in the van, his mouth sealed by thick gaffer tape.

The panic reared up and he snorted a breath in through his nose.

He blinked to find focus. He was laid out on the floor, prone on a sheet of plastic. Polythene. He had been stripped to the waist and his cuffed hands had been forced behind his back.

He tried to speak, shout, scream. Nothing came. Just a muffled cry from the back of his throat.

Movement from behind. Something heavy pressing on his lower back. It was the man, kneeling, pinning him down.

How much time had passed? Sam twisted his head up and around, straining for clarity, more detail. But the back of the van was windowless.

The cuffs and the weight of the man kept him steady.

'If you struggle, if you move, it will be worse.'

Behind him, the man shifted around, settling into position, rustling the polythene.

Then he was still, considering something.

Outside, Buddy's barking staggered the silence. Intermittent now. Running out of hope.

From behind, the man gripped Sam's neck, holding his head still. He was surprisingly strong.

With the bodily pressure and the hand and the cuffs, Sam was practically immobilised. He stared out at the folds of plastic. Crumpled peaks and valleys. He screwed his eyes shut, rapid breaths rasping in and out of his nostrils.

'I'm sorry, Sam.'

An impact, somewhere in the middle of his back. Sharp.

A tingling. Electrical?

The tingling receded, replaced by a rising heat.

Burning. Unbearable, unthinkable burning. From the inside.

'I'm so sorry.'

16

Sawyer opened his office door and leaned against the frame. Keating stood up-front by Shepherd, arms folded. He angled his head, beckoning, and Sawyer moved out to take a spot nearer the action. He had slept badly, barely at all, drifting in and out of baffling dreams. The MIT floor was packed and lively, but there was a distance, a surreal sheen that hung over the room like a mist. Faces leered: hostile and alien, washed out by the mid-morning light.

Shepherd said something to Bloom about press management. Keating confirmed Bloom's response.

Sally O'Callaghan reported. Something about soil samples being inconclusive. It was all fuzzy and amorphous, drowned out by his inner chatter. The sharpest image from his dreams: his mother, lifting him up, spinning him round. He was laughing at the dizziness, the thrill at the lack of control. She swept him close to the ground and his legs swam in the air, desperate for contact with the ground. She spun him twice, three times, denying his landing, before setting him down. And then his father. Roaring. Growling. Telling him he was going to get him. His mother shouting.

'Run! Don't look back.'

'DI Sawyer asked me to look into Susan's heart transplant'. Walker stood up near the front and turned to the detectives. The mention of his name jolted Sawyer into focus. 'I spoke to Ronald Bishop. He said that the heart became available when a forty-six-year-old man died in a gym accident in Bole Hill, Sheffield. They were asked if they wanted to know more but declined. Susan was taken to the heart unit at Wythenshawe where the operation was performed the same day.'

Sawyer pushed off the door frame and walked to the front. 'Why were they told the donor age?'

Walker faltered. 'He said it was to make the risk clear. Apparently, there's a slight concern about heart donors aged thirty-five to fifty, but the benefits in her case outweighed the risk.'

'What about the religious angle?' said Shepherd.

Walker nodded. 'I did some research on that.'

'Googled it,' said Sawyer. He glanced at Keating, didn't get the look.

Walker was unfazed. 'Actually, I spoke to a friend of my dad's. A theology teacher. He said that all the main religions either endorse organ donation or see it as a matter for the individual. Apart from Japanese Shinto, where the dead body is considered to be impure and dangerous, and so it's difficult to get consent from bereaved families for donation or dissection.' He looked at his notepad. 'They have this thing called the "itai", which is like the bond between the dead person and the bereaved. It can't be broken, and "injuring" the body by removing organs would violate the bond.'

'Interesting,' said Sawyer. 'But it feels like a dead end. We think we know where she was killed and we know the weapon and method. We still don't know why. Get more on the donor. The gym accident.'

'There must be more in Susan's relationship history,' said Shepherd. 'We're hardly likely to get a clear picture from her husband. He says they were solid, but she might have been doing a good job hiding something.'

Sawyer nodded. 'Dig deeper. Old flames. Crushes. Illicit encounters. Talk to the other people in her walking group and book club. And get Rhodes working overtime on the CCTV. All routes mapped, all businesses with CCTV investigated. Every second of footage analysed. Finding the vehicle might be our only hope of finding the killer.'

He turned and headed back to his office.

'How was Dean Logan?' said Moran.

Sawyer stopped. 'What?' He stared at Moran, but he didn't look up.

'I saw you'd signed him in yesterday. Is he helping with the enquiry?' Moran raised his head, looked around the room, avoiding Sawyer.

'A personal matter,' said Sawyer. 'Unrelated to the case. He chanced it, but got nothing.' He walked over to Moran's desk. 'DC Moran, it might be an idea to focus on casework, rather than snooping on your superiors.'

'Sawyer,' said Keating.

At last, Moran looked at Sawyer. He took off his wire-frame glasses and pecked something off one of the lenses. 'Just saw it in passing. I wondered if Logan had some insight you were interested in. And I agree, sir. We *all* need to keep totally focused on the case.' He smiled.

Sawyer held eye contact and returned the smile. 'Get down to the Batcave. With Rhodes. I want you and your totally focused mind to work through that CCTV footage. Every minute. Every second. No natural light until you've found me that vehicle.'

17

Sawyer drove out of Buxton and stopped at the High Peak Bookstore, a bookshop and café in a converted warehouse on the edge of Sterndale Moor. He bought a fresh copy of *The Gift Of Fear* and pushed on down to Alstonefield, playing the third My Bloody Valentine album at a volume loud enough to get the Mini's windows buzzing.

He stopped at The George, and grazed on a ploughman's lunch, dipping in and out of the book.

Denial is a save now, pay later scheme.

He gazed out of the window, across the fields, down to Dovedale. The George was propped on a limestone plateau between the Dove and Manifold gorges, and he felt the tug of the valley. Always, the ache for the pristine past. Infinite and uncluttered. He could make it to the cave in an hour on foot. Ten minutes by car.

But he had an appointment.

He had expected something more formal, similar to a dentist's surgery: a refitted detached house with its own car park. But the address took him to a generic estate of modern semis just outside the neighbouring village of Stanshope.

The front door had no bell, so he rapped on the letterbox, sparking a volley of yapping from inside. As he waited, he noticed the modest brass plaque on the wall by the door.

GOLDMAN COUNSELLING CENTRE

The door creaked open, and a slight, elderly woman stood in the doorway, clutching a wriggling Jack Russell: black-and-white body, rusty brown face.

Sawyer brightened and petted the dog. 'I have an appointment. With Alex?'

The woman smiled. She was late sixties, with a blow-dried helmet of battleship-grey hair. Her clothes were bland and colour-matched: fawn blouse shirt over a beige roll-neck; tasselled check shawl around her neck.

She leaned forward and studied Sawyer with her watery eyes. 'Mr Sawyer, isn't it? Please come through.'

She turned and led him through a dog-musty hallway. The walls were hidden behind framed academic certificates and undersized art prints: mediocre landscape watercolours, sterile pet portraits. The woman ushered the dog into a kitchen area at the end of the corridor and closed the door behind it. She opened another door and gestured towards what looked like a sitting room.

'Please go through.'

He led the way. The room was large and clean and uncluttered: a vast, throne-like mauve armchair in one corner; black chaise longue tucked along the near wall;

coffee table with box of tissues, water jug, glasses. A tray sat on a curvy-legged side table by the armchair: steaming teapot, cups, plate of biscuits.

The woman closed the door behind them. 'Would you like some tea, Mr Sawyer?'

'Jake is fine. No, thank you. I'll take a biscuit, though.'

She smiled. 'Take them all if you like. My husband lays all of this out before sessions. I think he's trying to fatten me up.' She took off her scarf and hung it over the back of the armchair.

'Your husband?'

She sat down. 'Thirty-five years this December. He's in antiques. Handles my admin and bookings.'

Sawyer sat on the edge of the chaise longue. 'You're Alex?'

She laughed. 'Ah! I see the confusion. Did Maggie not tell you? Is it a problem?'

'What?'

'A female therapist. Some men—'

'No. Of course not.'

'That's good. I find the clients who do struggle with it are the ones who assumed I was male.' She poured herself some tea. 'Anyway, this is just an initial chat, to get a sense of what kind of work might be useful. No charge.'

Sawyer looked around. The wall art here was a more tasteful variant of the pieces in the hall: more landscapes and animals, but rendered in idiosyncratic styles. Sheepdog herding sheep. Slow-shutter photo of a waterfall. A city at night: vast, blurry blobs of neon. Aiming for Van Gogh. 'I'm not really—'

'Why are you here, Jake? What do you want out of this?'

He sucked in a deep breath, took a few seconds to release it. 'I'd like to sleep a bit better, for one.'

Alex poured in some milk and stirred. The tinkling teaspoon jarred against the silence. 'And why don't you sleep well?'

'I just... I find it difficult to switch off my brain.'

She nodded. 'There must be plenty of unpleasant images in there, given your job.'

'Did Maggie explain my line of work?' Alex nodded. 'I suppose so. I take Temazepam.'

'Is it just general activity? Or is there something broader? A problem? Something you'd like to change?'

'Yes.'

She blew on the tea, tried a sip, winced. 'And how are you addressing the problem? Self-medication?'

'It's more of a confusion than a problem. I had a difficult case earlier this year, during which I suffered from what I think was a panic attack. But I've never felt anything like it before. I've never experienced anything close to panic, or anxiety.'

'Or fear?' Alex set the cup down on her side table. 'You have every reason to feel fear, given what happened to you when you were a child.'

A cold rush through his veins. Again, the sheen. The strangeness of it all. The woman, with her smile and her tea. What *was* this? Why would he be sitting here? 'It was the first time I can remember feeling it, or at least what I'd always imagined it felt like.'

'Tell me about what happened when you were a child. I'd like to hear what *you* think of it.'

He sighed. 'Already? Childhood stuff?'

Alex nodded. 'I understand your frustration. It is a bit of a cliché. And most people have pretty dull and trauma-free childhoods. But you're not most people are you, Jake?'

'My mother was murdered.' He was surprised to feel a rush of irritation. 'The man who did it tried to kill me and

92

my brother. I was six, my brother was eight. He also killed my dog.'

Alex didn't flinch. 'What breed?'

'Jack Russell.'

'What was the dog's name?'

'Henry.'

'And my Molly reminds you of him?'

'A bit.'

'You were quick to reach out, to pet her.'

He shrugged. 'I like Jack Russells.'

'So do I. What do you like about them?'

'They're crazy.'

She paused. 'Your mother's murder. The memory, the pain. It's returning to you now? Making it difficult to sleep?'

'Yes.'

Alex tried the tea again, slurped. 'I have rather a big question. It might seem obvious. Why is this only coming up now? Something that happened thirty years ago.'

'Isn't that why I'm here?'

'I don't know. You're telling me.'

'I've been working in London. It used to be difficult, when I worked here. In Buxton. Then I moved away and it seemed to get easier.'

'And now you're back, close to where it all happened, it seems to be returning?' He nodded. 'What do you mean by "it", exactly?'

'The images, sounds, the sense of the day.'

She nodded, enthused. 'The sense? How about the sensations? The emotions? How you felt?'

'I don't really get that. It's more—'

'The events?'

'Yes.'

Alex reached over to a cabinet and pulled out a sheet of

paper. 'Thank you, Jake. That's a great start. Before we go any further, I would like you to do a bit of homework. Nothing too scary, just a questionnaire. It's called the Beck Anxiety Inventory. You might have done it before?' He took the paper, shook his head. 'It's a useful tool to kickstart our work. It will show me how much this disturbance is impacting your life, impairing your functioning. You can fill in the paper version and post it, or do it online and email me. The address is on there.'

'I'll do it online.'

Alex smiled. 'The men always do.' She stood up. Sawyer mirrored her. 'I look forward to it. Could you send it over tomorrow and come and see me again on Friday? Could you make it earlier? At 2pm?'

Sawyer realised she was the first person to not express her sorrow for his loss and for what had happened to him. It was a welcome change. 'Yes. See you again on Friday. Nice to meet you.'

'You too, Jake. It was an absolute pleasure.'

They shook hands and Sawyer opened the door. Molly scurried to the other side of the kitchen door and scratched at the floor, whimpering. Sawyer turned.

Alex was writing something in a careworn old notebook. 'I'm sure we can help,' she said.

'We?'

She looked up. 'Yes. A bit of me. But mostly you.'

18

Sawyer drove up to Longnor village and bought cod and chips from the Manifold Fish & Chip Shop. He parked on the cobbled town square and lifted the chips into his mouth, one by one, staring up at the 1903 table of market tolls above the door of the craft shop. Four pence for a horse, a penny for a pig.

Simpler times.

He called Shepherd. 'I'm not coming in again this afternoon, unless there's any big development.'

Shepherd paused on the other end. 'Okay. There has been a bit of movement.'

Sawyer screwed up the fish and chip paper. 'Go on.'

'The gym accident was at the Xercise4Less gym in Sheffield last year. Forty-six-year-old male. Timings work with Susan's transplant. Roy Tyler. He was taken to the Northern General. They induced a coma but he died overnight. Donors have to die in hospital. It ensures the organs are fresh and well preserved. They have to move fast.'

'So, Susan would have been admitted to Wythenshawe and Tyler's heart posted up there?'

'Well, probably not DHL, but yeah.'

Sawyer opened the car window to air out the essence of vinegar. A blast of peaty wind swept in. He tipped his head back. 'Anything on her romantic history? From the walking group or book club?'

'Myers checked the walkers. I spoke to a couple of the book club members. Nobody had any suspicions of her being romantically linked to anyone other than her husband. No sense of any friction from any of the walkers or readers. Rhodes and Moran are analysing private CCTV around all the relevant routes. Moran isn't the brightest soul in the team at the moment. Quite a bromance you've got going there.'

Sawyer snorted. 'Good detective. Just picking the wrong fight.'

'I would have thought that Drummond could cover his battles by himself.'

'There's probably a moral outrage somewhere in there. Maybe his missus left him for someone who looks like me.' He took a breath, watched an elderly man with a walking stick hobble away from the craft shop. 'Tell him to look for a small vehicle. Not a big van.'

'Why?'

'He's efficient. Scrupulous. He'll go for something with no excess. It'll probably be dark in colour, too. Harder to pin down the model at night, in case it does get caught on camera somewhere. Call me if you need to.'

He hung up and took out Alex's questionnaire.

The Beck Anxiety Inventory.

The sheet contained a list of anxiety symptoms, which he was instructed to identify over the course of the previous month and grade across a four-point scale: zero (*didn't bother me at all*); one (*mild, didn't bother me much*); two (*moderate, not pleasant at times*); three (*severe, bothered me a lot*).

He looked down the list. Numbness or tingling... Dizzy or lightheaded... Feeling of choking... Hands trembling...

He could be a good boy. Go back to the cottage, do his homework.

Or he could do the other thing.

———

Sawyer parked a couple of streets away and walked along the Monyash road, away from Bakewell town centre. It took five minutes to reach Eva Gregory's house: a dirty-white semi, crouched behind a telegraph pole at the near end of a drab estate. It was the most conspicuous home of the bunch: larger, with a bigger front garden.

He lurked for a while, then strolled up to the front door and rang the bell. The door opened before the tone had faded. A wiry man in a black polo shirt stepped onto the porch.

The man hitched up his thin-framed rectangular glasses and squinted at Sawyer, deepening his double frown lines. 'Detective Inspector Sawyer. What an unexpected delight.'

'The pleasure's all yours.'

Dale Strickland laughed. He leaned against the door frame and folded his arms. 'I never got the chance to thank you for the part you played in ensuring my son's safety. If there's ever anything you need, I'm forever in your debt.'

His speech was measured, calm, almost rehearsed. But something feral flickered behind the eyes. He was shorter than average, but held himself upright with his chin raised. Expectant, arrogant. He let his gaze drift away from Sawyer, as if he was already bored with the encounter.

'Thanks,' said Sawyer. 'Just doing my job. Cleaning up your fallout.'

Strickland didn't react. 'You're being modest. That man

was a total maniac. Who knows what harm he could have done to others? I expect you got a gold star on your record for catching him?'

'He did some bad things, yes.'

Strickland caught Sawyer's eye. 'He'll suffer in prison.'

'Is that a promise?'

He smiled. 'It's an observation.'

Sawyer stepped forward, one foot on the bottom step of the porch. 'People who get in your way usually suffer, don't they, Dale?'

'After a fair warning.'

'How about Jason Haig? Did he get a warning?'

Strickland screwed up his face in exaggerated confusion. 'I can't say I know the name.'

'The guy who was driving the car that accidentally hit Luka.'

'Is this an official visit, Mr Sawyer? Or just a bit of extracurricular harassment?'

Sawyer stepped up onto the bottom step. 'This might be a tough one to understand, Dale, but it's not about you.'

Strickland smiled. 'Eva's out. Shopping.' Footsteps on the stairs in the hall, descending. 'So, is this a bit of aftercare? Don't you have specialist people for that? Head-shrinkers?' He smiled and eased off the door frame, scrubbed at his cropped grey hair. 'Detective Inspector Sawyer. Luka's fine. Eva's fine.' Strickland lifted his hands and held them a few inches from Sawyer's face. He brought the palms together repeatedly, in a slow, sarcastic handclap. 'Bravo. You got the bad guy. You did your job. Now, I respectfully request that you run along and get back to protecting the locals from aggressive cows.'

A small boy—skinny, with messy blond hair and red-framed glasses—eased around Strickland's legs. He was sullen and wary, but brightened at the sight of Sawyer. 'Hello, Jake.'

'Hey, Luka. How are you doing? Wasn't it your birthday recently?'

Luka frowned. 'That was ages ago.' He shrugged. 'Got a PlayStation.'

'Nice. I'm a gamer, too. I like the older games, though. You all better now? Back at school?'

He nodded, glanced up at his father. 'I have to take tablets. And I see a man sometimes at lunch.'

'A counsellor,' said Strickland, checking something on his phone. 'Some state-approved do-gooder.'

'He's alright,' said Luka. 'He doesn't shout.'

Sawyer looked up at Strickland, whose eyes stayed glued to his phone. 'And how is your mum?'

Luka nodded. 'She's okay. Sometimes, she's sad.'

Strickland put his phone away. 'She's fine.'

'When are you doing my first lesson?' said Luka.

Sawyer frowned, confused. 'Lesson?'

'Unlocking things without keys. Like you did in the cave with the handcuffs. You promised!'

Strickland stepped in front of Luka. 'That's secret stuff, son. Police work. Detective Sawyer was only joking.'

'No,' said Sawyer. 'I wasn't. I keep my promises. I'll teach you soon, Luka. Maybe when things are a bit less complicated. One or two things in the way at the moment.' He glanced at Strickland again. This time he got a look.

'Get back inside, Luka,' said Strickland. 'Homework.' He nudged Luka back into the house and edged out onto the top step. Sawyer was at a lower level, but the height difference set them face to face, like boxers at a weigh-in. 'I'm going to be crystal clear, Mr Sawyer. Your *work* here is done, and if you try to make contact with my wife or son again, then I will have to take action.'

Sawyer nodded, maintaining eye contact. 'And since you're being clear, can you just clarify what the nature of that action might be?'

'Have you read *The Art Of War*?'

'Yes. Sun Tzu. Chinese general and philosopher. Respected military manual, often used in business strategy. What's your point, Dale? Been Googling?'

If Strickland was surprised, he hid it well. 'Sun Tzu said, "All warfare is based on deception."' He raised his eyebrows.

Sawyer laughed. 'So, if I talk to Luka or Eva, then you'll get me, but you're not going to tell me how. Here's another Sun Tzu quote for you: "Avoid what is strong and strike at what is weak." That's more your style, isn't it, Dale?' He joined Strickland on the top step and loomed over him. 'But you really should pick on someone your own size.'

19

He walked down the verge, to the edge of the Tarmac path, and squatted down to rest behind some bushes. He took the chestnut-brown balaclava out of the backpack and rolled it down over his face.

The low autumn sun cast a golden dazzle over the railway track. Sawyer gazed across the burnished moorland beyond the station outbuildings and waited. No music this time. Just the sound of himself. His slow and steady breathing.

A shroud of cloud settled over the Kinder high ground, guttering the sunlight.

A dog barked somewhere, and another rebuked it.

The track rattled. The 17:14 from Sheffield.

He waited.

This time, he kept the stopwatch in his pocket and counted down the seconds out loud. It would be imprecise, and the dusk would reduce the driver's visibility.

The risk was higher.

But still, he felt no dread. No anticipation.

This time, there was only wonder. A terrible relish at the thought of no more thought. Only oblivion.

He thought of 'Aubade': Larkin's black-eyed meditation on death. 'The anaesthetic from which none come round.'

Sawyer sprang to his feet and jumped down to the path.

Ahead, the lights of the level crossing flashed red and yellow. The boom barrier was already down.

The rails pinged and popped. The train had long since crossed the river and turned the corner onto the straight stretch of track.

He had waited too long.

He wouldn't make it.

He ran hard. Top speed. Leaving nothing behind. He was in a race now.

At the crossing, he hurdled the fence and weaved around the barrier.

The train horn blasted its warning.

He sprinted for the crossing point and looked to the side.

He crunched through the trackside gravel and glanced to his right.

The train was almost on him.

Too large. Too close.

Too real.

He had miscalculated.

The driver again, leaning out of his cab, shouting.

The horn. Deafening now.

He had misjudged the time, the distance.

A flash of his mother.

His brother, crumpled on the ground.

His dog.

Metal on bone.

'Why?'

If her killer was still out there, he would learn of Sawyer's death. He would smile with relief.

He might even claim it as his own work. Thirty-year-old business, finally finished.

'Don't look back!'

He ducked down and found an extra burst of speed.

The train roared forward, seconds away.

Sawyer lunged for the track, dug his heel into the rail. He jumped across, swinging his arms for momentum.

He felt the *whump* of the train car as it punched through the air behind him.

He toppled into the trackside scrub and lay on his side, balled up, knees pressed into his face. Foetal in the mud. Panting.

He tuned in to himself. This time, there was something to feel.

Not fear.

Disappointment.

———

Back at the cottage, Sawyer stripped down to his underwear and worked on the wooden man, slamming his arms against the stubby poles. Too fast, too strong. No quality or precision.

He turned to the full-length mirror by his bed and assumed the Wing Chun horse stance. He worked through a few centreline punching exercises, locking his elbows with each thrust.

Left-right. Left-right-left-right. Two, then four, then eight.

He increased the punch speed until the blows were more like flurries, loose and undisciplined.

He closed his eyes and abandoned the controlled counts for a continuous roll of left-right punches. Strike after strike. Exhausting himself.

The force of the motion staggered him out of the stance and he dipped forward.

A right punch crunched into the mirror. Sawyer froze and opened his eyes. There was a fist-sized hole in the centre of a cobweb of shattered glass. Two rivulets of blood oozed through the channels of the fracture and found the smooth surface below. They trickled down, side by side, glinting in the lamplight.

Cursing, he headed to the bathroom. The mirror had cut through the skin of his right hand, leaving splinters of glass embedded in the flesh between his fingers. He picked out the glass, rinsed away the blood and wrapped a gauze bandage around the wounded area.

He shambled back into the bedroom, turned off the light and slumped down onto the bed. He lay back, not bothering to shuffle up to rest his head on the pillow.

Sawyer's hand flared in pain, and he thought of paracetamol, ibuprofen. But he lay there, still, focusing on the sensation, the jagged throbbing around his knuckles. Again, the pleasure of pain. His own pain. Unique. Uncomplicated. Without mystery. Nothing more than his physiology reporting on the injury. Proof that his body, at least, wanted to live.

Outside, a barn owl screeched, as if in comment. It repeated the call every few seconds: a territorial warning. Stay away. Keep your distance.

The rhythm of the calling carried him to a deep, dreamless sleep.

———

And then he was awake: wide-eyed, with a pulsing headache.

It was still dark outside, but the blackness in the room

had softened to a damp grey. The owl was long gone, replaced by the halting twitters of a few early risers.

Why was he so suddenly alert?

A new rhythm: short bursts of vibration, one every couple of seconds.

His phone, on the sitting room table.

Sawyer rolled off the bed and staggered out through the open door. The microwave clock told him it was just after 6am.

The phone danced across the table. He rescued it as it reached the edge.

Shepherd.

20

'Male, early forties.' Shepherd scaled the stone wall and led Sawyer into a patch of dew-sodden woodland off the A57 near Hollow Meadows. 'We think it's Sam Palmer. Football manager.'

Sawyer fell in alongside him. 'Think?'

'We'll check ID, obviously, but one of the forensics recognised him. He's a fan of Palmer's team. Chesterfield. Conference Premier Division.'

'Fourth tier?'

'Fifth.' Shepherd glanced down at Sawyer's bandaged hand. 'Defending someone's honour?'

'Slashed it on a tear in my punch bag.'

Shepherd whistled. 'You've worn out a punch bag? I'm not sure if that's good or bad.'

'Bad.'

They flashed their warrant cards at the officer on the outer cordon. He nodded, and Shepherd held up the scene tape for Sawyer to duck under.

'COD?' said Sawyer, as they edged down a slope towards a copse of amber trees.

'Waiting for you. Scene is secure. Sally's team has been

busy. Delivery was the same as Susan Bishop.'

They crossed a single-track lane and passed round the back of the Scientific Services Unit van.

The tent squatted in the centre of the copse. The blend of colours made Sawyer feel queasy: Paladin glare, watery dawn haze, blue-and-white tent fabric. A swarm of FSIs—more than usual—were sweeping the inner cordon, consulting with the turquoise-suited Sally O'Callaghan. The manager waved them through.

'DI Sawyer!' Sally bustled forward. 'A beautiful morning for murder.'

Sawyer nodded. 'Sally. Dog walker?'

'Surprisingly not. Runner. Says he saw the body when he took a rest in the trees. A white lie. We found a patch of fresh piss.'

Sally led them through into the tent. Two masked FSIs —presumably Sally's key generals—were waiting inside. One handed Sawyer a pair of latex gloves, while the other —the one from Fairholmes with the calm eyes—ushered Sally into the corner for a discussion about body transportation.

Shepherd leaned close to Sawyer. 'Where do they get these geeks?'

Sawyer shrugged. 'Bored researchers?' He peeled on the gloves and crouched beside the black holdall. 'No effort to conceal?'

'Seems like it was left out in the open. Although this place is hardly Times Square.'

Sawyer opened the whole zip before looking at the body. Like Susan Bishop, the man was naked, face up, and wrapped tight in polythene, sealed with the same silvery grey gaffer tape. He was white, middle-aged, overweight, with a modest patch of thinning brown hair. Remarkably unremarkable. His hands had been crossed at the wrists, concealing the area between his legs. No blood, no obvious injury.

Sally joined them. 'Again,' said Sawyer. 'Meticulous. Tape cut into even sections. Clean and stripped. Private parts covered.' He leaned in and squinted at the body through the polythene. 'Bruising around the wrists and mouth, forehead.' He unpeeled a section of the polythene and studied the man's torso, sifting through his brittle body hair. 'Whatever the madness behind his method, he's certainly consistent. That'll help us catch him.' He stood up. 'Nothing on the front. Help me turn him over.'

Shepherd took a pair of gloves from the FSI, and together they eased the body up and over onto its front. It slapped into place with so much force it almost rolled a second time. Shepherd stood upright and watched as Sawyer ran his gloved hands over the contours of the man's back.

'Anything?' said Sally.

Sawyer nodded, but didn't turn or stand. 'Something.'

———

Later that morning, Shepherd gathered the team in the main office and tacked a picture of the victim next to Susan Bishop on the whiteboard. He was about to turn and speak when Sawyer burst out of his office and strode to the front, carrying a folder.

He held up his bandaged hand to silence the chatter. 'This is Samuel Mark Palmer. He was forty-one years of age.' He stopped at the whiteboard, slapped the folder down on a desk, and faced the detectives. 'You killed him. You subdued him and you took him to a private place where you lay him on a sheet of polythene. You cuffed him and covered his mouth with gaffer tape. You turned him onto his front and you stabbed him, once. You waited for him to die. You cauterised the wound with a soldering iron. You cleaned up. You removed the tape and the cuffs. You transferred him to another sheet of polythene and you laid out his hands, covering his crotch area. You wrapped him up tight and you slotted him into an extra-large black holdall, which you dumped in woodland off the A57.' Sawyer placed his hands on the desk in front and leaned forward. His eyes were crazed and raging. '*Why*? Why did you do all of this? Why did you do it this way? Who was Sam Palmer to you? Did you know him personally? We need to answer these questions before we have another body on our hands.'

Walker waved a hand. 'I don't think he knew either of them personally, sir.'

Sawyer perched on the desk. 'Why?'

'It's all too intimate. The nudity. There's a lot of work. Cleaning the bodies, cauterising, removing clothes. Normally, when a killer knows the victim in a case like this, you either see rage or cruelty or, at the other end of the scale, a sense of shame and disgust. They want to get it over with and get out of there. This is measured, thorough.'

'Calm,' said Sawyer.

Shepherd nodded. 'Why stab Susan in the front but Sam in the back?'

'The inconsistency should interest us,' said Sawyer. 'But I want full beams on victimology. Connect these two people. What's the killer's beef with an ex-TV star who enjoys gardening, walking and reading, and a low league football manager? We know a lot about Susan Bishop. Tell me more about Sam Palmer. Find the links. Get everything into HOLMES. We'll have deeper forensics later, but there's no immediate evidence of sexual assault. As I've said before, I don't see any of the big three here. Domination,

109

manipulation, control. He needs these people to be dead, and I need to know why.'

Myers spoke up. 'What do we know about Palmer's last movements?'

Shepherd looked through his notes. 'FLOs spoke to his girlfriend, Judy. He took a session at the Chesterfield training ground on Monday evening. ANPR caught his car at a temporary light near Baslow at around 8:50pm. He called Judy around half an hour later, from the Angler's Rest in Bamford. She says he seemed fine, optimistic. After that, ANPR catches him on the northern edge of Bamford at around 10:30. His car is parked outside his house, so we assume he drove straight home from the pub. Timings fit. Nothing at the house. Forensics are all over the car as we speak.'

Sawyer turned to Walker. 'Focus on Palmer. I want a full bio. Anything stand out from his football connections? Any link to Susan or Ronald Bishop? Go to the Angler's Rest. Anything unusual? Was he acting strange? Did he meet anyone?'

Karl Rhodes, the station's digital media advisor, crept in at the back of the room and walked along the line of offices. He was skinny and elvish, with a tidy moustache and a flat, pitted nose. 'Sorry to interrupt. Got a plate match for a van we caught on a shop camera in Tideswell on the night Susan Bishop was murdered.' He handed Sawyer a grainy printout that showed a small, dark-coloured van, turning into a side street. 'It's a Peugeot Partner. Nice little mover.'

'And it's stolen,' said Moran, flashing a bleary look at Sawyer. 'Two months ago, from a lay-by near Bakewell. No ANPR since. We've been over everything from the surrounding area, and this is the only catch. I've barely been at home for the last two days. That fucking thing might cost me my marriage.'

Sawyer smiled. 'It's a price worth paying. You should be happy, Moran. You found the killer's vehicle. It's a breakthrough. All your own work!'

'Fuck off!' Rhodes' venom startled Sawyer. 'He sat there on his laptop most of the time. I was doing the grafting.'

Moran scoffed. 'I was working on other angles. Updating HOLMES.'

'It sounds like the beginning of a beautiful friendship,' said Sawyer. 'You can do it all again. Starting now. Focus on the Bamford and Baslow area and the routes to and from Hollow Meadows on the night Sam Palmer was last seen alive. Couple of days either side, in case our man did some casing.'

Moran sighed and slumped back in his chair. 'What happened to the hand, sir?'

'Overuse,' said Sawyer, eyeing Moran, denying him the obvious joke.

Rhodes' eyes widened at the sight of the picture on the whiteboard. '*Sam Palmer*? Chesterfield boss?' Sawyer nodded. 'Fuck me! What was it, a fan? It's been a patchy start to their season but killing the manager seems a bit extreme.'

'Do you follow them?' said Shepherd.

Rhodes shrugged. 'Got a mate who does. Been to a few games. Hard-working side but not that pretty. Palmer liked a drink, that's for sure. Y'know. The old euphemism. Bit of a rogue. Hellraiser. Translates as "piss artist". There's a video online of him having a pitchside scrap with an opposition manager. Fucking hilarious. I would rather watch a fight between two middle-aged men in bad suits than a professional boxing match, any day.'

Stephen Bloom got to his feet. 'Minor football celebrity. This will increase press interest. We should call a conference. Get on the front foot.'

'Not yet,' said Sawyer. 'Let's see if that van turns up again and work the Palmer angle, including this opposition manager. Maybe there's a grudge there?'

Rhodes shook his head. 'Nah. I think it was over a heavy tackle. Shook hands after. I remember his assistant manager saying the other fella told Palmer to calm down. Then he made the drinking gesture. Palmer didn't like that. Handbags. Doesn't sound like much of a motive for murder to me. He did a George Best, though, didn't he?'

'How do you mean?' said Sawyer.

'Yeah. He's been off for a while. Fucked himself with the booze. According to my mate, he wrote an open letter to the fans in a programme, about how the doctors told him he didn't have long if he carried on. Some surgeons won't do it, though. For alcoholics.'

'Do what?' said Shepherd.

'He got himself a new liver. Transplant.'

21

Sawyer took the Mini down through the central Peaks and, miraculously, found a spot in the Tissington Trail car park. He sat with the engine running for a while, mesmerised by the music ('Magpie' by The Unthanks), then got out and walked up the hill and down into town.

He paused at the steps of the Town Hall and read the flapping banner above the entrance.

AUTUMN ART FESTIVAL
Ashbourne Town Hall Ballroom
October 9th-12th

A line of six promo shots of local artists stared down at him: three vaguely familiar, two unknown. The sixth, Harold Sawyer, had tamed his floppy thatch of hair, although it still seemed oddly lopsided, almost completely grey at the temples; an off-kilter frame for his furrowed brow and unfathomable green eyes (his gift to his son). He had opted for a slight side-on angle, hinting at his aquiline profile. He scowled into the lens with poise and suspicion.

Sawyer steeled himself and climbed the steps.

———

The vast Victorian-era ballroom swarmed with the Derbyshire fine-arts cognoscenti: champagne flutes, Sunday best, a backwash of chatter blending with syrupy classical music. It was a private viewing, ahead of the festival's opening that evening. Strictly by invitation only. The artworks—mostly oils and watercolours—were arranged on separate easels, with the artists walled into individual zones behind pop-up partitions.

An elderly gent in a dark morning suit and bow tie greeted Sawyer at the entrance desk. 'Hello there. Could I get your name, please?' Sawyer held up his warrant card and the man startled, but instantly regained his composure. 'Is there a problem?'

'Well. I'm more of a sculpture man myself.' The greeter looked confused. Sawyer shot him a smile. 'I'm here to speak to one of the artists.'

'He's okay, Arnold!'

Harold waved and shouted from the far end of the hall. Arnold looked put out, but stepped aside and forced a smile.

Sawyer walked through to his father's section, and Harold pulled him into a hefty hug. He was shorter than Sawyer, but the contact was a reminder of his steel and strength: oddly undiminished for a man at the back end of his sixties. Sawyer recalled a moment of arm wrestling in a pub beer garden. He would have been four or five years old. His mother: indulgent, radiant, urging Harold to go easy. His father's arm like a tree trunk: implacable, unbudgeable, even as Sawyer wrapped the fingers of both hands around the knuckles and jerked and pulled.

'What a lovely surprise, Jake. You should have said you were coming.'

'You should have invited me. Then I wouldn't have had to gatecrash.'

Harold laughed, wheezing slightly. Sawyer caught a glimpse of his vintage, rippling to the surface of the fitted navy suit: a little too young for him, too metropolitan for the parochial setting. 'Didn't think it would be your scene. It's so lovely to see you, son. How are you? I read about the Crawley case. That's a hell of a shunt along towards DCI.'

'It wasn't a career move, Dad.'

Harold caught his eye, read him. 'Of course not. It's a pleasant side effect, though.'

A young woman in a maroon mini-dress walked over from the entrance and hovered at the edge of their conversation, too close to be ignored. She took an iPad out of a shoulder bag and held it up for Harold's attention.

'Son. Five minutes. Sorry. I need to look at this.' He turned to the woman.

Sawyer wandered over to the largest of Harold's canvases: a vast abstract, rendered in violent smudges and splashes. Greens and blues and pinks. There was something vaguely oceanic in there. Wild water, churned by storm winds. He took out a boiled sweet—a chocolate lime—and slid it into his mouth. He leaned in close to the work, as if studying it for clues.

'Rather good, isn't it?'

Another woman had sidled over. Fortyish and elegant in a white suit jacket, jeans and tan ankle boots. 'Provincial work can be a bit patchy.' She edged close enough for Sawyer to catch a gust of expensive perfume. 'And most of this stuff is barely on the bright side of average. But I do like *this*.'

She gazed into the painting for a few seconds, holding

the silence, then turned to Sawyer and held out a hand. 'Clara McKee. I write about art for the *Manchester Evening News*.'

He shook. 'Jake Sawyer. I'm a civil servant.'

Clara nodded. 'Sawyer? Are you...'

He nodded. 'Son.'

'Ah! Do you share your father's artistry?'

An attendant proffered a tray of drinks. Clara took a glass of wine, but Sawyer waved him away. 'I tried to paint, but I was held back, really.'

'Oh?'

'Yes. Lack of talent. So unfair.'

She laughed. Too loud and braying. Sawyer winced. 'Skipped a generation! Well, I'm an admirer of your father's work. Do you enjoy it?'

He angled his head at the painting. 'I think so. I suppose I wonder about how he makes the decisions over where to put the paint. Why one colour and not another?'

'Ah, but that's the pleasure of abstract art. The mystery. I doubt the artist would be able to articulate any of that. He wouldn't know himself.' She stepped closer to the painting. 'I suppose it's a form of self-examination. I wouldn't go so far as to call it therapy, but I think the two are related. For me, art is the ultimate way to transcend the fate that awaits us all.' She stepped back and turned to him. 'You may have photographs, of people you love. But they actually tell you little of the person in the picture. Particularly, if the shot is posed, prepared. What is more revealing and, I would say, lasting, is how an artist chooses to express himself, project his ideas and feelings in whatever form. The brain that moved the brush may have long since been absorbed back into the minerals of the Earth, but the work is immortal, eternal. That's why so many people gather to see the *Mona*

Lisa. It's actually quite an ordinary painting. But there's a fascination in how a seventy-seven by fifty-three centimetre piece of canvas can somehow transcend its creator and all his inner complexities.' She took a sip of wine.

Sawyer squinted at her. 'But, as you say, it can be revealing. The choices made. All those micro decisions. If you want to understand an artist, you look at the work.'

Clara abandoned her sip, almost spluttering. 'I couldn't agree more! The work reveals more than the boring old obituary. The life, the biography. That's full of facts. The work is full of *secrets*.'

———

Sawyer joined his father at a table in the corner of his section. He slid a leaflet out of a fan arranged around the edge of the table. Several pages, quality paper, photographs of the works, contact details for purchase enquiries. The banner photograph of Harold stared out from the back page, above a few words of context, including a cute line about how he had switched from criminal investigation to self-expression.

'Not like you to come south of the wall, Dad.'

Harold sat back, smiled, poured out a bottle of San Miguel. 'You mean the north-south divide at Castleton?'

Sawyer nodded. 'From Midhope to Ashbourne. Inching closer to London.'

'Fuck that. We're *technically* outside the National Park here. That's plenty for me. It's giving me hives.' He took a drink. 'Did you get an evaluation after the Crawley case?'

'I'm of sound mind.'

'And body? What's with the hand?'

'Punch bag. Caught it on a rip.' Sawyer crunched

through the last of another chocolate lime, grimacing at the bitter centre.

'What's your choice of candy, these days?'

'*Candy?*'

'Sorry. Been talking to American dealers.'

'Chocolate limes. Varies.'

Harold snorted. 'Well. I suppose I was wrong. All that nagging about your teeth falling out.' He sipped his beer. 'When you were a teenager, Jake, you used to come to my study. Say hello. It made me smile, watching you gauge how much small talk you needed to cover before you could ask for the thing you actually wanted.'

'I'm not here for money.'

Harold nodded. 'Chris Hill should leave you alone for a while. I've covered the finances for Michael's care.'

'We should get him a speech therapist.'

'You think we didn't try that?'

'He spoke to me.'

Harold narrowed his eyes. 'Michael? Spoke?'

'He said he remembered Mum saying something to the killer.'

Harold took a slow sip of beer, kept his eyes on Sawyer. 'What did she say?'

'She said, "*Why?*"'

'And this is a breakthrough, how?'

'You say "Why?" to someone you know. You say, "Stop!" or, "No!" or, "Please!" to someone you don't know. Someone who's attacking you with a hammer.'

'Jake...'

'Why did you try to stop Marcus Klein's release?'

Harold didn't miss a beat. 'Because he murdered my wife, your mother. She knew *him*, Jake. They taught at the same school together. That explains what she said. If she said it. Michael is hardly what you'd call a reliable witness.'

'And who would be? The Almighty himself?'

Harold sighed. 'Already? We're going there?'

'How about Owen Casey?'

The name jolted Harold. He screwed his eyes shut, dropped his head. To Sawyer, it looked like a pantomime; displaying an effort to recall. But his father would know about his son's sensitivity to lies, or the sugaring of truth.

Sawyer helped him out. 'Repeat burglar from around the time you were at Buxton.'

Harold opened his eyes and fixed Sawyer with a steady gaze. 'I don't remember him, no.'

'Irish traveller. Part of a group that settled in Uttoxeter in the seventies and eighties. You probably called them "gypos" in your day. Or "pikeys". They don't call them that any more. I don't even think they do much travelling.'

'And you think he killed your mother?'

'No, I don't. But I thought you might remember the name, give me an idea about where I might find him. I think he was involved in framing Klein. If I can find Casey, I might be able to catch the end of the thread, follow it back.'

Harold kept his eyes locked on his son. 'You're asking a sixty-seven-year-old man if he can think back thirty years and give you information on some petty thief who *might* be able to help with the framing of a convicted murderer? I said it before, Jake. Can you not see how crazy this is? How counterproductive?'

Sawyer stiffened. 'You're in denial. *That's* the crazy bit. You've locked it all away, told yourself justice has been served, taken refuge in the same old biblical bullshit.' He waved his hand around at the paintings. 'And what *is* this? Catharsis?' He leaned across the table. 'You tell me to move on and accept things. But I think that deep, deep down, you know that Klein didn't do it.' He sat back. Harold glared at him. 'I get it, Dad. You're old now. You want peace and quiet. You're following the Flaubert model. Be ordinary in your life so you can be extraordinary in your art. Here's the thing, though. *I'm* not ready to rest yet. Not ready to let it rest.' He leaned in. '"*Why?*". Mum never got an answer to her question. But I will.'

22

Sawyer fitted his phone into the dashboard cradle and slotted in the ignition key. He paused, before turning. He had wanted to see his father face to face, to get a live reaction to his mention of Casey. At the time of his mother's death, his father had been working at Buxton, under Keating, and it was conceivable that Sawyer's current DCI might have sanctioned unofficial informants, and his father might want that particular soil to stay undisturbed. But Harold's response to Casey's name was genuine: he didn't know him, and he seemed baffled and disturbed by Sawyer's continued obsession. Maggie had said that if he was in the middle of a breakdown, he'd be the last to know. Was this the first twinge of self-awareness? Was it all an elaborate conspiracy story he was telling himself to muffle the pain?

He pulled out of the car park, passed beneath a canopy of rusty trees, and turned right onto Mappleton Road, rolling down between the low pastures: a sunken spread of olive green that would soon be twinkling with frost.

His phone rang: an unrecognised number. He set it to speaker and answered.

'Sir? It's Walker. DS Shepherd has asked me to brief you.'

Sawyer smiled. 'Pestering paid off, eh?'

'I don't—'

'Brief away.'

Walker cleared his throat. 'Frazer Drummond has preliminary findings on Sam Palmer. Single stab wound. Internal bleeding. Says he proposes death by haemorrhagic shock. The mark on his forehead suggests Palmer was hit by something first. Bruising around wrists and mouth similar to Susan Bishop's.'

Sawyer passed a cyclist, giving him a generous berth. The man—elderly—waved as he passed. 'Where did the knife penetrate?'

'According to Drummond, he "scored a direct hit" on the liver with a blade that was long enough to pass directly through. Nothing internal removed.'

'Apart from the blood. Did you look into Palmer? Was Rhodes right about his liver transplant?'

'Hundred per cent. He went off the rails. Drink-driving in 2016. Assaulted the arresting officer. Fines. Banned for a year. Came out he was on Antabuse. There was a minor press fuss about a chronic alcoholic getting a transplant. Brought it on himself, all that. But it doesn't look like he did anything untoward.'

Sawyer pushed a button in the door and rolled down the window. The outside air rushed in, sharp and chilled. He turned up the phone speaker volume. 'Now we're getting somewhere. How about Rhodes and Moran?'

'Still nothing on the van we saw at Tideswell. I showed it to Palmer's girlfriend. She didn't recognise it. Couldn't find any direct link between Palmer and Susan Bishop.'

'We know where Susan's heart came from. Now we

need more on the source of Sam's alcohol-free liver. Check with—'

'I already looked into that, sir.'

Sawyer raised his eyebrows. 'Nice. And?'

'Palmer didn't want any details or contact with the donor. So we can't get the info there. The transplants were performed at different hospitals. Susan got her heart at Wythenshawe. Palmer's op happened at St James's University Hospital in Leeds. It all depends on the unit facilities. And here's the interesting bit.'

'They both happened on the same day?'

Walker paused. 'Almost. Susan's heart op was April 10th last year. Palmer's liver on April 11th. They would have both been on the lists and the organs would have become available somewhere nearby.'

Sawyer nodded. 'Shepherd told me the donors have to die in hospital so the organs remain viable.' He turned onto a straight, clear road which led back into the National Park. 'Did both organs originate from the same hospital? Bishop's heart came from Sheffield Northern General, yes?'

'That's right. Manchester and Leeds wouldn't confirm. Confidential. But they use a specialist ambulance service called Pulseline. Their records show organ dispatch from Sheffield to Manchester on April 10th and to Leeds on 11th.'

'Excellent. So let's talk to Sheffield. Find out where Palmer's liver came from.'

Walker hesitated. 'Shepherd tried that. They said the person we need to talk to isn't there until tomorrow.'

'Okay, I'll go with him in the morning.'

'Sir...'

Sawyer sighed. 'No. We don't need three people. It's not a drugs raid. I know you're keen, DC Walker, and you've done some fine work. But I need to be smart with resource.

This isn't on-the-job training. Work with Moran and Rhodes. Find me that van. If we can connect it to both scenes, then we can push it at the press conference. Someone will have seen it parked up somewhere. Then we'll have an address, and *then* you can tag along and see some fireworks.'

————

Sawyer spent the evening at the cottage, butterflying around various distractions, never quite settling enough to become absorbed. Videogames, online articles, Wing Chun forms. He sprawled on the sofa in his workout vest and tracksuit trousers, and played an old Future Sound of London album. He tried to dip into *The Gift of Fear*, but his eyes kept sliding off the page.

Barefoot, he padded into the kitchen and dug out an oversized bag of salt and vinegar crisps. He leaned in close to the small window and peered out. It was late, and there was nothing to see: just unpolluted blackness, with a few distant speckles of light from the sparse suburbs of Chisworth and Holehouse.

Two slow, solid raps on the front door.

He glanced at the microwave clock. 23:10. Nobody came calling, on phone or in person, with good news at this time.

He walked to the door and listened.

Shuffling feet just outside. More than one person.

He opened the door.

Two men stood in the doorway. The one nearest the step was tall, maybe six-five, and bulky. Strong-looking. His colleague was almost as tall, but more heavyset. Cheap suits, expensive haircuts. The shorter one was bald, with an arch little goatee, while the other was clean shaven, with the tendrils of a tattoo design curling up the side of his neck. They looked like reconstructed bouncers.

Sawyer quickly checked them up and down. Empty hands. The short one had something bulky in his inside pocket; the tall one looked clean. 'Bit late for canvassing.'

'What?' Tall one.

'Or are you preaching? For Jehovah?'

The short one stepped forward. 'We're not stopping, Mr Sawyer.'

Sawyer smiled. 'How's your boss?'

Tall one. 'We don't have a "boss"'.

'Freelance goons, eh? Good for you. The gig economy is pretty seductive. Must be tough getting a mortgage, though.'

No smiles. The short one held out his hands, palms up. 'This time, we'll keep it nice. We're hoping you can help us solve a problem.'

'Lads. It's late. I'm tired. Two questions. One. What's the problem? Two. Can I get you both a glass of warm milk?'

The tall one stepped up into the house, just over the threshold. He leaned in close to Sawyer. He was wearing at least half a bottle of Joop! cologne. 'You need to stay away from her.'

'Who?'

'You know.'

Sawyer nodded and put on a stern face. 'And might I enquire whose interests you're representing in this matter?'

'We know you're a copper,' said the short one. 'But that don't mean nothing to us.'

'Doesn't,' said Sawyer.

'Eh?'

'Doesn't. Not "don't". And that's a double negative. It should be, "That doesn't mean *anything* to us."

The tall one squinted, his eyes flitting to his colleague. 'You're not untouchable, Mr Sawyer. You're not the only one with long arms.'

Sawyer shook his head. 'So you work for Mr Tickle?' He braced, ready to move. He was expecting at least an attempt at a stomach punch.

The short one leaned in. 'You know who we're talking about. Like we say, this time we're nice.'

'And what happens next time? Naughty?'

'Next time,' said the tall one, 'we'll cut something off you.'

23

'Big night?' Shepherd side-glanced at his passenger, keeping his hands at the regulation ten to two position.

'Not sleeping well,' said Sawyer, staring out at the shorn farmland on Sheffield's western fringe.

'You in pain?'

Sawyer turned. 'What?'

Shepherd kept his eyes on the road. 'With the hand.'

'Oh. No. That's fine. Just the usual deep-rooted existential terror. Nothing to worry about.'

Shepherd got the message. No talking. He slid a CD —*Leftism* by Leftfield—into the ancient sound system and steered the mustard yellow Range Rover deeper into the city. The fields fell away, replaced by modular estates, chain pubs, hypermarkets, industrial blight. They passed the rows of compact terraces around the back of the Hillsborough football stadium.

He stopped at a light and looked at Sawyer: slumped onto his left, arms folded. 'Did you go? To Hillsborough? Too young for it?'

Sawyer shrugged. 'I was six. My dad was a mess, trying

to keep things together. Football wasn't really a thing then. I saw it on TV, though. Weird season, with the Michael Thomas goal at the end. Fucking cruel. It poisoned us.'

Shepherd checked the satnav and pulled out onto the road for the Northern General. 'No league title since.'

'Thanks for the reminder. At least we've gone close a few times.'

Shepherd smiled. He was getting through. 'Hey. With Everton, there's no weight of expectation. It's all about the chequebooks these days, anyway.'

Sawyer sat up in his seat, in mock surprise. 'Fuck! You're right. Money is ruining football. I'd never thought of it that way.'

Shepherd didn't dignify the sarcasm. 'Busy one, then? Yesterday? Couldn't switch off?'

'Saw my dad. That always puts a strain on the relationship.'

Shepherd nodded. 'Walker is good. Soon be a DS.'

'For sure. Don't tell him that, though.'

'Bit rough round the edges. Spoke over Keating a couple of times at the press conference.'

'Really? I bet he loved that.'

'Called him in for "a word" after.'

Sawyer laughed. 'I don't think we'll find the van. Not distinctive enough. And he's too sharp to leave it in a drive or take it to Tesco. He might have used a different vehicle in both murders. It's just busy work. Logging dead-end calls, tracing and eliminating.'

'Logan was there, badgering me about whether we can "confidently keep the public safe".'

'That's an easy one. No, we can't. Safer, but not safe. Our biggest chance is to work backwards. Look at what he's doing, the presentation, the method, the themes.'

Shepherd lowered the music volume. 'Two stab wounds. Both victims had recent organ transplants. Method is a link, but the transplant thing could be coincidence.'

'At the moment, yes. But both transplanted organs originated from the same hospital.'

————

They bought coffee at the cafeteria and found a table in a quiet corner, away from the vast window that overlooked the car park. Sawyer prodded at his pecan pastry. He took a bite, made a face, and flopped it back onto the plate.

'You leaving that?' said Shepherd.

'I thought you were on a new regime. Yoga or whatever.'

'Pilates. And, yes. I'm not hungry. Just surprised to see you turn down something sweet.'

Sawyer stood up, looking over Shepherd's shoulder. '*Too* sweet. Even for me.' He raised a hand.

Shepherd smiled. 'You have quite a camp wave.'

He stood and turned. A young woman in a dark blue nurse uniform approached their table. Mousey brown hair folded over one ear, nervous smile. She hesitated at the edge of the serving counter, and Sawyer caught her taking a quick look around the room, then out of the window. It reminded him of an ex-SAS friend who had to routinely check the exits in any new public area before he could relax.

The woman held out her hand. 'Are you the police?'

'Surely it's not that obvious,' said Sawyer, shaking. 'Amy Scott?'

She smiled and shook Shepherd's hand. 'Yes. Hello.' She was struggling to mask her nerves.

'I'm Detective Inspector Sawyer, this is Detective Sergeant Shepherd. There's nothing to worry about. We just wanted to speak to someone about a specific matter, and we were advised that you might be best placed to help.'

'I'll do what I can, of course.'

'Can I get you a coffee?' said Shepherd.

Amy waved him away. 'No. I'm fine. Just really busy.'

They sat down.

A beat. Shepherd looked at Sawyer, stirring his coffee, and got the eyebrows. He turned to Amy. 'Ms Scott. You're involved in the administration around organ donation at the hospital. Is that right?' She nodded and crossed her legs, hands clasped together over one knee. 'Could you tell us a bit about your role? About how it all works?'

Amy took a breath. 'I'm a Specialist Nurse, Organ Donation. They call us SNODs. We maintain lines of communication with the transplant surgeons, recipient transplant co-ordinators, other relevant staff in the donation centres. We liaise with NHS Blood and Transplant on all the relevant documentation, including audit requirements. And if I have any time left after all that, and I don't, then I work on promotion and education of health care professionals and the general public, about the benefits of organ and tissue donation.'

Shepherd nodded. 'And so you're right at the frontline when it comes to harvesting the organs of the recently deceased?'

Amy winced. 'A lot of donor families and medical staff consider the term "harvesting" offensive. It can also put people off. We use "donated" in everyday comms, and the clinical community uses "retrieved". So, the teams of surgeons who are sent to donors are all part of the National Organ *Retrieval* service.'

'Okay. So, assuming the potential donor is on the... National Organ Register?'

Amy nodded. 'Organ Donation Register. ODR.'

'Right. Assuming a recently deceased person was on the ODR, and they died at this hospital, then you would be involved in the retrieval of their organs?'

Amy glanced at Sawyer. He was picking the pecan nuts out of the pastry. 'Yes, I would. I would check they're on the register, and discuss the possibility of donation with the family. Even if the deceased person is already registered, then I will still need to seek family approval. It's a myth that your donation wishes will be blindly followed after your death. If the family blocks the donation for whatever reason, then it won't go ahead.'

'And would you ask families about donation, even if the deceased *wasn't* on the ODR?'

'Of course. The ODR is just a way of recording a person's wishes. It's not legally binding. Once we have the family's blessing, then information about the patient is transmitted electronically to relevant hospitals. Then, the transplant surgeons can decide whether to accept the organs or not. Obviously, organs are not retrieved unless they are accepted for transplant.'

'They're never just retrieved and then offered?'

'No. Bodies are not preserved. Once brain death is confirmed, then the deceased may spend hours, or sometimes a day or two, on ventilation to support organ function before donation. Once the ventilator is switched off, then death naturally occurs, and retrieval begins.'

Shepherd took out his notepad. 'And how long does that process usually take?'

'From the point where the family agrees to donation up to the operation going ahead? Minimum of a few hours, maximum of one to two days. It's all about preparing and co-ordinating the two surgical teams.'

'And one body, one deceased person, can donate several organs?'

'Yes. The organs will be transported to units around the country. Kidneys, heart, lungs, liver, small bowel, pancreas. Also, tissue. Eyes, heart valves, bone, skin, veins, tendons. The only complication is cornea transplant. The whole eye is retrieved, but only the cornea, the clear lens on the front of the eye, is transplanted. Not the iris or any other parts.'

'Ms Scott,' said Sawyer, still picking at the pastry. 'We're investigating a double murder in the Derbyshire area, and we've discovered that both victims received a transplant organ which originated at this hospital, last year. A heart and a liver.'

Amy's eyes widened. She looked from Shepherd to Sawyer. 'That is possible. We've coordinated hundreds of donations over the last eighteen months.'

Sawyer pushed the plate aside and leaned forward. 'I have a question. The answer could prove to be extremely helpful to the investigation. Could you give us the details of the liver donor? I'd like to explore the possibility of connections between the—'

'I couldn't do that. I'm sorry. We operate on strict grounds of confidentiality. The families of the donor and recipient sometimes choose to maintain a relationship, but we're not at liberty to make that public knowledge.'

Shepherd flicked through his notepad. 'We know from the husband of one of the victims that the heart came from a Roy Tyler, aged forty-six. He was injured at a gym in Bole Hill, and brought here, in April last year.'

Amy shuffled in place, agitated. 'I'm sorry, but...' She lowered her voice. 'I appreciate you're doing a difficult job, but I can't see how I can help.'

Sawyer smiled. 'You can give us the details of Sam Palmer's liver donor, Amy. We can get the medical records unsealed and released with a court order. But it's messy and time-consuming. Surely you can see how your information might open up the enquiry?'

'Yes, but I have to operate under a strict clinical code. And we would need to coordinate with hospital administration and the NHSBT authority.' She got to her feet. Sawyer and Shepherd mirrored her. She looked over her shoulder, took out her pocket watch. 'I'm so sorry, but I really have to get back to work. I hope I've been helpful.' She shook their hands. 'Look. I'll speak to NHSBT and my managers here.'

Shepherd wrote down a number on his pad and handed the paper to Amy. 'Thank you. Please give us a call as soon as you can. I'm sure you can appreciate the seriousness of—'

'Of course! It was lovely to meet you both. Thank you.' She turned, stumbling over a low chair, and hurried out of the café.

Sawyer caught Shepherd's eye. He tilted his head slowly from side to side in assessment.

Shepherd shrugged. 'She doesn't have the authority. Makes sense.'

Sawyer sat, tore off a chunk of pastry and popped it into his mouth. 'We'll work around it. It would help if we could get the donation info confirmed, but let's do the learning while we wait. Find out more about Roy Tyler. See if anything interesting pops up.'

'Can we get Drummond to get DNA samples from Susan Bishop's heart and Sam Palmer's liver? Cross-reference?'

'Probably, but that sounds like a lot of variables and legal hoops to jump through. If we can find a way to get the information from Amy, it will save a lot of time. And I'm interested in her in another way.' Shepherd eyed him. 'Not that. She wasn't busy or pushed for time. I'm interested because she was absolutely terrified.'

24

'Bodies, DI Sawyer.'

Keating had his back turned, tapping away at his corner computer. He glanced over his shoulder.

'Sir?' Sawyer took a seat.

'Too many of them. *Two* too many. What are your leads?'

'Forensics are scraps. At least the two bodies give us more potential. I'm trying to establish a link between the victims. And they both had recent organ transplant operations, so we're looking into possible angles there. I have a contact but we might need a court order.'

Keating pivoted his chair and faced Sawyer. 'Any more?'

'That's it, sir. At the moment.'

Keating scowled and smoothed down his neat crop of white hair. 'Means? Method? Motivation?'

'We know he can afford to buy a knife, and he's smart enough to steal a vehicle. Method? He subdues, incapacitates, delivers a single stab wound, which he cauterises. Death from haemorrhagic shock. He's extremely meticulous, clean, no tracks. He does the killing in the vehicle then transports the body, wrapped in plastic, to somewhere away from CCTV or ANPR.'

'Motivation? Anything in the presentation?'

Sawyer closed his eyes, looked over the bodies in his mind's eye. 'He cleans them, positions them so they're covering their private areas.'

'So he has some respect for the victims?'

'Possibly.'

'Why so clean and fastidious? Why is he cauterising the wounds? Why not multiple stabs? Is he stalking easy prey, or killing to make a wider point? Like Crawley.'

'All of this should open up if we get more victims.'

Keating sat back. 'So, when I meet with the Chief Constable tomorrow, I tell him we're working hard on the case, but we need a few more murders to happen before we can catch the offender?'

'No, sir. I'm confident that we'll find something in the connection between Susan Bishop and Sam Palmer.'

Keating nodded. 'Well, that's a relief. Do let me know.' He angled his head. 'And how about yourself?'

Sawyer read his gaze: curious, cautious. 'You mean post-Crawley? I'm fine. A few glitches, but otherwise okay.'

'Glitches?'

'Nothing to worry about.'

'I trust the glitches aren't compromising the investigation in any way?'

'Absolutely not, sir.'

'You could take a TRiM assessment. If you feel you need it.'

Sawyer shook his head.

They savoured a few seconds of silence. Keating opened a file folder. He took a chunky fountain pen and made a few notes on the outside. 'Klein is out.'

'Yes.'

'Your father tried to stop it.'

'I suppose he believes life should mean life. Part of his newfound sense of religious justice.'

Keating looked up. 'A few months ago, you asked me for access to the old file, but you haven't signed it out. Not officially, anyway.'

Sawyer broke eye contact and glanced out of the window. Iron-grey sky. A couple of pigeons, wheeling. He looked back. 'As you said, sir, I'm concentrating on the here and now.'

Keating nodded. 'Don't overload yourself. Hand some more off to Shepherd. He's capable. Walker is coming through, too.' He opened the folder, slipped on a pair of thick-framed reading glasses. 'I'm sure you're making progress in the case, DI Sawyer.' He looked up, over the top of his glasses. 'But I would at least like a *suspect* sometime soon.'

———

Sawyer strode out into the main office. 'Updates! Good news, please.' He perched on the desk near the whiteboard. 'Moran. How's the basement bromance with Rhodes developing?'

Moran glared at him. 'We've covered every inch of the relevant areas at the key times. No sign of the van anywhere.'

'*Any* van? Anything similar?' Moran shook his head. Sawyer nodded. 'He would have used something different, anyway. Thanks for your efforts.'

Moran forced a smile, nodded towards Walker. 'We didn't need another body down there, either.'

'Bit musky?'

Moran shrugged. 'Not a smart use of resource.'

'You weren't finding anything with two people,' said Sawyer. 'We added a body. You didn't find anything with three. Therefore, assuming you've done your job well, there's nothing to find. That's good information in itself. Look into recently stolen vans of a similar size.' He turned to Shepherd. 'How about Palmer's car?'

'Sally's team swept the house and surrounding area,' said Shepherd. 'Checked his car. Nothing but a few blonde hairs. His girlfriend.'

'How about Sam Palmer and Susan Bishop? Connections?'

Myers waved his pen. 'Nothing, sir. There's no evidence that they knew each other or ever crossed paths. DS Shepherd asked me to look into Susan's heart donor, Roy Tyler. He had a record. Back in 1991, when he was twenty, he was a lorry driver. Sentenced to ten years for causing death by dangerous driving. Three people killed in a crash on the A53 near Brandside. Night-time, bad weather. He was released on licence in 1996.' He checked his notes. 'Looks like he went back to working as a driver for various firms, then retrained.'

Shepherd addressed the team. 'We know that Susan Bishop received Tyler's heart. We went to see the specialist nurse at Sheffield Northern General. She couldn't confirm anything about Sam Palmer's liver—'

'But we'll work round it,' said Sawyer. 'Maybe get a court order if we need to. The transplants might be a coincidence, and we still don't know if there's any connection, but it might open up the picture. The killer stabbed Susan through the heart and Palmer in the back. Both wounds penetrated the transplanted organs.'

Walker waved a hand. 'Maybe it was easier to keep Sam Palmer quiet by stabbing him in the back. But Susan was different.'

Sawyer shook his head. 'We know for sure that Susan's heart and Sam's liver came from Sheffield Hospital. And the nurse we spoke to wasn't happy. Way too eager to get away.'

'Look into the methods more?' said Walker. 'Why is he so clean and careful? Why the hands covering the genitals?'

'Surgeon?' said Moran. 'Someone connected to surgery? Unfazed by bodies or death, but used to keeping things hygienic?'

Sawyer raised his eyebrows. 'Fair shout. Moran, let's get you some fresh air. Work with Walker. Find me all the names of the surgeons who perform transplant operations in relevant local hospitals. Focus on the ones who might have performed the Bishop and Palmer transplants, at Wythenshawe and Leeds. Any red flags, connections. Myers, find more on Tyler if you can. And look into deaths registered at Sheffield Northern General in the days leading up to Sam Palmer's liver transplant. Get me some potential matches for his donor. His op was on April 11th. The nurse told us that they keep life support on, and the organs viable, for a couple of days maximum after the patient has died.'

Myers nodded. 'So, deaths on the 8th, 9th and 10th.'

Sawyer headed into his office. 'Perfect. We need some angles, new leads. Think lateral.'

He closed the door behind him and flopped into his chair. He took a breath and listened. Office bustle from the main room. Keating next door: speaking, pausing, speaking again. A phone conversation. Too quiet to discern detail.

He scrolled down his phone contact list and tapped the name. The call connected after a couple of rings.

'This is Ainsworth. Can I help?'

'I hope so, Professor.'

'Jake? So good to hear from you. How's the world of rural law enforcement?'

Sawyer snorted. 'Busier than you might think.'

'I'm working with your friend, Richard Jensen. The chap I met at the end of the Crawley case.'

Sawyer sat back in his chair and lifted his feet onto the desk. There was something soothing and paternal about Donald Ainsworth's Scottish lilt. 'You still at Strathclyde? I thought you said you were moving away from parapsychology.'

Ainsworth laughed. 'The Persinger Unit is still a concern, but yes. The scales have been lifted from my eyes. I'm focusing on psychology. My core discipline. Shifting away from the supernatural.'

'Not if you're working with Jensen. He's quite an enigma.'

'It's a fine combination. The scientist and the sceptic. We're working on a book about the history of my paranormal challenge here. Examining the methods of charlatans and mediums. Fascinating stuff. Richard wants to do a podcast. Now...' Sawyer could hear him shuffling around, finding a seat. 'How can I help?'

'I thought you might be able to give me a fresh take on something. A current case. I have two murders. Both the work of the same killer, I'm certain. Each body has been stripped, cleaned and presented naked, wrapped in polythene. The victims' hands have been positioned so they cover private areas: breasts in the case of the female victim, crotch area in the case of the male. Each has only one stab wound, which has been cauterised. Death in both cases was by haemorrhagic shock. Internal bleeding, unsustainably low blood pressure. No sexual assault, and we can't find a scrap of forensic evidence anywhere.'

Ainsworth sighed. 'I have no qualification in criminology, Jake. But, as you're aware, I have done some work in psychopathology.'

'What's your initial feeling about what I've just told you? What comes to mind? Unfiltered.'

'The lack of anger. The composure.'

Sawyer shifted his feet off the desk and sat forward. 'You mean in the cleanliness?'

'Yes. And the single stab wounds. It's... *efficient*. There's no agenda. The cauterisation and hygiene perhaps suggests someone with a surgical or medical connection?'

'We're looking into that.'

'Or perhaps even butchery. There's also the possibility that he may have a pathological need to keep the process sterile. Something obsessive that may not even connect directly to the method of murder.'

'You mean like OCD?'

'Perhaps. OCD is more complex than just wanting everything to be clean, though. If it's not pathological, then perhaps this impulse might come from his work. Again, something medical or surgical seems most likely.' Ainsworth paused. 'But the thing that really leaps out at me is the hands covering the private areas. That doesn't feel like compassion to me. It seems more specific, more acute.'

Sawyer bristled with nervous energy. He stood and walked to the window, looked out at the dormant football stadium. 'Acute? In what way?'

'I wonder if the poor people are... inconveniently naked. Like he's covering them up not to maintain their dignity, but to ease his own embarrassment. He has to strip them and present them as naked, out of necessity. But there's an over-compensation. He wants to make it clear that this isn't sexual. Intimate. It's... and I'm sorry to put it this way, Jake. It's just a *job* he has to do.'

Sawyer nodded. 'Nothing personal.'

25

Sawyer drove back to Edale, hoping to snatch some downtime before the evening briefing. He wove up along the narrow Hayfield Road, too fast, flanked by the undulating moorland, soundtracked by his epic 'Favourite Songs' Spotify playlist. As ever, the shuffle algorithm acted like an inspired but demented DJ: Journey, then Portishead, then Eno, then John Denver, then, of all things, 'You Make Me Feel (Mighty Real)'. But the shifting mood meshed with the seasonal limbo of the landscape: unsettled, restless, everything in motion. The purple flush of heather—a three-week microseason—had been muted by an avalanche of sandy bracken, and Sawyer felt the familiar, woozy sense of nature dimming the lights for the long night ahead.

The music changed to something serene and ambient, and his eyelids drooped for a second. The soporific roar of the road. The siren call of sleep. Of oblivion. He could let it all go, let it steal over him. Or he could jerk the wheel violently to the left, lurch into the roadside ditch, crunch into the dry-stone wall, flip the car into the fields. A fleeting spike of agony, perhaps, and then, that everlasting anaesthetic.

The music dropped out, replaced by his ringtone. He looked at the screen, tapped the Accept icon.

Eva's voice filled the car. 'You shouldn't come to the house.'

'I didn't know he was going to be there.'

'That's why you shouldn't come to the house.'

He turned off, into Hayfield village, towards the cottage. 'You come to see me, then. You know where I am.'

The music faded back in. She had already ended the call.

———

He drove over the driveway bridge, parked up and killed the engine. The silence was complete, deafening. It was still a couple of hours from nightfall, but a plume of black cloud had rolled in over Kinder, casting a premature dusk over the road.

A few raindrops pecked at the windscreen. He closed his eyes.

He was with his dog, with Henry, further along the lane. Ahead of Michael and his mother.

He dug his fingers into a cluster of lemon-yellow buttercups and rolled them around, fluttering the petals together.

Henry bustled through the long green grass and stuck his nose into the petals, picking up scent.

Behind, a shout from Michael. Sawyer heard nothing but his brother's voice, but Henry sensed more. He jolted his head round, on alert.

Another shout from Michael. Then a laugh. Or a cry?

Henry bolted, back along the lane.

He ran after him.

The colours of deep summer. Rich and real. The bluest

blues, greenest greens. His mother: the gleaming orange of her jacket; her black, black hair.

And red. Beads of red, scattered over the shorter grass at the top of the verge. Smears of red across his brother's face.

His brother, lying in the grass, on his side. The powder blue of his T-shirt.

His mother, crawling towards Michael, reaching for him.

Red on her face, too.

Was it a game? What were the rules?

His dog. Barking, barking, barking.

Someone else there, too. A man in a mask. Just his eyes and mouth. Gloves. Holding a hammer.

He ran for his brother and felt the man at his back.

A hand on his collar.

He stumbled forward. Something clunked against the back of his head.

The colours dimmed. All was black for a moment. A minute? Five?

Intense, unbearable pain. At the back of his head, the base of his neck.

He rose up and looked around, the images swooping and warping.

'Jake! Run, my darling. Don't look back!'

Henry jumped up at the man but he pushed him away, gripped his collar.

He watched as the man brought down the hammer.

Metal on bone. Then silence from his dog.

The man turned to his mother.

And now, for the first time, Sawyer caught himself in the moment. In the present day. Aware that he was locked inside an abysmal dreamworld, but somehow in control of his actions. No longer just an observer.

He felt the back of his head, warm and wet.

The pain reared up.

He knew what came next. He would fall to the ground, touch the grass, feel the soil. Smell it, taste it.

He fought the familiar narrative and, instead, ran for the man.

But his mother didn't acknowledge him.

He saw something new: her hand, pushing away her black hair, swiping the blood from her eyes.

He leapt at the man's arm as he raised the hammer.

But there was no effect. He brought it down.

His mother reached up, half-blocking the blow, catching the head of the hammer with her wrist.

Metal on bone.

She screamed and reached for him with her other hand.

She pulled off the mask.

Rain. Clattering at the windscreen.

Darkness now. Inside and outside the car.

Sawyer was slumped to the side, his shoulder numb, his mouth dry and bitter. How long had he slept for?

There was a thrill at the lucid nature of the nightmare, but also frustration at the abrupt ending. Had he unearthed a fresh insight or just fictionalised detail he hadn't even seen at the time? A few extra seconds might have given him more.

But there was no way back in now.

He stumbled out of the car and ran to the porch, through the rain, dense and drenching.

Inside, he cupped his hands under the kitchen tap and splashed water over his face. He filled a glass and drank it dry, without pausing for breath, then mopped his face with a tea towel. The rain spattered against the front window.

And there was another, unfamiliar, noise.

Sawyer froze and slowly moved the tea towel away from his face.

145

Again. A high-pitched squeak. Plaintive, questioning.

He opened the back door and a slender cat strutted into the kitchen, its fur matted with water. It was mostly black with white patches around its head, and a neat, beard-like blot of black under its chin. It looked up at him, miaowed, and curled itself around his shins.

He spoke to it in sing-song, petted it. The cat immediately broke into a loud, continuous purr and tilted its head up to accommodate Sawyer's fingers as he scratched it under the chin.

He opened the wall cupboard. Mainly condiments and cereals, a couple of tins of rice pudding. He pushed aside a four-pack of baked beans and fished out a tin of tuna. The cat ramped up its purr volume and threaded itself around his legs in a figure of eight.

Sawyer forked the tuna onto a small plate and set it down by the door. The cat nosedived into the food. He filled a cereal bowl with water and nudged it in beside the plate. The cat looked up and considered the water for a second, then dug back into the tuna.

Microwave clock.

Just after seven. He had slept for almost two hours.

He took a can of Coke out of the fridge and sat on the edge of the sofa, watching the cat, pondering his nightmare.

He switched his phone to speaker and called Shepherd. It rang and rang. He placed the handset on the coffee table and lay back, sipping the Coke.

The cat had finished the food and was now lapping at the water. Life pared down to its essence: the base layers of Maslow's pyramid. Food and water. Warmth, rest. Safety, security. The cat aspired to nothing more, and its finely tuned instinct for danger kept it alive to repeat the cycle and, ultimately, to produce others. Death would come for it eventually, but only when the cat was good and ready. It would retreat from the living world and hide in a cool, dark place. A submission. A passive suicide. Death would need to cheat to take it before then: a speeding car, a double-crossing human, a house fire. He thought of Susan Bishop and Sam Palmer. Ambushed by death. Had they not been given the opportunity to see it coming? Or had they misinterpreted its approach? Mistook it for something else?

'*Why?*'

'Sir!' Shepherd's voice broke through. 'Sorry. Call of nature.'

Sawyer slurped his drink. 'I don't thank you for the image, but I'm grateful to get your full attention.'

'Too echoey in there, anyway. You would have known.'

'Let's move on. Any updates?'

'Moran has a couple of leads on stolen vans. Nothing on ANPR, so he's working with Rhodes to match them with CCTV. Relevant areas and times. It's a bastard of a job.'

The cat slinked over, hopped up on the sofa next to Sawyer and began to wash itself. 'He can take some leave when we're done. What about the transplant surgeons? Anything there?'

'All checks out. Nothing interesting about the surgeons who performed the Bishop and Palmer ops at Wythenshawe and Leeds. Myers has five potential matches for Palmer's liver donor. They all fit the accepted parameters for age.'

The phone bleeped. Sawyer checked the screen. Call waiting. 'Okay. Work through them and check for any connections. And find me that van.'

He switched to the other call. 'Max?'

'Jake. Good time to talk?'

'For you, Max, any time is good.'

DI Reeves indulged him with a laugh. 'Got something for you. The Casey name has come up in an investigation.

Public order offences on the Isle of Dogs. Unlicensed boxing.'

'Bare knuckle? Is that legal?'

'Technically, yes. But there's no regulatory body, so it's the Wild West. Some places have associations to keep it above board at decent venues, but there's still a lot of underground fights. Warehouses, garages. We mostly bump up against it for public order offences.'

'When the fights spill out of the ring.'

Reeves snorted. 'Exactly. Which they do, a lot. So, it kicks off at this fucking nasty old gym in the Isle of Dogs. Most of 'em leg it, but we get a few collars for possession, possession with intent. Mostly home-grown cannabis. Some speed. The gym owner was desperate to keep his legit licence, so he spilled on the network. And it's fucking *national*, Sawyer. Seedings, leader boards. Fights arranged over social media. One poor bastard died in a fight back in February down here in Radlett. Middle of fucking nowhere. Head injury. He was gone before the ambulance even found the place. So, this gym owner says he has a "relationship" with a family up in the Midlands. Derbyshire area. Looks like the top boy is one Ryan Casey. Seventy-odd but made of fucking steel. He's got two sons, Wesley and Ronan. He pimps them round the circuit. They're like rock stars. They turn up, beat the shit out of someone and Ryan handles the figures. He's pretty much the main connection north of Birmingham.'

The rain was easing. Sawyer's ear caught a hint of engine noise on the road outside. 'Right. So, what's the link with Owen?' He stood up. The cat dived off the sofa and slid under the coffee table.

'Owen Casey's name didn't come up in the gym investigation, but Ryan is Owen's uncle. Ryan's brother Billy died a few years back.'

Sawyer walked to the window and peered out through the edge of the blind, without moving it. A large white Mercedes was wedged up on the far side pavement with its lights off, engine running. 'So do you know if Owen is still with us?'

'No word either way. But I've got an address. Round your manor. Bonsall?'

'Matlock. Not far.'

'I'll text it. Do I get a gold star now?'

Sawyer smiled. 'You can have the whole sticker pack, Max. Thank you.'

Reeves slurped a drink. 'Best of luck, my friend. I hope you get some joy with this. And take it easy. These fuckers might not be too friendly with coppers.'

'I can look after myself.'

The car turned on its lights. It pulled out into the road, spun its tyres in a patch of rainwater, and drove away.

26

Simon Brock directed the taxi into the drive of his stone-built cottage on the edge of Hollinsclough. The driver parked in front of the single-storey annex and got out to retrieve the luggage from the boot. Simon sighed and looked out of the window at the former farmhouse: a rugged construction of charcoal-grey stone with incongruous refitted windows. The building shimmered in the morning mist. Home, sweet home.

It was too large for one man, even one who had grown as large as Simon. But he filled the space with regular—and legendary—'soirées'. Mostly gatherings of local literary types, old colleagues and students from Cambridge, and friends from his previous life, when the house had been the ideal homestead for a couple in early retirement.

He had bought the place ten years earlier, after his agent had sold the TV rights to his first series of five novels. In the end, only two of the stories were filmed, but the money funded the restoration, and the publicity had boosted his profile. He now enjoyed a comfortable life on sales royalties, with a new title added to the mix every year.

With difficulty, he climbed out of the car and looked

over the annex building, catching his breath. He had converted the old calf shed into a writing workshop, and had settled into a rhythm of bashing out his first drafts in there over winter. It was a womb-like haven of splendid isolation, with blissful underfloor heating. He often worked deep into the night, usually ending the sessions with a short stagger from his chair and a flop down into the double bed. His son had pestered him to rent the place out on Airbnb over summer, but the very idea was a violation, and he was in no need of either the company or the money.

Simon took his small case from the driver, paid him— including a generous tip—and shuffled towards the main house. He was a conspicuous figure, always impeccably dressed in tailored suit and Paisley tie, Full Windsor. He had a vast bald head with a grey beard tightly trimmed around a bear-trap jaw, and stood at six foot five, with immense, jutting shoulders which often carried his two young granddaughters during his son's Christmas and summer visits. It was a tradition: he would greet the girls in a crouch, and they would take a shoulder each, giggling as he rose to his full height, and bore them indoors, perched like parrots. He would perhaps enjoy that at least one more time.

He was a rugby man at Cambridge—a prop, of course —and he had briefly played the sport semi-professionally, before a knee injury had drawn him to the sedentary pleasures of storytelling. But his hedonistic appetites had always been at odds with the self-denial of sporting endeavour. He had been an unfailing epicurean. A drinker, an eater, an imbiber and inhaler of all. An arch consumer of the full tasting menu of life. He had been a two packs a day man—no filter—until his respiratory system had finally rebelled at the end of his fifties.

Simon unlocked the door and walked into the hall. He

was tired from the early flight, but his head was full of ideas for his new book, and he was keen to get something down before picking up his dogs from the nearby boarding centre.

He dumped his case by the door and flicked the switch on the wall outside, illuminating a modest sitting room: low ceiling with exposed beams, small corner television, wicker dog beds, bookshelves, a couple of ageing armchairs, working fireplace with a propped poker. A folding wooden side table sat snug beneath a large window that, in daylight, looked down towards the limestone knoll of Chrome Hill and the southern fringes of Buxton.

He ignored the man sitting in the chair by the table and took up his notepad from the mantel shelf by the door. He settled into an armchair, slid a pen out of his inside pocket and opened the pad.

Simon turned a few pages, found his outline notes. He spoke without looking up. 'Would you mind telling me what you're doing in my home?' His voice was loud and resonant, with no waver.

No answer. He looked up from the pad. The man was now leaning forward in the chair, elbows on knees. He held a large kitchen knife between his feet, with the point of its long, broad blade prodded into the floorboards. He twisted the handle, turning the blade. Light flashed off the metal.

'Simon Brock,' said the man. He was short, wiry, impish; engulfed by the high-backed chair. He wore surgical scrubs: short-sleeved sky-blue tunic, lightweight trousers, slippers with polythene covers. Latex gloves. 'You've kept me waiting.' In contrast to Simon, his voice was quiet and calm, higher in pitch. There was no malevolence in his eyes; they were open, accommodating, curious.

Simon nodded. 'Sorry about that. Flight was a little delayed. Who *are* you?'

'You know who I am. You'll have read about me.'

Simon set the notepad aside. 'A copycat killer?'

The man squinted in confusion. 'No. I'm the antagonist, Simon. You know all about those.'

Simon scoffed. 'You look like you can barely lift that knife, let alone stab people and carry their bodies around. You're a fantasist and you need to get out of my home before I call the police. I have good contacts with the police, you know.'

The man smiled. 'I'm sure. I read the first novel in your latest series. Not sure I have the stomach for the other six.'

'Seven.' Simon took out his phone.

'Please, put that away.'

Simon placed the phone on his notepad.

'I liked the story. I like the way you made use of the local folklore. On top of all the juicy murders, of course. That's what feeds the commuters' Kindles, right? The dark stuff.'

Simon nodded. 'Most people lead conventional lives, which is why so many are drawn to the unconventional and transgressive in their imaginary worlds. Crime, sci-fi, fantasy. It all serves a similar purpose.' He picked up the phone and swiped the screen to unlock it.

'That's your wife, I take it.' The man nodded at a photograph above the fireplace: a younger Simon in formal wear, standing beside a slight middle-aged woman in a powder-blue summer dress. Both smiling.

'Amelia. The cliché applies. My fiercest critic. Dead four years now. Cancer.' He looked down at the phone screen and accessed the call keypad.

The man lifted the knife from the floor and pointed it at Simon. 'Put. The phone away. Now.' His tone was more irritated than malicious.

Simon chuckled and slipped the phone back into his pocket. 'So you *can* lift that thing.'

The man reached underneath the table and pushed a shoebox across the floor to Simon. 'Put those on.'

Simon edged the lid of the box aside and saw the contents: a pair of handcuffs. He sat back in his seat. 'Look. Whoever you are, whatever this is about, there's something I need to tell you. I'm not a healthy man. I used to smoke forty cigarettes a day, and I suppose I've paid the price. I don't want to die like this, but I would like you to know that I don't fear death. I've faced it for many years now, and it's come close to taking me several times. I've felt its bony fingers around my throat. Doctors have employed many techniques to keep me going, and I'm grateful for their efforts. But I've had to make so many sacrifices. I've been forced to compromise on all of the things I love. Food, smoking, drinking. And now they tell me that it's all been for nothing. Death has found me again. And this time, apparently, there's no medical method of turning it away. I don't know why you're here, or what you intend to do. But you've certainly given me the urge to taste the pleasures of life, for just a little longer. May I?'

He pointed to another mantel shelf, near the fireplace, with a tray of spirit bottles and a small stack of tumblers.

The man shook his head. 'Put them on.'

Simon smiled. 'Come *on*. One last toast?' He rose from the chair, slowly, and edged over to the drinks tray. He poured from an ornate, oval bottle, keeping an eye on the man, on the knife. He took a sip and threw back his head in pleasure. 'Remy Martin. Louis XIII. A feast for the senses. Spicy and floral. Would you care for some?' The man gestured to the chair with the knife. Simon didn't move. He took another sip. 'Damned death! There's no escaping it.' He turned to face the man, moving his body in front of the propped fire poker. 'It finds us all, eventually. I have managed to delay it until now, with medical treatment.

Others choose to take control, through suicide. Life, though. That's different. It just comes. And of course, it brings us into existence. It's upon us before we know it, before we ask for it. It's the unstoppable force. I'm sure you know the phrase, "life finds a way".' He raised the glass with one hand, reached back to the poker with the other. 'To life! Stronger than death!'

'Put down the glass,' said the man. 'Move away from that poker and sit in the chair. Put the handcuffs on.'

Simon finished the rest of the cognac in one gulp. He winced. 'Creative Writing 101. If you're really the antagonist, then what's your motivation? You can't just be some boring, cartoonish psychopath. We might not agree with what you're doing on a moral level, but we have to at least *sympathise*, yes?'

The man sighed. 'Ten... nine...'

Simon stumbled away from the fireplace and sat back down in the chair. He could feel the alcohol flaring through his blood, soothing him. He picked up the handcuffs and turned them over in his fingers.

'Eight... seven...'

'Is this where I offer you money?'

'It's not about money,' said the man. 'Not even close.'

27

Karl Rhodes turned to the bank of monitors flattened against the recessed wall in his basement office at Buxton police station. Sawyer leaned forward and squinted into the screen. The room was cramped and overheated, with a continuous hiss from the computers' cooler fans.

Rhodes looked up at Sawyer and grinned, bearing a rickety set of off-white teeth. 'You're welcome.'

Sawyer stood upright and flashed a look at Moran, who had fashioned a temporary desk in the far corner.

Moran nodded. 'One of the stolen vans. Local shop CCTV. About an hour before Palmer got to his house.'

'The van was waiting for him when he got back from the pub,' said Shepherd, hovering by the staircase.

Sawyer took a seat, in one of Rhodes' prehistoric wheeled office chairs. 'And, given the lack of scene forensics, it doesn't look like he made it inside. Walker called it. Mobile murder lab. He catches the victims where they live, literally. He kills and prepares them in the van, dumps them somewhere else.'

'Does this actually tell us much that we don't already know?' said Moran.

Sawyer nodded. 'It opens up the profile. He's organised. Premeditated. He has a plan and he carries it through carefully, meticulously. He's self-aware, unemotional. He'll be intelligent, employed, educated, skilled, orderly, cunning and controlled. He'll have some degree of charm and emotional intelligence. Organised killers work hard to cover their tracks.'

'He's certainly done that,' said Shepherd.

'He'll be monitoring the investigation, watching the media. The scenes are so clean because he'll be forensically savvy.'

Rhodes scoffed. 'Fucking *CSI* has a lot to answer for.'

'Organised killers often return to the scenes to observe, when the police and forensics teams are doing their work. Gloating. Plenty of killers have been caught by checks on the public around scenes.'

'Like I said, he *needs* to do this. For some wider reason. It's not psychotic. It's not sexual deviance. It's not domination, manipulation, control. He's in control of his impulses. Which makes him harder to catch.' Footsteps on the stairs. Walker entered the room. It was a cramped space for two. Now it held five. He hung back, listening to Sawyer. 'We have a clear MO now, so the signature is the key. It reveals his motive.'

'But there are lots of signatures,' said Walker. 'Which one is most significant?'

'Single stab wound,' said Sawyer. 'Cauterised wound. Nude body. Cleaned body, no blood on the outside. Polythene. Cuffs. Tape. We've seen all of this, twice now. But what does it tell us about who he is and why he's doing it?'

'And how long is he going to keep at it?' said Moran.

Sawyer turned to Shepherd. 'Brief the others. I have an appointment. Moran, I want an ANPR check for this van.

See if it comes up anywhere else. And get me the records for similar vehicles stolen recently. In case he's planning a third.'

28

'Your homework was on time.' Alex smiled, reached over from the mauve armchair and poured the tea. 'Is that carried forward from your school days?'

Sawyer settled onto the chaise longue but stayed upright; the thought of reclining felt like a cliché. 'Not really. It was just short. Easy.'

Alex paged through her notes and nodded. 'You scored very low.' She looked up. 'For anxiety.'

'Is that bad?'

She laughed. 'It's not a competition. And, no, it's not bad. Interesting, though. Sometimes, the absence of something can tell us a lot. Still, Beck is a little blunt for our purposes. I have a more specific questionnaire for you. The Impact of Events scale. It's used to assess PTSD.' He stayed silent, eyed the plate of biscuits on Alex's tea tray. 'Shall we talk about fear, Jake?'

'It's not something I know a lot about.'

Alex stirred her tea. 'And that isn't phoney bravery with you, is it? You really mean that.'

'Yes, I do. I'm reading about it. Maggie gave me a book. *The Gift of Fear.*'

She nodded. 'I know it: de Becker. He's good, even though it's effectively an advert for his protection business. Sound thinking.'

'He says a lot of it is instinct.'

'Yes. We underestimate our impulses. The conscious thought that you're in danger comes later than the feeling. Two-hundred milliseconds. The brain alerts you to danger before you can assess, intellectualise. If we'd had to rely on conscious threat assessment, we'd have died out long ago. It's true across nature. A weasel smells the air. An octopus puts out its tentacle. We have an incredibly complex brain that conducts all of that without our involvement. We flatter ourselves. It's like all of our emotions, really. They're just thoughts with bells on. In one sense, a faulty fear response can be helpful. You'll be immune to certain types of persuasion, manipulation. Fear sells. Just ask journalists.'

'I try to avoid them.'

She sipped her tea. 'How do you feel, in a situation that you know is potentially hazardous?'

Sawyer looked around the room, searching the paintings for an answer. 'I want to prevent bad things, bad consequences. I see them. I understand the implications.'

'Yes, but you don't *feel* it, do you? Your primal response doesn't give you those vital milliseconds.'

'No. I've trained my brain, though. To observe tells, signs. I've worked on my reflexes.'

'With martial arts?'

'Yes.'

Alex set down her cup and wrote something in her notes. 'Do you think you're disabled, Jake?'

'No. Just differently abled.'

She looked up. No smile. 'So, because of these coping strategies you've formed to compensate, you don't feel compromised?' He shook his head. 'How about this?' She put down the pad. 'Does your own lack of fear response cloud your judgement, perhaps? You're wired in to the signs yourself, but does your behaviour put *other people* in danger?' She eyed his bandaged hand.

He sighed. 'Am I reckless?'

'What do you think?'

Sawyer leaned forward and took one of the biscuits: a Jammie Dodger. 'I sometimes just feel... incompatible with the world.'

'Like the operating system has advanced beyond you? Like you're an outmoded program?'

He crunched into the biscuit. 'No. The other way round. Like the world is the obsolete operating system, and I'm always having to slow down, compromise, filter, underclock myself to match the slower pace of everything. It's exhausting.'

Alex watched him, smiling. 'You say you've trained your brain. Do you not *feel* anything, in stressful situations? Confrontational moments?'

'Sometimes, there's a tingling sensation. Like my body is reacting to something. But it's... out of reach. I can sense it, but I can't *feel* it.'

'Interpret it?'

'Yes.'

Alex took out her phone and navigated to something. 'What happened to your hand, Jake?'

'Training thing. Missed a mark.'

She looked up, narrowed her eyes. 'YouTube.' She handed over the phone. 'Watch that.'

Sawyer looked at the title of the video: *Why Whispering Gives Some People The Tingles*. 'Is this ASMR?'

'Yes. Autonomous Sensory Meridian Response. A tingling feeling when hearing whispers or certain repetitive sounds. It's still being researched, but some people see it as a form of benign seizure, perhaps connected to empathy.'

He handed the phone back to her. 'I've tried it.'

'And?'

'It just gave me a vague, tingly feeling of bullshit. Pseudoscience. The sort of thing that didn't exist before the internet.'

She took the phone and set it down on the table, keeping her eyes on him. 'I think your brain function is fine. That's shown by the sensations, the panic attack you mentioned. But it's interesting that you can't make clear sense of it. Maybe there is some damage or disruption. You have the same hardware as the rest of us, Jake. Empathy, impulse control, emotion, decision-making. Anterior cingulate cortex. Fusiform gyrus. Superior temporal gyrus. Amygdala. But something is disrupted, compromised. You said you were self-medicating?'

'I suppose. Just—'

'Taking risks? Seeking out danger? Thrill?'

'I'm trying to...' Again, he searched the room, the walls. 'Feel it again. The panic. The fear.'

She frowned. 'Because that normalises you, right? Shows you're unbroken. How is it working out?'

'Not well.'

'Do you worry that you might be sociopathic? Even psychopathic?'

He snorted. 'Of course I don't.'

Alex raised an eyebrow at his reaction. 'Difficulty with empathy. Risk-taking. Easily bored. Charming but manipulative. Acute emotional intelligence and an understanding of how to push buttons to get what you want. Maybe a touch of narcissism? Inflated sense of self?'

He watched her, smiling. 'It all sounds like my job description.'

'Psychopaths are usually happy to commit crimes to get what they want. I assume you don't cut corners to solve cases? Play it on the edge?'

He leaned forward. 'By definition, a psychopath wouldn't be concerned about whether or not he was a psychopath.'

Alex didn't smile. She looked down and wrote something in her pad, taking her time. Sawyer recognised the technique from interrogation training: intimidate with silence. He also knew the counter: patience.

She looked up. 'Do you like women, Jake?'

'I'm straight, if that's what you mean.'

'Is that what you think I mean? What do you look for in a woman? What attracts you?'

He sighed. 'Someone who reminds me of my mother.'

Alex smiled, nodded. 'Thank you for cutting to the chase. But these sessions are going to be of limited use if you only tell me what you think I want to hear. Do you go for strong women? Vulnerable women?'

'I'm not afraid of strong women.'

She laid the pad on her knee and rested her hands on top, fingers clasped. 'Why would you be? You know they can't hurt you. Not physically, at least.' Sawyer licked his finger and dabbed at the biscuit crumbs on his knee. 'And how about when you look in the mirror? Or fall asleep at night? Do you like what you see? Are you happy with your thoughts?'

He didn't look up. 'Thoughts?'

'The things you don't share with anyone else. The things that go through your head as you drift off.'

'I don't see frolicking puppies and kittens, if that's what you mean.'

'Why did you shave your head?'

He frowned. 'When?'

'Maggie mentioned it. Did you just fancy a change? Or was your hair something to remove from the list of things you had to manage? The feeling of not being able to cope? Of looking for things you can—'

'—throw out of the boat.'

She nodded. 'Yes! Exactly.' Alex had momentum now. She leaned forward. Sawyer felt like a nervous paddler, aware of a gathering wave. 'Would you think it's fair to say, Jake, that your life has been pretty much defined by death? Your cases. All those puzzles to solve. All instigated by death.'

'You've got a theme, yes.'

She unclasped her hands and held her arms out briefly, as if waiting for a hug. 'But here's the thing! You're the *survivor*, Jake.' She sprang up and wandered over to a bookshelf, surprising Sawyer with her spritely movement. 'Behind it all, is the one puzzle you can't solve. The one case you can't close.' She reached the bookcase and turned. 'I don't think there's anything physically wrong with your brain. I think you're traumatised. The six-year-old who witnessed something too terrible to contemplate. He's still inside you. Frozen. And you can't unfreeze, get on with your own life, until he's—'

'—melted?'

'It's an unpleasant image, but it serves our purpose.' Alex walked back to her chair and sat down. 'So, we're going to work together on that.' She gestured out of the window. 'It's perhaps not the kind of thing you would want to do on a beautiful autumn afternoon, but I'd like you to take me through the whole thing. The day it happened. Every little event you remember. And then I want to know what happened next. Your life before and after.'

Sawyer tilted back his head. 'So you want me to talk you through my difficult childhood?'

'There may be *some* neurological impairment, given how you were assaulted. But I feel your difficulties are all based on the heightened drama of that appalling day. I want to try something with you. It's a technique used in trauma therapy, called "reliving". It can be painful, but extremely effective, to break free from the origins of the trauma. But you don't mind a little pain. You eat pain for breakfast, right?'

'I prefer Weetabix.'

Alex smiled. 'All of that will come later, though. For now, why don't you lie back on the couch and tell me about your mother?'

29

Sawyer bought a cheese sandwich in Stanshope village and drove down into the Manifold Valley. He parked at Wetton Mill and walked along the old railway line. There was something about the case that was nagging him, simmering at the back of his mind, and there was only one place to see if he could bring it to the boil.

The therapy had left him drained and leaden, but he pressed on up the steps carved into the crag and edged up the rocky slope into the mouth of Thor's Cave. A party of walkers in fluorescent waterproofs were gathered in the central chamber; they eyed him as he clambered past in his work suit and shoes. He found his usual place, near the natural slitted window that looked down onto the valley, and gazed out at the soft afternoon light, filtered by drizzle.

The walkers settled into the open space at the top of the slope. They all sat down on raised sections of rock, apart from a broad, bearded man in an unsullied North Face jacket, dabbing at the screen of his phone. He read aloud to the group. 'The cave entrance is ten metres high. Apparently, it was occupied as long as ten thousand years ago, probably until Roman or Saxon times. So it's one of the oldest sites of human activity in the area.'

Sawyer blocked them out, shifted their murmuring to the background. He pondered the details of the case, trying to identify the source of his irritation.

No sexual motive. Both victims received organs from donors who died at the same hospital. Was there a connection to the hospital? To the nurse? Was that all a dead end? Pure coincidence? Possibly. They were both local to the area and so Sheffield would be the natural source.

The bearded man continued. 'The name doesn't come from the Norse Thunder God. It's taken from the word "tor", which fits the geology.'

No official religions had a problem with organ donation, but was this a lone God freak with issues around artificially prolonging life? Why keep everything so clean? No blood? Why cauterise the wounds? Wrap them in polythene? Cover the private areas?

No external damage. Minimal damage. Efficient.

'But of course, it's the legend that persists. Not the boring reality.'

He thought of Ainsworth's comment. 'Inconveniently naked.'

'They've found stone tools here. And the remains of extinct animals.'

There was always something left behind.

———

He hurried down the steps and speed-walked back to the car. As he rose out of the valley at Hulme End, his phone found service and he called Shepherd.

'Sir. Been trying to reach you. Nothing major. Moran

says he's got nothing from ANPR for the van in the CCTV.'

'He abandons the vehicles somewhere once they're used. Somewhere private. Any other recent stolen vans matching the type?'

'Yes. But no ANPR hits yet.'

Sawyer turned onto the A515, the central North to South arterial road which bisected the National Park. He squeezed the accelerator, aiming for Monyash and the Barrel Inn. 'I assume Moran is cheerily checking the stolen vehicles for CCTV?'

'Of course.'

'Any links coming through from Myers for the potential liver donors? Connections to Susan Bishop?'

'As I mentioned before, there are five potentials based on deaths at Sheffield at times which fit Palmer's transplant. Working on links to Bishop and Palmer.'

Sawyer took a packet of salt and vinegar crisps out of the dash and opened it with his teeth. 'Six.'

'Sir?'

'Six matches. Including Roy Tyler.'

Shepherd hesitated. 'Susan Bishop's heart donor?'

'Right. I assume he fits the bill in terms of age and parameters. But we don't know anything about the condition of these people, their viability for transplants. And, anyway—'

'It could be a blind alley. The transplant thing.'

Sawyer pulled in to the Barrel Inn car park and unwrapped the bandage from his hand; the cuts were healed but still sore. Klein sat on the wooden bench that looked down towards the fields around Eyam, already veiled by dusk. A few lights twinkled from the farm buildings, with a denser constellation from Bakewell forming on the horizon. 'Get Sally in on the briefing tomorrow. We're groping in the dark with victimology. We need to review the scenes, the forensics. The fact that he leaves us nothing tells us something.'

30

They took the back lanes, bypassing Bakewell. Klein was silent, head resting against the window, gazing out. Sawyer slowed behind a hay lorry and flicked on the Mini's headlights. The beams glared against the bales, stacked impossibly high. He monitored the lorry as it wheezed up an incline. It wouldn't take much to topple the pile: an error in the tethering, a clunk into an unseen pothole. The bales would dislodge and tumble down onto the car, pestling Sawyer and Klein through the chassis and into the concrete below. It would take all night to scrape them out, to excavate them from the pulverised metal and glass. He imagined the inquest: cop and criminal, out for a night drive. The son of a murdered woman, delivering her killer to a vigilante justice.

'That's Robin Hood's Stride,' said Klein, pointing at a shadowy cluster of rocks at the back of the fields. 'Gritstone. Not far to Cratcliffe Tor. Stone circle. Used to hang out there.' He sighed. 'So long ago.' He took off his cap and laid it across his knees. 'They filmed a scene from *The Princess Bride* there. I remember going to see it at the old cinema in Leek. The summer before.... Went there with Jess a couple of times.'

'Were you close to her?'

Klein nodded. 'We were lovers, Mr Robbins. Let's not be coy. My parents moved to Wardlow halfway through my A levels. I scraped through and studied at Manchester. Teacher training. I worked with her and we became close.'

'Did you know she was married?'

'Yes. Unhappily. Do you remember back at the prison, when I told you that Jess had said she'd got herself into something and was trying to get out of it?'

Sawyer nodded. 'Her marriage?'

'I wonder if there was something more. Unhappy people often build themselves multiple distractions.'

The hay lorry pulled into a lay-by and turned on its hazard lights. Sawyer overtook, giving it a friendly double-blast on the horn. He turned off towards Elton and Matlock. 'Did she mention anyone else?'

'No. She never spoke about her marriage. But I had the sense there were secrets there. And not the kind of secrets you confide to a young supply teacher. An inbetweener.'

Sawyer glanced over. Klein had taken off his glasses and was wiping the lenses with the end of his shirt. He was again struck by how old he looked, how *spent*. It was common for long-term prisoners to struggle after their release: away from the insulating isolation of the prison walls, the longing for freedom could be replaced by a sense of exposure, and a panic over the lack of structure. 'How are you coping in general? It must be quite an adjustment for you.'

Klein startled and turned to Sawyer. 'Sorry. Miles away. I feel like a *child* again. In cars.' He settled in his seat. 'It's... not an overnight transition. Incarceration is terrible at first. The worst thing in the world. Over time, of course, it normalises. It becomes all you know. You live to the rhythm of roll-calls and spins.'

'Cell search.'

'Yes. And now, here in "The Out", it all seems so open-ended. All these people, on their own timelines, doing whatever the hell they like, whenever the hell they like.' He replaced his glasses. 'Are we going to be okay here, Mr Robbins? I've heard that Traveller communities can be quite hostile to outsiders.'

Sawyer shrugged. 'They're just marginalised. Their lifestyle doesn't conveniently fit in, and they've been antagonised rather than accommodated. You can hardly blame them for circling the wagons. It's like everything else. You can't demand respect if you don't give it.'

———

The address given by Reeves led to a dilapidated farm in Slaley, on the edge of Bonsall. The main gate opened to a muddy and cratered dirt track, so Sawyer left the car on a verge off the narrow adjoining lane. They side-stepped along a fringe of grass below the property's stone boundary wall. The outbuildings had mostly been converted for storage—old cars, building materials—but one had been refashioned into a makeshift gymnasium, with stacks of barbells and dented punch-bags.

The farmhouse was low-lit and quiet, but music throbbed from the woodland behind the farm. As Sawyer reached the end of the track, he could see a cluster of white caravans flickering in firelight. Shouting. Laughing. Cheering. A crowd jostled near the fire. Groups of twos and threes milled around nearby, some seated at tables.

'Look,' said Klein. 'I'd be happy to wait in the car. Really.'

Sawyer squinted at him. He was only half-joking. 'It'll help us to establish trust, rolling out the guy who suffered because of police injustice.'

A bald, heavyset man in an ill-fitting suit walked over from the farmhouse porch. 'Yiz lost, lads?' He spoke quickly, the words blurring into each other.

'Hoping to talk to Ryan,' said Sawyer. 'Ryan Casey?'

The man looked from Sawyer to Klein and back again. 'Coppers, eh?'

'I'm an author, writing a book about this man.' He gestured to Klein, who dipped his head. 'He's the victim of police malpractice and I think Ryan can help me with the case.'

The man folded his arms; most of the skin was hidden beneath tapestries of amateur tattoos.

Sawyer kept going. 'He's been in prison for thirty years. He's looking to clear his name. He's innocent.'

The man coughed, and styled it into mocking laughter. 'Aren't we fuckin' all?' He gathered himself. 'Money in this?'

'We might be able to work something out. But I can't guarantee—'

'Fuck yiz, then.' The man turned his back on them and headed back towards the house.

'We can definitely work something out,' said Klein.

The man kept walking, didn't turn. He held up an index finger. 'He's got the right answer! Ryan's out back. Follow me.'

———

He led them around the back of the farmhouse to a roofed veranda with raised decking. Cliques of burly men sat at white plastic tables cluttered with glasses and beer bottles.

173

A battered old barbecue flared and sizzled beneath a pop-up gazebo, tended by a walking whale of a man who wore a string vest, despite the chill in the air. Wafts of sweat, cheap sausage, fake designer perfume. Music—deep, bassy hip-hop—rattled the wood beneath their feet. Small children scampered in and out of the house, shepherded by women and teenagers. Two piebald ponies grazed in a stubbly field by the caravan camp.

The suited man turned and beckoned Sawyer and Klein to a large table in the corner, where an elderly man sat flanked by two larger, younger colleagues, both wearing tight black T-shirts which exposed their tattoos: Celtic designs, with tendrils curling around the contours of hard-won muscles. One of them turned, saw the suited man, and lifted himself to his feet, slow and calm. His hair was shaven at the back and sides, with a neat frizzy patch on top. He bent forward and glared at Sawyer and Klein.

The elderly man waved a hand. 'Visitors, Joe?'

Sawyer stepped towards the muscled man. 'Ryan? Could you spare us a few minutes?'

Ryan Casey sat back in his chair. He was well into his seventies, but had worn the years well: held his shape, kept his hair (thin on top, with something dangerously close to a mullet round the back). He looked a little unevolved—crude, simian features, with a flattened nose and wide mouth—but there was guile behind the deep-set eyes. 'No problem, son. Sit yourselves down. Keep it quick, mind.'

The muscled man stepped aside and pulled out two chairs, away from the table. The message was clear: a qualified welcome, open to evaluation.

Sawyer and Klein took their seats, as a shout went up. A group of men had gathered by the veranda. One threw two coins in the air while the others surrounded the ground where they fell, cheering or groaning at the outcome.

Casey called to a passing young woman, chasing a small girl in a floral dress. 'Drinks, darling!' She nodded, scooped up the girl, and disappeared into the house.

'Not the music I expected,' said Sawyer.

Casey nodded. 'The traditional stuff comes out later. All that maudlin shit sounds better with a bit of whisky in you.'

He lit a cigarette, held the silence.

More cheering from the men.

Sawyer turned. 'What's the game?'

'You not played Two-Up?' said Casey. 'Bit of gambling. The spinner throws up the coins. Everyone bets on two heads, two tails, or one of each.' He took a drag on his cigarette and yanked it out of his mouth, prodding into the air. The woman reappeared and set down three open bottles of beer. Casey nodded at her and she smiled back. Long hair, platinum blonde, unwashed. She seemed a little too refined for the surroundings.

Sawyer edged his chair closer to the table. 'Ryan. My name is Lloyd Robbins and this is Marcus Klein. I'm an author. I'm writing a book about Marcus. He was wrongly convicted of murder, a long time ago. We're working to clear his name.'

Casey frowned. 'Only one of yiz knows that, though, right? That he was wrongly convicted.'

'I know it,' said Klein. 'I've spent thirty years in prison knowing it.'

Casey glanced at Klein, returned to Sawyer. 'And what's this got to do with us?'

Sawyer picked up one of the beers and took a sip. Warm. 'I'd really like to talk to Owen. Your nephew. We think he might remember a couple of things that could help us re-open the case or quash the conviction, get compensation. We could come to an arrangement.'

Casey looked doubtful. 'I haven't seen Owen in years. He used to help us with the fights up in the northeast. The boys might know. My boys. They're down at the ring.' He stood up. It took him a few seconds to steady himself, then he strode around the table and turned towards the caravans. Sawyer glanced at Klein; they both got up and followed, with the muscled man shadowing behind.

'Big fight here on Sunday,' said Casey. 'It's going to be quite the party. One or two little rumbles tonight but nothing heavy. McDonaghs have been slagging us off, sending videos. My boy Wesley is going to take on their champ. Head of the family. Calls himself Big Joe.'

He took them past the bonfire into the woodland. They ducked under a jumble of low branches and emerged into a clearing, where a makeshift boxing ring had been set up: two lengths of rope wrapped tight around four corner poles. A tall bamboo torch burned at each corner, casting a pale light over the crowd: all men. The ring was occupied with two topless fighters, circling each other, stepping in for occasional cautious swings. Both were flabby and bottom heavy, with no muscle tone. The crowd watched them in reverent silence, cheering the rare connecting shots.

Casey approached two men leaning on the rope at the far end of the ring. They were similar in size and bearing to the muscled bodyguards on the veranda, but more contained, relaxed. He held up a hand, motioning for Sawyer and Klein to hang back. They stopped by one of the corner torches, the bodyguard waiting behind.

Klein leaned in to Sawyer and kept his voice low. 'Not happy, Mr Robbins!'

Sawyer looked at him. 'It's fine. Just a quick tour.'

The two men at the ring turned as Casey approached. As he spoke to them, he hitched a thumb over his shoulder. They looked up, caught sight of Sawyer and Klein. After a few seconds of discussion, they nodded to Casey, and all three approached.

'These are my lads,' said Casey, bright and genial. 'Wesley's the big one. Ronan's the nearly-as-big one.'

Sawyer leaned in and shook the hand of the tallest man, matching his firm grip. 'Lloyd Robbins. This is Marcus Klein.'

The man nodded. No smile. 'Wesley.' He was shaven-headed, with a shaggy black beard and aloof, curious eyes.

His brother—shorter, with an untidy scrub of reddish blond hair—forced a smile and held off the handshakes with his raised palm. 'Ronan. What's the score, fellas? You looking for Owen?'

Sawyer nodded. 'Hoping he can help us balance the scales of justice.'

Ronan smiled, revealing a couple of missing teeth. He regarded Sawyer with a predatory scowl. 'It's a lifelong struggle, Mr Robbins.'

Sawyer turned to Wesley. 'You ready for the fight? Hope the opposition is a bit more of a challenge.' He nodded to the current spectacle in the ring. The larger of the two fighters had stumbled to the ground and was being hauled to his feet by his supporters.

Wesley shook his head. 'No contest. Fuckin' "Big Joe".'

'Fat bastard,' said Ronan. 'Nothin' else big on him, that's for sure.' He nodded to Klein. 'Where d'ya do your time?'

'Few different places. They moved me to low security. Had to survive a few scrapes.'

'Kept your nose clean, eh?' said Wesley. 'You really not do it?'

'Really not.'

Wesley glanced at Ronan. 'What do you want with Owen, Mr Robbins?'

'He was in a bit of bother at the time. Long time ago. Thirty-odd years. Minor stuff. We think he might know something that can help us find out who did do it.'

Casey finished his cigarette and ground it into the grass. 'I have to say, there's a strong smell of bacon back here. And I'm not talking about the fuckin' barbecue.'

Sawyer smiled. 'No police. We tried them but they don't want to know. Case is closed for them. Thirty years old. We think Owen might be able to unlock it. I'd be grateful for your help.'

Ronan snorted. 'Can you put a number on that gratitude?'

'Depends on how quickly we can talk to Owen.'

Wesley chewed his lip. 'You a fight fan, Mr Robbins?'

Sawyer shrugged. 'A bit. Boxing. MMA. Not quite up on this scene, though.'

He caught a movement from Ronan and shifted his weight, stepping to the side, deflecting Ronan's haymaker punch with an open-palmed *pak sao* block. He could tell from the lack of power in the strike that Ronan had meant to intimidate rather than fully connect, but Sawyer's deflection was strong and effective, leaving him off balance and exposed for a simple follow-up attack to the side of his knee, body, temple. Instead, he shifted back, into Jeet Kune Do fighting stance: side-on, elbows tucked, fists raised.

Ronan stood off Sawyer and turned to his brother, beaming. 'Got a fuckin' live one here!'

Wesley looked on, eyebrows raised. 'That's some hand speed for a writer, fella. So if you're Batman,' he nodded to Klein, 'how does Robin shape up?'

Klein held up his hands, palms out, and took a step back. 'Please...'

Ryan Casey let loose a wheezy laugh and stepped between Sawyer and Ronan. 'Let's keep it civil, gents.'

Sawyer shifted out of fighting stance and Ronan backed away. Casey pinched at his forehead. 'Look. Do you really think I'm going to give up my nephew to a couple of strangers based on some sob story?'

'We need something from you first,' said Wesley. 'I've got just the thing. Something to establish a bit of trust. Looks like you can handle yourself, Mr Robbins.' He gestured towards a tall, wiry man standing at the ringside. 'That's Charlie. He's an up and comer. You give us ten minutes and we'll call it.'

Sawyer shook his head. 'I try to avoid fighting.'

Ronan scoffed. 'Fucker thinks he's Bruce Lee or something.'

'He was a childhood hero, yes. The art of fighting without fighting. Look. I'm willing to pay to make contact with Owen. However you want to play it. You can mediate, pass on my questions. I don't even have to meet him in person. I'm just interested in something he might know. Think of it as a business deal. A finder's fee.' He took out a notepad and wrote out his number. 'Whatever you can get me. A number. An address. An email address.' He handed the paper to Casey. 'Easy money.'

———

Klein was silent on the way back to the car. He took the lead for the awkward crossing of the muddy dirt track, steadying himself on the stone wall.

He glanced back at Sawyer. 'At first, I thought you shouldn't fight. In prison. On top of the horror of having my life taken away, I had to deal with the other prisoners. And I had to learn quickly. When you first go inside, you're like a blank slate to them. They want to know what kind of person you are. And in prison, there are only two types.

Wolves and sheep. The strong and the weak. It shouldn't be like that, but it is. Wolves don't often attack other wolves, but they will target sheep every waking hour of the day. So, the first time you get into a confrontation, you have to show that you're not a sheep. You don't have to win the fight. That's not the point. You just have to fight. You don't need to become a predator, but you must be willing to fight if you want to avoid being marked as prey.'

They reached the Mini. 'They know they have something we need,' said Sawyer. 'If I'd done what they wanted back there, that puts them in complete control and they can string us along forever. You've already wasted thirty years on this. Ryan Casey knows where his nephew is, no doubt. We need to find him, and find out if he was involved in stealing the hammer that killed Jessica Sawyer. And we might have to use the art of fighting without fighting.'

31

Amy Scott paid the cab driver and wriggled out onto the pavement. She was in first date mode: knee-length cocktail dress, comfortable heels (no risk of totter), light Karen Millen coat. Not too much on show, but a display of good taste with a confident promise of more to come.

The name had wrinkled her nose—Nigel—but he had been surprisingly good value for a Soulmates type. Decent looks, testing the limits early with edgy humour, decisive, no prepared lines. Black mark for slurping his spaghetti, but he'd redeemed himself by not making a show of paying.

She smoothed herself down and checked her phone. Ten minutes early. Myra was a reliable sitter and Amy knew she was on parole after the recent late returns.

She walked to the steps leading up to her door, head fizzing from the wine. Early shift tomorrow. Kick Myra out, herbal tea, few episodes of *Suits*... She would resist the urge to text or reply tonight. Always better to drift off to sleep with her thoughts full of potential.

At the bottom of the steps, a flush of anxiety. She turned, and walked down the street to the Corsa, parked beneath a streetlight. As she approached, she squinted and studied the windscreen area. Nothing. She moved to the back of the car. All clear.

Amy walked back to the house and began to climb the steps, allowing herself a moment of relief. Halfway up, she fumbled in her handbag for the door key. The motion sensor flicked on the porch security light, causing her to look up at the front door.

Her stomach rolled with nausea.

32

Sawyer watched as Shepherd gathered the core team for the morning briefing. Saturday faces. Sunken cheeks, distant eyes. He had worked on stalled cases before—some of them remained unsolved—and he recognised the gathering frustration. Humiliation, too. Like all good detectives, they had a well-practised weapon against cynicism: they took it all personally. It was a battle of wits and wills. One week in, and they were no closer to catching their tormentor.

He settled on the edge of a desk at the front and unwrapped a boiled sweet. Shepherd caught his eye and he nodded. DC Walker took a chair near the front and turned it slightly, half-facing the others. Sally O'Callaghan leaned on Keating's locked door.

'Updates,' said Shepherd. 'DC Myers. Where are we with the Palmer liver donor?'

Myers sighed. 'Nothing coming up for any of them. No records. No connections to Bishop or Palmer. No links to each other. Deaths and background all pretty mundane. Feels like we're chasing our tail on this one.'

'What about Tyler?' said Sawyer. 'Bishop's heart donor.'

'I have a bit more on that.' DC Walker got to his feet, and moved in next to Shepherd, ready to address the group.

Sawyer held up a hand. 'DC Walker. DS Shepherd is case lead. *He's* running the briefing.'

Walker looked confused for a second, and then woke to Sawyer's meaning. He smiled. 'Of course, sir.' He sat down again. 'The inquest into Tyler's gym accident holds up. Weightlifting. His spotter fumbled the barbell. Crushed his neck. Induced coma. Died at Sheffield later that day. Interesting background, though. The crash he did time for back in the nineties. Three deaths in two cars. Young couple, Faye and Tony Hansen, and an older woman, Maureen Warren. Tyler's girlfriend, Rebecca Morton, testified that she was giving him a hand job at the time. Judge wasn't having it. Ten years.'

Sawyer nodded. 'She tried to get him off by confessing that she was getting him off.'

Laughter. Not appropriate, but they needed to vent.

'He did five years, right?'

'Yes,' said Walker. 'Out on licence in 1996.'

'Get more on the couple and the older woman,' said Shepherd. 'Connections to Bishop. I'd like to talk to Tyler's girlfriend, too.'

Sawyer popped the sweet into his mouth. 'Any sightings of the recently stolen cars?'

'Nothing,' said Moran.

'Forensics?'

Sally shook her head. Sawyer squeezed his eyes closed.

'DI Sawyer,' said Sally, 'I've been working this job for many years now, and I have never seen scenes so clean. We've found nothing meaningful on the bodies, in the bodies, at the deposition sites, at the victim houses and vehicles, at the suspected killing locations. We have to go wider. Conduct new searches further from the centre.'

Sawyer opened his eyes, stood, and stalked away to his office. 'DS Shepherd, talk to the Sheffield nurse. If she still pushes back, get busy with a court order for the donor records. I want to know who gave Palmer his alcohol-free liver. Walker, keep on the Tyler victimology. Full bios on the deceased. Talk to his girlfriend. Moran, find me those recently stolen cars.' Moran started to protest, but Sawyer silenced him with a wave. 'Go from scratch. Where were they left when they were stolen? Track all the ANPR data you can find and triangulate. It might give us some idea about his workflow.'

As Sawyer reached his office door, Stephen Bloom got to his feet.

Sawyer glared at him. 'Tell them they'll get a conference when we have something new to say.' He paused. 'Okay. Prepare something for tomorrow. To run if we get another blank on the stolen cars.'

'Dean Logan's been in touch, sir,' said Bloom.

'And?'

'He seemed happy, for once. Said to tell you personally that he's working on the story and it's progressing well.'

Sawyer stared at him. 'Sally. A word.'

He entered his office and gazed down at his desk, tracing the patterns in the leather texture, thoughts churning.

'Jake.' Sally, from behind.

He nodded and crashed down onto his chair. Sally closed the door behind her.

Sawyer propped his elbows on the desk and covered his face with his hands. He slid his palms apart like curtains, providing an opening for his mouth. 'Is it good?'

Sally approached the desk. 'Sorry?'

'The thing you want to tell me in private. Is it a good

thing?' He dropped his hands and looked up at her, smiling. 'Or is it a bad thing?'

She looked nervous. 'Good thing. I think. Do you want the full-fat science or the Dorling Kindersley version with nice illustrations?'

'Stick to the detail I need to know. Easy on the Latin, if possible.'

She gave a thin smile. 'I had an independent analyst run a couple of tests on the Sam Palmer body scene and the road outside his house.'

'Why independent?'

'I'll get to that. We found a chemical trace, using chromatography and spectrometry. Methods of determining unknown substances, detecting trace elements. We use a specialist company to deep-clean scenes. CTS Decon. Comes from "Crime and Trauma Scene Decontamination."'

Sawyer slumped onto the desk. 'More illustrations!'

'They use some pretty specialist chemicals to sterilise scenes. Death has that smell. You know it. You never get used to it. Rotting eggs, sulphur, faeces, mothballs. Depends on the stage of decontamination. Once it gets into something porous, there's no shifting it. You need to throw away the thing and get a new one.' She sat down. 'But non-porous material is easier. Three-step cleaning process with pretty standard chemicals. But we found traces of an industrial strength detergent. It's thorough. And expensive. You can get it online, but it would be unusual. You'd need specialist knowledge to use it safely.'

Sawyer crunched into his sweet. 'And you found this *before* the company had completed its clean-up?'

Sally nodded. 'And here's the really interesting bit. We have plenty of techniques to find even the tiniest trace of blood. Luminol, phenolphthalin, haemoglobin test. But when you absolutely, positively, have to remove all trace of blood, then you can use detergent with active oxygen to stop the blood being detected. Which is exactly what we found at the Palmer scenes.'

'So if you put both those things together...'

Sally lowered her voice. 'This is not a standard layman attempt to conceal evidence with Dettol and a scrubbing brush. This is fucking hardcore.'

'An insider? Someone from CTS Decon, or another crime scene clean-up company?'

Sally said nothing.

Sawyer took a moment to digest it all. 'Can you trust your "independent" analyst"?'

'With my life. Known him for many years.'

'And can you run a similar test on the Bishop scene?'

She bowed her head. 'It's already been cleaned.'

Sawyer nodded. 'By CTS?'

'Yes.'

'Keep this off HOLMES. One to one for now. Just you and me.'

'What about Shepherd?'

He shook his head. 'Can you get me a list of CTS employees without them knowing?'

'Easy. It's a small operation. Three or four people. You could get them from the website.'

'I'll take a look. See if anything connects.' He stared ahead as Sally got up and walked to the door. She opened it and he turned to her, nodded. She smiled and left, closing the door behind her.

Sawyer took out his phone and checked the time. He made a call. It connected almost immediately. 'How's my timing?'

'Pretty good,' said Maggie. 'Considerate, for you.'

'I figured you'd be between clients.'

'You make it sound more exciting than it is.' A door closed and another opened. She was moving into her home office, for privacy.

He turned away from the main MIT office and faced the window. 'Have you spoken to Alex?'

'You've seen her? That's good, Jake.'

He scoffed. 'Don't make out that you don't know.'

'Why would I? Client-patient confidentiality, remember? So happy to hear. We can't discuss it, of course. It cuts both ways. But you must be getting something out of it, or you wouldn't have mentioned it.'

'Why can't you talk in the sitting room?'

She hesitated. 'Justin. You know the sensitivities. Did you see the thing about Donald Ainsworth?'

'Nice subject change. What thing? I spoke to him in the week. Just a steer on the case.'

'I read that he won substantial damages from Beck. He made a personal claim, alongside the University's suit for reputation damage.'

Sawyer smiled. Two taps on his door. He glanced behind and waved Shepherd in. 'Sometimes, the nice guys come first.'

'Beck had to pay costs, too.'

He turned and looked up. The sight of Shepherd's pale face wiped away his smile. His eyes were staring, and he was clearly struggling to keep his breathing steady. 'Sorry, Mags. Got to go.'

'Is that all you can spare, these days? Two minutes?'

Sawyer raised his eyebrows in question; Shepherd shook his head.

'Breakfast tomorrow?' she said.

'Course. See you at nine.'

She hung up. Sawyer kept the phone pressed to his ear for a few more seconds, savouring the bliss of ignorance.

PART TWO

LOVELESS

33

The man lay face-down, half-buried in the roadside ditch. He was immense: well over six feet, with an endless torso smothered in dense clumps of silvery hair. The flesh had shifted and sagged to one side, clinging to the frame in layered rolls.

Sawyer peeled away the tape and opened out the polythene. He flattened it to the side, forming a makeshift groundsheet. He crouched and traced his gloved fingers through the hairs on the back, shifting and flattening to reveal the skin beneath.

He nodded to Shepherd. They wedged their hands under the man's body and slowly rolled him onto his back. He slapped onto the polythene and stared sightlessly at the roof of the forensic tent.

'ID?' said Sawyer.

Sally held up a smartphone-sized electronic device. 'New toy. Mobile fingerprint scanner. We got a hit from IDENT1.'

'He punched someone at a book signing in Birmingham a couple of years ago,' said Shepherd. 'Fiery type, evidently. Writer. Simon Brock. Sixty-two. Lived locally. Hollinsclough. Myers is checking him out.'

Sawyer nodded. 'What kind of writer?'

'Novels,' said Sally. 'Crime thrillers. Apparently, he was friendly with one of the DCs. Chapman. Read his books before they were published. Checks the facts.'

Sawyer held her eye for a second. 'Two wounds, this time. Both cauterised like before. Upper back. Just below his shoulder blades.'

There was a sudden noise: a descending note, like a constrained trumpet blast.

'Death fart,' said Sally. 'Cellular breakdown. Escaping gases. Nature taking its course.'

Shepherd gagged, and turned away.

Sawyer crouched near the head. He brushed a hand across Simon Brock's face and closed his eyes. Again, the hands had been arranged to cover the area between the legs. The arms had shifted slightly in turning the body over, but rigor mortis kept them in position.

He turned to Sally. 'Anything?'

'Same as the first one. Multiple tyre tracks. Impossible. Same with footprints. I'll keep my team here all day. Zone, line, spiral searches. Multiple sweeps.'

Sawyer caught her eye again, nodded. He stood up, handed his gloves to an assistant FSI, and ducked out of the tent. He squelched across to the low stone wall, trailed by Shepherd. They stopped and looked out past the cordon edge, across the tumbling hay fields and the village of Flash: the highest in Britain.

'I'd put TOD at less than twenty-four hours,' said Sawyer.

'Farmer found him,' said Shepherd. 'Saw the polythene. Nice of him to leave the body a short drive from the station. Why so close to the road, though?'

'Have you seen the size of him? He must have rolled him out of the van and dragged him over the wall.'

'No holdall this time.'

Sawyer nodded. 'He's getting bolder.'

Sally came out and joined them. 'You do seem to bring the body count, Sawyer. Before you came back, the sharpest unpleasantness around these parts was a bit of contention between the Bakewell tart and pudding brigades. Now it's like the fucking Bronx in the 1970s.'

Sawyer turned. 'Get Simon to Drummond. Let's go see where he lived, and probably died.'

34

They checked in with the scene manager and walked through the hall. Wood panelling, ornate ceiling, mantlepiece with propped photographs: Simon sprawled on grass, laughing and wrestling with two young girls; Simon at some formal gathering, shaking hands with a frail-looking John Thaw. It smelt of polish and sweet tobacco and dog.

Sawyer twitched his nose. 'Family?'

'Wife died a few years ago,' said Shepherd, leaning in to the photographs. 'Cancer. Adult son, lives in York. Couple of granddaughters. Brazilian housekeeper says she cleans once every two weeks. He uses the annex as a writing shed. His son, Jonathan, is on his way.'

'Who spoke to the housekeeper?'

'Walker. He's working with the FSIs out back. Sally told me he asked her if he could get involved. Wants to learn.'

Sawyer shook his head. 'You should keep him on paperwork. He'll have your job.'

They moved into the sitting room. Two FSIs were wriggling out of their Tyvek suits and packing their gear into holdalls. One spoke to Shepherd. 'Scene fully documented, sir.'

'DI Sawyer is the ranking officer.'

'Sorry, sir.'

'Found anything?' said Sawyer.

'Few fibres. Lump of chewed chewing gum in the back garden. Filing it up for a briefing with Ms O'Callaghan.'

They moved out. Sawyer glanced at Shepherd. 'Pretty sizeist. Thinking the big guy must be the boss.'

Shepherd ignored him. 'Simon Brock doesn't strike me as a chewing gum type.'

'More of a snuff man.' Sawyer looked around the room. All was calm, undisturbed. He nodded to the dog beds. 'Pets?'

'Two dogs. Still in kennels. Taxi dropped him off early yesterday morning.'

'Do we know where he was?'

'Not yet.'

They headed past the fireplace into the small kitchen. Walker sat at the table, typing on a laptop. He stood up as Sawyer and Shepherd entered. Two more FSIs were finishing up by a floor-to-ceiling window that looked out onto a small back garden with wild fields behind.

'Looks like he forced the back door,' said Walker. 'He's tried to repair the lock but he couldn't disguise the splintering in the frame.'

'I'd say some kind of chisel or screwdriver,' said one of the FSIs.

'He made his first mistake,' said Shepherd.

Sawyer studied the lock. It was a good repair job, but not perfect. 'Take it off. Get it tested and sourced. With a bit of luck, we might be able to catch him buying it.' He studied a wall calendar by the cooker. 'MMF?'

'Sorry?' said Shepherd.

'He's blocked out the last three days with "MMF".'

Walker smiled. 'I checked that. "Murder Most Foul". A crime writing festival in Copenhagen.'

Sawyer nodded. 'Our man staked out the place, saw the calendar through the window. He subdued Brock, forced him out to the van. We know the rest, more or less.'

'Why not just wait for him outside?' said Shepherd. 'Like he did with Palmer?'

'He had the dates nice and clear. Probably checked the flights. Might as well get inside and make himself comfortable. Gave himself plenty of time to replace the lock. And like I said, he's getting bolder. Hopefully, a bit arrogant.'

'We now officially have a serial killer,' said Walker.

Shepherd sighed. 'Serial or spree?'

'He's frequent,' said Sawyer. 'But there's a tempo. An agenda. We need to find the motive, the connection between the victims. At least we now have one more to work with.'

35

They gathered back at Buxton: a full house, this time. Even Keating had diverted from his Saturday fly fishing at Ladybower; he stood at the back, managing to look grave and presidential, despite the civilian dress.

Sawyer tacked a photo of Simon Brock to the whiteboard, alongside images of Susan Bishop and Sam Palmer.

He turned to the team. 'Connections? A novelist, an ex-TV star, a football manager.'

'Entertainment business?' said Walker.

Moran waved his pen. 'First names all begin with "S"?'

Shepherd glanced at him; he wasn't even joking. 'Good news is that this time we have a few forensic scraps. Fibres, and a piece of chewed chewing gum in the garden of the Brock house. He also forced the lock and tried to hide it. Replaced it with a new one.'

'Same method as the other vics,' said Sawyer. 'Two stab wounds this time, though. Beneath the shoulder blades. Both cauterised.'

Keating's voice boomed out. 'He stabbed a woman in the front, but the men in the back. Might be significant.'

Sawyer nodded, clearly unconvinced. 'Moran, include the Brock house and deposition scene into your work with the stolen vans. Sightings, CCTV, ANPR.' His phone buzzed with a text. He checked it. Sally.

CTS employee alibis all check out. :(
Deep cleaners? Specialists?

He sighed and looked up: to expectant faces. 'Sally's team are working on findings from the Brock house and conducting searches in the area near Flash. She's also broadening the search around the Bishop and Palmer locations.'

'We're turning in circles,' said Keating. 'Stephen, set up another conference for this afternoon. We need sightings of the vehicles, anything around the scenes.'

Bloom nodded, made a few notes. A pulse of silent despair rippled around the room.

Shepherd cut in, too loud. 'I called Sheffield, about the Palmer liver donor. The nurse we spoke to isn't on shift today. She's at home.'

'Go with DC Walker,' said Sawyer. 'If she can give us a name, it's another ingredient for the mix. Might stir something up. If not, get the court order. I thought the nurse might be hiding something. But maybe Occam's razor applies, and she's just being difficult. Obviously, the donor is dead, so their records won't be so restricted. There might be family objections, though.'

Walker got to his feet. 'I looked into Tyler. The lorry driver who donated Susan Bishop's heart. Nothing interesting about the three people who died in the crash. His girlfriend, Rebecca Morton, moved to London a couple of years into his five-year sentence.'

Sawyer sighed. 'Let's wait for Drummond's report on

Brock, and see what forensics bring up on the findings and the lock.'

His phone buzzed again. It was a call, this time. Maggie. Shepherd wrapped up, and Sawyer disappeared into his office, feeling Keating's eyes on him.

He closed the door and answered. 'Hey. We'll have to ditch breakfast tomorrow.'

'I spoke to Jonathan Brock,' said Maggie. 'Simon's son.' Her voice sounded thin, distant.

Sawyer sat down. 'How is he?'

'You always ask that. How do you think he is?'

'Sorry.'

'He mentioned something about his father. I thought you'd want to know. He was pretty unwell. Heavy smoker. Chronic obstructive pulmonary disease. He had an operation last year, but it didn't work. He was pretty much terminal. Less than a year left.'

'Operation?'

'Transplant. Both lungs.'

36

Sawyer wove the Mini through the dawdling Saturday traffic outside Hollow Meadows. Shepherd fiddled with his phone, scowling.

Sawyer looked over. 'What are you doing?'

'Trying to connect to the sound system. Bluetooth. It's not having it.'

An Audi hooted as Sawyer cut into its lane to beat an amber light. 'What's wrong with this?'

Shepherd eyed him. 'It sounds like Grampa Simpson.'

'To your philistine ears, maybe. This is "The Story Of The Blues" by Wah! A forgotten classic. What are *you* looking for? You look like a Springsteen type.'

Shepherd gave up and pocketed the phone. He sighed and stared out of his window. The Derbyshire fields yielded to South Yorkshire suburbs.

'Walker not happy at being left behind,' said Shepherd.

'Executive decision. Bit of deskwork is good for him. He's a star, but he's burning a bit too brightly.'

Shepherd smiled. 'You've been watching too much *Blade Runner.*'

They turned off, into an enclave of handsome semis.

'Brock's double lung transplant happened on the same day as Susan Bishop's heart op,' said Sawyer. 'Same hospital, too. Wythenshawe. His son said Simon didn't want to know any details. But I do. All the organs have come from Sheffield within a two-day timeframe.'

They drove into Crosspool. The semis blended to fish bars and charity shops. Functional flat blocks.

'The nurse could just hide behind procedure again. We might need that court order.'

Sawyer smiled. 'That's Walker's deskwork. Let's see what wins. Legal procedure or good old-fashioned gentle interrogation.'

———

Amy Scott settled on the cushioned seat beneath the bay window. The net curtains muted the honeyed light from a low afternoon sun, casting her in fuzzy silhouette. 'Can we make it quick? I have to pick up Ava in half an hour. Playdate.'

The sitting room was bright and tidy and smelt of paint and lavender. Modest TV, smart speaker, couple of unfilled Billy bookcases. A waist-high easel was propped on a patch of newspaper in the corner, beside a stool, palette board and side table.

'You an artist?' said Shepherd, lowering himself onto the sofa.

She laughed. 'God, no. That's Ava's. She's eight.'

Sawyer nosed through the book spines. Medical non-fiction, Jane Austen, Joe Wicks, a few thrillers and cookbooks. 'Sorry to bother you at home, Amy. But we have quite an urgent line of enquiry. I think you can help us.'

Amy sighed. 'I told you at the hospital. There's nothing

I can do. I can't just share details of medical records. I would lose my job.' She laughed again, nervous. 'I... honestly don't know what you're doing here.' She looked from Sawyer to Shepherd and back again.

Sawyer tilted a book spine towards him: *Bel Canto*. 'We wouldn't normally bother you on a Saturday. But we've got three dead people. Stabbed. They all received transplant organs from your hospital. You're the Specialist Nurse in charge of organ donation.' He turned and sat down on the stool by the easel. 'So, can you see why we made the journey?'

Amy stared ahead.

'Ava's dad not around?' said Shepherd.

She caught herself and blinked. 'Junior doctor. He wasn't interested in being a parent. I was.'

'Look,' said Sawyer. 'I know you're in a rush. But can you answer me one simple question?'

She found a smile. 'I'll try. I want to help. Of course...'

'What are you scared of?'

Her shoulders slumped. 'What do you mean? Generally?'

'No. Not generally. You don't seem like a jobsworth to me, Amy. You know the sort I mean. *Grey* people. The types who hide behind bureaucracy. They point at signs, quote paragraphs in the rulebook. They think life can be ordered, modulated, kept inside the guidelines. I'm not saying I blame them. Life is pretty messy, right? Some people just need to know who's in charge.' He drew the stool forward. 'I don't think you're in charge here, Amy. And I'm not talking about the hospital hierarchy, the rulebook writers, the legislators. I don't think you do what you do because of a passion for "best practice". I think you do what you do because you're a decent human being. You want to help save lives. So, I'm going to ask again. It's an appeal for honesty. Because every second we sit here, another life is in danger. We can help you. Protect you, if needed. So, one more time. What are you scared of?'

Amy dropped her gaze. She clenched her hands in her lap. Her breathing deepened: juddering inhales, exhales of exasperation. The room went still.

They sat there in silence for almost a minute.

'He said that Ava would die if I said anything.'

Sawyer looked at Shepherd. 'Who did, Amy?'

She kept her eyes on her hands. Her fingers knotted and writhed. '*He* did. Whoever. I don't know. I've never met him. It's just messages. And he sends me things.'

Shepherd leaned forward. 'What things?'

37

Sawyer and Shepherd stood together at the MIT whiteboard. Three long-stem red roses had been laid out, side by side, on a spare desk. They were pruned, pristine. The petals were a deep, sensuous red, almost black.

The team gathered around. Sawyer leaned forward and planted his hands on the desk. 'These have been sent, one by one, over the past week, to Amy Scott, a Specialist Nurse at Sheffield Hospital. She deals with the processes around organ donation, for the people who die at that hospital.'

'Two of the roses were left on her car,' said Shepherd. 'The other was taped to her front door. Timings correspond to the killings.'

'Messages? Cards?' said Moran.

Sawyer nodded. 'The first rose came with a message, reminding Amy of an "arrangement". She was contacted at work late last year by a man who wanted the details of all the organ donations in April. Recipients, donors. She was told to put a document into a waterproof tub and hide it under a rock near a kissing gate on a walking route near Stanage Edge. Which she did.'

'Or else?' said Myers.

Sawyer looked up at the ceiling. 'Or else he was going to kill her eight-year-old daughter, Ava. As well as the roses, he called her school a few days ago, around the time of Sam Palmer's murder. To remind her.'

A female DC, Fleming, spoke up. 'So what was he after? Control over Amy?'

'He was being deliberately broad,' said Shepherd. 'He was only interested in one donor.'

Sawyer unrolled a blown-up printout of a section of the BBC News website, retrieved from the previous July. He tacked it to the board beneath the images of the three victims. A grainy image of a young male—spotty, bad haircut, glaring into camera—sat beneath the headline.

THE KILLER WHO GAVE THE GIFT OF LIFE

'It's in HOLMES,' said Sawyer. 'Read it. A companion piece to a radio documentary that was broadcast last July. Meet Roy Tyler. Deceased. Ex-lorry driver. Our man must have heard the documentary or read this piece. It talks about the crash that killed three, and how, twenty-six years later, he died at Sheffield after the gym accident and saved the lives of five people.'

Shepherd moved to the side of the whiteboard. 'The piece only mentions vague details of the recipients. Sex, age.' He pointed at the victim images. 'We now know that Susan Bishop received Roy Tyler's heart, Sam Palmer got his liver, and Simon Brock received both his lungs.'

Sawyer pinned up two more images: a nervous-looking middle-aged woman with pale skin and long auburn hair, and a younger man in a workout vest, heavily muscled. The man had tilted back his head to look down his nose at the camera. Sawyer pointed at each in turn. 'Jamie Ingram. Twenty-five. Received one of Roy Tyler's kidneys at the unit in Sheffield Northern General. Kim Lyons. Forty-eight. Received Roy Tyler's corneas at Manchester Eye Hospital. We've issued an Osman Warning, and Amy and Ava Scott are now under protection. We need to do the same for Jamie and Kim, as soon as possible. The killer is clearly targeting any individual who has received organs or tissue from Roy Tyler. We need to find out why. Is it related to the lorry crash? Let's look deeper into those three victims. I'll check out Rebecca Morton, Tyler's girlfriend.'

'The hand-job queen,' said Moran.

Walker stepped closer to the board. 'What about the other kidney?'

Shepherd glanced at Sawyer. 'It was donated to a fifty-year-old woman at Sheffield Hospital. She didn't survive the op. Never left hospital. GVHD. Graft Versus Host Disease. Her body rejected it, basically.'

'Let's dig deeper into that lorry crash,' said Sawyer. 'Find me the girlfriend. Get me more on Tyler. Surviving relatives, connections. We have the jump on him now. We need to know more about the madness behind his methods. Why does he not want Roy Tyler's organ recipients to survive? Moran, the flowers are hand-delivered. Ditch the car-chasing and work on CCTV for the relevant dates around Amy's house. Get timings from DS Shepherd. Also take a look near Amy's kid's school last Monday. He didn't show up in person, but he might have been staking out nearby. Street CCTV, local businesses. Anyone looking out of place, lingering, in vehicles. And see if you can find something on the document drop-off spot. Might get lucky and catch him on camera nearby.'

Moran sighed. 'Catch him on the world famous extensive CCTV coverage around Stanage Edge?'

Sawyer ignored him. 'It's crucial that we keep this line of investigation confidential. We have every reason to believe that Amy and her daughter will be in danger if it gets out that she's revealed anything to us. Stephen, cancel the press conference. Media blackout.'

38

A titanic mothership hovered into the playfield from off-screen, supported by hundreds of smaller attack craft. It sent out a target crosshair that honed in on Sawyer's ship, spraying lethal geometries of pulsing yellow points. He dodged the onslaught, and picked off a swarm of reinforcements as they swooped on his position. A female commentator exulted in Japanese, shouting to be heard over the impacts and detonations.

He had killed all the lights in the cottage, and was sitting, topless and cross-legged on the sofa, pulled in close to the TV. A Buddha of Bullet Hell. He counterattacked in strategic bursts, maximising his score. His face and torso flared red and yellow and blue in the game's lights.

While Sawyer's instincts and reflexes kept him alive onscreen, his active thoughts were busy elsewhere, illuminated by his hyper-focus on the game.

The case images bobbed on the edge of his vision: the victim photographs, the pallid faces, the texture of the cauterised wounds. He saw the hands: arranged, presented. The dead, covering themselves. Eternally coy.

Nothing personal.

He paused the game and bathed in the light for a while, gazing into the frozen pandemonium.

A car outside, slowing on the road by the cottage.

He called Shepherd. The phone rang for a while and he was close to hanging up and resuming the game when the call connected.

'Sir.'

Background office buzz.

Sawyer set the phone on speaker and wriggled into a faded black Underworld T-shirt. 'Sorry to call late.'

'It's fine. Still here, anyway. Drummond's report on Brock. Death from haemorrhagic shock like the first two. Stab wounds. One in each lung.'

Sawyer took in a breath, held it for a couple of seconds, released. 'There's anger. Is he attacking the things that are keeping them alive? Could still be about the vics and not Tyler.'

'Sally's team are working on the fibres and gum from outside Brock's house.'

'They can get DNA from the gum.'

'I know,' said Shepherd, excited. 'They solved a cold case with chewing gum DNA last year. Birmingham somewhere. Oswald. Or maybe Osmond...'

'Back in the room, Detective. Tyler's girlfriend?'

'Myers has got a London address.'

'I'll take that tomorrow. I can work old Met contacts.'

Outside, the car turned and crossed the driveway bridge, parking next to the Mini.

Shepherd opened and closed a door. Going into his office. 'The deceased in Tyler's lorry crash. Faye and Tony Hansen, Maureen Warren. I've got DCs contacting living relatives. No children or siblings. Tony's brother lives in Zurich. Faye had a sister, Sophie. Lives in Leek. Married, two grown-up daughters. Maureen's husband, Jim, died ten years ago, two weeks after his second wife went. Emphysema.'

'Shepherd, you do have that special way of cheering me up sometimes. Moran and the CCTV?'

'Nothing yet. Keeping him down in the dungeon with Rhodes isn't doing a lot for his self-esteem, though. Not helping with your interpersonal disconnect, either.'

Outside, the car turned off its engine.

'I'll take that under advisement.'

Shepherd snorted. 'Oh, and Keating is hopping about you cancelling the conference. Says we need to engage. Had a rant about how the press always fill the silence with bullshit. He wants to get public eyes on the vehicles while we protect the organ recipients and Amy. He wants you in tomorrow morning.'

'He's right. Fair call. Tell Bloom. Happy with the protection detail?'

'I have DCs overseeing, advising on precautions. Officers at all locations. Possible observation points. We've issued jackpot alarms linked to the control room. Jamie Ingram, the kidney guy, he's not happy with it. Says he can take care of himself. DC showed him the morgue shots, with the wounds. Didn't bother him. He said, "They'll have to get close to stab *me*." He does some martial art or something. You'd love him.'

'Let's check in with them tomorrow. See you in the morning.'

The car door closed. Footsteps, heading for the house.

One person.

They paused on the porch.

Three short, light taps.

The microwave clock read 21:50.

He stood close to the decaying wooden door. It was solid, but ill-fitted, and he caught a hint of Eva's perfume.

Eloquent, subtle. Pheromonic. Not an artificial top layer, but a seamless aspect of her look and poise.

He opened the door. She lurked around the side of the frame, as if ready to pounce. She was long and undulating: an arresting mix of formal and casual. Knee-length skirt; sneakers; designer-looking leather jacket; charcoal-black hair pinned over one shoulder.

She pushed up the bridge of her dark brown Tom Fords with her index finger. The nerdiness of the gesture chafed with her overall elegance; it made her even more appealing. Sawyer thought it seemed a little choreographed, but no less effective.

Eva looked at him. 'Good time?'

'As in, "Am I looking for one?"'

'As in, "Is it a good time?"'

'It's late, Eva. I was just about to turn in for the night.'

He smiled. She raised her eyebrows, chiding him, and stepped past into the house.

He closed the door and followed her inside.

She took in the sitting room: paused videogame flickering on the TV; coffee table cluttered with plates and packets; half-empty mugs and glasses dotted around like ornaments. 'You're such a boy.'

'This is me relaxing. You doorstepped me. It's not meant for external observation. I feel quite violated, actually. Drink?'

She held up a bottle wrapped in brown paper. 'I bought wine.'

Sawyer turned off the TV. He cleared away the crockery and transferred the rest of the junk into a carrier bag. 'I'll find a couple of clean glasses.'

'Good luck.'

He thrust the carrier bag into the kitchen pedal bin. 'Sarcasm suits you.'

'I wish I could say the same about your T-shirt.'

He laughed. 'Like I said, this is private me. Unobserved. I bet you've got a few band T-shirts you bring out on laundry day. I'm going with Simply Red.'

'Fuck off!' She smiled, studied his T-shirt. A jumble of white letters: some solid, some faded. The solid ones formed the phrase, *INTO THE BLOOD*. 'Actually. It's acceptable. Could pass as a fashion thing. At least there's no band picture.'

He produced two long-stem wine glasses and rinsed them under the cold tap.

Eva took off her jacket and hung it over a chair. 'I'm going to smoke.' She opened a fresh packet of Marlboro Golds. 'It's not like it'll ruin the ambience.' She slid a cigarette between her lips and lit it with the short, steady flame from a tiny lighter. 'How's the case?'

He shrugged. 'Grim.'

A sharp, scratching sound from the back door. Eva caught it. 'What's that?'

Sawyer smiled and opened the door. The black-and-white cat padded in, imperious. It made straight for Eva and threaded itself around her ankles in a figure of eight, purring.

She crouched and petted it. 'What a beauty! Is he yours? He? She?'

'He. I think he sees *me* as *his*. He's called Bruce.'

She gave him a look. 'I don't know why people name cats. It's not like they come when you call.'

'Yeah, they do. But in their own time, at their own pace. I like that. Cats are like adults. They can look after themselves. You can take them or leave them. Dogs are toddlers. Eating and shitting machines. Constantly needing attention.'

'You told me you had a dog when you were little.'

Sawyer unwrapped the wine. 'Yeah. They're good for kids. And lonely older people.'

Bruce broke away and headed for a dish of tuna on the floor in the far corner of the kitchen. Eva followed, and petted him while he ate. She looked around, peeking through the open door that led to the bedroom, then sat down on the sofa arm and blew out a jet of blue-black smoke. It swirled and dissolved in the lamplight.

Sawyer opened the wine. 'Whispering Angel? Rosé?'

'Yeah,' said Eva. 'Bit of a social *faux pas*. Off-season wine. Can you see past it?'

He smiled and poured out two glasses. 'You shouldn't have come. But I'm glad you did.'

She took her glass, sipped. 'I parked my car at a friend's place a couple of days ago. Took a bus there and drove here.'

'So you *do* accept that Dale is dangerous?'

'Of course I do. But I don't know as much as you probably suspect.'

'He sent some friends over.'

'What? Here?'

He nodded, sipped his wine. 'Yeah. Just bluster.'

'Luka said you came to the house. Sensible!'

'Dale is a bully. You beat bullies by refusing to be a victim.'

She sighed. 'I didn't come here to talk about Dale.'

Sawyer ran a palm across the fuzz of hair on the top of his head. 'I need to shower. Couple of minutes. If it's a bit boysy in here, you could wait in the bedroom.'

Eva laughed. 'Is that your best line? I suppose that weird wooden dummy thing *is* pretty sexy.' She stood up, set down her glass on the coffee table. She walked over and stood before him, still holding her cigarette. The smoke spiralled upward, coiling around them.

Up close, Sawyer could see the colour of her lipstick: deep, dark red. Almost black. Like Amy's roses.

He leaned forward. She pulled back, froze for a second, then angled her head, submitting to the kiss.

———

While Eva slept, Sawyer threw on his bathrobe and crept out to the sitting room. Bruce had curled into a tight ball on the sofa; he pricked an ear as Sawyer entered.

Two discarded wine glasses sat on the coffee table, one with a floating cigarette butt.

He unlocked the front door and walked down to Eva's silver Mazda, parked behind the orange Mini. It was still dark; a few hours to dawn, with a bite to the air. He looked up and down the lane: clear and silent. A light wind ruffled the trees.

He bent down by the Mazda and felt under the rim of the driver-side wheel arch, probing with his fingers. He did the same for the other three wheels. Nothing. He took out his phone and switched on the torchlight. He crouched and peered underneath the chassis, sweeping the beam from back to front.

The light picked out a small oblong protruding from the metal. He gripped it, jiggled, and pulled it clear. It was about the size of his hand: a solid black box with two round metal discs. A micro-magnetic GPS tracker.

39

Shepherd parked the Range Rover at the side of the road, behind a tank-like Alfa Romeo SUV: new-looking.

Sawyer whistled. 'Is that his car? What does he do?'

'Runs some training company. We have officers stationed here and at Kim Lyons and Amy Scott's places. DC Walker is here, overseeing.'

An officer checked their ID and they stepped through a low gate onto the garden path. Jamie Ingram's house was part of a patch of contemporary semis just outside the village of Youlgreave. To give the buildings a rustic, stone-built look, they had been constructed with chalky brickwork in varying shades of brown and white. It was how the buildings might look if Las Vegas ever developed a themed Peak District hotel.

'Do you run?' A deep but petulant voice from inside.

'Not regularly, sir. But I'm fit enough to keep up with you.'

Sawyer and Shepherd showed their ID to another officer at the front door and followed the commotion into the sitting room. It was poky, with a low ceiling and functional, show-home furnishing. The walls were covered in framed certificates: ugly and beige with gold trim; bold and red with Japanese characters. Signatures, exultations.

Jamie Ingram stood in the centre of the room, in shorts and T-shirt, clutching a plastic water bottle that had been shaped to fit snug around his fist. He was short but beefy: heavily muscled, with a thin flap of blond hair he had combed forward in an attempt to disguise premature balding. He wore a fitness tracker on his wrist, and his T-shirt was fitted, to emphasise his inflated pecs and biceps.

DC Walker sat at a table near the window, on his laptop. Another officer stood face to face with Ingram. 'Sir. It's our job to keep you safe. We would appreciate it if you could delay your run while we wait for some sportswear to arrive. I will then be able to accompany you—'

'So I'm effectively under fucking house arrest? Look. I run every day, in the woods. Two minutes up the road. It's beautiful, okay? I know it better than the fucking squirrels. If anyone wanted to attack me, they would have to do some serious reconnaissance work, and they would have to catch me first. And then they would have to fight me. See these?' He gestured at the walls. 'Judo. Taekwondo. Karate. This one's for the Staffordshire Iron Man. One-mile swim, fifty-six-mile cycle, thirteen-mile run.' He waved a hand at Sawyer and Shepherd. 'Who's this? My pace-setters?'

Shepherd held out a hand. 'DS Shepherd. This is DI Sawyer.'

Walker registered Sawyer and Shepherd, and leapt to his feet.

Ingram returned Shepherd's handshake, briefly. 'Look. I appreciate you are doing your jobs, but this is incredibly disruptive and totally over the top.'

Sawyer stepped into the room, between Ingram and the

standing officer. 'Could you sit down for a second, Mr Ingram? Please. Just give us a couple of minutes.'

Ingram fixed Sawyer with a flinty glare. Crystal blue eyes. A vein pulsed at his temple. 'Two minutes!' He slumped onto the sofa. 'Then I'm gone.'

Sawyer pulled a chair from the table and sat opposite. 'Tell me about your kidney.'

Ingram spluttered. 'The new one? I waited nearly two years for it. Dialysis. Blood clots. They think the disease was something to do with blood pressure. A gift from my father. What is this, a GP consult?'

'Just trying to get a full picture. And you've been well for a while now?'

'I have. I take immunosuppressants, but everything is fine.' He pointed at the certificate again. 'I ran the Iron Man within six months of the op. Beat my previous time, too. It'll take more than chronic kidney disease to kill me.'

'It made you stronger,' said Shepherd.

Ingram smiled. 'I feel fine. What's this got to do with the so-called "threat" against my life?'

Sawyer pulled the chair closer. 'We're investigating a series of murders that appear to be linked with organ donation. Did you know an individual called Roy Tyler?'

'Haven't heard the name, no.'

'How about Susan Bishop? Sam Palmer? Simon Brock?'

'Only from what I've seen on the news. Sam Palmer was a disgrace. He should never had received that liver. He ruined himself.'

Sawyer glanced at Shepherd. 'He was an alcoholic. Substance addiction, not lifestyle choice.'

Ingram scoffed. 'Willpower. Self-actualisation. We all have control over our choices, officer.'

'Detective,' said Sawyer.

'I'm not saying that some people don't struggle with impulse control, but the idea that you're a passive slave to your urges... It's a cop-out.'

Sawyer nodded. 'You seem quite agitated that you're being stopped from exercising.'

'That's different.'

'So you have no personal connection to any of these people?'

Ingram shook his head. 'No, I don't, and I really do believe that this is all rather heavy-handed. What problem could I possibly pose for someone, just because I happen to have been treated for a kidney condition?'

'That's what we're working on,' said Shepherd. 'But in the meantime, as you say, it's our job to keep you safe.'

Ingram smiled and nodded his head slowly. 'Detectives. I have a black belt in Shotokan karate, third dan. High level certifications in Judo, Taekwondo—'

Sawyer held up a hand. 'Mr Ingram. We're not talking about classical combat. This person is not going to pay you the courtesy of telling you what he's going to do before he does it.'

Ingram laughed. 'No, but he's going to have to—'

'Catch you first, yes. You said. This isn't about tournament fighting or modulated endurance. We're dealing with a dangerous, highly intelligent multiple murderer—'

'Who, so far, has got the better of a woman, an overweight middle-aged man, and an obese—'

'I run,' said Walker. 'I'll go with you.' He got up and made for the front door. 'My house is five minutes' drive away. I'll get changed. Be back before you know it.'

Sawyer looked at Shepherd, shrugged.

Walker hurried out of the house, up the path.

Sawyer tilted his head and took Shepherd aside, into the

hallway. 'I want an observation point across the street. Plenty of options for location. Take over a house if you need to. Shed or outbuilding. Do the same for Kim Lyons and Amy Scott. Our man won't know that we know. This has to be covert. If he comes calling, we need to be ready.'

40

Kim Lyons set down three mugs of tea and joined Sawyer and Shepherd at the kitchen table. She was slight, and strangely ageless, with fringed, auburn hair which hung limp at her shoulders, as if she had one day indulged in an expensive bob cut but hadn't bothered to maintain it. She crept around the room slowly, touching her fingertips to the edges of tables and chairs.

She produced a square Family Circle biscuit tin and opened the lid. Sawyer was disappointed to see it had been repurposed as a container for some kind of flapjack tray-bake, cut into strips. He took a piece, anyway. 'How long have you owned this place, Ms Lyons?'

'Many years now. It used to be a working farm and we took a few courses, me and Jay, my then husband. It was cheap and we thought we could pick up where the previous owners left off. It wasn't to be.'

'Were you both from the Peak District?' said Shepherd.

'Jay was. Buxton. I come from Congleton. It's a suburb of Stoke. I met him at a student gig. We were both studying Fine Art. We married young. Twenty-two.'

The words wafted from her. Kim's voice was dreamy,

conspiratorial. Almost a whisper. She kept her eyes on the kitchen window, as if monitoring the sheep in the facing fields that sloped down to Longnor.

Shepherd sipped his tea, slurping. Sawyer glanced at him. 'And you're no longer together?'

A shaggy mongrel dog padded in, and Kim petted it, scrunching her slender fingers into its fur. 'I'm afraid not. I... We couldn't have children.' She dipped her head, caught herself. 'He's rather an accomplished chef, these days. He works at Fischer's, in Baslow. He lives there now, with someone new. We haven't been together for many years. He left a few days after I turned forty. Turned. Like milk.' She took a sip of tea. 'I live in this little farmhouse and rent out the main building. Airbnb. HomeAway.'

Sawyer nodded. 'It would be helpful if you could keep the house free of guests for the time being.' He gestured to DC Fleming and the uniformed officer down the hall in the sitting room. 'We may need to keep officers stationed here for a while. I hope that's not a problem.'

She smiled. 'I understand.'

'We will set up an observation point nearby, and one officer will stay with you here. DC Fleming will check in daily. You have your alarm. It's a remote signalling device. Keep it with you at all times. If you activate it, the police control room will be alerted and the officers at the observation point will respond and call in back-up units.'

Kim sighed. 'Why on Earth would someone want to attack me, anyway?'

'We don't actually know that, Ms Lyons. At the moment, we're working on the assumption that the offender is specifically targeting people who have received transplanted organs and tissue, from the same hospital. Possibly the same person.'

'Well. If he wants the tissue back, he'll be disappointed

with my corneas. There was no explanation for why my sight started to fail. I had a strange 'misting' effect around everything. Distortions. It got worse and I had the transplant in April last year at Manchester. But I'm afraid I've suffered countless related problems and I've now been told that the degeneration is irreversible. This time next year, I'll be completely blind.' She leaned forward. 'Are you seriously telling me that someone might want to kill me, because I've tried to improve my eyesight?'

'Do these names mean anything to you?' said Sawyer. 'Susan Bishop. Sam Palmer. Simon Brock.'

She shook her head. 'I think I've read one of Simon Brock's novels, but I didn't know him personally or anything. Same with the others.'

'How about Roy Tyler?'

'No.' Kim stood up and moved to the window, guiding herself by the table edges. 'Beautiful day out there. I was planning on doing some gardening.' She turned. 'Is that allowed?'

Sawyer nodded. 'Your protection officer might hover a bit. Comment on the greenness of your fingers.'

She smiled. 'Some people see autumn as the melancholy season, but it's actually rather magical. It's nature taking stock, clearing the path for renewal, making a break from the past. And then winter is the repose before the rebirth of spring. Strange to think that this will be the last autumn I get to see the world like this. The green turning to gold. The dying light.' She caught herself. 'Sorry. It's my frustrated inner artist. Like all artists, I'm a bit obsessed with light.'

'Edward Hopper,' said Sawyer.

Kim nodded, delighted. 'Yes! He said that he wanted "to paint sunlight on the side of a house". I suppose he was talking about the elusive nature of light. How difficult it is to recreate.' She turned, and held out the egg-shaped attack alarm given to her by the protection officer. 'Detectives, I would like you all to leave now, please. And take this. I don't wish to be protected. I'm not afraid.'

41

Sawyer and Shepherd drove through the clattering rain into Buxton town centre. They parked at the police building and ran inside, heads bowed. The lift door was open as they entered reception, drenched and steaming.

As they rode up to the first floor, Sawyer checked his phone. No messages from Eva. He sighed and glanced at Shepherd, crammed into the corner between two uniforms. 'I should have seen it earlier.'

'Seen what?'

'The organ donation thing. We would have moved quicker if I'd called it.'

Shepherd shook his head. 'Doesn't sound like a Stoic talking to me. Regret. Looking back.'

'I saw it, but I couldn't see past it, couldn't make the connections. It's like my brain was fogged over.'

'Lot on your mind?'

Sawyer didn't answer. The uniforms exchanged a look.

The lift opened. Sawyer and Shepherd strode out across the MIT floor, brushing water from their jackets.

'The boss in on a Sunday?' said Shepherd, nodding at

Keating's office. Their DCI was at his desk, in discussion with Stephen Bloom.

'Press conference prep. Call a briefing when he's done.'

Sawyer ducked into his office and closed the door. He hitched off his soggy jacket and hung it on the back of the chair. Outside, the rain had already given way to a mid-morning blush of sunshine. A different-coloured traffic light on the way from Longnor, and they wouldn't have got wet. He sat down, and tuned in to his drifting thoughts. Tiny margins. Choices. Consequences. Chaos theory. Micro decisions, reaching out and shaping the future.

He opened his laptop and logged in to the Police National Database. He typed 'REBECCA MORTON' into the search box and filtered out the hits by age and location. He cross-referenced the results with the address given by Walker.

———

Keating took up a spot by the whiteboard. 'Press conference at 1pm. We'll be focusing on the vans, looking for sightings around the victims' homes and where the bodies were found. I cannot emphasise enough the importance of the blackout on the knowledge gleaned from the nurse, Amy Scott. She's under protection, but I'd rather keep the odds in our favour. And on top of the risks, if he is targeting the two remaining recipients of Tyler's organs, then it's obviously better that he doesn't know we have them under observation.'

Shepherd tapped the victim photos. 'We know that he isn't shy about approaching their homes. With a bit of luck, we'll spot him staking out or watching. Then we can arrest and it will all unravel without any more bodies.'

'Kim Lyons and Jamie Ingram are both refusing close

protection,' said Sawyer. 'But we have OPs outside their homes. They're both aware. Ingram won't accept anything, but I convinced Kim Lyons to at least keep her attack alarm. I'm concerned about Ingram, as he's a runner. He's shared his regime with us, though, and he knows to vary his routine and route. DCs overseeing both observation points. Fleming with Lyons, Walker with Ingram.'

Shepherd looked around the room and found Sally O'Callaghan. 'Where are we with forensics?'

She sighed. 'Nothing yet from the fibres at the Brock scene. We have a DNA match from the gum but no match on NDNAD.'

'Moran? Any CCTV from the Amy Scott document drop site, or her home? Kid's school?'

'No cameras at the drop site or around her road. Plenty by the school but nobody standing out.'

Myers cleared his throat. 'Did some work on Tyler and the lorry crash. No connections with Maureen Warren. As I said, her husband died ten years ago, no kids. The couple who died are a bit more interesting, though. Faye and Tony Hansen. Faye's sister, Sophie, and her partner Andrew. In their fifties now. Got back from a holiday yesterday. I was going to speak to them this morning.'

'Why interesting?' said Sawyer.

'Looks like they married four years before the crash that killed Faye. Census data shows they've lived in the same house near Leek since then. Twenty-nine years.'

'This is the interesting bit coming up, right?' said Sawyer.

Myers gave a wry smile. 'They registered two births. One in 1988, one in 1986. Girls. Nicola and Grace. And then, in 1991, five days after the crash that killed Sophie's sister, they registered a boy at Leek Registration Office. Joseph.

'Adds up,' said Keating. 'But I'm still not interested.'

'You checked the hospitals,' said Sawyer. 'A week or so before the registration.' Myers nodded. 'Sophie Dawson wasn't admitted to any of them.'

Shepherd squinted, working it out. 'The baby wasn't hers?'

'It was her sister's,' said Sawyer. 'Joseph Dawson was delivered on the day of the crash. He survived his mother's death.'

'Looks like they became his guardians,' said Myers.

Sawyer beamed at him. 'This *is* interesting. No need to go see them. I'll cover it with DS Shepherd later.' Sawyer gazed out at the others and held a few seconds of silence. 'Lorry crash kills a young couple. The woman is pregnant. The baby survives, gets taken in by her sister. He grows up. He hunts down the man responsible for the crash, but discovers that he's died.'

'He's denied his revenge,' said Shepherd.

Sawyer nodded. 'But he can't bear the idea that the driver has donated his organs. In his mind, he's still "alive" inside the recipients. In a way, he's cheated death. And so the only way to get justice, to rebalance the universe, is to neutralise the organs, by killing the recipients. And, for extra satisfaction, he works out a pure and efficient method to deliver the killing blows directly to the offending organs. In a sense, he gets to kill the man responsible for his parents' death multiple times. Revenge might be sweet when served cold, but it's even sweeter if you can space it out into multiple servings.'

'But the people with the organs...' said Walker. 'They're innocent.'

Sawyer shook his head. 'For him, that's irrelevant. They're just collateral. He has them cover themselves to give them a bit of dignity in death, but that's as far as he'll go.'

Keating perched on the edge of a desk. 'So, how can we be so sure that this is all directly related to the lorry crash? It still might be someone else who has a different beef with Tyler.'

'I checked with PND,' said Sawyer. 'About Rebecca Morton. Tyler's girlfriend. She tried to ease the sentence by confessing she had distracted him with a hand-job. The BBC piece we found on Tyler's organ donation is coy on that, but the details were widely reported at the time. Rebecca Morton was found dead in a garage in Wembley, four weeks ago. She was a junkie, so I imagine the Met will focus on her dealer network. She'd been tied to a chair. Bled to death.'

Shepherd winced. 'Messy?'

'No. Wound cauterised. Not a speck of forensics.'

'Stabbed?' said Keating.

Sawyer let his gaze wander to the window. 'He cut off her hand.'

42

Sophie Dawson led Sawyer and Shepherd into the sitting room, while her husband bundled their dog—a majestic red setter—into the kitchen.

She smiled. 'Sorry about the fuss. He's not normally this unsettled. Only just out of kennels.'

'Where did you go?' said Shepherd.

'Had a week in Iceland! Now the girls are grown up, we have a bit more free time. So we're going to all the places we didn't manage when they were younger.'

She was a compact and petite woman who had held her looks well into middle age: neat blonde hair tucked over one ear; searching, sympathetic eyes. She was flustered and a little sweaty, in downtime dress: grey fleece, battered jeans.

Andrew Dawson followed them into the room. He had a similar outdoors look, but had gone for a darker fleece. He was large and rounded, with ruddy cheeks and wispy grey eyebrows. Together, they had a comical, twin-like appearance. Little and large.

'We've just come back from our walk,' said Andrew. His breath was laboured, almost a rasp. 'Can I get you a drink of something?'

Sawyer held up a hand. 'We're good, thanks. Sorry to bother you on a Sunday.'

Sophie fussed with the sofa, brushing it down. 'I've *told* him not to get up on here.'

'You mean the dog?' said Shepherd, smiling.

Sophie looked at him, missing the joke. 'Yes. Hopefully he'll stop moulting now the weather is getting chillier. Are you sure we can't make you some tea or coffee?'

'Absolutely fine,' said Sawyer.

Sophie gestured to the sofa. 'Please, sit down. Is everything okay? How can we help?'

Andrew and Sophie took to an armchair each; Sawyer and Shepherd sank into the spongey sofa.

Sawyer looked around the room. Clean and uncluttered. No chintz. Dining table with two placemats and settings; blocked fireplace; work desk and iMac. Farrow & Ball tones. The furniture looked high-end, not flatpack.

'What do you do?' said Shepherd.

'Family business,' said Andrew, taking a sip from a glass of water. 'Property refitting and conversions. Occasional original builds.' He mopped his brow with a handkerchief. Sawyer was worried that he was about to keel over.

'We also own a rental cottage up near Chatsworth,' says Sophie. 'Andrew's parents' old home.'

'You've lived here in Leek for some time?' said Sawyer.

Andrew nodded. 'Almost thirty years.'

'We wanted to talk to you about something that happened quite some time ago. We think it might be related to an ongoing case.'

Shepherd sat forward. 'It's about your sister, Mrs Dawson. Faye.'

Her shoulders sagged and she closed her eyes. When she opened them again, they seemed glazed and remote. 'What would you like to know?'

'I'm very sorry about what happened to Faye and Tony,' said Sawyer. 'But I need to find out a bit more about Joseph. Her son.'

Sophie dropped her head. Andrew got up and perched on the edge of her armchair. He wrapped an arm around his wife. 'How is he? Is he in trouble?'

'We'd like answers to those questions ourselves, Mr Dawson.'

Sophie raised her head again. Her gaze had hardened. 'We gave him his father's middle name. Joseph. They told us that Faye had already gone, by the time they got her to A&E. Tony died at the scene. It was a terrible, terrible crash. The man wasn't paying attention. Joseph had to have CPR when he first came out, and he was on a ventilator. Spent the first three months of his life alone, in hospital.'

'Controlled environment,' said Andrew.

Shepherd glanced at Sawyer. 'Can you tell us a bit about your life with Joseph? Are you still in touch?'

Andrew took over, his tone harsher. 'No, we're not. He chose to go his own way.'

'We became his guardians,' said Sophie. 'After what happened.' She grimaced. 'He was *so small*. Hard to believe that he could have survived. Joseph had a special diet. Nutritional support. Health visitors in and out. I was grieving for my sister and we had two young daughters to look after.'

'Nicola and Grace,' said Sawyer.

Sophie looked up and smiled. 'Yes. They have their own lives now.'

Shepherd nodded. 'Grandchildren?'

She laughed and shook her head. 'Oh, now you are ageing us!'

Andrew reached for Sophie's hand. He squeezed and patted her wrist. 'We had a bit of Empty Nest Syndrome, didn't we? But life is good now. Why are you interested in Joseph?'

'Tell me more about him,' said Sawyer. 'What happened in the years after the crash?'

Sophie gulped in a breath, steeling herself. 'We did what we had to. Legally adopted him as guardians. The girls were delighted to have a little brother.'

'A new toy,' said Andrew, with a faint smile.

Sophie nodded. 'We got through it. Joseph was a little sickly in those early years, but he filled out. He was always the smallest boy in the group, though. Toddler, juniors, big school. Still. Joseph was *clever*, wasn't he?' She looked up to Andrew; his smile broadened for her benefit. 'He used to love the library. He would get out so many books.'

'I never believed he actually read them,' said Andrew.

'He did! He used to talk to me about them, on the way to school.' She drifted, reaching for her memories. A sadness flashed across her eyes. 'He loved science fiction, and real science. He started to read lots of true crime when he was a teenager. He bought a few of his favourite books when he started to get his own money. We still have them. Top shelf over there. All books that Joseph bought for himself.'

Sawyer stood up and walked over to the bookcase.

'What was he like as a person?' said Shepherd. 'Was he kind? Funny?'

'Of course!' Sophie was adamant, almost outraged. 'He was a delight. He was a little obsessive about his routines. Always concerned if things changed too much, or the rules of a situation weren't clear. I would imagine, these days, he might be diagnosed with something or other. But, yes. He was a lively young boy. A pleasure to live with.'

Sawyer ran his finger across the spines on the top shelf. Philip K. Dick. Isaac Asimov. Heinlein. Vonnegut. *The*

Stainless Steel Rat. The majority were books by JG Ballard: a short story anthology, plus a run of his early novels. *Concrete Island, The Unlimited Dream Company, High-Rise, Crash.*

'When did you tell him about his real parents?' said Sawyer.

Sophie dropped her head.

Andrew sighed. 'We left it rather late, I'm afraid. When he was sixteen, we gave him some money that we'd kept aside from Faye and Tony's will, and told him that he wasn't our biological son. He took it very badly. Said he felt his life had been a lie, that he was going to "start again". We were shocked. There was a lot of resentment and rage flying around.'

'What about the crash?' said Sawyer. 'Did you tell him the details?'

Sophie looked up. 'No. We just said that they'd died in a car accident. He refused to listen to anything else. We tried. The girls were graduating. Grace was going through tough times herself, trying to find a job, a way in the world. Joseph withdrew and he left home not soon after. He said he would be in touch, but... nothing since.'

'My God,' said Andrew. 'That was over ten years ago.'

Sophie pulled a tissue from a box on the table and dabbed at her eyes. 'Grace moved back in for a year or so. Nicola came back for a while, too. Everything moved on. We still look at the news, fearful that we're going to see that something's happened to him.'

'Do you have any photos of Joseph?' said Shepherd.

'We have a few things from his school days,' said Andrew. 'Family holidays. He stopped going away with us when he was around fourteen, though.'

In the kitchen, the dog scrabbled and whined. Andrew hauled himself to his feet and waddled to the door. He paused, but didn't turn, resting against the dining table. 'So, go on. What's happened to him? Just tell us. We would like to know. He was a part of our lives for so long.'

'We're pretty sure he's alive and well,' said Shepherd.

'Oh, that's good to hear,' said Sophie. 'It would be lovely to see him again. To try and heal those old wounds. I would give anything to speak to him.'

'So would we,' said Sawyer.

43

Sawyer dodged the press conference and gave Myers and a group of DCs the job of finding Joseph Dawson. The name was broad, and they would need to trawl through the electoral roll, social networks, arrest records. Refine by age, location. Trace and eliminate. The clearest photograph was a shot of Joseph on a beach with Grace and Nicola; he stood astride an elaborate sandcastle in red-and-black striped trunks, holding a blue spade aloft, mouth open in triumph. The girls stood either side, smiling for the camera. Joseph was the shorter of the three by some distance, and skinny to the point of skeletal, with a mop of dark hair swept aside by the sea breeze. Andrew Dawson had said he was twelve, maybe thirteen in the picture, but he looked much younger.

Sawyer closed the window blind, shutting out the gloomy afternoon, already agitating for nightfall. He slumped into his office chair and flipped open his laptop. Among his new emails was a PDF of Rebecca Morton's case file from the Met. On the opening page, there was an arrest photograph clipped to the corner, taken a few months before her death. Possession, Offering to Supply. Rebecca was gaunt and long-necked, with a tangle of gravy-brown hair. She stared out at him, bored and dubious.

From the forensic report, the killer had subdued her, silenced her with gaffer tape and stripped her. He had then cut off her hand. The cut had been clean and singular, probably executed with a cleaver or heavy knife. The wound had been fully cauterised, which would have taken some time. The killer had waited for her to die, and removed the tape. But she had not been wrapped in polythene, and, according to the FOA account, the garage floor was saturated with blood. Forensics also discovered splinters of bone, presumably from the force of the amputation. The severed hand wasn't found.

The anger and logic resonated with the case: attack the cause of the accident, the source of Tyler's distraction. But the scene was messier. He had left no direct forensic links, but he had been less focused on cleaning up and, unlike the others, the body had been left at the murder site. He may have been disturbed or worried that he was about to be disturbed. But it felt more like a first attack, to be refined and perfected with subsequent victims.

Two taps on the door. Sawyer nodded at Shepherd through the glass, and he walked in.

He closed the laptop. 'Pretty quick for a conference. Keating lose his voice or something?'

Shepherd took a seat. 'Sunday. No new revelations. Just a dry appeal for information. No victim relatives to gawp at.'

'How's Myers doing with the Joseph Dawson search?'

Shepherd took out a banana and unpeeled it. He took a bite, offered it to Sawyer, who scowled and shook his head. 'Hundreds of hits. Trace and eliminate will take days, maybe weeks. He had money. He could be anywhere.'

Sawyer nodded. 'And *anyone*. Anything from the OPs?'

'Give them time. He's hardly likely to attack in broad daylight. They're good. They won't miss anything. Kim Lyons is low maintenance, but Ingram is a pain. It's almost as if he's relishing the chance for a fight.'

'He's an idiot. Unlike the killer. My old instructor once told me that you can spend all day at the gym, refine your techniques, hone your reflexes. But the best weapon is always the mind.'

Shepherd finished the banana and curled the peel into a ball. 'We have the jump on him. He doesn't know what we know. Three possible targets, all covered. If there's any sign of him approaching or staking out, we'll pick him up. The attacks have been frequent so far. There's every chance he'll come out of the woodwork in the next day or two.'

'Was Logan at the conference?'

Shepherd nodded.

'He's doing a story on me.'

'You mean your history? Your mum?'

'As he sees it, yes.'

'Is that why you're avoiding the conferences? He'll see that. He's like the Eye of fucking Sauron.'

Sawyer stared him out for a second. 'Has he spoken to you?'

'About your story? No. Do you seriously think I'd tell him anything?'

'No. Just curious about his angles.'

Shepherd stood up. 'Leave him to it.' He lingered, prompting a response. But Sawyer stayed silent. 'I'll stay in touch with the OPs, keep grinding at the leads. Don't worry about me. Seriously. I live to work.' Sawyer finally gave up a half-smile. 'Plans for the evening?'

Sawyer tilted his head. 'The usual. Staring at the walls. Paralysing existential dread.'

Shepherd raised his eyebrows.

Sawyer sighed and shook himself alert. He beamed at Shepherd. 'Not really. Going to a party.'

44

Sawyer drove his forearms into the stubby poles of the wooden man dummy. He ramped up the exercise steadily: from slow and methodical strikes to hone technique, to quick flurries which would improve co-ordination, rhythm, hand speed. He rested, then settled himself in front of the new full-length mirror and worked through the third Wing Chun form, *biu jee* (darting fingers). Sharp, efficient finger and elbow strikes to develop power. Emergency techniques to escape grapples and defend against weapons. Agility, turning, footwork.

He showered, and dressed in his best civilian-looking clothes: jeans, weathered old Vans, grey Sherpa jacket. He fed himself (spaghetti) and Bruce (ghastly sachet of glutinous meat) and climbed into the Mini for the journey to Bonsall: solo this time.

He cued up a night drive album—*Second Toughest In The Infants* by Underworld—and checked his phone messages. Still nothing from Eva. Was this their relationship rules being established? Random dangerous liaisons with radio silence to follow until the coast cleared?

———

At the farm in Slaley, Sawyer left the car on the verge in the adjoining lane and walked along the dirt track towards the main house. He squinted through a fine mist of rain, and his nose twitched at the savoury waft of barbecued meat.

Little had changed since his visit with Klein two days earlier: music from the woodland at the farm fringes; firelight flashing across the white caravans. This time, though, as he reached the farmhouse porch, two men stood up from a table and approached. They were tall and wide, with better suits than the Friday night guard. The shorter of the two carried a walkie-talkie.

'Evening, fellas,' said Sawyer. 'I was here a couple of nights back. Ryan invited me.'

They glanced at each other. 'Did he?' said the tall one. 'Who the fuck are ya?'

'Lloyd Robbins. I'm a writer.'

The short one grimaced, then laughed. 'Covering the show for *The Times*, eh?'

Sawyer smiled. 'Not that kind of writer.'

The short one turned away and muttered something into the walkie talkie. He listened to the response and nodded to the tall one.

They glared at Sawyer, holding the moment.

The tall one stepped forward. 'Twenty-five to get in.'

Sawyer shook his head. 'Strange to invite someone to a party and then charge them an entry fee.'

'Yeah?' said the short one. 'That's just how it fuckin' works.'

'Even for potential business partners of your boss?'

The short one edged forward, in line with his colleague. 'Twenty-five quid, big man. Whoever you are. There's no fuckin' VIP area, okay?'

The front door opened behind the men, and Ronan Casey emerged, also suited. He had cut his red hair short, and Sawyer could smell his spicy cologne almost at the moment he opened the door. He took his time walking over, then stopped between them and laid a stare on Sawyer. 'What's the beef, boys?'

They shuffled aside, giving Ronan space.

'No beef, Ronan,' said the tall one. 'Just coddin' the man. Says he's a writer. Says Ryan invited him.'

Ronan smiled. 'He's not a writer. He's a fighter.'

———

Sawyer followed Ronan around the back of the farmhouse, past the veranda. A group of men were playing Two-Up at the usual spot. Surely not the same ones? They cheered and jeered the results of the coin tosses.

'You missed the fun, Mr Robbins,' said Ronan. 'Wesley put the McDonagh cunt down half an hour ago. Barely took him a minute. Left him with a face like a butcher's block, though.'

'So, what now?'

'Few side fights later, maybe. His family are all phoney-friendly now, but the beef videos will come in tomorrow, demanding a rematch.' He laughed, wheezy. 'Big Joe was boasting about his "iron fists". Said he'd been soaking them in petrol to make them harder.'

'That's bullshit.'

Ronan turned, incredulous. 'Of course, it's fuckin' bullshit! Didn't make any difference in the end, anyway. He barely touched us.'

They walked along the edge of the pony field, past the bonfire and into the woodland. Groups of white plastic tables had been set up at the far ends of the makeshift boxing ring. Music pounded from a rusted old ghetto blaster: swaggering hip-hop, obnoxious trap, occasional squalls of tinny techno. Ryan Casey—suited—sat at the near end, with Wesley Casey—still topless from the fight— bent forward, in conversation with three seconds, each wearing a dark purple hoodie with the word *CASEY* gold-embossed in enormous Gothic script. The McDonagh group sat huddled around the tables at the far end. A couple of teenagers play-boxed in the ring.

Ryan caught sight of Sawyer and turned to face him. He tapped Wesley on the shoulder and he composed himself.

Sawyer nodded at Wesley. 'Congratulations. Sorry I missed it.'

Ryan lit a cigarette and flapped away the smoke. 'Mr Robbins, you are a cheeky fucker, alright.'

Sawyer shook his hand. 'I need your help, Ryan. Mr Klein lost thirty years of his life to a police mistake. Your nephew can help me put that right.'

Wesley glared up at Sawyer. He was a little puffy round the eyes, but had barely sustained a scratch from the fight. 'Proper little superhero, aren't ya?'

Ryan gestured towards a chair and Sawyer sat down. 'All this,' he swept a hand across the ring, 'it's all based on beefs, Mr Robbins. Arguments. Feuds between families and clans. Grudges. Some of it goes back so far that nobody can fuckin' remember the original disagreement. Sometimes it's as simple as something some fucker said in a pub about some other fucker's wife or girlfriend or dog. So it gets settled, in a ring, or on some patch of wasteland or down a country lane. Brothers fighting brothers. Cousins fighting cousins. You send your clan man out, you beat their clan man, you move on.' He slurped at his bottle of beer. 'Thing is, it never works out that way. It just keeps going and going. It changes form, becomes about something else, gets passed on down the generations. Sometimes, it all breaks out and the fighters get targeted by family "associates". Proper bad guys. But that's just the dark side. The thing that keeps it going, the unbreakable bond, that's also our way of protecting ourselves.'

'Family,' said Sawyer.

'Deeper than that!' He took a drag on his cigarette. The tobacco flare lit up his features; he was red-faced, over-refreshed. 'I'm talking about culture. *Our* culture. It's like an invisible thing. A network. The people get old and die, but the beef gets passed on. The culture lives on. It's bigger than us. We all need something bigger than us, don't you think? For some, that question of afterlife or no afterlife... it just doesn't cut it.'

Sawyer dragged his chair close to Ryan. 'But this is what I'm trying to *do*. Two families have suffered terrible pain. One with a man robbed of his freedom for so long, and another robbed of a mother. A young woman in the prime of her life. I believe that Owen is the key. *Your* family can help me settle this beef.'

Ryan shook his head. 'The Caseys settle Casey beefs.'

Sawyer sat back. 'Call it business, then. We can pay you.'

Ryan drew in a deep breath through his nose. 'You don't know our price yet, Mr Robbins.'

A commotion rose up from the McDonagh table. A tall, wiry character sprang to his feet and tore off his T-shirt, revealing a surprisingly muscled torso.

'Here we fuckin' go,' said Wesley. 'Danny McDonagh. Joe's baby brother. Thick as pigshit in the neck of a bottle.'

Danny was pointing at the Casey crew, opening his arms out wide, tipping his head back in defiance. 'Hey!

Hey! No class. No fuckin' class! Yiz got a lucky shot on an old man, Wesley Casey. Don't make you a fighter.'

Wesley waved him away. 'Behave yerself.'

Danny kept it up. 'Honour! Honour!' He pointed at the ring, beating his fist into his chest. 'You and me!'

Ronan stepped forward. He called to the defeated McDonagh champ and patriarch, sitting bruised and bowed at the centre of his group. 'Joe! If you want another taste, your boy can take on our cousin, Lloyd.' He turned and grinned at Sawyer. 'Get the fuck in there, Mr Robbins. Shut this fucker up, will ya?'

Ryan hauled himself upright. He stumbled over to Ronan and clapped an arm round his shoulder. 'No, no, no. We can't risk the name. Let him blow himself out. He's a gobshite.'

Ronan shifted away from his father and called to the McDonaghs. 'Yiz are shitting out, then?'

Wesley got up and steadied Ryan back to his seat. He sat slumped, glaring at Ronan, breathing heavily.

'Come on, then!' Danny climbed through the rope into the ring. He hustled the teenagers out and pointed at Sawyer. 'Get this Lloyd fucker in with me. Yiz'll see a proper fight!'

Ronan looked down at Sawyer and angled his head towards the ring. Sawyer sighed. He stood up and took off his jacket. Wesley lifted it away and draped it over the back of his chair.

The group of onlookers gave a cheer and shuffled forward. Joe McDonagh raised his head as his family and seconds leapt to their feet, whooping and waving. The sparring teenagers ran back towards the farmhouse, shouting.

A stocky but elderly man in a white dress shirt and yellow tie stepped in front of Sawyer. He crouched and looked him in the eye, studying. 'I'm Chris, son. You okay for this? You had a drink?'

'No drink,' said Sawyer. 'Let's go.' He lifted off his T-shirt, revealing a lean, lightly muscled torso that looked flimsy compared with Danny's bulky, gym-pumped definition.

He climbed through the ropes in a daze of disbelief. And again: nothing. No apprehension or anxiety. Just the familiar internal chill; a numbness. More spectators gathered, herded in by the teenagers. The crowd bayed and roared, but it seemed to Sawyer that they were gathered around the exit of a long, thin tunnel: a squirming huddle, their shrieking mouths inches from his ears, but their bodies distant.

Chris stepped into the ring, between Danny and Sawyer. Danny danced and waved at the crowd. Up close, he was taller than Sawyer, with long, beefy arms. He was barefoot, in shabby grey sweatpants. One of the McDonagh group restrained him and wrapped his fists in gauze bandage.

Sawyer dropped his gaze to the ground and the churned-up grass and mud, glinting in the light from the ring's corner torches. Chris wrapped the protective bandage round his hands and bobbed his head around, trying to make eye contact. But Sawyer held his focus, and sank into the familiar glow: inner calm in the face of chaos.

One of the crowd called out. 'That some Egyptian shit?' They were referring to his tattoo. Camera phones flashed.

The Caseys in the embossed hoodies gathered around the corner of the ring near to Ryan, who was now leaned forward, elbows on knees, staring up at the ring.

Chris pulled Sawyer and Danny close, within touching distance. 'Let's have a fair fight, boys. No biting. No hits with the head. Show fair play, now. There's no rounds. No gloves, no rest. I'm here to keep it fair, but I'm not allowed to stop it. You keep going until one of you says he's had enough, okay?'

They nodded, and Chris shoved them apart. Sawyer backed away, keeping his eyes on Danny. It was a wise move; as soon as Chris was clear, Danny lurched forward and pulled back his elbow, winding up a right hook.

Sawyer switched into JKD fighting stance and side-stepped, turning to face Danny in case he corrected himself for a follow-up attack. But he stumbled, overbalanced, and had to steady himself with a hand to the ground.

A cheer went up: more for the audacity of the attempt than for Sawyer's agility and anticipation.

Sawyer righted himself and held up his fists: clenched, thumbs tucked. One defensive, close to his face; the other angled forward, ready to strike. He danced on the balls of his feet, getting a feel for the give in the ground. He would need to favour the firmer sections nearer the edges; the solid foothold was worth the risk of getting caught on the ropes.

Danny bobbed forward. He kept his fists low, near his chin, but was smart enough to keep his head moving in dips and circles. He drew back his right elbow again. Sawyer stepped into his left side, on a diagonal, and Danny tottered, striking at air.

The crowd jeered as Sawyer shifted his stance instantly to face Danny side-on, fists up and ready. Danny steadied himself on the ground again, keeping his head down, open to a shot. But Sawyer waited for what he knew would come from Danny's humiliation: an all-out attempt to land something.

Danny stayed bent forward, turning his head to look up at his opponent. Sawyer saw him drop his right shoulder. He grunted and whipped his body up and around, bringing the punch with him: a full-on haymaker. Sawyer shuffled back, diagonally, feeling a whip in the air as Danny's fist swung past his chin. Now, Danny was twisted around, with the right side of his face exposed.

Sawyer pushed off his back foot and jerked the full power of his core up and to the right, thrusting a direct jab into the left side of Danny's face. Danny's head snapped to the right and he dropped down into the mud. Sawyer shuffled back, still in fighting stance, pointing his fists down, ready for retribution.

Danny's seconds rushed over and dragged him to his feet. He pushed them away and lifted his fists back in front of his face. But the light had gone out of his eyes. He blundered around, confused, as if he was struggling to locate Sawyer. On instinct, he twisted back his arm for another punch. But the movement overbalanced him and he staggered backwards, sat down in the mud, and fell onto his back, unconscious.

Chris held his arms up high and waved them left and right, in crossover.

Cheers and jeers from the crowd. Sawyer winced beneath a shower of warm beer. Uproar from the McDonagh side, as Joe and the other family members gathered around Danny, reviving him.

Hands on Sawyer's shoulders, pulling him to the ropes. Ronan Casey. Outside the ring, Wesley grabbed Sawyer's hand and threaded him through to a beaming Ryan.

The McDonaghs dragged Danny to the other side and propped him up on the ropes, rousing him with splashes of water. He winced as he came round, and held a hand to his jaw which seemed to be stuck half-open. Joe looked him over and shook his head. He shouted to one of the teenagers, who took out his phone and made a call.

Ryan Casey pulled Sawyer into a bear hug. 'A good, good fight, son. Floatin' like fuckin' Ali in there.'

Ronan laughed and locked an arm round his brother's neck. 'Looks like they're calling him an ambulance.'

Ryan leapt to his feet, suddenly sober. 'Come on, boys. Get this ring cleared. Torches out.'

Wesley slapped Sawyer on the shoulder. 'I didn't even *see* that punch!' He spoke to his father, gesturing back at Sawyer. 'Thought he was a streak of piss, this one. But you know what? He's a fuckin' beast.'

Ryan smiled and nodded. 'He's a *Casey*.'

———

Sawyer sank low in the Mini, as the ambulance jinked its way up the lane and turned into the farm. It juddered along the dirt track, directed by a mixed group of Caseys and McDonaghs.

He phoned Klein. It was late, and he was surprised when the call connected immediately.

'Mr Robbins?' He sounded surprised, vague. Sawyer thought of Alex's line about self-medication.

'Just a quick update. I saw the Caseys again. There's an old bothy near Magpie Mine in Sheldon.'

'The ruined place?'

'Yes. Ryan Casey tells me that the bothy is sometimes used by travellers and homeless. It's also used as a neutral meeting spot. Organising fights, settling disputes. There's a meeting there tomorrow afternoon. Owen Casey is going to be there. I can pick you up at three? Usual place. We find Casey, see what he knows. All shall be well.'

Klein shuffled around, coughed. 'I thought Ryan said he hadn't seen Owen in years?'

'He lied. People do that.'

45

Dry soil, on his lips. The sunlit world around: fading up, swelling into focus.

The sickening silence.

He raised his arm, dug his fingers into the earth, hauled himself up onto his knees.

He coughed, spraying soil and blood. Her blood?

His brother lay motionless. Powder-blue T-shirt. More blood. Like paint, scattered across the grass.

His dog. Flat, on his side, legs out straight. Like he was asleep by the fire at home.

He crawled forward. Every movement triggered a spike of agony from the wound at the back of his head.

His mother. Black hair. Orange jacket. Red, red, red.

Her face. Always kind, always open and curious. Always alert to the love she might give. Now replaced by something collapsed and unspeakable.

The man with the hammer had gone.

A woman's scream, ripping through him.

His brother jolted at the sound.

He reached out and rested his fingers on the palm of his mother's upturned hand. Warm. Wet.

Behind, a man talking. Urgent.
A woman. Whimpering.
Her hand on his back. He shrugged it away.

Sawyer opened his eyes. Something was wrong. It was too bright for an autumn morning. Bruce paced around the bed, miaowing, pining for food. Sawyer winced at the pain from the hand that had punched Danny.

He reached for his phone, saw the time, and jerked upright.

He scurried around, diving into clothes. As he brushed his teeth, Bruce protested from outside the door, as if chiding him for indulging in hygiene when he was half an hour late for work.

He fed and watered the cat, and hurried out to the car.

Phone. Text to Keating.

Flat tyre. Nightmare. Be in soon.

―――――

Sawyer threw the Mini around the narrow lanes, taking corners at top speed, scouring the asphalt. His hand throbbed; the skin around the knuckle had already turned an alarming dark purple, despite the bandage protection. He let his thoughts drift to the case: there was something off-key about Rebecca Morton's murder. It didn't sit neatly along the rest of the narrative. The revenge logic made sense, along with the wounding and cauterisation. But there was too much left behind. Too much mess, and with little evidence that he had been disturbed and forced to abandon the scene.

Like the man in the balaclava: so present in his recent nightmare, but absent in his long, exhausted sleep last night. He had taken the hammer, slipped off the edge.

Could Owen Casey help Sawyer pull him back into the frame?

He made the half-hour drive to Buxton in less than twenty minutes. The MIT floor was busy, and someone had written 'JOSEPH DAWSON' above the photographs on the whiteboard.

He dashed down the corridor between the desks, catching a wry smile from Moran, and slipped into Keating's office. Shepherd and Sally O'Callaghan stood at the desk.

Keating opened his arms out wide. 'Honoured by your presence, DI Sawyer! I'm afraid that DS Shepherd has had to brief the team without your steadying—'

'He's local.' Sawyer leaned on Keating's desk and addressed all three. 'He had time to clean up the Rebecca Morton scene, but he didn't bother. He didn't even bother to move the body. That was London, though. Here, he's a lot more careful. Surgical. He's determined to cover his tracks, leave no trace. The proximity is spooking him.'

Shepherd studied him, squinting. 'I'm not so sure, sir. He has left us things. At the Brock scene. The fibres, gum.'

Sawyer looked at Sally.

She shrugged. 'Fibres are from a generic brand of carpet. No DNA match.'

'Probably because he's not on record,' said Shepherd.

Sawyer nodded. 'Or it's not even his DNA.' Blank looks. 'He planted them, to throw us off. Hard to imagine he would clean up everything else so meticulously, but leave something he knew we would find... unless he wanted us to find it. Sally found traces of a specialist clean-up chemical at the Palmer scenes. We kept it private because we wanted to check out one of our own contractors, the clean-up company, CTS Decon. Their employees checked out, but if our man is willing to go to the trouble of obtaining a specialist chemical to decontaminate the scenes, why would he leave chewing gum and fibres behind?' He turned to Sally. 'What about the lock? The one he replaced at Simon Brock's house?'

'No forensics on it.'

Shepherd shook his head. 'We checked recent purchases at local shops. Indies and chains. Hundreds. Some cash, some card. There's an intel cell working on it, but it could take weeks to narrow down, check CCTV. Some of the shops won't have CCTV.'

Sawyer sighed. 'He's clever enough to use a shop without CCTV and pay cash. Go lateral. Have the cell check those instead. We might get a description. E-fit.' He stood up off the desk. 'Sorry I'm late, by the way.'

'All quiet from the observation points,' said Shepherd. 'Ingram is still being an arsehole. But Walker is handling him well. Kim Lyons' mother came to visit. Amy and Ava Scott are happy to have the officers around.'

'What about Dawson?'

'Still tracing, still eliminating. I spoke to Sophie and Andrew about the money they transferred from his parents. Five figures.'

'Account trace?' said Sawyer.

Shepherd shook his head. 'He emptied it a few months after he left home.'

'Not enough to sustain him over ten years. He must have done something with his life.'

'Might have changed his name,' said Sally. 'Easily done. You can do it by deed poll from the age of sixteen or seventeen, I think.'

Keating stood up and took up his cap from the desk. The overhead light bleached the grey from his hair, rendering it a furry film of white. 'Chief Constable meeting.' He nodded at Sawyer. 'I'd like a word with my DI alone now, please.'

Sally and Shepherd left. Keating walked to his window and looked out. 'Tyre really flat? Or did the dog eat it?'

'Really flat.'

'Which one?'

He was looking down at the parking area, and Sawyer couldn't be sure that he wouldn't check. 'Wasn't as bad as I thought. Just had to put some air in it.'

Keating turned. 'So not really flat?'

'As it turned out, no.'

'DI Sawyer. I know you seem to think press conferences are optional, but I'd appreciate it if you would at least adhere to the agreed working hours. We're not exactly nine to five round here, but we're in the middle of a complex case that is drawing national attention. Conduct leaks out. We have to be airtight.'

Sawyer nodded. 'Sir.'

Keating approached him. 'You'll forgive me for wondering why your hand is injured for the second time in seven days.'

'Hitting things. Exercise. Overdoing it.'

Keating nodded. 'More "glitches"?' He straightened his cap. 'Your extracurricular activities are none of my business, of course. But they're starting to impact on my investigations. Consider this an informal verbal warning. I'm sure it's not your first.'

46

The guest in Room 38 angled his head at the gentle knock on his half-open door. Chris Hill, Operations Manager at Rosemary House, edged into the room. Hill had the look of a flustered local councillor: unflattering, off-the-peg suit; fuzzy ginger facial hair caught between stubble and beard. He wore a pair of baroque half-moon glasses, and was in the habit of hitching them down the bridge of his nose and tipping his head forward when he wanted to make a point.

Sawyer hung back in the corridor, feeling queasy at the institutional odours: ageing linoleum and boiled food, with a whiff of faeces from the communal toilet opposite his brother's room.

He stepped inside, where the smell wasn't much better: old socks and cheap coffee. As ever, Michael sat before his muted TV, wall-mounted at head height. The screen showed a recording of an old football match—eighties, judging by the strip and height of the shorts—but Michael kept his gaze down on a handheld gaming device, which trilled and bleeped as he played.

'We haven't been too well lately,' said Hill. He pulled a cord at the window and raised the slatted blind, over-lighting the charmless en suite room. 'A bit irritable, perhaps. Oh well. Every day a fresh start, eh, Michael?' Without waiting for a response, Hill turned to Sawyer. 'Would you mind keeping it quick? We have a training session in fifteen minutes, and we need to secure the rooms.' Again, no wait for a response. 'Many thanks to your father for settling the fees, by the way.'

As he left, Sawyer heard his bright demeanour slip as he berated a young orderly over preparations for the meeting. Their voices faded as they moved along the corridor, until they were silenced by the double doors which led to reception.

Sawyer picked up an angular wooden seat and moved it around into Michael's potential eyeline. He sat down on the cushion: solid and unyielding. 'Still playing that one? Is there a global leader board? You can't be far off the top spot.'

Michael glanced up and nodded. His handheld fell into a tantrum of discordant twittering. He recoiled in anger, and tossed it onto his bed. He looked up at the TV.

'Mike.' Sawyer shifted closer. 'I'd like to get you a speech therapist. I know we've tried them before, but sometimes you have to try things more than once.'

Michael looked at him. He had gained more weight in recent weeks, and cultivated an unruly thatch of beard: black around his lips, grey at the edges. He squinted, muting the green of his eyes. Sawyer raised his eyebrows, hoping for more words, but Michael just strained and grimaced, as if swallowing something unpleasant. He held up his hand and splayed out his fingers and thumb.

'Five?' said Sawyer. 'That many? Let's try again. Maybe you just haven't met the one who's right for you yet. Let's build on what happened a few weeks ago. Now you know you can do it, yes?'

Michael turned back to the screen, paused, then nodded his head in rapid jerks.

'Like I promised, Mike. I'm going to help you get your life back.'

Michael reached to his bedside table for an opened can of Dr Pepper, exposing the diagonal ladder of scars down his inner forearm. Some of the rungs were made up of single, straight swipes, while others had been carved in place with jabs and scratches. He took a drink, shrugged.

Sawyer pushed on; he was used to the rules, the gestures. 'I might have found someone who can help.' This time, Michael shook his head. 'Mike, I think he's the one who stole the weapon, to frame Klein. He's our link to the killer. I don't think he did it, but he could help us find who did. Maybe there's enough time passed now. Maybe he feels safer.'

Michael sighed. His shoulders slumped. He clenched his hands in his lap and threaded his fingers together, writhing them around.

Sawyer shuffled in close and rested a hand on his brother's fingers. 'You said she asked him *why*. Mike? *She knew him*. I think she knew him well. She pulled off his mask, didn't she? You must have seen that.' He leaned forward, deep into his brother's personal space, making himself un-ignorable. 'What did he look like? You saw him, yes? *Yes?*'

Michael's fingers stopped moving. He raised his eyes to Sawyer. A sheen of tears muted the bright green of his irises.

He shook his head.

47

On the drive down to Sheldon, Sawyer scrolled through his phone contacts and tapped one of the names. He set the phone to speaker and slotted it in the dashboard dock. The reply was almost instant, and the caller's stentorian tone seemed to rattle the bodywork.

'Detective Sawyer. To what do I owe this pain?'

'You know how I only call when I need something?'

He heard Frazer Drummond shuffle some papers, flick a switch. 'Uhuh. And why break the habit of a lifetime?'

'Talk to me about detergent. With active oxygen.'

A pause. 'As my son Ben says, "JFGI".'

'I've done that. Googled it. But I'm old-fashioned, Frazer. I prefer the opinion of an expert over the online mind hive.'

'Flattery might work with the lonely MILFs of Ladbroke Grove, Sawyer. But it's lost on me.'

He slowed for a cattle grid, stayed silent.

Drummond sighed. 'At industrial strength, it's the hard stuff. You don't just buy a batch of that at Superdrug. He's done his research. He knows how the forensics work. He's a step ahead. Usually, they'll splash around the Domestos. Bit of Cif to make sure. Who does your clean-up?'

'Company called CTS Decon. Checks out.'

Drummond clicked his tongue. 'You not spoken to Sally about this?'

'Of course. Just looking for a second opinion.'

'Might not be a professional connection. He just needs to be cosy with chemistry. He's stacking them up, though. Can you do me a favour and catch this fucker before the weekend? Daughter's birthday party.'

Sawyer's phone pinged with a text message.

'House full of teenagers?'

Drummond snorted. 'Oh, yes. The boys, I can handle. The girls frighten the life out of me. And there's fireworks. I fucking *hate* fireworks.'

'Is there anything you don't hate?'

Drummond thought for a while. 'Montoya Cabernet. Ruby red. Black cherry and blueberry on the nose. Plum and vanilla finish. With a sweet, tender lamb, and honey roast vegetables from a wood-fired oven.'

Sawyer smiled. 'Anything else?'

'A spot of walking and birding around the Gouthwaite Valley. My wife, my kids. But that really is it. Listen. Love to chat, but you know how it is. Dead people.'

'Your favourite sort.'

Drummond cackled and hung up.

Sawyer checked his phone message. Eva.

Not ignoring you. Hold back for a while. Dale acting off. Suspicious? xx

He sighed, and accelerated through a flooded dip near a farm entrance, drenching the Mini in muddy water. He called Shepherd.

'Sir. How was the "word" with Keating?'

'It was more his words than my words. I'm busy this afternoon, but I want you to talk to Myers. While he's tracing Joseph Dawsons, get him to cross-reference with chemistry graduates. Stick to colleges and unis in the North and Midlands.'

'Is this the scene clean-up angle? The one we only found out about today?'

Sawyer paused, hoping it would transmit his irritation. 'I told you, we had to keep it quiet because we were looking into one of our own contractors.'

'With respect, sir—'

'Don't say that, Shepherd. Please. Let's take our mutual respect as read, yes? No need to apologise for frankness.'

'I'm the direct report for the DCs on this case. I should know—'

'You do know. Now. Before, I made the decision that you didn't need to know. As *your* direct report. Myers, please. Chemistry. Stay on target. We can kiss and make up later.'

He hung up, angered by his need to have the last word.

————

Sawyer picked up Klein at the Barrel and they drove on to Sheldon in near silence. Klein looked frail and haunted, as if the adventure was all a bit too much for him.

They turned in to the road alongside the Magpie Mine site. Sawyer glanced at Klein as he jinked around the potholes. 'How's your living situation, Marcus?'

Klein managed a faint smile. 'First name terms at last!' He lifted his glasses and rubbed at his eyes. 'It's okay. I have the place to myself until just before Christmas. My brother is away.'

'Is something bothering you?'

He shook his head. 'No. Not at all.'

'I don't believe you.'

Klein turned to him. 'You don't *believe* me?'

'No. I've interviewed lots of people over the years. You get used to the little tells and body language leaks.'

Klein sighed. 'It's strange. I'm having trouble adjusting. Nothing serious. Struggling with the small things. The maintenance. Day by day. The supplies, the consumables.'

'The things that were done for you on the inside?'

'Yes. Prison does have its positives.'

Sawyer steered into the parking area. 'That's one of the freedoms they take away. The right to make those small choices. The little decisions that make up the days. Brand of toothpaste. When to go to bed. What to eat and when.'

Klein laughed, without humour. 'There's also... You'll probably laugh. But I'm really feeling the paranoia. Like someone is watching me. Or following me.'

'Today?'

'Since I've been out. Noises. Looks from people in public. I'm hyper-sensitive to cars behind me, waiting for them to turn off so I can be sure they're not following.'

'It'll take time. All this? It's just the real world. Life. Freedom.' Sawyer smiled. 'You wanted it. You've got it. But you can't just pick up where you left off. You have to rebuild. Start at the foundations.'

Klein closed and opened his eyes. 'Mr Robbins. For all that I appreciate your help and your support, you're forgetting one thing. You might *believe* that I didn't murder Jess, but I *know* that I didn't. For certain.' He looked at Sawyer. 'And there's one other person who also carries that certainty. And this freedom.'

They walked along a scruffy public pathway; it was Open Access Land, but designed to distance observers from the fractured outbuildings of the disused mine.

Klein cupped a hand to his forehead, shielding his eyes from the sinking sun. 'They used this place to suck lead out of the earth in Victorian times. But then they had to pump the water out, and it became unprofitable.'

Sawyer gazed out across the broad, flat field. The brick ruins brooded in the afternoon shadows; a clutter of chipped pottery, gnawed down by the elements. The buildings were mostly low and roofless, gathered around a central engine house with a cylindrical chimney that loomed like an obelisk. The place was a fossil; a monument to obsolete industry, marooned in the centre of the very ground it was built to exploit.

'I read there was a murder here,' said Sawyer. 'A rivalry with another mine or something.'

Klein scoffed. 'Probably an industrial accident. And the tale has grown with the telling. There's a lot of that round here. The ghost tours feed off it.'

It was already past three. The mine was deserted, but for the occasional hiking couple cutting through from Bakewell and Ashford. They passed the rickety winding house, and picked around the central buildings. Anything with a roof had been bricked up, apart from an empty corrugated shed and a restored two-storey house: firmly secured. Klein pointed to a sign on its door.

STRICTLY PRIVATE PROPERTY
PDMHS

'PDMHS?' said Sawyer.

Klein thought for a few seconds. 'Peak District Mine Historical Society. It'll be their field centre.' A squall of wind raised his wispy grey hair and he dug his hands into his jacket pocket. 'There's no "bothy" here, Mr Robbins. No secret meeting. I think we've been had. Maybe it's time to switch strategy. Try the art of fighting *with* fighting.'

————

They walked back to the roadside parking area. As they stumbled down a rocky slope onto the main path, Klein froze and placed a hand on Sawyer's shoulder.

He took out his phone and showed the screen to Sawyer. It was blank. 'Don't look up. I'm sure that's the one! I've seen it before, near my brother's place.'

Sawyer kept his head tilted down towards the screen. He lifted his eyes and looked across at the distant parking area, just visible behind the tall perimeter hedge. It was close to dusk, and he had to squint to focus. A large burgundy BMW was parked next to his Mini. They were too far away to read the number plate.

'I'm *sure*, Mr Robbins. I'm sure that's the same one.'

'Can you take a picture?' said Sawyer. 'We can zoom in later.'

The car engine started and its lights came on.

Klein opened his camera app. But by the time he had raised the phone, the car had pulled away.

48

At the cottage, Sawyer executed the second Wing Chun form, *Chum Kiu*, and slowly ran through his post-workout stretches. He walked into the bathroom and opened both taps, full. He was eager to sink into the frothy water and power down for the night. There was too much in motion. The killer, the Caseys, Eva, Michael, Klein.

The car. It wasn't the one he had seen outside the house on the rainy night. But he had seen it before somewhere. A while ago. Somewhere stationary.

He picked up *The Gift Of Fear* from his bedside table and walked through into the bathroom. He stopped, listened. It was about this time that Bruce would usually emerge, scratching at the door for food.

Nothing.

He carried on into the bathroom. The water thundered down, full volume. He took a bottle down from a shelf over the sink, opened it, sniffed it. Coconut. He squirted too much into the base of the stream and stood there for a while, transfixed by the bloom of bubbles.

He turned off the taps and stabbed his fingers through his thickening hair. He was about to strip, when he heard a familiar drilling sound. He looked out and saw his phone jerking across the wood of the coffee table. The microwave clock read 10:40pm.

He rushed into the sitting room and picked up the phone.

It was Keating.

'Sir?'

'DI Sawyer.' He was gruff, angry. He drew in a breath, composing himself. 'I've just seen the end of tonight's BBC news. The regional section.' He spat out the words in short, angry bursts. 'The main story. From one of tomorrow's newspapers.'

'Logan?'

'I assume so. I took a picture of the screen. Check your messages.'

Sawyer's stomach lurched. 'Do I need to come in?'

'If it's not. Too. Much. Trouble.'

He hung up.

Sawyer looked at his inbox and opened the message from Keating. The picture attachment showed a wavy TV screen with the front page of the *Derbyshire Times*. The main image was a large shot of three red roses lined up side by side. Above them were three smaller square images in a neat row, with photographs of Susan Bishop, Sam Palmer and Simon Brock.

The headline screamed out.

EXCLUSIVE! RED ROSE KILLER TAUNTS HERO COP

Shit.

As soon as the killer saw this, he would know that Amy had spoken to the police. How much time did they have? Had he been watching the programme, too? Amy's protection detail was geared towards catching him staking her out, but the threat against her had now been stepped up.

As he threw on his shoes and jacket, he heard a car cross the driveway bridge and turn off its engine.

A single set of footsteps approached the front door.

Two slow, strong raps.

Only one person. He could handle that.

He opened the door.

It was Shaun, from the Barrel Inn. He had scrubbed up a bit: thick blazer over the black polo-neck. 'Evening. *Tough guy.*'

Sawyer shrugged. 'You don't write. You don't call.'

Shaun nodded. 'Still a smartarse.'

Sawyer checked him over. The jumper was fitted; no unnatural stretch around the waist. Clean. Bulge in one pocket. Car keys. For the first time, Sawyer was struck by the size of Shaun's hands: chunky fingers, flexing in and out of fists. 'I don't mean to be rude, but now's not a good time.' He turned off the light and moved to step out onto the porch.

Shaun shifted to the side, blocking his path. 'We won't keep you long. Just a quick thing.'

Sawyer moved forward. They were inches apart; face to face. 'We?'

'Let's play nice, fellas.'

Sawyer looked around Shaun, to the white Mercedes parked in front of the Mini, blocking him in. An equally hefty man climbed out of the passenger seat, followed by a shorter, wirier colleague on the other side. It was the short man who had spoken. He was holding a small pistol.

Sawyer squinted into the darkness. 'Is that a Glock?'

The man smiled. 'It is! Austrian. Purchased from an Irish associate, if you're interested.' Hint of a Scottish accent. He was handsome, in a good suit. Yellow tie. Blond hair in a tidy block on top of his head, short at the sides. His colleague was the biggest of the three: square-jawed and angry-looking. Shaven headed, like Shaun. Blazer and white shirt. He had a small gym bag over one shoulder.

'Not at the moment,' said Sawyer. 'I've got to go out. If you'd leave me your card, I'll be sure to get back to you at the earliest convenient opportunity.'

The short man waved the gun towards the cottage interior. 'Let's pop inside. As the man says, we'll make it quick. I can't guarantee it will be painless, though.'

Sawyer backed into the sitting room and turned the light on. Shaun stepped inside, followed by the other two. The biggest man closed the door behind them.

'So, is this an upgrade?' said Sawyer. 'You sent the Reminder guys and now you're the Final Warning team?'

The man with the gun kept it on his hip, pointed at Sawyer. 'We don't follow that system. It's more of a fast track from warning to sanction. We're the debt collectors.'

'And for whose benefit are you collecting the debt?'

The man glared at him, flashed a forced smile. 'Now. You already know Shaun. I'm Marco, and this is Hector. Doesn't speak a lot of English. He's more a man of action.'

Sawyer laughed. 'What *is* this? Some new hidden camera show? The dumb goon, the mute muscle, and you. The brains of the operation? Or are you all sharing just the one brain cell?'

Marco smiled.

'Go on, then. This is where you nod at one of the other two and they give me a slap.'

Marco lost his smile. 'Are you left or right, Mr Sawyer?'

'I'm apolitical. It's all about Stoicism for me. And the milk of human kindness.'

'I mean physically. Which one is your wanking hand?'

'I have to use both.'

Shaun nodded at Sawyer. 'It's the right. I remember from the pub.'

Hector lifted the bag off his shoulder and pulled out a length of thick rope.

'I won't lie to you,' said Marco. 'This isn't going to be the most pleasant evening of your life. But you can make it slightly less unpleasant.' Shaun dragged a chair over from the kitchen. 'Here's the plan. I'm going to stand here, pointing this loaded gun at you, while Marco and Shaun tie you to that chair.'

Marco took a heavy-looking chisel and a round-headed mallet out of the bag.

'Is this a sex thing?' said Sawyer. 'Can't you just stick to each other? Leave me out of it?'

'We said we'd cut something off you if you didn't listen,' said Shaun.

Marco nodded. 'We're going to take your right thumb. The one you use to send phone messages.'

'To Eva? I like it. Poetic justice.'

Marco ignored him. 'And if you somehow manage to keep sending messages—'

Sawyer snorted. 'By, say, using the other thumb?'

'Yes. Then we'll be back for that one later.'

Marco and Shaun shouldered into Sawyer and grabbed an arm each. They hustled him to the chair and forced him to sit. Marco took a step back, keeping the gun on him.

Sawyer nodded to the mallet and chisel. 'Do you have to use such a big hammer? Won't that split the wood?'

Marco shook his head. 'Distributes the impact quite evenly, actually. Less stress on the—'

'Chiseller?' said Sawyer.

Marco nodded. 'And if you miss with a small-headed hammer... Well. It gets *really* messy.'

Hector held Sawyer's arms to the frame of the chair while Shaun began to wrap the rope around his legs.

'We're not savages,' said Marco. 'Shaun will hold your hand down on that coffee table. Marco will do the business. It'll be nice and quick. Then we'll be on our way and you'll be free to call for help. With your left hand. Seriously. If you just let us get on with it, we'll be gone before you know it. We've done this before, you know.'

'No anaesthetic?' said Sawyer.

'As I say, it'll sting a bit. But you'll live. Wrap a towel round it to stop the bleeding. We will be taking the offending digit with us, though.' He shrugged. 'It's a trophy thing.'

Sawyer nodded. 'Proof that the job is done.'

Marco smiled.

Shaun threaded the rope underneath the chair and wove it up and round, over Sawyer's legs.

'Any advice for aftercare?' said Sawyer. 'Oils or ointments?'

Marco squinted at Sawyer, equally amused and bemused. 'Maybe a touch of Vaseline. At least.'

'You do realise that cutting the thumb off a high-ranking police officer constitutes an assault. That's a serious offence.'

Shaun looked up. 'It doesn't count if you're not "executing your duty".' He stood up and moved around in front of Sawyer, momentarily blocking Hector's vision.

Sawyer lurched forward and drove his shoulder into Shaun, pushing with his full force, using Shaun's weight against him. He overbalanced and toppled backwards, into Hector. As they stumbled together, Sawyer jerked his legs up, freeing them from the rope. He reached behind and grabbed the kitchen chair.

Hector made a move for him, but Sawyer was quicker.

He swung the chair around, smashing the heavy seat into the side of Hector's head. The big man bellowed in outrage and dropped to the floor, dazed but still conscious.

Sawyer stepped to the side, giving himself more room. He swung the chair again, this time at Marco. It wasn't as strong a connection, but it hit him across the shoulder, jolting him sideways and forcing him to drop the gun, which, inconveniently, slid across the floor towards Hector, who had pulled himself up onto all-fours.

Sawyer kicked the gun away and drove his knee into the side of Hector's head, swinging the full strength of his core into the impact. Hector sank to the floor, unconscious.

Now, Shaun was on him, bursting forward. Sawyer switched to JKD fighting stance and shuffled back and to the side, allowing Shaun's forward momentum to stagger him. Shaun turned and drew back his right arm, telegraphing his punch. Sawyer neutered it with an inside forearm block and stepped inside, hoping to down him with an elbow strike. But Shaun was quick, and grabbed Sawyer's left arm, readying a second punch. They grappled for a second, as Marco climbed over the sofa, in search of the gun.

Shaun had pulled Sawyer in close, clearly hoping to overpower him with brute strength. Body odour. Tobacco breath. Sawyer drew his head away, as Shaun jerked him to the side, trying to wrestle him to the ground. Shaun had the advantage in bulk, and once they were on the floor, Sawyer would be sucked into a time-consuming grapple.

Marco crouched down by the kitchen table, fumbling for the gun.

Shaun jerked Sawyer to the side again. One more of those and he would have him down, and be on top. He smiled, his mouth close enough for Sawyer to see a thread of cosmetic silver fillings across his front teeth. 'Nice try.' He jerked again. 'Tough guy.'

Sawyer lifted the car keys from Shaun's pocket. He strained the muscle in his neck, pulling it back. He nodded down, crunching his forehead into Shaun's nose. Shaun cried out, and released Sawyer's arm. He stumbled back, and Sawyer hit him with a finger thrust to his eyes: brutal and direct, like a snake strike. Shaun fell away, howling and clutching his face.

Marco was on the floor, reaching underneath the sink unit.

Sawyer bolted for the front door.

Across the porch, to the Mercedes.

He squeezed the transponder button and the car's lights flashed.

He opened the driver's door.

A gunshot resounded from behind. Muzzle flash lighting up the night.

Marco stood at the front door, pointing the gun at him, head drooped but alert. 'Don't fucking move!' Inside, Shaun roared in fury.

Sawyer stared at him, breathing hard. He glanced inside the car. Push button start. He slipped inside and closed the door, ducked down, squeezed his foot on the brake pedal.

Muffled gunshot. Another muzzle flash.

A bullet crunched into the bodywork on the passenger side. It was oddly anticlimactic; as if it had been hit by a heavy rock.

Sawyer pushed the start button. The engine growled into life.

Another shot skimmed the roof of the car. Marco moved forward on the porch, holding the Glock at eye level, aiming along the barrel.

Sawyer slid deep in the driver seat, head below the level

of the windows. He pushed hard on the accelerator and reversed onto the road.

As he swung the car around, Marco scored a direct hit on the windscreen. The bullet punched a hole through the centre, sending out a spray of jagged fracture lines.

Sawyer shifted gear and squeezed the accelerator, staying low in the seat. The car screeched away. As he rounded the corner, he looked in the wing mirror and saw Shaun standing on the porch next to Marco, watching.

———

He drove to the Edale station car park, turned off the lights and engine, and sat there in the quiet, in the dark.

Every inch of his skin felt raw and tender, and the familiar tingling had reared up in the base of his neck. He inhaled, held it. He covered his ears with his hands and listened to the accelerated thump of his heart. He exhaled, lowered his hands to his legs. Wetness on the left leg, near the thigh. He turned on the interior light.

Red, red, red. Spreading out from the top of his trouser leg. His fingers found the scorched fabric, the bullet hole. Warm. The smell of singed fabric, burnt flesh.

Sawyer took out his phone and checked the time 11:17. The late Sheffield train would be arriving in three minutes.

He opened the door and tumbled out. Now, at last, the pain flashed across his leg, through his groin, up into his torso. A deep and deadly burning.

He limped across the car park, to the verge. He climbed the perimeter fence, his wounded leg sending out rapid pulses of pain.

Sweat, now. Tickling his forehead, prickling the edges of his mouth.

Train lights. Vibrating track.

He shuffled down the verge onto the Tarmac path, close to the level crossing.

It was his first time: being shot. It was worse than he had imagined. The burning intensified with every step, and every step seemed heavier than the last. He could flush it all away here: the pain, the puzzles. He could step away from the whole righteous farce; bow out before the great decline of middle-age. Leave behind a work in progress.

He limped over the boom barrier and stepped onto the track.

Alex's voice drifted in. *'I think you're traumatised.'*

He turned and walked, stepping over the sleepers, towards the onrushing train.

'The six-year-old who witnessed something too terrible to contemplate.'

A blast on the train horn. He kept walking. The lights from the train getting closer, brighter.

And then, his mother. Another work in progress.

'Why?'

He would never know the answer. He would never know the reason for the question.

Another blast on the horn. The driver, leaning out of the cab. Waving, shouting.

He stepped up his pace.

'Jake! Run, my darling. Don't look back!'

Sawyer veered away from the train. He jumped over the rail, crunching into the trackside gravel, broke into a run for the shrubland, his leg blaring with pain.

From behind, the *whump* of the passing train.

He fell forward, gasping for breath. Dizzy now. Trembling.

He took out his phone, felt his trouser leg. Warm and wet.

His mother's upturned hand.

'Sir?' Shepherd sounded groggy.

'Step up the protection.'

'Protection?'

'On Amy and her daughter.'

Sawyer swallowed, groping for the words. 'Do it now. Don't wait until morning. *Have you got that*?'

Shepherd paused. 'Are you okay, sir? It's really late. Have you been *drinking*?'

He was suddenly so tired. He closed his eyes.

'Sir?'

'And feed my cat.'

49

White light. Voices.

'How is he?' Deep, vaguely Welsh. Keating.

Then, a new voice. Clipped. High-born. 'He's lost quite a lot of blood. Gunshot wound. No bullet. Must have passed through. Just shy of the femoral artery. Mild hypovolemic shock. Dehydrated. He's stable. He's also incredibly lucky. Couple of millimetres difference and he wouldn't have even made it here.'

Sawyer wanted to stay there: at rest, unreachable. But he forced his eyes open. He was in an overheated hospital room. A ward, judging by the noise outside the closed curtain around his bed. Keating stood at the foot of the bed, in off-duty clothes, talking to a younger man in a white shirt and striped tie with a stethoscope and lanyard badge around his neck.

Sawyer found his voice. 'For a minute there, I thought I might be in heaven.'

'Maybe you are,' said Keating.

'That's your God complex talking.' His voice was thin, his throat dry. 'Protection,' he said to Keating. 'Amy and the others.'

'It's in hand. All fine. Your DS has it under control.'

Sawyer reached to his bedside table and sipped from his plastic glass of warm water. He took in too much and spluttered. 'Newspaper?'

'Next on my list. Thumbscrews for Bloom.'

The doctor stepped forward. 'Morning! I'm Dr Harford. I'm one of the senior A&E doctors. You're in Cavendish Hospital, Buxton. How are you feeling, Mr Sawyer?'

Sawyer read the man's lanyard: *Dr George Harford*. 'I'm feeling okay. Bit sleepy. You're the guy who saved my life, right?'

The doctor laughed, and checked him over. 'Hardly. Just plugged a leak. You're on saline for now. You've had some morphine. And some blood.' He wrote on the clipboard at the end of the bed, looked up. 'You were shot, Mr Sawyer. I'm happy for you to go home, but you must rest.' He glanced at Keating. 'Whatever you're... dealing with, it's important that you give your body time to recover. And your mind. You may be feeling calm now, but you've been through a great deal of shock.' Sawyer nodded, his thoughts spooling back through the scene at his house. 'Someone will be in soon with more painkillers, and to check your dressing. You may need to change it yourself later.'

Sawyer shrugged. 'I'm a big boy.'

The doctor narrowed his eyes. 'You *will* need some time. Couple of weeks.' He nodded at Keating and slipped through the curtain.

'Close one,' said Keating.

'I heard.'

'"Close", as in, "would have probably bled to death if the train driver hadn't reported some maniac on the track near Edale."'

He looked down at his gown, examined the bandage around his thigh. 'How did I get here?'

'Dispatch sent police and ambulance. Picked up the maniac. By the side of the track.' Sawyer dropped his head, rubbed and stretched the skin around his eyes. 'I called your father.'

'Good catch-up?'

Keating sat down beside the bed. 'I haven't seen him for a long time. He's doing well for himself, but worried.'

'About?'

'About you. Wants me to update him.'

'Like old times?' Sawyer gently squeezed at his wound and winced at the jolt of pain. 'Tell him I'm fine. Tell him the doctor says I'm fine. He has a thing for higher powers.'

'I spoke to the officer who found you. The train driver said they've had trouble at that stretch lately. Someone running across the tracks. Playing chicken, or something. They're lobbying for more security. A closed crossing.' He pulled his chair closer. 'Jake, if you were in my shoes, you would be asking what the fuck is going on.'

Sawyer hitched himself upright against his pillow. 'Well, I'm not you. But don't think I haven't fantasised.'

'Maggie wants you to call her. I promised to let her know once I'd seen you.'

He nodded. 'Shepherd?'

'He went to your house. Door was open. Looks like someone left in a hurry. He says the place was clear. Bit studenty.'

'Studenty?'

Keating looked at his watch. 'His word. Evidence of an altercation. Furniture disturbed. Tyre tracks on the drive. Skid-marks. Bullet shells.'

Sawyer stared ahead, recalibrating. 'I was attacked in my home. I got away in the attackers' car.'

'And where is that now?'

'I left it in the station car park. White Mercedes.'

'There was a transponder key in your pocket. Shepherd took your house keys, secured your place. We had a look around near the station. No cars.'

'They must have had a tracker on it. Dupe key. Picked it up before you got there. What time is it, anyway? How long have I been here?'

'Nine-thirty. You arrived just after midnight. Considerate of you to do all of this at a civilised hour. Whatever *this* is.'

Sawyer sighed. 'It's personal. I'll fix it.' He looked at Keating. 'I'm fine. I'll re-focus.'

Keating bristled. 'You are not fine. *This* is not fine.'

'You know it's pointless to insist I go home and watch YouTube for two weeks?'

'I do. But Shepherd is to take on the bulk of the work. We've moved Amy and Ava Scott to a safe house. Kim Lyons is co-operating, but Jamie Ingram is a character. Another bloody unreconstructed male who thinks he's the master of the universe.' He took out a set of house keys and lobbed them onto the bedside table. 'From Shepherd.' He sighed. 'Leave this to him for now. I need you strong. You've been weakened. Your body needs to renew itself. You've lost blood.'

Sawyer smiled. 'Ain't got time to bleed.'

'*Predator*. Now that I *have* seen.'

———

After Keating had left, Sawyer lay there for a while, listening to the activity outside the curtain: chattering staff, footsteps squeaking on linoleum, bleating children, the tannoy's muffled appeals. The sounds of human beings caring, repairing, keeping each other going. The urgency of life; the eternal wrestle to delay death. They had pieced him together here before, thirty years earlier, as a shattered six-year-old. He remembered the adults' hollowed eyes and drained faces; the probing lights, the head-shakes. The way they peered at him, looked *into* him, searching for signs of survival, prising him back up, out of the dark, to face the horror of his freshly upside-down world.

He dozed, drifting in and out of consciousness. Images clashed and warped. The doctor's lanyard badge photo. The monolithic mine buildings. The train lights. Joseph Dawson holding the blue spade high above his head.

He pivoted out of bed, dressed, and signed himself out. In the cab back to the cottage, he checked his phone. Missed call from Shepherd. Messages from Maggie, his father. Nothing from Eva.

The cottage felt surreal, unchanged. The chairs and kitchen table were back in place. Shepherd had cleared up some of the coffee table clutter, and even washed the dishes. There were no calling cards or sinister notes, and the Mini was untouched. A saucer of cat food lay on the kitchen floor; the half-empty can sat on the top shelf of the barren fridge.

His attackers would have called for another car, tracked the Mercedes, picked it up from the station. With Shaun, and the European Health Insurance card, he had a clear connection to Dale. But it would be tough to directly connect him to the assault.

He made tea and buttery white toast, and hobbled over to the sofa. The wound in his thigh rebuked him for the effort as he eased himself down and called Shepherd.

Background office noise. 'Sir. Are you out?'

Sawyer sipped his tea. 'What's this Lily's Kitchen shit?'

'It was all they had at the farm shop. It's eco-friendly.'

'I'll never get him back on Whiskas now.'

The background noise dropped as Shepherd closed his office door. 'It ain't cheap, either. I'll be adding it to my housekeeping fee.'

Sawyer laughed and looked around the sitting room. There was something vague and unwelcoming about the place, as if it belonged to someone else. His head felt fuzzy from the morphine. 'I'm taking the day off. But, obviously, I'm still "on".'

'What *happened*?'

'Unrelated to the case. I've pissed someone off. He sent round some people to let me know it would be a good idea to stop pissing him off. I'm fine. Thanks for your help. I owe you.'

'Yeah. £1.40 for the cat food, for starters.' Shepherd paused. 'Targets are protected. Walker is still with Jamie Ingram. I have a separate team with Amy and Ava at a safe house. Kim Lyons has reluctantly agreed to have the officers in the house. The Observation Points are in position. If he comes within fifty feet of any of the places, we'll know about it in plenty of time to act.'

'If we bring him in, we'll still need to make a case.'

'Of course. Still nothing on forensic leads, though. Nothing from local shops on recent purchases of the type of lock he replaced at Simon Brock's house.'

Sawyer flexed and unflexed his right hand. The bruising had eased, but the joints had stiffened. 'He must have staked it, bought it somewhere distant. Online, maybe. How is Myers doing with the name trace? Have you checked chemistry graduates?'

'Still going. Nothing. Sally mentioned that Dawson might have changed his name.'

'It's likely. Andrew said that he wanted to "start again".'

'A rebirth?'

Sawyer reclined on the sofa. The urge to sleep swept over him, and he sat back upright. 'I tried to track deed poll records on a previous case, find out someone's old name from the post-deed poll change. Impossible.'

'Why?'

'There's no obligation to announce the name-change. Even if you're researching, say, *when* a person changed their name, you only find a trail of records in their original name and another trail starting from their new name. There's usually no single document that links the two. We could send someone to the National Archives in Kew to search the indexes. Focus on the likely dates he might have registered the name change. We might get lucky and the index will include a note that refers to the new name, but it's not guaranteed.'

'And it will take a lot of hunting through documents?'

Sawyer crunched into the toast. It tasted metallic, alien. 'It will. You can't search the indexes online. Get a researcher down to London. Or send Moran.'

'Are you trying to get him to hate you?'

'Okay. Send Walker.'

'He's on decent terms with Jamie Ingram. I'd rather have him covering there. And you know how he's been pushing to be at the pointy end.'

Sawyer blinked away another tug of sleep. 'Just get someone, anyone, to do the digging. If we can find his current name, we can start to eliminate, narrow down his location, and hopefully pick him up bloodlessly.' He paused, grasping for his next words.

Shepherd cut in. 'Rest up. Keating told me he wanted me to take on the bulk of the work while you recover.'

Sawyer's eyes drooped again. 'So get on with it.'

———————

50

'You look tired, Jake.'

He kept his eyes on the carpeted floor. 'Busy week.'

Alex leaned forward. 'How's your sleep?'

Sawyer reached for the plate of biscuits on the side table. Teatime assortment. Bright colours. Foil wraps. Chocolate coating. Icing. He took a dark chocolate digestive. 'My sleep is interesting. I had a dream about the murder. The first lucid dream. I knew what it was. I knew what was happening. I tried to help. I tried to—'

'Stop it?'

'Yes. Usually, I'm just watching. Powerless.'

Alex nodded. She was wearing a bottle-green shawl with buttons down one arm. Cape-like. No notepad this time. 'And how are you doing with the fear? Are you still chasing it? Any luck?'

'Plenty of scary situations. No fear.'

Alex slipped on a pair of silver-framed glasses. 'When you say, "no fear", I wonder if you really mean "no feeling".'

'Maybe.'

'Are you concerned about your choices? The distractions you're seeking?'

He crunched into the biscuit. 'Not really. But everyone else seems to be.'

She picked up a book from her side table. 'How are you getting on with women?'

'Again? This?'

'Where else can you examine it safely? Isn't that what you're here for?'

He sighed. 'I've got my eye on someone, yes. Is that normal?'

'We're told not to say "normal" now.'

'Neurotypical?'

'Yes. And I suppose it is.' She held up the book: a copy of *The Gift Of Fear*. 'I've been re-reading this. There's a part where he talks about stalking. Unwanted attention.'

'I fancy someone. I'm pursuing them. That's neurotypical, right? Sexual attraction. Stalking is about control.'

Alex smiled and turned to a marked page. She read out loud. '*Young women should know this. Persistence only proves persistence. It does not prove love. The fact that a romantic pursuer is relentless doesn't mean you are special. It means he is troubled.*'

He stared at her, silent.

'I also read an astute quote the other day. Somewhere online. It said that the problem is never the problem. It's the *response* to the problem that's almost always the real problem.'

Sawyer nodded. 'I like that. Very Stoic. Did you buy these biscuits especially for me? For the "frozen" inner child?'

'This woman you have your eye on. Does she remind you of your mother?'

'In some ways.'

His phone buzzed in his pocket.

'Seeking distraction and drama. It isn't helping. What you need to do is to turn and face yourself. Know yourself as an adult. Like I said, I think you *are* frozen, and I want to start the process of thawing. The thing I talked about last time. Reliving. You've already taken me through what happened on the day of your mother's murder. We're now going to go one step further.' She pulled out a small digital recorder. 'We're going to record you, walking through it, step by step.'

'Hypnosis?'

'No. That's not the aim. But it's along the same lines. You're going to take me through it in the first-person present. Immerse yourself in the reality of the moment. Lots of sensory detail. "I'm walking down the lane", "I can see this", "I can feel this", "I can smell this".'

Sawyer reached into his pocket and squeezed the button on his phone, turning it off. 'Why?'

'Because, in your mind, it's all chaos. Horror. Confusion. Your brain can't process it.'

He sat forward. 'Jung said, "In all chaos there is a cosmos".'

Alex smiled. '"In all disorder, a secret order." That's what we're going to do. Clear away the chaos. Find the order. The first stage is to turn the event into something your brain can cope with. A clear, linear story. A narrative. You're currently processing the murder as a six-year-old. The goal is to get it clear in your mind and then *reframe* it as something you can reprocess as an adult. Once we have that, then we can pack it away.'

'And all shall be well.'

She squinted at him. 'It can't just be forgotten. At the moment, your mother's murder is a horrendous mix of professional and personal. We have to get it to a place where you can "solve" it as a case, without the trauma and confusion of the personal dimension. If it gets too stressful, we can come back to safety at any time, get re-grounded.'

———

It took Sawyer half an hour to recount his story into Alex's recorder. As he spoke, the daylight dimmed outside her window, and it was close to dusk by the time he had finished. He kept his voice soft and calm, but always on the edge of emotion. All the while, Alex sat there in absolute silence, never prompting.

When he reached the end, and had stayed silent for a while, Alex leaned over and switched off the recorder. 'Thank you, Jake. Now we have something we can really work with. I want you to take it away and listen to it. At least two times before our next session. Which moments are the hot spots, the most distressing moments? The points where you *feel* the most intensely? Remember, we're looking to reframe those parts. That was then, when you were a child. This is now. You're an adult. It's only when you see this story from an adult perspective that we can move on to the final stage. Then you'll still carry it inside you, as a painful memory, but it will no longer be something which makes it impossible to live a normal life, in the here and now.'

Sawyer took the recorder and stood up. 'Final stage?'

She nodded. 'That's when we go there in person. To the lane. To the place where it happened.'

———

Outside, he climbed into the Mini and switched his phone back on. His heart raced; he could feel the pounding against his shirt. The images fluttered: his brother's body, his mother's hand, the raised hammer. But, despite Alex's logic, he wasn't interested in fixing his own mind. He just hoped the reliving would unlock more detail, give him some sight of the man behind the balaclava.

He checked his phone. Several missed calls from Walker. He called the number.

'Sir?' Walker sounded frantic. 'Are you there? Sorry. Here? Are you on your way?'

Sawyer started the engine. 'Are you with Jamie Ingram?'

Commotion in the background. Walker speaking to someone. 'Hello? Yes. I mean, no. I'm at Jamie Ingram's *place*, yes.'

'I'm about fifteen minutes away. What's up?'

'I couldn't reach DS Shepherd at the safe house. He just called. Said he can be here in half an hour.'

Sawyer's phone buzzed. Probably Shepherd.

He pulled the car away and turned on the lights. He shouldered the phone. 'What's happened?'

'It's Ingram. We've been running together. Up in the woods behind the house. Mornings and evenings, around this time. He was complaining yesterday about how I was slowing him down. I went to the toilet. Just for a couple of minutes. He's gone, sir. By himself.'

Sawyer squeezed the accelerator. His leg flashed with pain. 'Where are the OP guys?'

'One is here with me. The other is looking for Ingram. I followed the route for a while, but it's getting dark. He could have gone anywhere.'

51

Jamie Ingram dropped his head and drove forward, bull-like, into the trees. It felt good to finally open the taps and push himself. The police guy was a casual runner: 5K twice a week. He was always off the pace: panting after 2K, suffering at 4. If the big, bad murderer had jumped out of a tree, he would hardly have been in any state to fight him off. If anything, the roles would be reversed: Jamie would be the one doing the protection.

He caught the trail by the ridge that sloped down towards the Primary School on Alport Lane. It was mulchy underfoot, and as the trees became too dense and low-hanging for comfortable running, he veered back onto the usual route: a circular track through open forest that would have him back in Youlgreave in fifteen minutes.

Jamie looked up through the spindly canopy. The sky was almost covered now, close to black. The race was on. He would need to really fly to be home by nightfall.

He squinted through the gloom, his attention caught by a blot of colour up ahead. As he got closer, he saw a figure in a yellow high-viz vest sprawled face down across a clump of fallen leaves, just off the track.

He slowed. The figure was short and slight. Male. He wore black tracksuit bottoms and bright red Nike trainers. All the gear looked new.

Lightweight. Probably his first run. Over-reached himself.

'You okay there?'

As Jamie approached, the figure rose onto all-fours, head down. He moaned and turned his head slightly. He was a young guy in his late twenties. Jamie suppressed a laugh at the man's yellow head sweatband, also new-looking.

'Probably low blood sugar,' said Jamie, holding out his hand. 'Let's get you up. Classic rookie mistake. You should start with short runs, mixed with periods of walking.'

The man stumbled to his feet and turned towards Jamie. He held up a red-and-black can, only slightly larger than his hand. A fine white spray billowed into Jamie's eyes. He cried out in surprise and twisted away. But the man followed his movement and kept spraying, keeping his aim on Jamie's eyes and nose. Jamie clamped his eyes shut and rubbed at his face, swiping away the liquid.

He tried to blink, to coax his eyes open. But his eyelids were in spasm, and hot liquid streamed down his cheeks. He dropped to one knee, roaring in agony. His eyes and face blazed with a paralysing heat, like instant sunburn. His nose streamed and he shook his head, shedding tears and snot.

The spraying stopped, and Jamie ducked his head away, terrified of another burst. The burning intensified, and he covered his eyes with both hands, protecting them from further spray while trying to force his eyelids open with his thumbs.

He jerked forward, and had to steady himself with a hand to the damp earth. He hit his head on something hard. He toppled, face first into a mound of brittle leaves.

52

'How long has he been gone?'

Walker closed his eyes. He was trembling, struggling to keep his breathing steady. 'Almost an hour now.'

'Jesus Christ.' Sawyer turned to the Observation Point officer: a hefty man with receding hair and a high forehead, gleaming with sweat. 'Where's the other guy? Has he seen anything? Heard anything?'

The man lifted his walkie talkie. 'Just checked in. Nothing.'

'Call him back here. I want both of you on the house. DS Shepherd will be here soon.'

'I'm sorry, sir,' said Walker. 'I didn't know. He knew we were there, said he didn't mind. I thought he was getting used to it all. He must have gone out of the back door.'

'How long are his evening runs?'

'Half an hour. Sometimes forty minutes. His early ones are longer.'

Sawyer thought for a second. 'Show me the route.'

Walker led the way, up to the end of the road and out to a wide field which rose away from the houses and blended to dense woodland. 'There's a path here. The trees thin out a bit. He walks onto the main track and follows it through the woods. There's a steep bit that probably gets you through to the main road over the ridge. We usually veer off, though. Circle the fields, end up at the road on this side. Then it's a five-minute walk back to Ingram's.'

Sawyer pushed forward, up into the trees. He tried to favour his good leg, but the ground was soft and uneven, and he stumbled over loose branches, wincing through the pain as he corrected himself.

'Are you okay, sir? What happened? Shepherd wouldn't say. One of the others said you'd been *shot*.'

Sawyer stopped to rest. 'Let's get through this and I'll tell you the whole gory story.' It was dark now, and he turned on his phone light.

Walker did likewise. 'I've never been shot.' He sounded regretful.

'I don't recommend it.'

They found the base of the walking track and climbed up to a more open path, parallel to the ridge. It was heavy going for Sawyer, and he struggled to hide his discomfort.

'We should split up,' said Walker.

'No, we should not.'

Walker looked at his phone. 'Decent service here. You could take the ridge. I could follow his typical running route. We can meet up further into the woods.'

'We could do that,' said Sawyer. 'But we're not going to.' His voice wavered. The pain was impossible to ignore now. 'Let's stick together. Get higher up. Hopefully, the lights from the road will give us—'

A shout, off in the distance, deeper into the woods. Male.

Walker turned to Sawyer. 'That's Jamie!' He sprang forward, stopped, turned again. 'Sir?'

'Wait! I'm okay. I can speed up once the ground levels off.'

Walker's eyes widened. 'We can't wait. We've got to go. Stay on the main trail and catch me up.'

'Walker! Stay here! You don't know—'

But he was sprinting away, his phone light bobbing like a firefly. 'He needs help now! Catch me up, sir.'

Sawyer sucked in a deep breath and drove himself forward, after Walker. Each right step rewarded him with a jagged flex of pain. He had to stop several times before he reached the level section of walking track where the trees thickened. No sign of Walker.

He hobbled on, keeping his phone light trained on the ground ahead. He was in so much pain now, he could barely put pressure on his right leg. Instead, he hopped forward on the left, scraping the right along the loamy ground, kicking away the undergrowth.

The ground inclined, and he stopped to listen. Traffic rumble, rising up from Alport Lane, over the ridge.

Footsteps. Crunching. Moving away, somewhere ahead and off to the right.

And something else. Spluttering. Coughing.

He pushed on, through retreating branches, into a broader stretch of track.

He called out, to the body lying prone in the middle of the path. It was Walker, clutching and clawing at his neck. He gazed up at Sawyer, his wide eyes drowned in tears, his mouth opening and closing like a beached fish.

Jamie Ingram's body lay off to the side, further into the trees. He lay face down, perfectly still. Ankles cuffed. Wrists cuffed behind his back.

Walker thrashed his legs above the ground, running in

mid-air. Sawyer called up his phone number-pad and dialled 999. He crouched by Walker and reached out for his hand, lifting it away from the wound in his throat. The hand was warm with his blood.

He thought of his mother's palm. The blood, beaded on the tips of the short grass. Smeared and splashed across the leaves and soil.

Walker pulled his hand away, pressed it onto the wound.

Sawyer gave Ingram's address to the emergency dispatcher, along with directions from there along the trail. He ran through the details quickly and clearly, gripping Walker's wrist, maintaining connection. There was so much blood, too much blood, cascading down Walker's neck, pooling around his shoulders. It slurped in and out of the cavity in his neck as he tried to breathe.

Sawyer hung up and lay his phone on the ground, light shining upward. He shrugged away his jacket and tore off his shirt, twisting it into a long rope of fabric. He lifted Walker's head and wrapped the shirt around his neck. He applied pressure to the area around the cut: plugging the gap, stemming the bleeding.

'Try to breathe slow, Matt. I know you're scared, but try to slow your breathing. I'm here. I'm doing what I can. I'm doing the right thing.'

Walker's eyes bulged with the effort of calming himself. He ground his legs into the dirt.

Sawyer rested a hand on Walker's forehead and leaned in close. 'Take yourself away somewhere, Matt. In your mind. Somewhere happy. Go there. Go away from this.' The eyes stared up, the gaze drifting away. '*Look at me.* Focus on me and take yourself there. I'm with you. I'll go with you. Away from the pain. You're over the worst now. The shock and the panic. Help will be here in a few minutes. We've just got to keep you calm. They'll put you together again. Then we can have words about you running off by yourself.'

He kept up the pressure on the wound. He knew it all depended on the depth of the cut. He could tell by the blood's relatively calm flow that the killer had missed the carotid artery. But there might still be too much blood loss, oxygen starvation.

Sirens. On the road over the ridge.

Walker was trembling now, going into shock. Sawyer kept eye contact, but Walker's legs had stopped thrashing.

'We'll get you back, Matt. You did a good thing. You tried to help. You tried to stop it. You couldn't do any more.'

The shirt was heavy with blood now. Sawyer applied more pressure, but Walker was still, his stare frozen.

He had tried to help. He had tried to stop it.

But he could do no more.

53

Sawyer and Shepherd sat opposite each other, heads bowed, in the corridor at Cavendish Hospital. Further down, by the nurse's station, the lift door opened. Keating burst out, saw them, and hurried along the corridor.

Sawyer and Shepherd stood in unison, and turned to face him. A nurse dashed out from behind the desk and followed Keating.

He anticipated her protest and shouted, without turning. 'Detective Chief Inspector Ivan Keating!'

Sawyer held up a hand, slowing him. 'He's alive. Critical. In theatre now. His throat was cut. Missed the main artery but nicked the windpipe. I got there minutes after it happened, sir. Did what I could.'

Keating's expression was black with fury. He stared at the floor in silence, waiting for more.

Shepherd looked at Sawyer. 'The doctor said they've stabilised him but it's impossible to—'

'Why was Detective Constable Walker alone?' Keating kept his gaze on the floor.

'I was with him,' said Sawyer. 'But I couldn't keep up, because of my leg. Ingram gave him the slip and went for a solo run. The killer must have been waiting for the opportunity. Walker probably disturbed him. He had to leave Ingram's body behind.'

Keating nodded. 'One of the OPs said that Walker tried to contact both of you, over half an hour before you got to Ingram's house.'

Shepherd cleared his throat. 'I was at the safe house with Amy and Ava Scott, sir. Didn't pick up the call straight away.'

Keating raised his eyes to Sawyer.

'I was resting,' said Sawyer. 'Your orders.'

'Ingram was pronounced dead at the scene,' said Shepherd. 'Stab wound. Lower back. Kidney. Didn't have time to bleed him out like the others, so he cut his throat, too. Much deeper than Walker. Myers and Moran are there with Sally's team.'

Sawyer stared past Keating. A group of nurses had gathered at the station, drawn by the commotion. 'He knew about the running routine. But he could have staked it out. I think he also knew that Ingram was refusing heavy protection, refusing to scale back his runs. He wouldn't have planned an ambush otherwise.' He turned to Shepherd. 'OP guys all check out?'

Shepherd sighed and shook his head. 'Watertight.'

'Reassign them to Kim Lyons' place. Immediately. He's near the end of his project now. He might be crazy enough to try and wrap it up tonight.'

'We should take her to a safe house.'

Keating shook his head. 'She won't go. Wants to stay in her own home. Double the OPs outside her place. Surveillance detail on a five-mile radius. Firearms officer on shift, on the door. Spot checks. Nobody gets within shouting distance of the place. And if anyone tries, I want to hear about it. DI Sawyer. Get back to your rest.'

Sawyer drove home in a trance, under a midnight blue sky. By the time he reached Edale, the desolate fields were glowing in the approaching sunrise, making him crave an extension of night. Extra time. The space to repair his mood, and gather himself for the terrors to come.

He slipped into the cottage and made himself a cup of tea, staring at his warped reflection in the hissing kettle. He stood still, and watched as it rattled to the boil, smothering his image with steam. He ached for purification, renewal.

He found a packet of paracetamol and limped into the bedroom with his tea. He set down the mug on the bedside table, and allowed himself to fall forward, face down into the mattress.

And then his phone was buzzing, and he was awake. Two hours swept away in an instant.

Sawyer twisted round onto his back and sat up. Weak morning light outside. Headache. Dry mouth.

He took two paracetamol with a gulp of cold tea and checked his phone. Shepherd.

Phone me back

He made the call. Shepherd answered immediately.

Sawyer drew in a breath, held it. 'Go on.'

'Survived the op. They've put him in an induced coma. Brain swelling. Looks like he was hit with something before having his throat cut. Maggie's here with his girlfriend.'

Sawyer exhaled. 'You still at the hospital?'

'Yeah. Managed to shut my eyes for an hour or so in the brightly lit relatives' room.'

Sawyer's leg sent out a pulse of pain. He rummaged in the drawer for ibuprofen. 'Did you manage to—'

'Haven't even seen him yet. He's gone, though. Intensive Care. I did ask the doctor, but he said there was no telling what might happen next. He might wake and be able to speak. He might be under for a few days, maybe even a couple of weeks.'

'Will he live? Will he survive it?'

'Doc said there might be cognitive impairment.' He went quiet for a few seconds. 'I'm going back to the office. Sorry about the cliché, but now it's personal. Let's get this bastard.'

'Twenty minutes.'

54

Sawyer stepped out of the lift, not bothering to disguise his limp. It was early, and only a few of the desks were taken. As he crossed the floor, he could feel Moran's sunken eyes on him, tracking his progress. Myers sat at a spare desk in the far corner, staring ahead, mesmerised by his kaleidoscopic screensaver.

Shepherd followed Sawyer into his office and closed the door. Sawyer wrapped his jacket around the back of his chair and sat down. 'Four murders. One attempt. What's new?'

'Firearms officer with Kim Lyons,' said Shepherd. 'Protection doubled. OPs round the front and back. I'm staying in the spare room. One of the other DCs, Murphy, is covering when I'm not there.'

'Missus not happy?'

Shepherd shook his head. 'Missus not happy. Moran went to the Archives at Kew. He found the end of Joseph Dawson's line in the indexes. April 2008. As you predicted, no document or note to indicate what he changed it to. We have a big list of names that were registered at that time, though. Myers cross-reffed it with local chemistry graduates, but no hits.'

Sawyer took Shepherd's tactical pen out of the pot and twiddled it around his fingers. 'He might have studied but not graduated. Let's get closer to the centre. Dawson himself. This thing about wanting to start again. He was angry at his given parents, rejecting them. Get someone to check the hospital records on the day he was born. Obstetricians on duty. Who might have delivered him? Get some names. Cross-check with the deed poll list.'

Shepherd nodded. 'Forensics from Ingram show he was hit with PAVA. Incapacitant spray.'

'So much for his certificates. Good, old-fashioned surprise attack.'

'Sally says the immediate scene is clean, but they're searching the surrounding woods. If he had to get away in a hurry, he might have left us something.'

Sawyer slotted the pen away. 'Get back to Kim Lyons. I need you to stay there and supervise.'

'She's pretty low maintenance.'

'She's also effectively under house arrest until this is over.'

———

When Shepherd had left, Sawyer closed his blind and dug out a pair of in-ear headphones. He connected them to his phone and cued up the recording of his reliving session with Alex. It was profoundly strange to hear his voice checking off all the details, including the colours, the weather, the sensory information.

I am walking down the lane... I can hear a plane, high in the sky... I am running back, too fast, tripping over my steps...

I can hear my mother's voice and my dog, barking... The sound makes me feel scared and sick... I can feel the heat of the sun... I can see the green of the grass, the red of the blood...'

He couldn't stop it. He couldn't help his mother. And he couldn't help Walker. Both times, he had been too late. Compromised. Powerless.

Of all the questions Alex had posed, one lingered.

'Does your behaviour put other people in danger?'

He listened some more.

'I am feeling dizzy... I am crawling on the ground... I can see a man holding a hammer...'

He stopped the recording. He was breathing hard.

He let his brain wander.

His mother asked her killer, "Why?" There was no indication that she had known Owen Casey. So, if he had taken the hammer from Marcus Klein's house, he was unlikely to be the killer. And the killing was too brutal and calculated for a man with a history of petty burglary. Someone must have asked him, forced him, to take the hammer. They had to be the killer. Or someone connected to the killer. Someone who could plant it as evidence. Or manipulate it later to incriminate Klein. Another informant? An *insider*?

He called Sally. She barely had time to say hello before he started to speak. 'Are you alone?'

'Sorry?'

'Can you be overheard?'

'I'm at the processing lab. Private office. Why?'

'We checked the staff on the crime-scene clean-up company, yes?'

She sighed, irritated. 'Yes. CTS Decon.'

Sawyer got up and walked to the window. 'What if the person using the hardcore cleaning chemical isn't involved in *cleaning* crime scenes but their work still brings them into contact with similar chemicals?'

She thought for a moment. 'Jake—'

'The chemical, the apparent insider knowledge, the change of methods...'

'You're not fucking serious?'

He opened the blind. Sunny. Short morning shadows. 'Remember the conversation we had in the tent at the Palmer scene? I talked about the killer being consistent. I said how it would help us to catch him.'

'Yes?'

'The FSIs were there, all around us. After that, we get the chewing gum and fibres at the Brock scene. Breaking in, changing the lock. *Changing his methods*. Less consistent. Intentionally trying to throw us off. I want a list of everyone you've employed as a forensic scene investigator, helper, assistant. Everything. Particularly those who have accompanied you to the scenes in this case.'

Sally took a breath, holding her temper. 'My team are subject to extensive background checks. They're regularly screened for psychological—'

'This is nothing personal on you. Please email me the list straight away. And don't let anyone on your team know you've sent it.'

55

Sawyer drove out of Buxton, climbing away from the tangled outskirts onto the broad A-road artery that connected to the High Peak. He played the album that defined his early teenage years: *Everything Must Go* by the Manic Street Preachers. Soaring art rock, fuelled by melancholy. It was the first record the band had released since the disappearance of their mercurial guitarist Richey Edwards, and the sense of loss and longing defined his bittersweet escape from a childhood poisoned by his mother's absence. Today, the breadth of the music meshed with the widescreen fields, spotlit by unseasonal sunshine.

He aimed for the village of Flash, sizing up the potential endgames: extrapolating, projecting options, gaming scenarios. The killer was pathological. He was determined to complete his work: erase all cellular evidence of the man who had denied him the chance to ever know his real parents. But what then? Move on? Wall it all off as an unpleasant duty?

He remembered the words of Dennis Crawley, his quarry in the previous case; a man also driven to murder out of a twisted desire to rebalance the universe. He had said that an eye for an eye was too final, that revenge was a stone in a lake, sending out ripples across future generations. An insatiable legacy.

For the first time, Sawyer was struck by a terrible thought. What if he *was* to discover his mother's killer? To confront the man who had demolished her delicate face with a hammer? Would an eye for an eye be enough for him? Would her killer's death be enough to break the spell that held his brother mute, that had turned his wise and funny father into a religious recluse? Would it unlock his own state of suspension? Unfreeze him?

———

The gate at the entrance to Kim Lyons' house was guarded by an authorised firearms officer in bullet-proof body armour, carrying a semi-automatic carbine rifle. Sawyer showed his warrant card. The man called through on his walkie-talkie. A plain clothes protection officer opened the front door and the AFO nodded Sawyer through.

Kim Lyons sat at the kitchen table, talking to a standing female firearms officer. She wore a chunky, rainbow-striped jumper and bright blue jeans. Was she favouring louder colours to compensate for her fading eyesight?

'Detective.' Kim pulled herself upright and walked over. She shook Sawyer's hand: her grip was limp, more like a pinch. 'A great deal of fuss for one person.' Her voice seemed even weaker. Watery.

'Ms Lyons. We have an ongoing situation and we have to prioritise your safety.'

She gave a sad little nod. 'Are you close to catching this person?'

'My boss would like you. I think so. I have some ideas.

We hope you won't have to suffer this inconvenience for much longer.'

She ran her fingers around the table and navigated to the far corner of the kitchen. The firearms officer stepped aside to let her through. 'Would you like some cake?' Kim took a plastic tub out of the fridge. She opened it, revealing a square sponge cake, coated in bright pink icing and cut into small slices.

'My kind of breakfast,' said Sawyer, picking out a slice. 'Thank you.'

Kim handed him a side plate and a sheet of kitchen roll. 'Your colleague is through there, in the sitting room. I can't get him to eat anything.'

Sawyer smiled. 'Doesn't do sugar. His body is a temple. Well, a parish church, maybe. Strict regime. How are you doing?'

She groped her way to the chair and sat down. 'Not terribly well, I'm afraid. Everything seems a little darker now. I keep squinting, blinking. Rubbing my eyes. Hoping it will get better. But it never does.' Kim looked up at him, her eyes darting, hungry for light. 'My ophthalmologist is very sweet. He tells me that people live perfectly good lives without sight. But I'm not sure I'm ready to accept that. There's so much beauty in the world. Too much to live on without it.'

The mongrel dog padded in; Sawyer petted it. 'Life can surprise you. It might feel you've reached the end of the road, but then you find a little path, and it leads you somewhere unexpected. You should always be open to the unexpected. Emily Dickinson, the poet, said a beautiful thing. "I dwell in possibility".'

Kim smiled. 'That is beautiful. But I think I've stopped fearing death, as the end, with nothing but void beyond. In one sense, fear of death is the fear of missing out, on all the things the living can enjoy. But I value my sight too much. The compromise would be impossible to bear. Have you heard of David Eagleman?'

'The neuroscientist?'

Kim seemed pleased. 'Yes! He wrote that we all have three deaths. The first, when the body ceases to function. The second, when the body is buried or otherwise discarded. And the third is the moment, sometime in the future, when your name is spoken for the last time. When you're forgotten by the living. I have no children, Detective. There's nobody to speak my name, to carry my genes, hold me in memory. I'm ready to be forgotten.'

'Your moment will come,' said Sawyer. 'As it will for all of us. But for now, I'm afraid it's my job to extend it into the future, to make sure you have the time to do unforgettable things.'

She gazed up at him. 'You sound more like a priest than a policeman. I lost my faith years ago. Catholic. I always enjoyed confession, though. So cleansing. I hope you have someone you can confess to.'

Sawyer smiled and turned away. He walked through, past the plain clothes officer. Shepherd sat at a wooden dining table, busy on his laptop.

'*Minecraft*?' said Sawyer.

Shepherd looked up, startled by his presence. 'Something happened?'

Sawyer dismissed the officer and closed the door. 'You online?'

'Yeah. Looking at the list of doctors from Myers. The ones working at Cavendish on the day of Joseph Dawson's birth. Two obstetricians. Edward Shaw and William Riley.'

Sawyer joined him at the laptop. 'Bring up the names from Moran. The deed poll name changes registered at the end of the Joseph Dawson timeline.' Shepherd opened a

PDF from his desktop: a smudgy photocopy, with a long list of names in alphabetical order of first name. Five Edwards. Three Williams. No Shaws or Rileys. He took out his phone and checked his email. Another list, from Sally. Sawyer scanned the names and set the phone down on the table, for Shepherd to see.

He took a bite of the cake, waited. Shepherd read through the list, cross-checked with his laptop screen. He looked up and raised his eyebrows.

Sawyer nodded. 'Remember the bookshelf?'

'Bring him in?'

'Get Myers to trace the name. Full story. There'll be an address, but he won't be there now. Not after Walker.'

'Public appeal?'

'I've got a better idea.'

56

They stood before Keating like a line of naughty children in the headmaster's office: Sawyer, Shepherd, Moran and Sally. Keating leaned forward on his desk, scrubbing a palm across his stubbled chin.

'We have to keep this tight,' said Sawyer. 'Just the key players. Nothing on HOLMES. I think he has inside information somehow. Maybe hacked HOLMES access. Maybe just what he's picked up from the scenes or second-hand from briefings.'

Sally stared down at the desk, at her file photograph of Edward Ballard: a photobooth shot, bright and bland. Ballard was perched in front of a corrugated, watery blue background. He peered into the lens, head tilted up slightly. He had frizzy brown hair, cropped short all over. Wide, pensive mouth with thin lips pressed together; round, dark-framed glasses which perfectly matched the radius of his eye sockets. His expression was curious, and there was a softness to his eyes. A sympathy. He seemed slight and scaled down, diminished in the centre of the image.

'He looks like an accountant,' said Moran. 'Or a fucking mortgage advisor.'

'It's just so difficult to believe. He's one of my best investigators. So sharp. And *kind*, too. Diligent.'

'This stuff doesn't always show on the outside,' said Sawyer.

'He's ditched the glasses,' said Sally, dreamy and distant.

Myers knocked on the door; Sawyer waved him in.

'There's nobody at the Hayfield flat block,' said Myers. 'His flat is on the ground floor. Looks empty, through the window. The landlord is around tomorrow morning.'

Keating shook his head. 'He's not obliged to let us in.'

'Harbouring?' said Shepherd.

Moran nodded. 'Perverting the course, at least.'

'He won't go back there,' said Sawyer. 'Not after what happened with Ingram and Walker.'

'It's crazy,' said Sally.

Sawyer looked at her. 'It's safe. For the target.'

'But not for you.'

'She'll only agree to it this way,' said Keating. He nodded to Myers. 'What else?'

'Edward Ballard. Twenty-seven. Studied Forensic Science at Wolverhampton Uni. First three years undergrad, fourth year Masters. Looks like he didn't complete the Masters. Worked clean-up at a Birmingham firm, Scene Clean. Then...' He looked at Sally; she kept her gaze fixed on Keating's desk. 'Started to work on Sally's team three years ago.'

'Did he attend the Ingram and Walker scene?' said Keating.

Sally shook her head. 'Called in sick the day before.'

'Busy staking out,' said Sawyer. 'Probably living in a new stolen van.' He unwrapped a black-and-white boiled sweet. 'The timeline adds up. I bet he saw the BBC article about Tyler last summer and it set him in motion. He contacted Amy Scott, forced her to reveal details of Tyler's organ recipients. He spent some time observing the targets, establishing routines. A few weeks ago, he travelled to London and murdered Rebecca Morton. Then he visited Susan Bishop, the first of the five who are keeping Tyler "alive", in his mind. He's meticulous, unwavering. Andrew and Sophie mentioned his obsessive nature. We've seen it in his presentation, the way he's tried to direct his attention to the offending organs. Leave no trace.' He squeezed the sweet into his mouth.

Keating stared up at him. 'One more time, Sally.'

She sighed. 'I email my team, explaining how Kim has requested that the heavy protection be removed, with one protection officer at the front of the house and one unarmed protection officer inside, while we prepare for transfer to a safe house tomorrow morning. I say the house is to be swept after Kim has left, for evidence of intruders or listening devices.'

'And we're confident that Ballard will see this email?' said Keating.

Sawyer shrugged. 'Belt and braces. Even if he doesn't, he will be watching as we remove the protection. There's only one route through to Kim's first-floor bedroom, which will be covered by the protection inside. Me. She's asked for me specifically.'

Keating nodded. 'You mean you pitched it to her, sold yourself.'

'Not like you to make friends, DI Sawyer,' said Moran.

Keating pointed at Myers. 'I want you as the officer out front. Sawyer, stay in touch. Regular check-ins with Myers. If something feels wrong, if Ballard shows, you call it in. You get help. Immediately. Clear?'

Sawyer stepped forward, towards Keating. 'This is our best chance of getting him. Kim Lyons is more than a loose end. Her continuing survival is unbearable for him. He needs to finish his work.'

57

Kim Lyons paused at the foot of the stairs. 'There's tea and cake in the kitchen. Please help yourself.'

Sawyer had pulled an armchair through to the hall. He sat in a pool of shadow in the corner, facing the door that led through to the porch and back garden. 'Thank you. I've got everything I need. We appreciate your co-operation. If our friend makes an appearance, I can have back-up here in seconds. But please keep your bedroom door locked. I have your number, so I'll inform you if there's any development.'

Kim smiled. 'You're very brave, Detective.'

'I'm fine. Leo's got my back.' He reached down and scratched the head of Kim's mongrel dog, curled up tight at the side of the armchair. His tail swished against Sawyer's ankles.

'He's not much of a guard dog, I'm afraid. He's getting on a bit now.'

Sawyer patted Leo's flabby torso. 'Let me know if you need anything. I realise this must be stressful, Ms Lyons. But it's under control. We have a watcher out front, and I have the back covered here. If nothing happens tonight, then we'll have to move you and take another approach.'

She forced a smile and slowly made her way up the stairs. Sawyer followed the footsteps as she moved into her bedroom, directly above. He looked down to the dog. 'Just you and me tonight, big man.' Leo lifted an ear.

He reached over to the table at the side of the chair, and opened his book. 'Let's see if we can finally get through this.'

––––––

An hour passed. Sawyer knew from his experience with stakeouts that he had to hold his mind in stasis. It was a mistake to try and keep it alert with hectic videogames or lively music; that would just tire it out. But he also couldn't afford to let it settle, sink too close to the edge of sleep.

He read, listened to low-volume music through one earpiece, played a few mildly taxing phone games.

The house was silent and still, apart from the metronomic *tick, tick, tick* of the kitchen wall clock. Its rhythm synced with Leo's wheezy breathing and Sawyer found himself tuning out, drifting.

He got up and walked into the kitchen, navigating only by low-brightness phone light. Leo followed him, curious.

The kitchen clock read 2:40.

He made a cup of black instant coffee and helped himself to a slice of the sponge cake. Leo looked up as he sliced, hopeful. Sawyer smiled and handed down a chunk. The dog inhaled it and immediately agitated for more. He found some ham in the fridge and tore off a few strips, laying them on the floor for Leo to snaffle in seconds.

Sawyer ate the cake standing up and swallowed two ibuprofen with a slug of water. He took the coffee back to his chair, riding a spike of pain whenever he applied pressure to his right leg.

A noise upstairs.

Kim's footsteps, moving across the ceiling towards the bathroom. After a few minutes, the toilet flushed, and she shuffled back.

Sawyer sent a message to Myers, out front, parked in an adjacent road.

All good?

After a few seconds, the reply came back.

Yes. Quiet.

Sawyer sat in the chair, staring into the darkness. He felt a sudden sense of panic, as if the idea to lure Ballard was flawed in a way that was just outside his perception.

He got up and crept to the end of the hallway, just in sight of the small conservatory with reading chair and bookshelf. The room looked out through French windows onto a decked porch and a large, well-tended garden beyond.

He looked back to the dark corner and his chair.

Tick, tick, tick.

Moonlight leaked in through the sitting room door, casting a pallid half-light over Leo, who snuffled in his sleep. Sawyer walked back and sat down, pondering his unfinished business.

He had Shaun's insurance card, but he would need to connect him to Dale, and prove his involvement in the assault. Dale was moving away, but clearly had no intention of letting Eva go. He thought of Alex's words, about unwanted attention. Was he already inside that realm? Forcing the issue, when the smarter choice would be to hang back?

He would pick things up with Ryan Casey once this was all over, one way or another. He imagined the laughter at the Magpie Mine goose chase, but felt more disappointment than humiliation. It was clear that the Caseys knew more about Owen than they were prepared to reveal right now.

His therapy with Alex had become more than just a favour to Maggie. But it disturbed him, how he was more concerned with using her to gain more detail about the attack on his mother than with improving his own mental health: finding something tangible that would open up a new angle, away from his journalist masquerade, and the hunt for the man who had helped the killer frame Klein.

Tick, tick, tick.

He breathed steadily, listening to his thoughts, monitoring his physical aches: the throbbing in his hand, the sharp pain in his leg, a tender spot on his forehead where he had butted Shaun.

He reached for the book again, checked the time.

3:35.

His eyes stung with fatigue. More coffee. Soon.

Sawyer allowed his body to recline slightly, submitting to the pull of sleep. He closed his eyes, sank a little deeper, forced himself back from the brink.

Upstairs, Kim shuffled across the floor again.

Bathroom door: opening, closing.

Leo growled at his feet: a low, continuous drilling. He whimpered a little in his sleep. Chasing imaginary cats.

His tail stirred, started to swish. He growled again.

Sawyer leaned forward. The moonlight from the sitting room reflected in the dog's open eyes. Not asleep any more.

A thought struck him, flipped his stomach. He stood and walked out to the conservatory, making himself visible to the French windows. He crouched, looking out to the porch and the single-storey extension where Kim kept the washing machine.

Sawyer walked back to the chair and nudged Leo to his feet. He bundled the dog into the sitting room and closed the door.

He listened. Some movement upstairs. No toilet flush.

Kim's footsteps, moving from bathroom to bedroom. Quicker than before. More purpose.

Sawyer scaled the two bottom steps and leaned around the corner of the staircase, staying silent. He edged his way up, stair by stair, conscious of potential creaks.

As he neared the top, he thought he heard more movement from Kim's bedroom. A brief shuffling. Then silence. The door was ajar, throwing a dim strip of lamplight over the landing.

Sawyer stepped forward and dabbed a finger at the door. It swung open, revealing the bed pushed against the far wall. Pink-and-white two-tone duvet, pulled to one side. No Kim.

He looked across the landing, to the bathroom. The door was closed. Solid light inside, bright around the edges. He had heard Kim go back to her bedroom. So why was the bathroom light still on, with the door closed? Had he dropped off to sleep? Missed her journey back again? And why no toilet flush?

Another room sat in the centre of the landing corridor. Spare? Office? He pressed his ear against it, listening. Nothing. He turned the handle slowly and pushed it open.

It was a spare bedroom. Unmade single bed, dresser with mirror. He inched his way to the window which overlooked the back garden. The net curtain flapped against the glass. One of the panes had been opened, admitting an outside chill. The lock had been forced. He looked out and down to the garden; the single-storey extension sat directly beneath the window. A bundle of rakish branches from a neighbouring tree obscured the roof, making the access difficult to see from the ground. From up here, it was clear that an intruder could climb up onto the extension and pull themselves up to the window.

A thud from the bathroom next door. He turned, on full alert, and edged back out onto the landing. He reached for the bathroom door handle, expecting it to be locked. But it turned, and he opened the door.

Kim Lyons lay on her back, in the bathtub, wearing only a thin blue nightdress. She was handcuffed, with her hands behind her back, and her mouth had been covered by a strip of gaffer tape. He caught the panic in her eyes as she nodded for the door, towards the space behind him.

He turned back, facing the bedroom door. Edward Ballard stood in the frame: head down, eyes glaring up at Sawyer. He was even shorter than Sawyer had imagined. Maybe no more than five-two. He wore a dark jumper, black jeans, black boots, and a blue-and-black striped beanie hat. His left hand—gloved—was in view, but his right was obscured behind the door.

His expression softened, and Sawyer recognised the kind eyes of the FSI who had handed him the latex gloves, back at the Susan Bishop crime scene.

Ballard angled his head and smiled, curling up one corner of his mouth. He had a shining black bruise around his left eye socket. Ingram must have winged him. Or Walker.

'Bright and fierce and fickle is the South,' said Ballard. His voice was calm, colourless. 'And dark and true and tender is the North.'

Sawyer smiled. 'Tennyson.'

'I read about you. "Hero cop". Quite a life. You've done well, considering. It's been a pleasure to work with you.'

'I can't say the feeling's mutual.'

Ballard smiled. 'We've both suffered. I saw you in the woods, limping.'

'Wear and tear. Anyway...' Sawyer clapped his hands together. 'Can't stand around talking all day.'

Ballard shook his head. 'We're just getting started.' He moved out from Kim's bedroom and walked towards Sawyer, keeping his right hand down, out of sight. He lunged forward, lifting the red-and-black can of incapacitant spray towards Sawyer's face.

Sawyer's first thought was to deflect Ballard's arm with an inside block, and hopefully get him to drop the can. But he couldn't risk Ballard catching him in the face before he could make the distance. He dropped his head and charged forward, keeping sight of Ballard's legs to maintain his bearing.

He heard the hiss of the spray, and felt the liquid settle on the back of his head, stinging his scalp. He rammed his dropped head into Ballard's body, pushing him into Kim's bedroom door, which snapped open with a loud crack. The can flew into the wall and clattered down the stairs.

Leo downstairs, barking.

They fell to the floor, grappling. Ballard was small, but he had immense core strength, and Sawyer struggled to get him under control.

Ballard jerked out of his grip and rolled away.

The light from Kim's bedside lamp was weak, and Ballard's all-black clothing camouflaged him in the darkness. Sawyer couldn't immediately see where he had rolled to.

A blur of movement to his right.

Ballard swung his arm around and drove a short-bladed knife into Sawyer's right thigh, inches from his bullet wound. Sawyer bellowed in agony and groped for Ballard's hand, hoping to hold and overpower him. But he jerked his arm away, pulling the knife free. He scurried out of the room, across the landing.

Sawyer writhed and clutched at the stab wound. The carpeted floor beneath his leg was already warm and wet. He planted his left foot down and forced himself upright.

Ballard crossed the landing and slipped into the bathroom.

Sawyer followed, shouldering into the door before Ballard could lock it, shoving him back into the room. He glanced down at his leg: too much blood.

He pushed into the bathroom.

Ballard was crouched by the bathtub. He had grabbed a fistful of Kim's hair in one hand, holding her head back. He held the bloodied knife in the other hand, poised at her throat. Kim had screwed her eyes shut; her body convulsing with fear.

Ballard smiled at Sawyer. He had barely broken a sweat, despite the tussle. 'I know what you're thinking. Femoral artery. I wouldn't worry. Complete transection is rare.' He looked down at Sawyer's leg, and the pooling blood. 'Although you *can* still bleed to death.'

Sawyer snatched a towel off the rail. He tied it tight around the top of his thigh, keeping his eyes on Ballard.

Ballard smiled and nodded his head. 'The article said you were present at your mother's murder. A child. Truly terrible.' His eyes narrowed, hardened. 'But then you still had your father. Most orphans are made. I was *born* an orphan. Denied the love of both my mother and father. Then, I was lied to. The love was tricked out of me.'

Sawyer steadied his breathing. Downstairs, Leo barked in bursts of two and three, paused for a few seconds, repeated. 'This is such a *mess*, Edward.' He waved a hand

317

across the bloodied floor, gestured to Kim. 'And you've been so tidy. So precise.'

Ballard darkened; the anger poking through his poise. He pinched his lips together, drew in a deep breath through his nose. 'That fucking nurse.' He composed himself, turned a curious gaze on Sawyer. 'How is your colleague? That was wrong. But I had to...' He trailed off. It struck Sawyer that his enquiry wasn't sarcastic; he seemed genuinely concerned for Walker.

Sawyer slid to the floor, back against the wall, keeping the bathroom door open. 'You know, Ed. In a way, you might say that Roy Tyler was your real father.' Ballard let his gaze sink to the floor. 'The crash resulted in the death of your parents. But it also induced your premature birth. You came into being as the result of his choices that night.'

Ballard jerked his head up. There was rage in his eyes now. 'Edward Shaw gave me life. He delivered me.'

'From evil? Do you see him as your father, or Our Father?'

'He's a surgeon. Not a god.'

'And how about you, Ed? Are you a god or a monster? What gives you the power over life and death?'

Ballard shook his head. 'I was a nobody. Born to nobody. The judge who sentenced Tyler—'

'Is he next? Are you going to take his tongue?'

Ballard raised his eyebrows. 'He died a few years ago. He said that, "No powers possessed by the court can lessen this terrible and devastating loss".' He leaned forward, spitting the words across the room. '*No powers.*' He sat back, resting his head against the wall, keeping the knife pointed at Kim's neck. 'They gave him ten years. Ten years for two people. It wasn't even the maximum allowed at the time, fourteen. He served five, and he was driving again after a two-year ban. That piece of filth killed three human beings with a lorry and they didn't even ban him from driving for life. So, when the law is impotent, and the sky is empty, when God himself is powerless to prevent the loss of innocents, then what's left but to take control?'

'Appoint yourself as the higher power?'

Ballard nodded. 'When the so-called forces of good fall so far short of the mark, what else can you do but deliver your own justice?'

'And you planned to kill him. But he was already dead. And so you had to wipe him out. You couldn't stand the *mess* of it. The fact that the man was gone, but his tissue lived on.' Sawyer pushed down on the stab wound, ground his teeth through the pain. His phone buzzed in his pocket. 'You say you were born a nobody, but do you know how unlikely it is that you were born at all? The odds are about one in four-hundred trillion. Your parents meeting in the first place, staying together, the sperm meeting the egg. You could go further back. The probability of all your ancestors reproducing. It's so unlikely, you *could* call it a miracle. Life is a wonderful thing. Some people see it as a gift from a divine being. But however you think it all begins, we keep doing it. Creating more people, more life. I've been alive for thirty-five years. In that time, three billion people have been added to the global population. Life is what we do. Despite all the horrors in the world, we just keep on bringing people into it. It all comes down to that old saying. Where there's life, there's hope. Humans like hope. It keeps us going. Your mother, Faye. She felt that.'

He shifted position, against the wall. Downstairs, Leo kept up the barking.

'What do you mean?' said Ballard.

'Your father, Tony. He died at the crash scene. But your mother carried a donor card, which was the old way of showing your wishes for your body after death. And because Faye died at the hospital, just before you were delivered, then she could donate her organs. Now that really *is* an act of higher power. Passing on your precious, unlikely life to someone else. And now, you can make that choice. Show mercy. Follow your mother's example and give someone the gift of life.'

Downstairs, Leo had fallen silent.

Ballard stared at Sawyer. 'To answer your question, I'm not a monster. I'm not going to stab a woman in the eyes.'

'But you can't leave the job unfinished, right?' Sawyer looked at Kim, foetal in the bathtub, eyes staring up and away from Ballard's knife, breathing through flared nostrils. 'This woman here. Kim. She's *over*. Her cornea transplant has failed. Her eyesight is degenerating. The last spark of the man who killed your mother and father is fading inside her, day by day, regardless of what you do now. Soon, there will be none of his living cells active. He'll be gone forever. Your work is *already done*. You're going to prison for a long time, Ed, I can't change that. But this woman here is your one source of hope. Spare her, and that decision will come back to you in the future, when you're looking for leniency. You'll serve your time and apply for parole, many years from now. You'll be a different person, desperate to live an independent life, after circling the exercise yard for decades. The choice you make here and now will be the difference between getting a shot at that life and being turned down and left to rot it out. You are the higher power, yes, and you can choose either an act of kindness or an act of pointless cruelty that will end one person's life and condemn you to a living death.'

Ballard's head drooped. He lowered the knife, away from Kim's throat.

A noise downstairs. Ballard didn't react. Sawyer pushed down on the towel, wincing. 'Your favourite author, Ed.

320

Your namesake. He said that he believed in the "non-existence of the past", and—'

'"The infinite possibilities of the present".'

Sawyer nodded. 'Roy Tyler is the past, Ed. He's non-existent. And here we all are, in the present. It's all we have. And here and now, you can make the right choice, out of all those infinite possibilities. Give me the knife. Give this woman her life. Give yourself some hope.'

Barking again, from downstairs. Ballard raised his eyes, listening.

More noise on the stairs. Bustle. Another bark. Footsteps.

Ballard jolted himself alert and looked around, startled. He gripped Kim's hair harder, forcing her head back, exposing her throat. He raised the knife again.

Leo scampered up the stairs, barking and growling. Footsteps behind him. Sawyer's stomach lurched; Myers must have heard the dog, sent him a message and entered the house when he didn't answer, releasing Leo from the sitting room.

The dog clattered through the door into the bathroom and leapt for Ballard. He pulled the knife away from Kim and raised it at the dog, but Leo clamped his jaws around his forearm. Ballard tugged his arm back, and dropped the knife in the bathtub. It skittered up the curved surface and settled beside Kim's body.

Leo growled and kept his grip on Ballard's arm, burrowing his paws into his body for purchase. Sawyer lifted his left leg, struggling to raise himself. He looked behind. Myers had reached the top of the stairs. 'Police!'

Ballard dug a left hook punch into the side of Leo's head. The dog whimpered, but kept his grip. An empty wine bottle, streaked with candle wax, sat on a shelf above the bath. Ballard dug his feet into the floor, running on the spot, trying to gain enough height to reach the bottle with his left hand. But Leo pulled at his arm, shaking it left and right, keeping him tethered. Ballard punched the dog again. Leo released the arm and cowered back, howling.

Sawyer managed to shift onto his left knee. His right leg flared with the pain of the stab wound, and he struggled to unfold it and get himself upright.

Myers reached the bathroom door. Ballard's can of incapacitant spray was in his hand. Sawyer snatched it and forced himself to his feet. He turned towards Ballard.

Kim had pulled up her knees and worked the cuffs around to her front. She gripped the knife in both hands, holding it on Ballard. He had forced his head back into the wall and stared down his nose at the point of the blade, millimetres from his throat. Kim's eyes were wide, fixed on Ballard. She breathed through her nose in rapid bursts.

Myers stepped into the room and grabbed Leo. The dog wriggled in his grip, but seemed subdued. Myers pulled Leo away and bundled him out of the room, closing the door and shutting him outside.

'Kim?' Sawyer reached out to her, palm up. She kept the knife fixed on Ballard's neck. He closed his eyes, forced his head further into the corner. Sawyer moved his hand towards Kim's face. She flashed him a wary look, retrained her eyes on Ballard. Sawyer peeled at the edge of the tape across her mouth and lifted it away slowly.

Kim opened her mouth wide, gulping down air. She licked her lips, spoke to Sawyer. 'You're wrong. I am not "over".' She pulled herself up, leaned closer to Ballard. '*You*. Complaining about how you were denied love. You don't deserve love. You don't deserve life.'

Sawyer snatched out his arm and held Kim firm by her wrists. She gasped and scowled at him. He paused, then relaxed his grip, opening his fingers. 'You make the choice, Kim. You have the power now, over life or death.'

Behind, Sawyer felt Myers make a move forward; he held up a hand to stand him down.

Ballard opened his eyes. He looked from Kim to Sawyer, weighing his options. Outside, Leo whined and scrabbled at the foot of the door.

Kim held the knife steady for a few seconds, then sighed. Sawyer felt her arm go limp. He closed his fingers around her wrist and slid the knife out of her hand, pulling it away from Ballard.

Myers moved in. He yanked Ballard to his feet and held him in an armlock.

Ballard tried a half-hearted struggle against the restraint, but soon relaxed. He raised his eyes to Sawyer. 'Detective, I know what comes next. I know I'm not obliged to say anything. But while we're still off the record... I hope you find some justice for your mother soon.'

58

FIVE DAYS LATER

Wardlow Mires was a one-street limestone village that sat in the centre of the National Park, on the North/South divide between the High and Dark Peak. Sawyer steered the Mini into the vast car park of the roadside Yondermann Café. It was early, and the morning mist lingered low over the flat farmland towards Eyam. The sky—so open and infinite in his childhood memory—had been sealed over by an opaque veil of grubby white cloud. He parked, and left the engine running for a few seconds, zoning out to the brooding baritone of Nick Cave. Interventionist gods, guiding angels, the power of love. He killed the engine and stepped out into the sodden air.

Alex sat at the table nearest the door, with a pot of tea and a novel: *Morvern Callar* by Alan Warner. She wore her standard beige roll-neck, with a brimmed grey beret. A fawn velvet overcoat hung over the back of the chair. She sprang to her feet and embraced him.

'Not stopping?' Sawyer nodded to her hat.

'It's cold. You feel it more as you get older. You'll see.'

'Looking forward to it.'

She smiled and waited for more. Sawyer dropped his head. 'Are you ready?'

'We'll soon find out.'

———

They walked out of the village, along the verge of the main road, and turned left at a Public Footpath sign. The track was unpaved, and they had to navigate around wide puddles and sopping mounds of mud.

'Wardlow is your home town, right?' said Alex.

'Yeah. This is one of the routes we used to take after my mum picked us up from the old school.'

Sawyer hung back, limping a little. Alex edged around a crater of folded mud. 'And have you been back before today? To the lane?'

Sawyer found a firmer section of path, and edged ahead. 'Yeah. Few months ago. It was dark, though. Didn't seem as real.'

'Looks like you're struggling. With the leg.'

He shrugged, didn't turn. 'I won't be training for any trail marathons anytime soon.'

They descended into sparse woodland, which opened out to a straight, paved lane that ran with open fields on one side and a line of trees on the other. Sawyer stopped and looked out across the flattened pastures. He drew the collar of his jacket up around his neck.

Alex came up behind him. 'I know the weather is hardly the same, but that shouldn't matter.' She took out her digital recorder. 'How are you feeling, Jake? Is this a good place to start?' He nodded. 'Okay. Take your time. Nice and steady.'

She pressed Play. Sawyer's voice.

'I am walking down the lane...'

They moved off, guided by the recording.

'It is warm, but my mouth is still cold from an ice lolly I just finished...'

Alex stayed behind Sawyer. She rested a hand on his shoulder.

'My mum is telling my brother not to touch something. Litter. Chocolate wrapper. My dog is barking at him. He is running past me now...'

Alex's voice. *'Your brother?'*

'The dog. I am chasing him...'

Sawyer walked faster, into the relative shade of a patch of overhanging branches.

'My dog is stopping and barking. He is running back towards my mother and brother. I am turning and following. I can hear a plane, high in the sky...'

Sawyer turned. His face was flushed red; eyes darting around, confused. Alex paused the recording. 'We can slow down if you like, Jake.'

He shook his head. She started the recorder again.

'I am running back, too fast, tripping over my steps...'

Sawyer broke into a half-run. He was compromised by his leg injury, but Alex still had to shift to keep up with him; her long blue coat flapping in the frosty wind.

'I can hear my mother's voice and my dog, barking...'

Sawyer hobbled off the side of the road, over the verge, into the edge of a field. He stopped, hung his head. Alex waited, watching him. Sawyer dropped to his knees and dug his hands into the grass. His shoulders heaved.

Alex's voice. *'How is that making you feel?'*

'The sound makes me feel scared, and sick.'

Alex startled at the sound of a shout, rising up from Sawyer. A roar of anguish, frustration. She stepped over the verge and followed him to the edge of the field.

'*I can feel the heat of the sun.*'

He looked up at her, eyes shining with tears. 'Turn it off.'

'*What can you see, Jake?*'

'*I can see the green—*'

'Turn it OFF!'

She stopped the recording. Sawyer tried to get up, stumbled, stayed on his knees. He had turned his head away, but Alex could tell from his movement that he was sobbing.

He sucked in a deep, ragged breath, and swiped at his cheeks with both hands. 'I can't.'

She rested a hand on his shoulder. 'Can't what?'

He shrugged her away. '*This*. I can feel it, but I can't *see* it. I can't see anything that helps. There's nothing here. Just a field and some trees. Why does it hurt so much?'

'Why does what hurt?'

'*Love.*' He turned to her, his face warped with rage.

Alex sighed. 'The fact that you're feeling it shows that you can heal. That you *will* heal. It's not the love itself that hurts, Jake. It's the loss. The longing. The denial of the urge to express love.' She crouched down beside him. 'But that's all life is, really. A fight between love and death. Death always wins in the end, of course. But it's love that makes it a hollow victory.'

59

In the Nut Tree, Maggie Spark sipped her black coffee. She reached over and snapped an edge off Sawyer's pastry.

Sawyer looked up at her. 'Do try some yourself. Don't be shy.'

Maggie squinted at the flaky crust and grimaced.

He smiled. 'Not for you?'

'It looks so dry.'

'It's a *palmier*. Traditional French pastry. And you call *me* a food philistine.'

She sat back. 'I don't know where to start, really. I was going to ask what you've been up to. But I should probably ask about what you *haven't* been up to.'

He shrugged, bit into the pastry. 'I got a cat.'

'That's the highlight of the past few weeks?'

'Well, I suppose he got me.'

'Name?'

He slurped his tea. 'Bruce.'

Maggie rolled her eyes. 'You've been shot, stabbed, god knows what else. You've solved a difficult case, apprehended an appalling multiple murderer.'

'Saved the life of a colleague. Don't forget that.'

'How is Walker?'

'Awake. Still in hospital. Shepherd went to see him. They need to do tests to measure his brain function. But he'll live.'

She nodded. 'We used to think that the brain couldn't repair itself, that cells don't regenerate. But now we know it's possible to regain function.'

A moment's silence. They held eye contact.

'How about me?' said Sawyer. 'Do you still think I'm having a breakdown? Shall I give you an update so you can report back to Keating?'

She scowled. 'You're being mean again. Would you rather people didn't care about you?' He shrugged. 'Have you felt what you experienced in the cave again? Panic? Fear?'

'No. Whatever it was, it's keeping its head down.'

'And Alex?'

'She's good.' He nodded. 'Thank you, Mags.'

Maggie smiled. 'It'll take time. But I'm so pleased you've started—'

He waved a hand. 'Please. Don't say anything about "journeys".'

She laughed, pushed her hands across the table and covered Sawyer's. 'Clichés are clichés for a reason. Sometimes they're full of truth.'

'Which is in itself a cliché.'

'It *is* a journey. And it might be a bumpy one.'

Sawyer laughed. 'There might be potholes. I might run out of petrol a few times. My ticket might not be valid.'

A group of fluoro-jacketed hikers bustled into the café, chased by a whistle of wind.

Maggie hugged herself. 'Jesus, it's getting cold. I'm thinking of moving, you know.'

'Where?'

329

'Somewhere warmer.'

'Serious?'

She stood up. 'More tea?' Sawyer nodded. 'I'll get it. Going for a wee. Then you can tell me about the case. And I can tell you about my separation.'

Maggie smiled at his shock and swished away. She ordered another coffee and tea from the counter and sidestepped into the poky unisex toilet.

As she washed her hands, her phone vibrated in her bag.

Outside, she picked up the drinks and walked back to the table.

Sawyer had gone.

She looked at her phone message.

Sorry. Emergency. x

60

Sawyer called Klein's number and set the phone on speaker in the dashboard mount. He pulled the Mini away from the Nut Tree and headed east, towards Matlock.

The call connected. 'Mr Robbins?'

'Can you get to the Barley Mow? It's a pub, only a few minutes from the Casey farm.'

'Now?'

'Soon as you can. Ryan Casey called. He says that Owen is willing to meet. I'm about ten minutes away.'

Klein was silent. Sawyer thought they might have lost connection. 'You still there?'

'Yes. How do we know this isn't another diversion?'

'We don't. But at least this time the facilities will be better. Their pies are good.'

Klein laughed. He sounded brighter. 'I can be there in half an hour.'

Sawyer waited, in the corner of the Barley Mow's main bar area by the front doors. At the far end, behind the bar, another door opened out to a fenced private car park. It was nearing midday, but the room was empty, apart from a couple of hardy solo punters with their pints and racing papers. It was a claustrophobic space, further shrunk by the suffocating clutter covering most of the wall and ceiling: beermats, local photographs, trophy plaques, sports emblems. A fading handwritten poster behind Sawyer's seat advertised the annual Barley Mow hen racing event.

The front door swung open and Klein walked in. He was more layered than usual, fitting the weather.

He took off his cap and sat down next to Sawyer. 'Any sign?' He used his sleeve to wipe condensation from his glasses.

Sawyer shook his head. 'Only a few minutes late. If they don't show this time, I might look into the licensing for their vehicles. Put some pressure on.'

Klein gave a grim smile. 'How would that help?'

Sawyer caught himself. 'I could report them. Or threaten to report them.'

'They don't seem the type to respond to threats. Drink?'

'I'm fine.'

Klein seemed deflated. 'I might have one if they don't show soon. Working late last night. Been doing some online teaching. Skype. Course writing. It's good to feel gainful again.'

'No trouble with background checks?'

'Not at all. I appreciate all you're doing, I really do. But I'm starting to think that I can maybe rebuild my reputation independently. Without the need to "clear my name".'

Sawyer winced at his air quotes. 'The conviction may still limit your opportunities in the long term.'

Klein shrugged. 'Easy does it. Build to each job by way

of the last. Eventually, it will be further and further behind me. I'm actually feeling rather optimistic. For the first time in years.'

Sawyer kept his eyes on the bar. 'Have you seen the car again?'

'No. I thought I saw it behind me today, but I'm pretty sure it was a different model. Same colour, though. I had my eye on it in the mirror, but it turned off a few minutes out of town.'

The door behind the bar crashed open. Ryan, Wesley and Ronan Casey led the way, flanked by the two men who had been guarding the farm on Sawyer's second visit. They flipped open the bar entrance and crowded into a booth.

Ronan spotted Sawyer. 'There he is! Wild Man Robbins.'

The others laughed, loud and theatrical.

'Mr Robbins.' Ryan Casey nodded. 'Mr Klein. What can I get you?'

Sawyer held up a hand. 'Staying sober, Ryan. You called me over in the middle of work.'

'Ah. Hell of a shame.'

A nervous-looking young woman emerged from behind the bar and took Ryan's drink orders. Wesley Casey called over. 'One for yerself, Chrissie!'

The door behind the bar opened again, and a short, wiry man walked through. He was in his late forties, dressed in cheap-looking blue jeans and a PVC jacket zipped up to his chin. His face was pitted with acne scars, and a bushy grey moustache twitched beneath his flattened nose. He squeezed into the far end of the booth, between Wesley and Ronan. The other two men sat in front at either side, creating a two-body buffer zone.

Ryan turned and beckoned to Sawyer and Klein. They headed over and pulled up a couple of chairs.

Ryan handed round the drinks. He plonked a pair of tumblers in front of Sawyer and Klein. 'Jameson. Can't have you not drinking, now.' He gestured towards the new man. 'Lads, this is my nephew, Owen. Owen, this is Mr Klein, Mr Robbins.'

'How was the mine, boys?' said Wesley.

Sniggering between Wesley and Ronan.

'I've always wanted to see it up close,' said Sawyer. 'Thanks for sending us somewhere interesting.'

They looked a little put out.

Owen Casey pointed at Sawyer, then Klein. 'Which one's the cunt who put down Danny McDonagh?' His voice was sharp, nasal.

Ryan slapped Sawyer on the shoulder. 'Broke his fuckin' jaw, no less.'

Another round of laughter.

Owen raised his glass. 'I'll drink to that!'

Klein eyed Sawyer, confused. Sawyer nodded at him, and they complied with the toast. The whiskey scorched his throat, but gave him a spike of resolve. He leaned forward and fixed a stare on Owen. He had shrunken, accusing eyes. Sawyer thought of the line from *Get Carter*: 'Pissholes in the snow.'

'Now,' said Owen. 'What do yiz fuckin' want from me?'

'Mr Casey. I'm writing a book about Mr Klein's case. He suffered a terrible injustice, thirty years ago.'

Owen nodded, impatient. It occurred to Sawyer that he was already drunk. 'Heard about that. The fuck's it got to do with me?'

'Mr Klein was wrongly convicted of the murder of a local woman. We believe you might have acquired an item for someone. Perhaps for the person who really committed the crime. He's obviously keen to find out more about this person. So he can clear his name.'

Owen frowned. He took a sip of his whiskey, swilled it round his mouth. 'What "item"?'

'A hammer,' said Sawyer. 'From Mr Klein's home. It was then used in the murder, and traced back to him.'

Owen slammed down his glass. 'Are you sayin' I *stole* this?'

Ronan spoke up. 'Owen's never stolen a fuckin' thing in his life, have you?' He broke into a smile and wrapped his arm around his cousin.

Owen smiled, sheepish. 'I might have done a bit of "liberation" to get by. But that's when I was a young boy. Respectable businessman, these days, mind.'

'I don't doubt it,' said Sawyer. He pulled his chair closer to the booth. 'But around June 1988, you were arrested for an aggravated burglary.' Sawyer could feel his tone slipping, but he was too close now to care. 'The police don't have any record of that arrest. For some reason, they didn't want it to go on record. But they forgot that you were mentioned in a separate victim's statement. That makes me think you did some kind of a deal. You did a job for one of the officers to get you off this serious charge. I think the job was to steal the hammer from Mr Klein's house. Is that right?'

Owen scowled, and cracked a smile. 'This is up in Buxton?' Sawyer nodded. 'I remember the fella from the house catching me. Fat fucker. I was out of shape, like. Police took me in. The guy who made the arrest was a young fella, and he left me in the cell for fuckin' ages. Then this other guy came in. Older. He said I was looking at five to ten years. I thought, fuck that! He sent the other one out, said I could do a job for him. Easy work.'

'What did he look like?'

Owen shrugged. 'Big guy. Hard to tell age. Thirties, forties. Everyone just looks old when you're a kid. I was nineteen, but I still felt like a kid. I don't know. Suit. Scruffy hair. Brown. Big fuck-off watch. Bushy moustache. Not much to remember, really.' He sipped his drink.

Sawyer edged further forward. 'What did he ask you to do?'

'Take a hammer. He described it. Black handle. Said it would probably be in a tool box or an outhouse somewhere. He wanted to know if I could get in and out without being seen or leaving evidence. I said, no problem. I'll be like a fuckin' shadow. He gave me an address. Place near Tideswell somewhere. Purple door.'

Sawyer looked at Klein. He nodded.

'Piece of piss, in the end. Got in through the back. It was in a little work-room area just off the kitchen. Sitting there on a workbench, out in the open. Not exactly a big treasure hunt. I met the guy in some pub car park, handed it over.' Owen drifted, caught himself. 'You know what, Mr Robbins. This fella didn't just get me off the charge. He paid me pretty well.'

'How did he get you off?'

'Fuck knows. He had me out of the cop shop in a couple of hours. Never spoke to anyone else after that. I did hear him arguing with someone outside, though. Another bloke.' Owen set down his glass. His hand was trembling.

'Did he say what he needed the hammer for?'

'No. And I didn't ask. He was sweetness and light when he was telling me the deal. In the car park after, though, he turned pretty fuckin' nasty. If I ever told anyone, then my miserable life wouldn't be worth living. Blah, blah, blah. It's not as if I would tell anyone, anyway. It was a sweet job. I had cash in my pocket and I wasn't banged up. It was an easy way out. I wasn't exactly connected to current affairs at

336

the time. I didn't even know about the woman's murder until a few years later. Look, fellas. This guy. He'll be crackin' on by now. You'd better get a move on if you want to question him. But what's the point? He's already lived ninety per cent of his life.'

Sawyer felt a jolt of anger. 'The ten per cent is important to me. And to Mr Klein. Owen? This man. What was his name? He must have introduced himself when he first came into the room. Do you remember his rank? Was he in uniform?'

Owen shook his head. 'No uniform.' He drained his glass and looked from Klein to Sawyer. 'I do remember his name, yeah. Surname, anyway.'

'What was it?'

He smiled. 'You know what? I'm getting the feeling this means a lot more to you than you're letting on, Mr Robbins. I've lived under this fella's threats for a long time now. Who's to say he's not still out there, keeping tabs on me?'

Sawyer raised up slightly in his seat. 'Owen. What was his *name*?'

Owen shook his head. 'I need guarantees. Compensation for all the distress I've suffered—'

Sawyer lunged out of his chair and climbed over Ryan Casey. Glasses scattered; one fell to the floor and smashed. He grabbed Owen by the lapels of his jacket. Wesley and one of the bodyguards hauled Sawyer away, holding him back.

'Easy now!' Ryan stepped around Sawyer and stood in front of Owen.

Sawyer wriggled away from the bodyguard, but Wesley managed to keep him back. He was flushed, raging. '*Distress*? You think *you've* suffered?'

Owen smiled. 'Get yourself under control, Mr

Robbins. This is a seller's market, yeah? You can't just come in here, ranting about "injustice". You come up with a number and I'll give you a name.'

Wesley and Ronan Casey took an arm each and dragged Sawyer back to the front door, shadowed by Klein. For the first few steps, he kicked at the floor. But as he reached the door, he calmed and went limp. Wesley and Ronan released him, and Wesley stood in the centre of the room, blocking his path.

Sawyer glared at them both. He closed his eyes, slowing his breathing.

'You might wanna cool off, Mr Robbins,' said Ronan. 'Long time ago to be caring so much.'

———

Outside, a low sun had cracked through the shroud of cloud. Sawyer stood with Klein at the edge of the car park, by a disused red telephone box. Sawyer leaned forward, resting his forehead against the cool glass.

'I can get some money together,' said Klein. 'He probably won't ask for much. I'll get Ryan's number. Make an offer.' Sawyer was silent. 'I didn't realise you were this passionate about the case.'

Sawyer stood up and turned. 'I'll help with the money. My publisher might be able to come up with something.'

Klein smiled. 'Why don't we stop this now, Mr Sawyer? I know who you are. I read the *Derbyshire Times* piece, with the section on your story. But I knew before then. Back at the Casey farm, you said, "all shall be well". That was Jess's phrase. She used to say it all the time. It was from some prayer.'

Sawyer nodded, sighed. 'You can see why—'

'Of course. It actually makes all of this easier. It's always been hard to believe that some stranger would come out of the blue and want to help me, after thirty years. Like I said, I'm ready to move on. I can see how I might start to rebuild things, have some kind of life again. But it does feel like we're close to the truth now. I'll make some calls. Find the money. Then we can get that name. And hopefully it won't lead us to a tombstone.'

61

Sawyer crawled the Mini along the dirt track that led to his father's house: a refurbished 1700s mining cottage, isolated on a hillside above Upper Midhope. He parked by Harold's laurel green Volvo and climbed out, eager to take in some air after the long drive. He walked to the end of the short path that led to the front door and looked down into the valley, where the Langsett Reservoir basked in the feeble sunshine, grey and swollen.

The door opened, and Harold appeared. His gangly German Shepherds, Rufus and Cain, bounded out to greet Sawyer.

'I swear you've got a hidden security camera somewhere around here,' said Sawyer, fussing the dogs. 'I come within ten feet of the place and you pop up like a bloody vampire.'

Harold smiled. 'Lovely to see you, too.'

Inside, Harold made tea and served it in his reading room with colossal French windows that looked out across the valley and the top end of the dirt track.

Sawyer stood by the windows and sipped from his mug. 'This is good.'

Harold nodded and fell into a sky-blue armchair beside

one of the walls of bookcases. 'Fresh leaf tea. Strained. Tea is one of the joys of life. It's worth a bit of care. Patience. Too many things are all about speed, these days. You can't fast-track your pleasures.' He studied his son. 'How are you, Jake? Are you healing?'

'Physically, yes. Took a beating in this case.'

'Got your man, though.'

'Not the one I'm *really* looking for.' He sat down, on the stool of a generic upright digital piano. 'This is new.'

'Always wanted to learn. It's relaxing, meditative. The guy who gives me lessons looks about twelve. When I first called him, he said, 'Good for you'. Cheeky fucker.'

Sawyer laughed. 'You have left it a bit late.'

'Like I say, patience. Rejoice in hope. Be patient in tribulation. Be constant in prayer.'

'Sounds like a lot of work to me.'

Harold sipped his tea. '*Romans.*'

'The Bible: a handbook for personal providence, and full of top tips for tea brewing. It's almost as if you're moulding its wisdom to fit your situation. Astrologers do that.'

Harold sighed. 'For once, can we stay away from religion? Find some common ground?'

Sawyer opened the piano lid. The keys were pristine: shining black, gleaming white. 'I dropped in on Michael last week.'

Harold raised his eyebrows, waiting for more.

'He's okay.'

'I'm just glad I managed to transfer the money without having to talk to that little shit, Chris Hill.'

'I still want to try speech therapy.'

Harold scoffed, irritated. 'Did he speak to you again?'

'No.'

'Well, there's not a lot for a therapist to work with,

surely?' He ran a hand through his long, greying hair. For all of his talk about patience, Sawyer had the impression he was eager to get back to something.

'How did the paintings do?'

Harold brightened. 'Good! Sold them all. Worked up some reproductions. They've sold, too. I got myself an agent, Arnold. You met him in Ashbourne. Bit tweedy, but he knows his stuff. So, who's this man you're *really* looking for? Owen Casey?'

Sawyer shook his head. 'I found him. Quite a charmer.'

'And did he help you "catch the end of the thread"?'

'I think he did, yes. He knows the name of the man I'm looking for. The man who killed your wife. Mum. He won't give me the name, though. Says he wants compensation.'

Harold nodded. 'So, this time you *are* here for money?'

'No. I have a couple of questions.'

'Do I need to get a lawyer?'

Sawyer ignored him. 'When you worked at Buxton, under Keating, who were the senior officers? In the run-up to the year of mum's death?'

Harold looked up to the ceiling. More pantomime of recall? 'I was a DC, then. Keating was DI. It was a standard station, though. No Murder Investigation Unit or whatever you call it, these days. There was a DCI, a Chief Superintendent. They don't have them any more, though.' He shook his head. 'I don't know. We never really saw the brass. They came and went. Not like these days, where I imagine Keating is hands-on.'

'Anyone with a moustache? Big watch?'

Harold shook his head. 'Nobody comes to mind.'

'And if you wanted to use an informant, who would handle that? How would it be signed off?'

'That's changed a lot, too. As you can imagine. Source

handling used to be a lot less formal. Off the books. Mainly to protect the sources.'

'You would need senior sign-off to get charges dropped, though?'

'Absolutely. Once an arrest has been processed and the charge is approved by CPS. You don't just wipe that clean. It would be noticed, even in a small station.'

Sawyer stood up, restless. 'So *did* you notice? Who arrested Casey? Who looked the other way, or was *told* to look the other way, so that somebody senior could do a deal with him?'

'I told you. I don't remember him. I don't remember him being arrested. You know, son. It would be nice if we could talk about other things during our limited get-togethers. Reminisce, share life experiences. Look to the future, instead of this pointless, divisive obsession.'

Sawyer nodded, in a trance. 'And here's a supplemental question. Why would a senior police officer want my mother dead? A schoolteacher?'

Harold paused before answering. He lowered his voice, measured out his words. 'Not a senior police officer. Another schoolteacher. Marcus Klein.' He leaned forward. '*Means*. He's young, he can wield the weapon, get away quickly. *Motive*. Jealousy, male rage, she was married. She rejected his advances. *Opportunity*. They worked together, had access to each other.'

'All hearsay.'

'All credible.' Harold raised his voice. 'More credible than this conspiracy theory you're peddling. A senior officer working together with a petty criminal. Casey has clocked you as a buyer of information. He's telling you what he thinks you want to hear, in exchange for a bit of money. And now he's holding out to get the price up. The crime has been committed. The killer has been convicted.

This is all a game, Jake. Don't play it. Don't *be* played like this.'

Sawyer moved away from the piano, heading for the door. 'I have a key card in my hand. I *will* get this name. This is me, persevering. Being patient.'

'It's a dead case, Jake!'

'It's a *cold* case!' Sawyer was shouting now. 'And I'm about to warm it up again. Whatever you choose to remember.'

———

Harold stood at the edge of the French windows and watched, as his son reversed around the Volvo and drove away, throwing up dirt from the track. When the final fragments of dust had settled, he turned and walked out to the back of the cottage, to his studio.

He browsed through his colour-coded shelving, and slid a small paint pot from the neat row on the yellow shelf. The pot rattled as he prised off the lid. He took out the key and unlocked the side room, which connected to a sturdy old outbuilding, around twenty feet square, with a stone floor and steps leading down to an old wine cellar. The building's central space was empty, but the walls were lined with stacked metal shelving, packed with supplies: neatly marked boxes containing groceries, medical materials, small electricals.

An old dresser had been pushed into the corner, perfectly fitted in the remaining space left by one of the shelving units. He took a notepad and pen from the top drawer and worked through the supply boxes, noting the month's depletions, marking items for order.

He closed the book and stood there for a while, letting his eyes drift to the heavy steel door which led down to the cellar. He had installed it himself, ten years ago, after torrential rain and floods had savaged the building and weakened the old door beyond repair. It had taken him most of one week: two days for acquisition and the marking of parts, five days for the installation: drilling into the brickwork, securing the frame, fitting the security cylinder. In one sense, it was an act of divinity, of omnipotence. So fitting, that he would toil for six days and rest on the seventh.

Harold locked the main door to the outbuilding and walked back into his studio. He replaced the key in the pot and set it alongside the others, twisting its position so that all the colour swatches formed a neat horizontal line, ascending in intensity from inky black to brilliant white.

Cain and Rufus sat outside the studio, looking up at him hopefully.

Harold smiled and ruffled their heads. 'Let's get you some lunch, boys.'

He headed outside, to a small garage with another hefty shelving unit which held various brands of dog food, biscuits and supplements: all items perfectly aligned in alphabetical order.

He pulled away a couple of tins and ducked out of the garage, under the folding metal door. He set down the tins on the floor, reached up with both hands, and pulled the door down, concealing the vehicle inside: a 2008 BMW X5. Burgundy.

Sawyer spent the weekend at home, recharging and recuperating. His leg wounds healed well, and he found a curious solace in the regular ritual of checking, cleaning, rebandaging. On Maggie's recommendation, he downloaded a recipe app and bought in a supply of quality ingredients from the local farm shop. For the first time since he'd left London, he planned his meals, prepared the ingredients, followed the recipes. The results were mixed, but Alex had suggested he focus on physical self-care for now, which would help build the mental strength for another try at her reliving therapy. Holism. Body and mind as one project.

On the Saturday evening, he set his Spotify 'Favourite Songs' playlist on shuffle and spent two hours cleaning the cottage, wearing a battered old Bruce Lee T-shirt, headphones and rubber gloves. He scoured beneath the toilet rim to Richard Hawley's 'Tonight The Streets Are Ours'. He dusted and polished to The KLF; hoovered to Robyn and Bat For Lashes. Later, he flopped down with a bowl of lemon and tomato salmon pasta, and called Klein.

No answer. He hung up without leaving a message. He was about to send a text when a waiting call cut through. Eva.

She half-whispered. 'Listen. Got to be quick. Can you meet somewhere on Tuesday? Near you is fine.'

'Rambler's Inn? Not far from here.'

'I'll find it.' She paused. 'I've got to go.'

'Wow. *That* quick? Why are we meeting out? You should come back here. I've cleaned the place. You'll be impressed.'

Eva sighed. 'Is that a serious question? I want to see you.' She lowered her voice. 'And that name you mentioned, Shaun Brooks. He works for Dale.'

'Can you prove it?'

'Dale had a going away party here the other day. I took lots of photos. He had a private meeting with Shaun and another guy. Looked serious. I've got to go. Five on Tuesday?'

'Keen! Bit early for me.'

An indulgent pause. He could see her smile; the coquettish eyes. Doubtful but indulgent. 'In the *evening*. Bye-bye.'

She hung up.

————

That night, Sawyer dreamt about his mother. The scene was different, the colours muted. And Alex was there, standing by the side of the field in her long coat and beret, making notes. He crawled towards his mother, through the blizzard of barking and screaming. He turned back, looking for encouragement from Alex. She nodded, urging him on. But then he was overhead, above it all; a drone's eye view.

And he could control his movement: hovering and diving at will. He zoomed down on Henry, on Michael. But he couldn't get close to his mother and the man in the balaclava. There was an invisible shield around them, preventing entry. He willed and willed, flying into it, bouncing back like an insect.

He turned to Alex. She nodded, insistent. He tried again. This time, his descent slowed, as if the air had turned viscous, fluid. But he was through, closing in on the man, as he smashed and smashed the hammer into his mother's face.

His mother had pulled away the balaclava.

'*Why?*'

And Sawyer caught a glimpse. The man's face, spattered with blood. Dark, heavy eyebrows. And the moustache. Black with an edging of grey. Deep-set eyes with brown irises, almost black. And there was nothing in them. He wasn't frantic or angry or aroused. He looked more irritated; annoyed that his work had been interrupted by the removal of his mask.

Sawyer was suddenly awake, but with no distress. He reached to his bedside table drawer and dug out a pencil and envelope. He sketched the man's face, filling in as much detail as he could remember. The result was impressionistic, and it may have been nothing more than a creation of his imagination. But it felt good to have something tangible in reality: a positive link, extracted from his night terrors.

———

On Sunday, he drove out to the Penny Pot Café near Barber Booth. He read his book, drank coffee, ate too much lemon drizzle cake. Outside, he turned away from the station and crossing barrier, and walked down, past the Rambler's Inn, into the chocolate-box hamlet of Edale. Tiny primary school, one pub, one general store, one flickering bar of 3G coverage. The weather was crisp and sunny, and he fell in with the flow of ramblers aiming for the base of Kinder Scout.

He climbed the south side, taking it slow, resting his leg. At the rocky slope near the summit, he forced himself into a scramble, pleased with his general fitness. At the top, he shivered in the stinging air and gazed back down into the folds of the valley, across the scarred moorland, cobbled by gritstone. A low bank of raincloud seethed overhead, and Sawyer pressed on along the edge of the ridge and found Jacob's Ladder, a set of precipitous stone steps which delivered him back to earth, just as the rain swooped down in anger.

He stopped for tea at a small café in Edale and called Klein again. Still no answer. Was he screening him now?

———

In the evening, as twilight settled outside, Sawyer sat around playing videogames and browsing through articles on his phone, struggling to settle. He fed Bruce and went out for a late run, following a circular route of farm trails around the back of the cottage, keeping his pace slow. He hopped over a break in a dry-stone wall and followed the edge of a field, tracked by a crowd of curious sheep. As the ground inclined away from the roadside trees, the sky opened out, and a spare firework popped above, its neon shards flaring in the gloom.

As he reached the cottage, he could see the headlights of a car approaching from Hayfield, along the Kinder Road.

He let himself in, freshened up, and poured a large glass of milk. He sipped it, listening.

The car slowed on the road outside, and pulled in, across the driveway bridge. It idled for a while, then fell silent.

Sawyer hung back in the kitchen and finished the milk. Surely Dale wouldn't send his men again, so soon?

The car door opened and closed. One set of footsteps approached the house. Five urgent raps. He braced and opened the door.

It was Keating, in uniform, holding his cap under one arm. 'DI Sawyer.' His expression was grim, but he forced a smile.

'Sir. Sunday night. I'm going for business over pleasure.'

'Perceptive, as ever. Can I come in?'

Sawyer stood aside and closed the door behind Keating. He took a chair at the kitchen table, obliging Sawyer to do likewise.

Sawyer eyed him. 'Drink?'

'No, thank you.'

'Is it Walker?'

He shook his head. 'They tell me he's rallied. Recovering well.'

'So...'

'It's you.'

Sawyer nodded. 'Dale Strickland?'

'He's filed an official complaint about harassment. But that's the least of your worries.' Keating laid his hat on the table. 'I asked Maggie to look out for you. A friendly check on your state of mind, based on a few of your professional decisions. But I've also been suspicious of your motives for coming back here. I asked Moran to keep an eye on you. We know you were tracking Klein, Jake. Getting close to him. Studying his rhythms.'

Sawyer squinted at him. 'Does Moran drive a burgundy BMW?'

'Not as far as I know. Seems a bit above his level.'

'He's hardly a partial observer. You know our history. Drummond's wife.'

Keating nodded. 'I do. For me, that was a good thing. I figured he wouldn't give you the benefit of the doubt. I know you visited Klein in prison a few months ago, under an assumed name. Lloyd Robbins. That would be enough to have you on a disciplinary charge by itself. You've also met him a number of times since. I assume he didn't know who you were? Where did you get the name from?'

'Apollo Robbins. My favourite pickpocket.' Sawyer ran a palm across his forehead. 'Look. Sir. Klein didn't kill my mother. You know how I feel about that. I've been trying to find out who did. I had to hide my identity because he was hardly likely to cooperate with the son of the woman he was convicted of murdering.'

'And did you take him with you on the trip to the Irish traveller camp?'

Sawyer flinched. 'Someone sent you a picture. I took him once. But not the time I got in the ring. I had to get their trust. They're close-knit. They have information. I can take you through it.'

Keating stood up. 'You should never have come back. We should have been smarter with your application. Seen the angle.' He walked to the front door and opened it. 'When did you last see Klein, Jake?'

'Couple of days ago. I was following a lead. Pub in Matlock.'

Car doors closing.

'And what did he do after that?'

Sawyer shook his head. 'No idea. Went back to his flat, I suppose. I've never been there. He told me he lives at his brother's place in Castleton.'

Footsteps outside. Several people.

Keating dropped his head. 'We found an item of yours at his place.'

Sawyer frowned and got to his feet. 'It must be something he took from my car, or—'

'He was found dead early this morning. At his flat. His brother found him.'

The room swayed. Sawyer reached a steadying hand to the table.

Bodies in the doorway. Shepherd and Moran.

Sawyer looked at them. Moran: glaring, with the hint of a smile. Shepherd: eyes on the floor.

Keating took a step towards Sawyer. 'After your meeting, Klein went back to his flat. He didn't report in to his scheduled parole interview the following morning.'

Sawyer felt the muscles in his legs go limp. He sank to his haunches, covered his face with his hands.

'He'd been tied up,' said Moran. 'And beaten.'

The words left Sawyer's mouth before he could stop them. 'With a hammer.'

Keating nodded. 'With a hammer.'

Sawyer rose up. 'Do it.'

Keating had the arrogance to put on his cap. 'Jake Sawyer, I am arresting you on suspicion of the murder of Marcus Klein.' Sawyer looked to Shepherd and Moran. Both were fixated on Keating now. 'You do not have to say anything. But it may harm your defence if you do not mention when questioned something which you later rely on in court. Anything you do say may be given in evidence.'

Shepherd produced a pair of handcuffs and stepped forward. 'Is there any point putting these on, sir?'

Sawyer smiled and held out his hands. Shepherd clicked the cuffs into place.

Moran stepped around them and stood next to Keating.

Shepherd turned and led the way.

Sawyer followed. Out of the door. Into the dark.

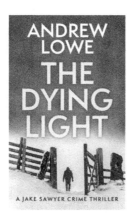

BOOK THREE IN THE **JAKE SAWYER** SERIES

JAKE SAWYER is out in the cold. As winter descends on the Peak District, he finds himself suspended from the force, accused of murder.

When two young children go missing, feared abducted, Sawyer must improvise to help solve the mystery. As the bodies of adults appear in remote locations, Sawyer suspects a chilling connection to the missing children. With time running out on his bail, he must fight to crack the cases and clear his name.

But then Sawyer uncovers the shocking truth behind his mother's murder, thirty years earlier: a truth that leads him to question his sanity, and threatens to tear his world apart.

https://books2read.com/thedyinglight

JOIN MY MAILING LIST

I occasionally send an email newsletter with details on forthcoming releases and anything else I think my readers might care about.

Sign up and I'll send you **a Jake Sawyer prequel novella**.

THE LONG DARK is set in the summer before the events of CREEPY CRAWLY. It's FREE and totally exclusive to mailing list subscribers.

Go here to get the book:
http://andrewlowewriter.com/longdark

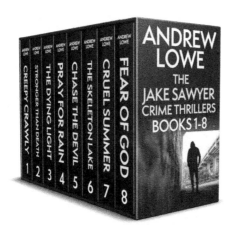

BOOKS 1-8 IN THE **JAKE SAWYER** SERIES

AVAILABLE IN EBOOK and PAPERBACK

READ NOW WITH **KINDLE UNLIMITED**

https://books2read.com/sawyerboxset4

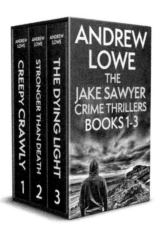

BOOKS 1-3 IN THE **JAKE SAWYER** SERIES

AVAILABLE IN EBOOK and PAPERBACK

READ NOW WITH **KINDLE UNLIMITED**

https://books2read.com/sawyerboxset1

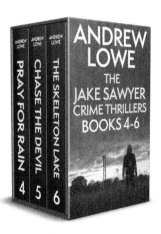

BOOKS 4-6 IN THE **JAKE SAWYER** SERIES

AVAILABLE IN EBOOK and PAPERBACK

READ NOW WITH **KINDLE UNLIMITED**

https://books2read.com/sawyerboxset2

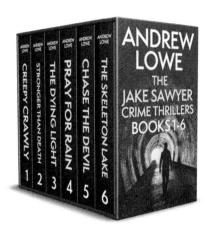

BOOKS 1-6 IN THE **JAKE SAWYER** SERIES

AVAILABLE IN EBOOK and PAPERBACK

READ NOW WITH **KINDLE UNLIMITED**

https://books2read.com/sawyerboxset3

ACKNOWLEDGMENTS

Dr Adrian Harrop for the red pen treatment on the medicals.

Stephen Bailey from NHSBT for patiently educating me on the extraordinary work of blood, organ and tissue donation professionals.

Detective Constable Ralph King for his prompt and precise answers to my incessant emails.

Bryony Sutherland for scrupulous editing and creative de-stressing.

Book Cover Shop for cover and website design.

Special thanks to **Julia** for listening to me go on about it all.

Andrew Lowe. London, 2018

PLEASE LEAVE A REVIEW

If you enjoyed **STRONGER THAN DEATH**, please take a couple of minutes to leave a review or rating on the book's **Amazon** page.

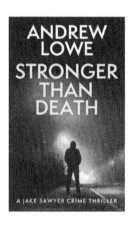

Honest reviews of my books help bring them to the attention of others, and connecting with readers is the number one thing that keeps me writing.

Go here to leave your review:
https://books2read.com/strongerthandeath

JOIN THE TEAM

Would you like the chance to read my books for free, before they're published?

Join my **Advance Reader** team, and I'll send you a copy of each book when it's finished.

Then, when the book is published, I'll ask you for feedback and an honest review. (No obligation, though.)

Go here to sign up:
andrewlowewriter.com/advancereaderteam

THE JAKE SAWYER SERIES

GLOSSARY

AFO – Authorised Firearms Officer. A UK police officer who has received training, and is authorised to carry and use firearms.

ALF – Animal Liberation Front. A political and social resistance movement that promotes non-violent direct action in protest against incidents of animal cruelty.

ANPR – Automatic Number Plate Recognition. A camera technology for automatically reading vehicle number plates.

AWOL – Absent without leave. Acronym.

BSE – Bovine Spongiform Encephalopahy. Colloquially known as 'mad cow disease'. A neurodegenerative condition in cattle.

CCRC – Criminal Cases Review Commission. Independent body which investigates suspected miscarriages of justice in England, Wales and NI.

CI – Confidential Informant. An individual who passes information to the police on guarantee of anonymity.

CID – Criminal Investigation Department. The branch of the UK police whose officers operate in plainclothes and specialise in serious crime.

COD – Cause of Death. Police acronym.

CPS – Crown Prosecution Service. The principle public agency for conducting criminal prosecutions in England and Wales.

CROP – Covert Rural Observation Post. A camouflaged surveillance operation, mostly used to detect or monitor criminal activity in rural areas.

CSI – Crime Scene Investigator. A professional responsible for collecting, cataloguing and preserving physical evidence from crime scenes.

CSO – Community Support Officer. Uniformed member of police staff in England and Wales. Non-warranted but granted certain police powers. Also known as PCSO.

D&D – Drunk & Disorderly. Minor public order offence in the UK (revised to 'Drunk and disorderly in a public place' in 2017).

EMDR – Eye Movement Desensitisation and Reprocessing. An interactive psychotherapy technique used to relieve psychological stress, particularly trauma and post-traumatic stress disorder.

ETD – Estimated Time of Death. Police acronym.

FLO – Family Liaison Officer. A specially trained officer or police employee who provides emotional support to the families of crime victims and gathers evidence and information to assist the police enquiry.

FOA – First Officer Attending. The first officer to arrive at a crime scene.

FSI – Forensic Science Investigator. An employee of the Scientific Services Unit, usually deployed at a crime scene to gather forensic evidence.

GMCA – Greater Manchester Combined Authority. Local government institution serving the ten metropolitan boroughs of the Greater Manchester area of the UK.

GMP – Greater Manchester Police. Territorial police force responsible for law enforcement within the county of Greater Manchester in North West England.

GPR – Ground Penetrating Radar. A non-intrusive geophysical method of surveying the sub-surface. Often used by police to investigate suspected buried remains.

HOLMES – Home Office Large Major Enquiry System. An IT database system used by UK police forces for the investigation of major incidents.

H&C – Hostage & Crisis Negotiator. Specially trained law enforcement officer or professional skilled in negotiation techniques to resolve high-stress situations such as hostage crises.

IDENT1 – The UK's central national database for holding, searching and comparing biometric information on those who come into contact with the police as detainees after arrest.

IMSI – International Mobile Subscriber Identity. A number sent by a mobile device that uniquely identifies the user of a cellular network.

IOPC – Independent Office for Police Conduct. Oversees the police complaints system in England and Wales.

ISC – Intelligence and Security Committee of Parliament. The committee of the UK Parliament responsible for oversight of the UK Intelligence Community.

MIT – Murder/Major Investigation Team. A specialised squad of detectives who investigate cases of murder, manslaughter, and attempted murder.

Misper – missing person. Police slang.

NCA – National Crime Agency. A UK law enforcement organisation. Sometimes dubbed the 'British

FBI', the NCA fights organised crime that spans regional and international borders.

NCB – National Central Bureau. An agency within an INTERPOL member country that links its national law enforcement with similar agencies in other countries.

NDNAD – National DNA Database. Administered by the Home Office in the UK.

NHS – National Health Service. Umbrella term for the three publicly funded healthcare systems of the UK (NHS England, NHS Scotland, NHS Wales).

NHSBT – NHS Blood and Transplant. A division of the UK National Health Service, dedicated to blood, organ and tissue donation.

OCG – Organised Crime Group. A structured group of individuals who work together to engage in illegal activities.

OP – Observation Point. The officer/observer locations in a surveillance operation.

Osman Warning – An alert of a death threat or high risk of murder issued by UK police, usually when there is intelligence of the threat but an arrest can't yet be carried out or justified.

PACE – Police and Criminal Evidence Act. An act of the UK Parliament which instituted a legislative framework for the powers of police officers in England and Wales.

PAVA – Pelargonic Acid Vanillylamide. Key component in an incapacitant spray dispensed from a handheld canister. Causes eye closure and severe pain.

PAYG – Pay As You Go. A mobile phone handset with no contract or commitment. Often referred to as a 'burner' due to its disposable nature.

PM – Post Mortem. Police acronym.

PNC – Police National Computer. A database which

allows law enforcement organisations across the UK to share intelligence on criminals.

PPE – Personal Protective Equipment designed to protect users against health or safety risks at work.

Presser – Press conference or media event.

RIPA – Regulation of Investigatory Powers Act. UK Act of Parliament which regulates the powers of public bodies to carry out surveillance and investigation. Introduced to take account of technological change such as the grown of the internet and data encryption.

SAP scale. A five-point scale, devised by the Sentencing Advisory Panel in the UK, to rate the severity of indecent images of children.

SIO – Senior Investigating Officer. The detective who heads an enquiry and is ultimately responsible for personnel management and tactical decisions.

SOCO – Scene of Crime Officer. Specialist forensic investigator who works with law enforcement agencies to collect and analyse evidence from crime scenes.

SSU – Scientific Services Unit. A police support team which collects and examines forensic evidence at the scene of a crime.

Tac-Med – Tactical Medic. Specially trained medical professional who provides advanced medical care and support during high-risk law enforcement operations.

TOD – Time of Death. Police acronym.

TRiM – Trauma Risk Management. Trauma-focused peer support system designed to assess and support employees who have experienced a traumatic, or potentially traumatic, event.

Urbex – urban exploration. Enthusiasts share images of man-made structures, usually abandoned buildings or hidden components of the man-made environment.

VPU – Vulnerable Prisoner Unit. The section of a UK prison which houses inmates who would be at risk of attack if kept in the mainstream prison population.

A WOMAN TO DIE FOR

AN EX WHO WOULD KILL TO GET HER BACK

Sam Bartley is living well. He's running his own personal trainer business, making progress in therapy, and he's planning to propose to his girlfriend, Amy.

When he sees a strange message on Amy's phone, Sam copies the number and sends an anonymous threat. But the sender replies, and Sam is sucked into a dangerous confrontation that will expose his steady, reliable life as a horrifying lie.

https://books2read.com/dontyouwantme

ALSO BY ANDREW LOWE

WHAT IF THE HOLIDAY OF YOUR DREAMS TURNED INTO YOUR WORST NIGHTMARE?

Joel Pearce is an average suburban family man looking to shake up his routine. With four close friends, he travels to a remote tropical paradise for a 'desert island survival experience': three weeks of indulgence and self-discovery.

But after their supplies disappear and they lose contact with the mainland, the rookie castaways start to suspect that the island is far from deserted.

https://books2read.com/savages

ABOUT THE AUTHOR

Andrew Lowe was born in the north of England. He has written for *The Guardian* and *Sunday Times*, and contributed to numerous books and magazines on films, music, TV, videogames, sex and shin splints.

He lives in the south of England, where he writes, edits other people's writing, and shepherds his two young sons down the path of righteousness.

His online home is andrewlowewriter.com

Follow him via the social media links below.

Email him at andrew@andrewlowewriter.com

For Andrew's editing and writing coach services, email him at andylowe99@gmail.com

facebook.com/andrewlowewriter

twitter.com/andylowe99

instagram.com/andylowe99

tiktok.com/@andrewlowewriter

bookbub.com/profile/andrew-lowe

amazon.com/stores/Andrew-Lowe/author/B00UAJGZZU

Printed in Great Britain
by Amazon